I0825373

CRITICAL ACCLAIM FOR THE DEFENDERS OF DEMBROCH

"Satisfyingly original... Epic, well written... More, please!"

— Diane Donovan, Midwest Book Review

"From cover to cover, this story will have you flipping pages faster than someone working at a copy center to find out what will happen next."

— Jon

"The book is a lot of fun! ...the prose flows like pure poetry."

— Anna (Goodreads starred-review)

"...an exciting adventure... A rich and compelling world... This one is for the whole family."

— Charles

"...incredible worldbuilding... Never a dull moment...races from point to point with excitement and a fresh appetite for adventure..."

— Reader's Favorite (starred review)

"...action-packed [and] adventurous... Relatable for adults as well as young adults."

— Jacob & Allie (Goodreads starred-review)

"You won't want to put this book down until it's finished."

— Matt

"...a great tale [with] many creative twists and turns."

— Lauren (Goodreads starred-review)

"Dembroch: a location every fantasy fan needs to add to their destination list."

— Kristine

The Defenders of Dembroch

ALSO BY PATRICK HARRIS

GUARDIAN OF THE PARADISE

THE WATERMAN CHRONICLES

#1: Rise of the Elementals
#2: Return of the Water
#3: Red in the Waters

SILVER RAIN

COMING SOON

THE DEFENDERS OF DEMBROCH

Book 2: The Sinner's Solemnities

A TOAST OF BLOOD

The Defenders of Dembroch

BOOK 1: THE AGE OF KNIGHTS AND DAMES

A Novel by

PATRICK HARRIS

Book Design by SunBurst Sagas
Map by Rhys Davies

Published and printed in the United States of America.

ISBN: 978-0-578-48290-3

Summary: Four long-lost friends take on daring, lethal, and magical quests to save a queen and her cursed kingdom.

1. Young Adult Fiction / Fantasy / General
2. Young Adult Fiction / Legends, Myths, Fables / Arthurian
3. Young Adult Fiction / Fantasy / Epic

www.AuthorPatrickHarris.com

DEDICATIONS

To my family near and far,
For showing me the corners of the world
And the unimpeachable strength of virtue.
No matter the distance, we're always together.

To my friends, life with you guys is like a day at Disneyland.
We don't need a map, we eat too many churros,
And, in the end, we stay up way too late.
Even in the old folks home, I doubt that will ever change.

To Dylan and Maverick and the new generation,
May you be brave and bold
And hold the fire of joy in your soul.
Rest well, for you will move mountains.

And for the queen of my heart, my McWife.
May we grow old, but never grow up,
And always seek our forever in every adventure.
I am yours until the end.

Verum
WHITTLESEA
Sand bar.
walkable during low tide
Watchmaker's Cottage
Bridgemaster
Amaranthine
Coral Canyon

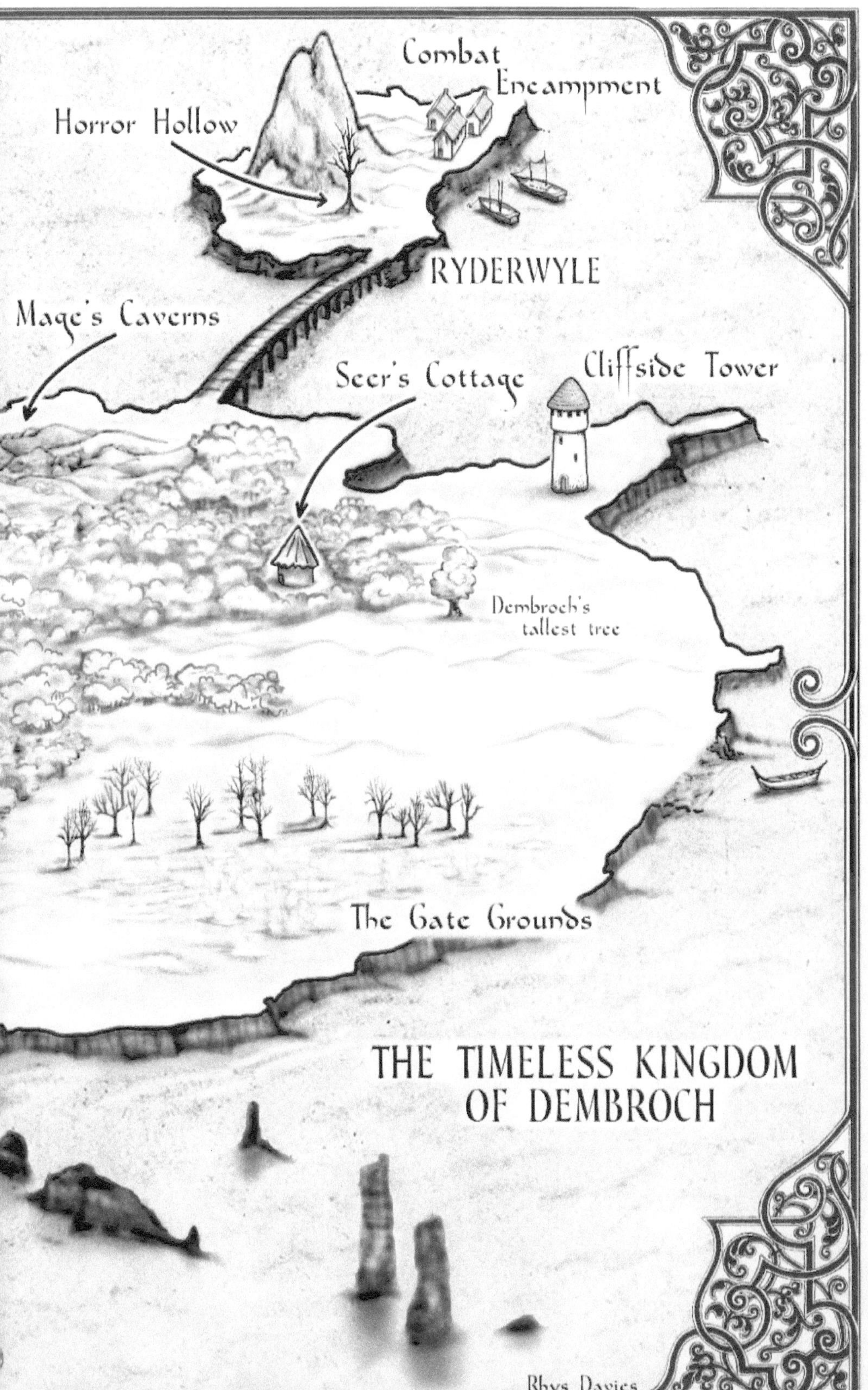
Combat
Encampment
Horror Hollow
RYDERWYLE
Mage's Caverns
Seer's Cottage
Cliffside Tower
Dembroch's
tallest tree
The Gate Grounds
THE TIMELESS KINGDOM
OF DEMBROCH
Rhys Davies

The Defenders of Dembroch

BOOK 1: THE AGE OF KNIGHTS AND DAMES

Once upon a time, King Arthur sought out his greatest foe, Morgan Le Faye and fought the final battle of their great war. After many days and nights, King Arthur bested the evil witch and offered her one final bequest. Rather than confess her crimes or show repentance, Morgan Le Fay cursed King Arthur and his lineage so that, by the age of thirty years, each would be stripped of their lands, people, and titles, and spend the rest of their days, however long, however short, fruitlessly seeking what they had lost.

King Arthur slew the witch and, burdened with this curse and his spoils of war, returned home to Camelot. There, he assembled the finest knights of his Round Table and, together, they scoured the globe for a way to break the curse. They sought many relics and artifacts, even the Holy Grail, until at last, the good king discovered the secret means to break the curse. But it was too late. Shortly after his discovery, King Arthur perished to his curse at the hands of Mordred, and he passed on to Avalon.

If only, if only, King Arthur had known earlier to seek out the kingdom of Dembroch, so that he and his family would have been spared the curse. For Dembroch is a wondrous place where a people toil, where the fairest magic burns around a castle royal. Where defenders protect flames six strong and seek out the helpless in need of healing their wrongs.

Seek it if you must, hunt its distant shores. Waiting for you, good men and women, will be the Timeless Kingdom of Dembroch forevermore.

– From the collection of recovered writings of
Sir Percival, the last of King Arthur's knights
Circa 557 A.D.

PROLOGUE

A New Tale of Dembroch

On a cold winter's night fit for carols and cheer, he told them a summer's tale of a queen and her kingdom. Wild red flames crackled in the fireplace. The room swelled gently with light; the grandfather clock ticked softly. Flurries of white collected on the sill.

Grandpapa sat in his chair, one giant bear claw of a hand holding up a book, the other twirling his gold-flecked pocket watch that always seemed to be stuck in the nine-o'-clock hour. A key dangled from the other end of the chain.

On the couch, the grandchildren listened raptly, eyes wide, ears perked, hearts thudding. It may have been past their bedtime, but sleep was the last thing on their minds.

The night had started like any other. After supper and games, Grandpapa had ushered them to the living room. From the shelf, he had pulled out a worn blue book and let it fall open wherever the pages would lie. As the grandchildren had curled up on the couch, he had begun another bedtime story of Dembroch.

But just as he'd began, Robbie and Lucy stopped him. The winter winds outside seemed to hush.

It wasn't that the grandchildren didn't want to hear a story, least of all one about Dembroch. They loved the Timeless Kingdom, you see, with its wild woods, towering castle turrets, wondrous magic, and nail-biting battles. But they had heard every story from Grandpapa's blue book at least a dozen times. They knew by heart the battle of Lady Ansel and the dragons, Sir Solomon's exile, Sir Tamas' quest to touch flames without being burnt, and King Arthur's search to break the curse on his lineage. The grandchildren loved these stories, one and all, but this night, they had longed for something new, something more.

"Tell us a new tale of Dembroch," the grandchildren pleaded. "A new bedtime story. One we've never heard before."

And so, with a sparkle in his eye and a mischievous grin, their Grandpapa left the room and returned with a new book, one the grandchildren had never seen before. It was a black leather journal, one you'd find in a used bookstore or left on the back seat of a bus. But the leather was dried and shabby, its cover dinged, scrapped, and burnt. Some of the pages were torn.

On its cover was a castle silhouette inscribed in flames. Now that, the symbol, the grandchildren knew well.

"This is not a tale for the lighthearted," Grandpapa told them, holding up the black book. "You'll have wished I'd told you a sweet story you knew so you would be rocked gently to sleep. But this tale is only for those of brave stock, thick skins, and bold hearts."

"What is it about?" Robbie asked nervously.

"Dembroch, of course," their Grandpapa replied, "but so much more. Within, you shall hear of the last knights and dames, magic and a terrible curse, a queen and kingdom in peril, lies that comfort and truths that scar. In these pages, magic dies and dead men walk. There are fires and fights, a monster of your worst nightmares. Clocks that don't tell time. Eyes that don't see. Invisible doors that take you far away. A witch... Is that adventure enough for you both?"

Robbie shuddered, but Lucy beamed.

"Tell it to us, Grandpapa," she pleaded. "Please."

"Only if your brother wants to listen, too," Grandpapa said.

Robbie hesitated. His sister elbowed him, and then he nodded vigorously.

"Alright then," Grandpapa said. "Let's begin."

He pulled their blankets up to their chins and took his place in the seat by the couch. From his pocket, he again pulled out his tiny, funny watch with the key on the end, and in his other hand, he cracked open the black book.

As the fire crackled and the grandfather clock ticked, as snow gathered on the sill and the cold winter's night grew colder, he told them a summer's tale they had never heard.

PART 1

Finding Dembroch

CHAPTER 1

The Siege of the Shallows

Deep in the castle library, the witch appeared out of thin air. Her blood-slicked hands clutched the king's chroniseal.

She was an atrocious creature, human by all accounts, but ravaged by age and time. Her skin was thin and spotted with scabs. Her eyes were hard and cruel. She was the woman death had forgotten, a terror that no man or woman dared follow, a witch named Sorgana.

It took a moment for Sorgana to gather her bearings. One second, she'd been surrounded by corpses and killers, caught in a vicious battle, and the next, she'd arrived here. The eerie calm after the chaos was unnerving. But she couldn't help it. She smiled, her lips curling devilishly.

She'd finally made it to Dembroch.

The old fool was right, she thought. Good thing, too. She'd shed plenty of blood to get the answers. But her joy was fleeting. There was much to be done.

She went on her way, as familiar with the library and the castle as a citizen of Dembroch would be. Before long, and after slaughtering anyone who crossed her path, she had exited the castle and gone to Coral Canyon, a deep fissure on the western side of Dembroch's main isle. She descended the canyon and, at the bottom, found turtles and fish playing among shallow pools. She snatched up a baby turtle and bit off its head, chewing ravenously. When she swallowed, her skin became fuller and her hair darker. The wrinkles disappeared; scabs healed.

Reinvigorated and visibly younger, the witch strode through the pools to her prize. Amongst the shallows was a strange black rock, and on its flat top, a bright, orange flame. Golden sparks, small as the eye could see, hung around the fire like frozen fireflies.

She approached the flame, holding a hand to it. Her fingertips grew warm and she had to pull away before she was burnt. But it was no matter. She had no need to touch the flame really, only to extinguish it.

She began to bend the reality of the world around her, manipulating the magic to unveil the true nature of the flame—it was not an ordinary fire. Not by any accounts.

No sooner had she discovered how to extinguish the flame—it was, as the old fool had said, quite complicated—the witch sensed a presence behind her. A large presence. She turned to find near one hundred of the kingdom's defenders standing at the ready, swords brandished, armor shining, all focused on her.

The witch could barely contain her glee. Formidable fighters though these knights and dames may be, they would be no match for her magic, her might, and...her monster.

The defenders called for her surrender. The witch cackled, thirsty for more blood, and with a snap of her fingers, her monster was released and the battle began.

In the massacre that followed, which would be known as the Siege of the Shallows, the witch decimated the forces of Dembroch's defenders. Her magic, both quick and razor sharp, cut through dozens. The witch's unleashed monster, the horrific Dreadnaught, devoured bodies whole before charging up the canyon walls and disappearing over the side to wreck more havoc.

The battle raged on. The flame on the black rock seemed to flicker with each fallen knight and dame.

Not long after it had begun, it was just the witch and a half dozen of the kingdom's last, best defenders. They were as talented at combat as the witch was at sorcery. She fought cruelly, but was soon subdued and at their mercy. After a lengthy argument about whether to kill her or not, the defenders took her back to the castle and to the queen.

Only the witch saw that, amongst the corpses and reddened shallows, the flame atop the black rock had diminished in strength and was now a flickering, wavering tongue, sputtering for life. A second later, it died. The frozen fireflies of sparks fell like stars from the sky.

Sorgana was dragged all the way back into the castle to a grand chamber with tables for dining and a throne for two. Only one person sat on the throne, a slender woman with long, golden tangles of hair, a sword hanging from her hip, and a fine metal crown atop her brow. In her hand, she held a metal contraption covered in dried blood—the king's chroniseal, the device that had brought the witch to Dembroch, which she had dropped in the library.

The witch sneered at the woman. This was Dembroch's last living monarch, Queen Coralee.

The remaining defenders, a scant half dozen, informed the queen of the witch's transgressions, including unwelcome infiltration of the kingdom, the murder of numerous defenders, the release of the Dreadnaught, the tampering of the flame, and the attack on the king, whose true fate was yet to be discovered.

"Lies! All lies!" the witch cried. "I have come to this kingdom to free you. All of you. A curse looms and anyone who remains shall be consumed by it."

There were murmurings, a stirring of fear.

"Silence," the queen interrupted. She observed the witch, measuring her words before speaking. "How do you know of this kingdom and its flames?"

"Your secrets are not so well kept," the witch replied.

"And who, pray tell, has shared the secrets of Dembroch with you?"

"Anyone will speak when enough blood has been shed," the witch replied, eyeing the king's chroniseal.

The queen screwed up her face to mask her true emotions. She kneaded her hands.

"What have you done with the king?"

"Wait and see," the witch simpered.

Queen Coralee jumped to conclusions: "Why would you dare strike this kingdom? Its people? Its leaders?"

"Have you no inkling?" the witch snarled. "Have you no memory of your transgressions? Don't you even recognize me?"

Queen Coralee's brow furrowed.

"I do not know you, witch," the queen said. "Enough with your trickery. What do you intend for my people?"

The witch's expression was the only answer anyone needed. It was full of bloodlust and contempt, a thirst for suffering.

"Take her away," the queen instructed. "Lock her in the last cell, seal it against any magic. I shall speak with her in due time."

And so, the witch was taken away, but she didn't mind. Her work was done for the time being. No cell could hold her any longer than she wanted to be held, and when the moment was right, she would strike again.

Back in the throne room, the queen consulted her viziers about the ongoing crisis. While the witch had been apprehended, the Dreadnaught was running loose on the main island and the flame in Coral Canyon was out.

"We must act quickly," Queen Coralee said. "Call upon the Watchmaker. He must find this witch's watch and discover what she intends. Consult the seer, see what must be done. Recover the fallen from the canyon. Prepare a proper service for the catacombs."

She held up the blood-coated chroniseal.

"And someone find my husband."

The viziers and remaining defenders did just that, heeding the queen's instructions to a tee. But much was for naught. Shortly after the Watchmaker received his instructions, the Dreadnaught attacked and every watch was taken, including the witch's. Defenders sought out the king, only to find his body lifeless and savagely beaten. His corpse was returned to the kingdom, as were his guard of defenders. A service was organized, but all the while, the kingdom was on high alert. A monster roamed their woods and a witch, unwilling to spill her secrets or admit to killing the king to gain access to the kingdom, remained locked in the castle's prison. Worst of all, the other flames of the kingdom were starting to flicker. The queen consulted the seer, but she had seen such a terrible future, she refused to look again and offered only tidings of doom. Desperate, the queen turned last to the mage, the elucidator and observer, first born of the island and long forgotten by its people, and he alone saw a path forward. He laid out four tasks that must be accomplished. They were daunting and nigh impossible. The few remaining defenders began to fall. Only a few remained. Civium began to whisper nervously to one another in the halls.

With nowhere else to turn, Queen Coralee issued the order. The kingdom needed help, and they needed to prepare for the worst. A scant trio of defenders could not protect Dembroch domestically and abroad, let alone hope to accomplish the mage's proposed courses of action.

"Send out the call to every corner of the globe," the queen commanded. "Every able-bodied, good-spirited man and woman, whosoever believes themselves worthy and able, are asked to become defenders of Dembroch and save our timeless kingdom."

CHAPTER 2

We Four Friends

Dembroch's request for aid was published in every paper around the world. Millions saw it, a few took it seriously. And my friends I were one of them.

We were about ten or so, little firecrackers of energy and imagination. There was Clay, taller than the rest of us and bold as brass, an all-American kid who had everything going for him. He liked Jenn, the new girl from the big city, who was brilliant and beautiful and happy. We came to tease Jenn for her uncanny eye to spot all things sparkly and shiny and her equally strong dislike of mud, goop, and germs. Meghan was my younger stepsister, a little pill sometimes, a couple years younger than the rest of us, but so confident and cool and sure of herself. She often did her own thing, but when it came down to it, she stood with us through thick and thin. And then there was me, Nick, the starry-eyed adventurer always looking to escape my classes and play in the woods with my friends.

We couldn't afford much back then, so playing pretend in the woods was our favorite thing to do. But if there was one thing worth saving up for, it was the orange cream malts at Dave's Diner.

Well...that was, until Dembroch.

We were in Dave's Diner that fateful day, sipping our well-earned malts, when Clay came charging through the door. Normally quite reserved, Clay was beside himself, insisting we read the listing he'd found in the newspaper's classifieds:

Immediate Assistance Needed

Dead is the king of Dembroch, as are many of our knights and dames. We call upon the noblest members of the public to aid our kingdom during this trying time and volunteer for our sovereign military order. Defenders are expected to guard the kingdom, the dowager queen, and her people at any cost. If you find yourself willing and able, deliver your statement of intention, letters of mark, $125, and a lock of your hair by post. Join the defenders of Dembroch. Save us.

Ah, I still remember the feeling when I first read it. I couldn't wait to be a knight. A defender of Dembroch. I yearned for it with every fiber of my being. And, in my heart, I thought about the queen, the desperate dowager seeking help. How I wanted to be her knight, I realized. How I needed to be. And all I had to do was save $125. That would be worth every penny.

My friends must have felt the same way. Jenn, Clay, Meghan, and I helped one another save up our money. Once we'd made enough, we collected everything we needed to apply and mailed it to Dembroch. We waited for ages it seemed until, finally, we received a reply.

We'd been accepted. Each of us were given a certificate naming us knights and dames of the kingdom by authority of the ruler, Queen Coralee. She gave us metal brooches, the seal of Dembroch, to wear at all times. They were beautiful, shining medals of a castle silhouette, encircled by a ring of flames with the kingdom motto, *Omnia Aeterno*, inscribed in the bottom. Lastly, she wrote each of us a letter. I thought for sure it was our summons, our call to the kingdom. But in it, we discovered a less amazing truth. Though my friends and I had been named knights and dames of Dembroch, we were placed in the Reserves.

I looked it up later just to be sure. To be in the reserves was like being benched during the game. You were there in case of emergency, a last call of sorts, doomed to sit and watch while the stars took the center stage. A couple hundred people had volunteered to help Dembroch, and the queen had called several of them into service. But not us. Not my friends. Not me.

I took it in stride, or tried to. Though we hadn't received a direct summons, we pined for the day in which we would be called. I still longed to go there, even if it took longer than expected. So, in the meantime, I started writing letters to Queen Coralee, promising to find her one day and save her kingdom.

Yeah, that's right, I liked her. Or the idea of her. I wanted to be her knight. And I felt sure that, if I kept writing to her, one day, she would call upon us. One day, Dembroch would need us.

But, someday never came. Dembroch, and the queen for that matter, never called for us. Years passed. My friends and I grew older and, worst of all, we grew apart. We stopped talking about Dembroch, then we stopped talking all together. I started spending more time alone, filling my time waiting and hoping for the kingdom that would never call...

Then, one day, out of the blue, near the end of high school, we received a package from Dembroch. I got the gang together and tore open the envelope to find—just a book. It was entitled *The Knights and Dames of Dembroch.* There was no letter, no explanation, just the book. I poured over it, suspecting a secret message or summons lay within, but there was nothing.

A few days later, the worst happened. We received a letter from Dembroch. I gathered my friends once more. Within was not a summons, no, nor an explanation of why we had received the book. It was a dismissal. The queen renounced our titles and disbanded the order of defenders. There was no clarification, no reason, just a dismissal and request we send back our medals.

I was so angry and ashamed. My friends laughed it off, admitting that they'd always thought this "Dembroch thing" was just a scam to get money from kids. Deep down, though, I knew it was real and I knew why we'd been removed from the order. My letters. I was positive that my letters, which had started innocently enough and perhaps turned into chaste little love letters to the queen, had spurred her to take our titles.

With no other evidence to the contrary, I lived with that guilt. Because of my childhood crush, we were dames and knights no more. I tried to make it up to my friends. I wrote many more letters, begging the queen to take us back, or at least my friends, but we never heard another word. All the while, my friends and I drifted further apart. A few years later, we graduated high school. Clay and Jenn ran off to Seattle and got married. My sister and I remained strong, promising to stay together through thick and thin. And then, as if fate had turned against us, we too were torn apart.

I remember it too well. Our parents arguing and shouting. The word 'divorce' being thrown out like a knife. The papers arriving. My stepmom moving out, dragging Meghan with her. The long talks with Meghan in the woods, consoling one another, promising that no matter what, we would stick together, brother and sister. And then, a few weeks later, when the divorce was finalized, Meghan's mom decided to move to Seattle. Meghan and I met in the forest, and she begged me to come with her. At that point, Jenn and Clay had been married a few years. Meghan was a year away from graduation. Dad was kicking me out of the house to live on my own. There was nothing left for me in little, ol'

Midvale. Except Dembroch. What if they sent for us? No one would be left in Midvale to answer their call.

"We're not defenders anymore!" Meg had cried. "We haven't been for years. You're waiting for nothing."

But I couldn't bring myself to leave. Sure, it had been more than a decade since we'd first volunteered, but someday, they would send for us.

"I'll stay," I had said. "I'll stand guard. I'll wait for the summons and call you all back when it's time."

She called me stupid, I called her a traitor. And in the end, Meghan stormed off and I was all alone in Midvale, pining for a kingdom that had never needed me, for a life I had wanted but been refused.

As the days and weeks passed into months and years, I thought often of Dembroch and its queen, wondering what had happened to her. I wondered if and when they would call upon my friends and I. Surely it would be the next day. Or the next. Or the next...

CHAPTER 3

The Clash at Cliffside Tower

Fifteen years later, the defenders of Dembroch huddled in the tower, awaiting the worst. Swords were held with the loose grip of inexperience. Haphazard pieces of armor clung to their bodies as sweat moistened their foreheads.

These men and women were most of the remaining members of the Reserves, volunteers from all walks of life, aspiring heroes, cowards, and charlatans. They hid in the Cliffside Tower, waiting for Sir Kenneth. Of these last Reserve defenders, Sir Kenneth alone had devised a final, desperate plan to save the kingdom and his fellow knights and dames. And though Sir Kenneth had come upon a great idea, it was ultimately ill-informed, shallow, and—to be blunt—stupid.

Sir Kenneth was deep in the Horror Hollow. His brilliant plan? To retrieve the fortissium blade, a sleek sword of black, indestructible metal. All around him, the monsters of the hollow hissed as though warning him to not take the blade from the Storm Stone. The blade too resisted him, sending jolts of electricity through his fingers. But, at long last, he rent the sword from the stone. As he did, the stone's dial was wrenched out of place and a blast of winter winds came out. The gales blew Sir Kenneth, sword in hand, out of the Horror Hollow. He found his feet and ran, headed for the skybridge. Around him, the mountainous terrain of Ryderwyle, normally green and lush, was quickly coated in snow and ice from the winter wrath unleashed. The monsters of Horror Hollow shrieked after him.

Huffing and puffing, Sir Kenneth made it to the skybridge, the path connecting the mountain island of Ryderwyle to Dembroch's main island over a channel of deep ocean. He sprinted across it. The fortissium blade was heavy in his grasp.

Just then, when the knight was almost across the skybridge, the Dreadnaught arrived. It slammed into the bridge, smashing it to smithereens. Like dominos, the bridge began to collapse. Sir Kenneth leapt just as the structure crumbled beneath him. He crashed into the water. Salt bit at his wounds and the cold cut to his bone, but he did not stop. Sword still held tightly, he swam along the channel to a calm inlet. He scaled the cliffs and ran deep into the woods.

Miraculously, Sir Kenneth made it back to Cliffside Tower. His fellow defenders cheered heartily at his arrival, but there was little time to celebrate. The Dreadnaught appeared right behind him, crashing through the trees. Sir Kenneth, too far away from the tower to beat the monster in a race, turned and stood his ground to face the beast. He bore his new sword offensively. The black metal glinted in the summer's heat.

The Dreadnaught kept charging. It roared. There was the buzz of a million ticks and clicks. And then, the sky turned black. Sir Kenneth's bravery faltered ever so slightly.

The monsters of Horror Hollow, repugnant beasts of fangs and fire and flight, had followed Sir Kenneth, the thief of their treasure. They bore down on him now, the Dreadnaught scuttling into the fray too, a million teeth aching to sink into the knight's flesh.

Sir Kenneth swung mightily with the fortissium blade, that indestructible sword that could cut through anything—should have cut through anything—and it glanced right off the monsters like water off a duck's back.

The knight did not get a second chance. He was swarmed by the monsters, lost in a sea of teeth and blood.

It was the last anyone saw of Sir Kenneth. There were shrieks and squelches, rips and tears. A second later, a severed arm, still clutching the black-bladed sword, flew high into the sky, fell through the tower's window, and landed with a splat in the upper room amongst the defenders. The blade was spattered in crimson blood. The fingers twitched.

No one tried to grab it. It was all too clear: the sword would not aid a thief, let alone these cowardly defenders.

Beyond the tower walls, the world seemed to rumble. No one had to look to know what was coming.

The monsters of the Horror Hollow landed on the tower's top. They clawed through, breaking into the upper room. At the same time, the Dreadnaught assaulted the walls, breaking large chunks away. The defenders fought for all it was worth, but they were indeed ill-equipped and inexperienced. Some were gobbled up by the Dreadnaught, others were skewered by the monsters of the hollow. It was an extermination, and the cries of terror and agony were the stuff of nightmares.

Across the island, in the kingdom's castle, a new nightmare was unfolding. Free of her prison cell of the last twenty-five years, Sorgana the witch burst into the throne room. There, the queen was begging her last remaining citizens to stay in the kingdom.

The witch cackled as she entered and, with a snap of her fingers and curt wave, sent the citizens flying to their deaths.

"Witch!" the queen shouted. She made to draw her sword.

CHAPTER 3

But Queen Coralee was too slow. The witch had already spoken an incantation and a weave of thorns wrapped around the queen tight as a blanket. She fell, crying out as the thorns stabbed her sides.

"How did you escape?" Queen Coralee cried.

"I had a hearty meal," the witch replied with a smack of her lips. "Magic lives in my veins as it lives in your island."

The queen seemed confused for a moment. "You do not manipulate Dembroch's magic? You dare hold magic—your own magic—*within* you?"

The witch giggled at the queen's lack of vision. "It's a power you would never dream of holding."

"How—why would you dare?"

"Tales for another time, my queen," the witch simpered. "Come with me, dear queen. Your kingdom cries for you."

The witch dragged the queen to the top of the castle's tallest tower. There, on the open-air balcony under the Reliquary, they saw the unfolding calamity.

All across the isles, the land itself seemed to be dying. Trees rotted and fell. Vineyards and grassy hills yellowed. Rumbles pulled the earth apart in deep fissures.

But the true horror was at the Cliffside Tower on the northeast headland. The tower was burning. An inferno blazed from its top. Rivers of boiling blood spilled out of the upper room and down the broken walls. The Dreadnaught was still tearing away, snatching up bodies.

"The defenders of Dembroch are dead," the witch proclaimed. "With it dies your kingdom's magic, and so too shall you."

She grabbed the queen by the head, squeezing her face. Savoring this perfect moment, Sorgana let the magic course through her. Her fingernails bore into the queen's skin. She declared the incantation she'd been reciting for more years than she could count.

The air seemed to be vacuumed from the world. The witch's youthful beauty decayed away, revealing her true, hideous form, as her magic was put to the test. In her grasp, the queen writhed in agony, screaming wordlessly.

Elsewhere, the last defender on Dembroch crawled across the inner room of the Cliffside Tower. She reached for the fortissium blade, which was pinned under a fellow dame's burning body. When she tried to pull it out, it shocked her and refused to be wielded. She died that way, pulling on the sword, as the monsters of Horror Hollow mobbed her.

The witch sensed this final death, felt the last breath as though she had been cheek-to-cheek with the dame. The kingdom felt it too as the mighty isles tremored.

And just then, as the witch's spell on the queen should have been completed and the witch should have been triumphant, it all stopped. The spell seemed to hit a wall, an unseen barrier. A blast of pain shot through the witch's hands and up into her temples. She gasped and released the queen. A deep cut had split across her forehead. Blood dripped from the wound.

Spitting with fury, the witch looked beyond the balcony's edge. The Cliffside Tower was a firestorm. No person could have still been alive. The magic must have been—

A flicker caught her eye. The witch spotted a different, smaller flame burning in the southeast. It was one of the magical flames and it was still alive.

"No!" she cried furiously.

She spun on the queen and was nearly skewered. The queen, unharmed by the botched spell and freed from thorns, had gotten to her feet, drawn her sword, and tried to stab the witch.

"Dembroch will never fall," the queen declared, pressing forward and swinging expertly. "So long as I am queen of these isles, and the defenders of Dembroch stand, this kingdom and its magic will never fall to you."

Queen Coralee swung again. Weakened from her attempted spell, the witch could only dance away. She circled the balcony, waiting for her energy to return, for her magic to flow once more at a level that would allow her protection and defense.

"You have shown your hand too soon," the queen said confidently. "Dembroch will not fall this day, if that is what you hoped. The poor defenders in the tower are not the last."

"You disbanded the order," the witch seethed.

"Their titles may be gone, but their duty and bonds still remain," the queen corrected. "The last defenders eagerly wait on distant shores for their summons. They are the fiercest warriors. Beyond compare. They know Dembroch's every secret, know every cavern and tree and blade of grass. They will know what happened on this day and they will come for your head, witch."

Sorgana did not seem intimidated by this. If anything, she looked ready for the challenge, happy to know why her spell had failed, and anxious to go about completing her plans.

"Let them come," she said gleefully. "I will slaughter them, and then your kingdom will truly fall."

Queen Coralee charged with her sword. The witch drew on what little strength and magic she had left to her devices. The castle quaked. The isles of Dembroch tremored. The Cliffside Tower burned. The defenders' bodies burnt to ash. The blood of eighty-some souls saturated the tower's grounds. And there, in the southeast Gate Grounds of the kingdom, one small, magical flame continued to burn.

CHAPTER 4

The Summons

He pushed through the crowds. His brow was slick with sweat and he longed to rest, but time was no friend to him.

As he pushed past, people stared. Maybe it was his clothes. Maybe it was his bright green eyes. Maybe it was the blood. No one was brave enough to stop him, and he was in too much of a hurry to care.

He made it—*finally*, he breathed, dark splotches passing through his eyesight—and hurried inside. The building was taller than any he'd ever seen and made of shining metal and glass. Inside, he begged to see her, insisted, shouted, but the gatekeeper would not allow it. He begrudgingly left the package, instructing the receptionist to give it to Lady Meghan at once.

And he was off again, bulldozing through the crowds, breathing hard, wiping the blood from his eyes, hurrying every chance he could.

CHAPTER 4

But it was for naught. The next two recipients, Sir Clayton and Lady Jennifer, were also unreachable. He left their packages, trusting that fate would deliver them to the right hands, and hurried on, marching into the forest, heading south. He had to find the one who would listen. The one who would unite the last defenders. The one who could save Dembroch.

I was the last person anyone would call, even as a last resort. No one sought me out intentionally. That's why it didn't make any sense to find someone waiting just for me.

I was halfway up the stairs to my condo—just a fancy name for my tiny, dingy, studio apartment on the fourth floor. Bangs were echoing down the stairwell. They were loud, incessant.

"Sir Nicholas!" someone shouted, their cries so desperate, I thought someone had died.

What was going on? I wondered. Was someone trying to break down a door? Were they calling for me?

Fearing a drug-addled trespasser or loathsome landlord demanding rent, I slunk back down the steps. I must have made a noise, because a head rose over the top of the stairs. It was a man, masked in shadow, but obviously big, burly, and angry. His eyes seemed to glow in the dim lighting.

Upon seeing me, the man ran toward me, descending the flight at a rapid pace.

I did the one thing I was good at in the face of danger: I shrunk on myself. I couldn't even bring myself to turn or run, let alone prepare for battle. I cowered, fearing the worst.

The person came to a stop a few steps above me. His breathing was labored. Dried blood covered his forehead and was smeared down his cheeks.

"Sir Nicholas Hutchinson?" the man said, his voice aged, gruff, and twanging with a foreign accent one-part Scottish and another unknown to my ears.

"Yes," I said nervously, though I'd never been called a sir before. Plenty of other names, but never sir.

I dared to look up.

Towering over me was a man with deep set eyes so green they seemed to glow, bloody and blistered cheekbones sharp as mountain bluffs, scrapes and scuffs all over his body from a long journey, and bristles of white hair poking out of his scalp and ears. He wore mustard yellow clothes made of leather and felt. I thought I saw something shining on his chest, but I didn't dare look anywhere but directly at him. He had the air of a man who had traveled too far for a glass of whiskey.

"Sir, are you—?" I stammered, eyeing the dried blood smeared over his cheeks. "Do you need an ambulance?"

Unexpectedly, the man swept into a deep, gracious bow.

"I have traveled quite far to see you," he said, his voice still deep, but carrying a note of jubilation. "I am Page Hybore of Whittlesea, servant of Queen Coralee and citizen of the Timeless Kingdom of Dembroch."

I couldn't help it. I gasped. Fireworks shot off in my mind. It felt as though I'd been shaken awake from a twenty-year slumber. Had I just heard right?

My eyes flew to Page Hybore's chest. The shine on his tunic was a medallion, circular in shape, a castle silhouette inscribed in a ring of flames. My heart seemed to freeze.

It was the sigil of Dembroch.

The name of Dembroch had not passed my lips in several years, nor had it crossed my mind much. My knight's brooch, first received at the age of ten, was tucked away four flights up, stowed in a box of knick-knacks, its allure forgotten alongside my hopes of regaining my physical fitness or achieving financial stability. The child who had once hoped and believed in Dembroch was now a grumpy old man, thirty-three years of age and at least three hundred in spirit, sharp in skepticism and forgetful of youth and joy.

"This is a joke," I said flatly.

The man named Page Hybore cocked his head.

"This is no joke, I assure you," he said. "Hear my words, Sir Nicholas. Dembroch summons you."

He reached into the breast pocket of his mustard tunic and withdrew a bound scroll and a pocket watch. He held them out to me.

"But–but I'm not a knight anymore," I stammered. "The queen—"

"The queen regrets her actions," Page Hybore said. "We saw a time of peace, a calm in the eye of the storm. But the kingdom is in dire straits, more so than ever, and on the verge of collapse. We have reclaimed a temporary calm, but it shall not last long, or so long as the last period. I was sent to collect you. I have traveled over land and sea, through bitter cold and blazing heat, to find you. If we—if Dembroch—is to survive the coming nights, it needs its last defenders."

My brain seemed to be short-circuiting. I wasn't fully understanding the page.

"Dem—Dembroch," I stuttered. "It's in trouble?"

Eyes glowing green, Page Hybore gave me another look, a suspicious one that seemed to wonder if I was playing a game and kidding him or testing him somehow.

"I'm sorry," I said. "It's just... What's happened?"

"There is much to explain, as you well know," the page replied. "Suffice it to say a terrible famine of sorts has befallen our kingdom and a witch threatens our lives every moment she breathes. Now, please, come with me."

"What about my friends?" I said, though I hadn't called them *friends* in years. These were surely the other Reserves he spoke of.

"I have already reached out to them," the page replied. "By now, they have received their summons and their chroniseal—"

"Their what?" I interrupted.

Page Hybore seemed impatient now. He held up the pocket watch.

"This is your watch," he said, then pointed to his chest. "When you affix it to your Dembroch sigil, it creates a chroniseal." He said the word slowly as though I were a child. "Press the winding crown and you shall be taken where you need to go. Now, if you please, Sir Nicholas, time is of the essence, a commodity we cannot afford to waste any longer. Come with me! Now!"

His last word caught in his throat. He clutched at his gullet and made a weird rasping noise. The next second, he fell onto me. He was heavier than I expected and we crashed to the ground. I wiggled out from under him and turned him over.

The man lay deathly still. His eyes, once vibrant and alive and flecked with green, were hazy and distant.

It took me a moment to realize it. The man was dead. Just like that. Dead. Gone.

"No," I said to myself. This man had more to say. He could not die. Not like this. I needed to know more.

Before I fully knew what I was doing, I was hammering on his chest. After several pushes, I gave him mouth-to-mouth. I breathed for all it was worth, willing the page to come back from the brink.

Suddenly, just as I was about to compress his chest again, Page Hybore jolted back to life. He coughed and spluttered before looking right at me. His eyes were a soft blue, which was odd considering how green they'd been before.

"Sir Nicholas," he gasped, holding his chest. "I—"

The words caught in his throat again. He shuddered violently and lay flat. His breathing became sickly and shallow. Trickles of blood ran from freshly opened blisters on his cheeks. He stared at the ceiling, mouthing without sound.

"Sir?" I stuttered. "Page Hybore? Are you—"

"Listen," he murmured, finally finding his voice, the words quiet and weak. "My Sinclair. My Emily. They lie hidden in Dembroch. They need your help. Tell them I love them. That I did this for them. Help her to find the safest shores. It's where..." His voice lost strength and I didn't quite hear the words—I thought he said fairest tragic or perhaps terraced magic. He took a rattling breath and, louder, said, "And the witch—"

Page Hybore grimaced and shook violently again. His eyes flashed green.

"Page Hybore!" I cried.

"Beware, Sir Nicholas," the page managed to say as he convulsed. "Save the kingdom. Save my—"

And suddenly, he lay still again. The green light left his eyes and they were blue once more, fading in vibrancy until they were dull and lifeless and blue. Bruises began to form under his chin, spreading up into his face. His bloody cheeks flowed red.

I sat in stunned silence, unable to process what I'd just seen. Page Hybore was dead again, and this time, deep down, I knew he wasn't coming back.

Wheels squeaked as Page Hybore's body, zipped up in a black body bag, was borne away on the coroner's stretcher. The police asked me what I knew, and I lied through my teeth until they had gone. Pushing past my curious neighbors, I locked myself into my apartment room and, from my pocket, pulled out the two items Page Hybore had given me.

Examining them, my heart beat fast. It was as though with Page Hybore's death, the child within me—that young, resilient, adventurous Nick that had been buried deep under my adult logic and sense—had risen once more, eager for the quest ahead. For the watch and the summons. For Dembroch.

The watch was made of a metal I'd never seen, a shining black speckled with gold flecks. It seemed an ordinary pocket watch, though it read eleven-o'clock when the correct time was seven, and the time would not change when I tried to reset it. Additionally, curiously, the back was not enclosed. I could see all the inner gears that clicked and spun in mechanical precision.

I turned my attention to the scroll. It read something like this:

Dead are the last defenders of Dembroch, helpless is the queen. In this, our darkest hour, we call upon you, our last knights and dames of the Reserve. Set your affairs in order and fly to the defense of your queen, her people, and this land. We pray for your safe voyage and shall expect you by first light of summer. Fly to us, our last knights and dames, and save your Timeless Kingdom of Dembroch.

I folded the note and sat on the edge of my bed. My hardened heart thudded away, breaking free of its skeptical shell. My mind spun like a leaf twirling down a river in the woods.

"It's real," I breathed aloud.

After all this time, Dembroch, my renounced knightship, the queen—they were all real.

My brain screeched to a halt as I thought of the queen named Coralee. I remembered my youthful yearning, my letters, and my childish crush. My cheeks burnt red though no one was around. For the first time in my life, I prayed she hadn't received any of my letters.

But it didn't matter. Not anymore. Dembroch was real and its queen was calling for help. My friends and I had to answer.

I recalled the faces of Clay, Jenn, and Meghan, my old childhood friends and stepsister, my fellow ex-defenders of Dembroch. I wondered if we could still be considered friends, now that they were all big wigs in Seattle and I was still here in Midvale. Clay ran his parents' store, Jenn was a psychiatrist with more problems than her patients, and Meghan was a CEO of a booming tech company. They seemed like strangers, and it didn't help we hadn't spoken in years.

Time to change that, I told myself, standing from the bed and reaching for my phone. After fifteen years, it was time to get the gang back together.

CHAPTER 5

A Reunion of Friends

A week later, as the longest day of the year gave way to night, Dave's Diner—the childhood haunt of my friends and I—was packed to the gills. Lagers crowned every table. Hearty laughter echoed off the walls. Friends and coworkers clinked glasses in cheers to the weekend. Ol' Dave, the bartender who seemed to outlive any customer who walked into his diner, greeted visitors with a cheery bellow.

For the first time in twenty-some years, four orange cream malts sat on the bar counter, thawing slowly. I sat at the farthest seat, keeping an eye on the diner's front door, thinking I should have ordered beers instead of our old childhood drink.

Over the arm of my chair hung my old satchel, one from my youth that I'd worn to look like a suave, swashbuckling adventurer. In the satchel, I had packed the book about Dembroch knights and dames, the gold-flecked pocket watch from Page Hybore, the handwritten summons from the queen, and my Dembroch sigil. It was everything I thought I'd need if my friends arrived and we really made it to Dembroch.

As I sat there, a thousand thoughts ran through my mind. Was it really real? Why had Dembroch and the queen and Page Hybore waited so long to call us? What dangers did they face? Could I dare to stand and fight whatever it may be?

I'd gone looking for Dembroch. After high school, after my friends went their separate ways, I'd collected all my savings and gone hunting. I saw such beautiful sights—mountains so high they touched the clouds, oceans bluer than the sky—and met people of new cultures, different worlds, and unique faiths. Every moment was like a spark from a raging fire in my soul, but the magic soon faded. For all my searching, I never found Dembroch. Never found anyone who had heard of it.

The money ran dry after a few years. So did my hope. I returned back home, the only place I'd ever known, and lived with my Dad. The love for Dembroch I'd harbored since a child started to rot. A few months later, Dad died. I was on my own then. For good. With nowhere else to go and no one else to depend on, I'd finally grown up. I stopped writing letters to the queen. I got a job as a local handyman, sold the house, and hid away from the disappointing world in my tiny apartment.

I didn't look back fondly on those times. I sank low. Even lower when the Internet had come around and I'd searched for Dembroch. All I'd found was an entry from an old encyclopedia, citing that Dembroch was a small island fishing community with less than a dozen citizens.

Such a small, boring, little land couldn't possibly need protection, I decided. Deep down, I started to wonder if, all this time, I'd been a naïve, gullible child, seeking a fairy tale in a sewer.

But here I sat, some ten years later—fifteen since high school, twenty-five since I'd first heard of Dembroch—and the kingdom was back in the forefront of my mind. How had I never found it? What could this tiny little island need help with?

CHAPTER 5

It all circled around, but it all kept coming back to Page Hybore. It was difficult to deny a dying man's final words.

The door to the diner opened. A motion-sensing frog croaked loudly to announce a new guest. I spun around—but it was just Old Sal from three streets down. He already looked several sheets to the wind, maybe even a whole comforter set.

"You look much harder at that door, you'll have to buy her a drink," said Ol' Dave.

I snapped out of it, exchanging a smile with the barman.

"What you thinking about so deeply?" he asked.

I shrugged. There was no sense in keeping it a secret.

"Remember that ad we found when we were kids? About the knights and dames?"

Ol' Dave grunted in remembrance. We'd caused quite a ruckus that day when Clay had shown us the newspaper clipping.

"It was real," I explained. "A guy from there found me last week—"

"Must have been the bloke who came 'round here looking for you," Ol' Dave mused. "Sent him that way."

"—and he died to tell me...that place we volunteered to protect...it's real. It's in trouble."

The bartender leaned closer to me, losing interest in his clientele further down the counter.

"I know, it's crazy," I said. "I'm not even sure if I believe it. It could be a lie."

"I've heard crazier. Seen stranger," Ol' Dave mused. "The way I see it, every story has a grain of salt, even the tallest tale. Every one of 'em has just a bit of truth. So maybe you were right when you were younger. Maybe that place is out there. So why haven't you gone yet?"

I shrugged again. "I know how to get there, but I don't want to go without...you know, the gang."

The door opened again, and I spun around again, but it was just some mill workers.

"Good of you to keep your word and get everyone together," Ol' Dave said. "Promises—real promises—are difficult to make and even harder to keep."

"They have to get here first," I said.

"And if they don't show?"

I didn't know how to answer that.

Down the counter, shouts came for more drinks. Ol' Dave hurried over to fix them up, leaving me with my thoughts. All the while, I kept an eye on the door. Several more patrons arrived, but none of them were my friends.

Another hour crept by. My spirits fell. I drained my malt and pushed my chair back from the counter, resigned to head home and figure things out on my own. At least then, if it was a prank or lie, I would be the only witness to my foolishness and gullibility.

Just then, as I threw my satchel over my shoulder, the diner's door opened. The frog croaked. I looked around, prepared for disappointment, but instead, I did a double-take. In the doorway stood my stepsister Meghan.

She had grown a foot taller since I'd seen her. Her hair was pulled back in a tight bun, and her face looked even tighter. When she saw me, she smiled a thin little smile and strode toward me, her pantsuit swishing crisply.

I met her halfway, wrapping her in a warm hug. She embraced me slower. It felt like hugging a cardboard cutout.

"Doing well, Nick?" she asked.

"Fine," I replied. "It's great to see you again, Meghan!"

"It's Meg," she corrected.

"Sorry," I said apologetically. "Come on, Meg! Have a malt! Or a beer. I can get you a beer if you want."

I led her to the counter. She accepted the malt and we toasted, making faces at the strong taste. Without abandon, I launched into conversation, asking how she was, what she'd been up to, how life was going. She wasn't incredibly talkative, and I sensed a tenseness in the air between us. When I asked what was wrong, her eyes narrowed.

"Why are we really here, Nick?" she asked.

I stammered, not yet ready to bring up Dembroch.

Just then, the door to the diner opened again. A croak of the frog ushered in a potbellied man and a skin-and-bones woman. The couple glanced around the bar, spotted Meg and I, and made their way toward us. The woman ambled along, but the man strode with purpose. His personality seemed to fill the room. It was obvious he was headed right for us, though I didn't know why until, with a jolt, I realized the couple was Clay and Jenn. Geeze, we'd all gotten old.

Clay practically tackled me with a hug. I was stunned to see how different he was. Age hadn't been kind. His buttoned shirt and tie strained around his potbelly and fleshy neck. Worry lines crisscrossed his face and grey peppered his hair, but despite it all, he seemed full of energy and life.

"Gosh, it's been too long!" Clay exclaimed, his voice louder and more confident than I remembered. "Would you look at us all? It's like we never left."

"Meghan?" asked Jenn, who had finally arrived beside us. Her voice was slow and sad.

"It's Meg," my sister replied.

Jenn acknowledged this sadly and the old friends greeted one another stiffly.

Like her husband, perhaps like me too, Jenn had grown significantly older. Though she had done up her hair and wore fancy clothes that outclassed the patrons of Dave's Diner, she had a distant look in her eye and a well-practiced frown. Her hair was thin, her face weary. She wore a wedding ring fit for a queen, its diamonds shining like a flashlight. Jenn had always like the shiny stuff.

"Thanks for coming," I said to her when we greeted.

"Clay insisted," Jenn replied. "I'd rather have stayed at home."

I tried to chuckle, but I realized she wasn't trying to be funny.

Suddenly, it hit me: we were all together. The four of us were once again at Dave's Diner on a Friday. And yet...only Clay was smiling. And he was the last one I'd expected to be ecstatic. Growing up, he'd always been the quiet, thoughtful, stoic friend. His energy and bravado seemed...well, I wasn't sure at the time, but he didn't seem like the Clay I knew.

So there we were, the four friends together again. We all stood opposite each other, Clay grinning, Meg crossing her arms, Jenn staring off into the distance, an atmosphere of uneasiness hanging amongst us like a faint, unpleasant stench that wouldn't go away.

I gestured to the malts.

"A drink for the good old days?" I asked.

"What good old days?" Meg asked.

"I'll say," Jenn mumbled, looking nonplussed.

Clay shrugged his shoulders. "Jenn and I can't stay long. Places to go, people to see. We just wanted to swing by and say hello. You've all been well?"

Meg mumbled in agreement. I didn't know where to begin with the recap of the last decade of my life, but I didn't have to try. A second later, Clay zipped up his coat and waved a farewell.

"Anyhow, it was great seeing you all. Have a great evening!"

"Hold on, wait," I said. "Do your old friend a favor and hang out for a minute."

"Favors take longer than a minute," Jenn said morosely.

"Maybe another time," Clay said. "Catch you later, buddy."

There was nothing else to be done, I realized. I had to make them stay. I had to tell them.

"Did you get the message from Dembroch?" I blurted out.

The reaction was small, but instantaneous. Clay tensed as though he were scared—his bravado vanished, and I could have sworn some hairs on his head went grey. Jenn groaned a sad little groan that only ghosts and abandoned puppies should make. Meg rolled her eyes ever so slightly.

CHAPTER 5

"That's what this is about," Meg muttered.

She turned to go.

"Wait!" I shouted. "Didn't you get the note?"

Meg rummaged through her purse and pulled out a rectangular piece of paper.

"This?" she asked, her voice mocking. "It was left at my office's front desk by a man who had to be escorted from the building. Who did you pay to do it?"

"What?" I said, completely confused.

"I know you wrote the note, Nicholas," Meg said, brimming with irritation I had never seen before. "Who did you pay to deliver the notes? The Renaissance Faire? Old Sal?"

"Aye!" Old Sal grumbled groggily from two tables over.

Clay pulled a similar note from his pockets.

"Wait. This was from you?" he asked softly, a deep hurt in his voice.

"Told you," Jenn said sullenly. She dug into her purse, but instead of pulling out a note, withdrew hand sanitizer. She squeezed a generous amount on her hands.

"No, no!" I shouted. I rummaged through my satchel and withdrew my own note. "I got one too, just like all of you. I asked you all to come here so we could go together."

Meg laughed harshly at me. It was like a car backfiring.

"Go?" Clay repeated.

"Very risky, Nicky," Jenn grumbled at me. "We could have died in a car accident on the way here, just for you to have your fun."

"That's a bit extreme," I said.

Clay hung his head.

"This is why I don't like people," he mumbled under his breath.

There was the Clay I remembered.

I stammered, frustrated. I couldn't believe how they were reacting. Weren't any of them the least bit interested or intrigued? Maybe it was because Page Hybore had only talked directly to me. If I could tell them what he'd told me...

"This is a waste of time," Meg said. She turned to leave again.

"*This* is an emergency," I said, jumping in front of her. "This note was delivered to me by a guy named Page Hybore. He was *from* Dembroch. And he died in my arms."

Jenn let out a dramatic gasp. "You killed him?" She took a step back as though I were diseased.

"He was already weak," I explained. "But he told me everything. Dembroch is in danger. The people who live there need our help."

"Help?" Clay interjected. "What type of help?"

"Like we could do anything to help them," Jenn groaned.

"It doesn't matter! There is no Dembroch to begin with!" Meg shouted, her cheeks flushing.

Clay put a hand on my shoulder, his puffed-up personality returning to the forefront.

"Nick, buddy," he said. "I know you're all worked up about this, but...even if Dembroch is out there—"

"It's not," Meg interjected.

"—we don't know where it is," he continued. "Or how to get there. It's a wild goose chase. We have better things to do with our time."

"Actually...," I said.

From my satchel, I pulled out the pocket watch Page Hybore had given me. I showed it to all my friends.

"Did you all get one?" I asked. "Page Hybore told me how to use it. I think it can get us straight to Dembroch."

Clay shook his head adamantly. "Be sensible, man. We can't just...leave. We have responsibilities."

"And we have a duty to Dembroch," I insisted. "We signed up to help them."

"And then they kicked us out," Jenn said. "Remember, we're not knights and dames anymore."

"It never existed!" Meg exclaimed, eyes bugging out. "Am I the only sane person in this room?"

CHAPTER 5

"Aye!" Old Sal grumbled at us. Our shouts were drawing glares and firing up the feisty drunks.

"It *does* exist," I insisted, my voice a bit quieter but no less pleading. "Dembroch is out there. And they need us. You guys gotta believe me."

Meg sighed heavily. I knew what that meant. She was about to go to any lengths to prove I was wrong and make me see reason.

"And a pocket watch will get us there?" she asked.

"I think so," I guessed, realizing how ludicrous it sounded.

"Okay, then," she said coolly. "Let's go."

"What?" Clay and Jenn said in tandem.

"We're going," Meg said. She gestured at me. "Right now. Take us there." She stopped just short of saying, "Prove me wrong."

"This is a bad idea," Jenn said tonelessly.

"I don't care," Meg continued. "Nick thinks he can trick us all by sending cute little messages and forcing us to meet. Well, I'm calling his bluff. There's no Dembroch. He should know because he wasted five years of his life looking for it. But if he still insists otherwise..."

She fastened the buttons on her suit and crossed her arms again.

I shrugged innocently and held up the pocket watch again, showing my friends the exposed gears.

"He said to connect the watch to our Dembroch sigils," I explained. "Together, they form a chroniseal."

"Great," Meg commented.

I pulled out my Dembroch medal and snapped the pocket watch onto it. The watch gears and sigil fit perfectly together.

"Then he said to press the winding crown," I explained. "That should be this button here on the top."

"Guys, wait," Clay said, his bravado disappearing again, his face a wrinkled wreck of nervousness.

"I don't want to die," Jenn bemoaned.

Unsure what would happen, fearing that nothing would, I pressed the button on the watch. This would have normally unclasped the watch's front and revealed the timepiece. Instead, the watch remained shut. But...nothing else happened. The gears within cranked loudly.

For a split second, dread filled my heart. I panicked—had Page Hybore lied? Had he forgotten to tell me something? Was I a fool? Was this all a lie?

Suddenly, a jolt of electricity shot out of the watch and passed through my whole body. A dizzy-spell hit me. Horizontal streams of color began to form around me.

"What in the world?" Clay murmured.

Assuming something big was about to happen, I reached out to my friends. Meg pulled away, but I grabbed a fistful of her suit and held tightly.

The world began to spin. Dave's Diner lost its detail, running into blurred lines. I felt my feet leave the solid floor.

And just like that, we disappeared from the bar. Not a single person noticed except Old Sal, who hiccupped and returned to his lovely liquor, and Ol' Dave, who *humph*ed in interest before he returned to tending his clients.

Like Ol' Dave had said, bartenders tended to hear and see stranger things. To the observant, sober eye, four adults disappearing in a flash of color was just another Friday night at Dave's Diner.

CHAPTER 6

Rough Landings

We spun for a few more seconds—I got very close to losing my lunch and the orange cream malt I'd had—until, suddenly, my feet touched ground again. Only my head kept spinning. The world came back into focus.

The four of us stood outdoors on a green slope curtained in thick mist. Lights of a far-off town passed in and out of sight. It was dark, even more so than Dave's Diner. High above, the moon glowed softly behind swirling clouds. Wherever we were, it was a different time of day, perhaps the opposite side of the planet, somewhere European. At least it was still Earth.

"What the hell?" Meg shouted.

"It's a little too cold to be hell," Jenn commented with a shiver. She dug into her purse and squeezed out another drop of hand sanitizer.

"Nick!" Clay exclaimed, his tie flapping in the wind. "Where are we?"

"I don't know!" I shouted, as confused as they were. It wasn't quite the peaceful, serene island kingdom I'd imagined. The weather was miserable, and the wind was cold; though on a sunny day, the grassy meadow by the ocean might have been an idyllic picnic spot. Was this really the Timeless Kingdom?

A blast of frigid air hit my face. Water speckled my cheeks. I scanned the landscape, searching for the source. A football field away, I saw a rocky shoreline and an ocean. Waves swelled dangerously in the high winds and crashed into the rocks. Amongst the chaos was a small, squat building with a dock leading out into the waters. I didn't know exactly what it was, but a building meant shelter, and it was much closer than the city lights.

"Come on!" I shouted, waving them toward the building.

"Wait!" Meg shouted after me. "Nick!"

We ran down the hill, slipping on the wet grass.

The building on the shore was a shack. Its wooden sidings were peeling away and dark from the moisture. A dock ran from the back of it, disappearing into the haze of the churning ocean. Three rowboats were tied to the dock, rocking in the windswept waves.

I tried the door, but it was locked. I thought about tearing it open, but we weren't that desperate yet.

The four of us flattened against the wood sidings, hiding from the weather.

"What the hell was that, Nick?" Meg shouted in my ear. "What did you do to us?"

"You told me to take you!" I replied, as shocked as she was.

"We're all going to die!" Jenn bemoaned.

"It'll be okay," Clay said. "No one's dying yet."

"What do you mean *yet*!"

"Screw this," I heard Meg mutter.

She reached into her pocket, withdrawing her Dembroch brooch and a pocket watch. I was so stunned to see she still had her medal that

CHAPTER 6

I didn't even think to stop her from connecting the two and clicking the top button.

"No!" I shouted, realizing too late what she was doing.

A flurry of color like a miniature rainbow tornado surrounded her. A split second later, the lights faded, and she was gone.

"What—Where did she go?!" Clay shouted.

"She died!" Jenn cried, sinking to her knees.

A second later, light flashed out in the meadow. Meg appeared, stumbling out of the column of color. She looked around wildly. Even from a football field away in the high winds, I heard her curse.

"Meg! This way!" I shouted.

She didn't seem to hear me. Instead, she pressed the button on the watch again. Lights appeared, swept her up, and deposited her right back where she'd been. More angry shouts reached our ears.

Meg stalked back toward us through the rain. All the while, she yelled at me.

"Nicholas Roger Hutchinson," she exclaimed, "take me back! Take me back right now!"

"I can't!" I replied. "The watch thing must only take us to—"

Meg lunged, grabbed my hand, and squeezed tight. My hand was compressed around the watch and medal contraption called a chroniseal. I felt my thumb press the watch's winding crown. Pulses of energy jumped through us, the world blurred together. I felt like I was flying on a merry-go-round, and then we were standing on the green slopes again, one hundred yards away from the shack, Jenn, and Clay.

"—here," I finished.

"Take me back!" Meg shouted through the wind.

"I don't think I can!" I called back. "It brings us *here* no matter what we do."

Meg threw her chroniseal on the ground, wrapped her hands into fists, and shrieked in anger. She looked to be at wit's end.

"How? How are you doing this?" she demanded. "Did you spike my drink? Did you drug me?" She was getting crazier by the second.

"No!" I insisted. "It's the watch. Page Hybore told me it would take us to Dembroch."

Meg visibly rolled her eyes.

"You have a better explanation?" I asked aloud. When she said nothing, I waved toward the shore. "Come on. We're getting sopping wet."

After picking up her chroniseal and giving it back to her, I led her back to the shack. All the while, I could practically hear her brain churning, studying her watch and medal, trying to riddle out how this was all possible.

As we walked, the clouds to the east began to lighten. The mist thinned. Dawn was coming. Back home, the sun had just been setting.

"What do we do?" Clay shouted when we were within earshot.

"Stand here and ponder life, obviously," Meg said grumpily.

"Let's look around," I said. "Find out where we are, or find someone who can tell us."

"I'll just stay here," Jenn said miserably. "Let me know if you find anything."

"Come on, Jenn," Clay insisted, pulling her to her feet and dragging her along. "Chin up, darling."

We circled the shack, looking for a clue or a sign. We found one—a literal sign—hanging from the dock, creaking in the wind. It read:

Ferry of Northern Scotland
Pick-ups at First of Every Hour from Dawn to Dusk

"Scotland!" Meg shrieked. "You took us to *Scotland*?"

I felt my heart drop.

"We're going to die!" Jenn moaned again.

"Stop saying that!" Meg shouted. "No one is going to die."

Suddenly, Jenn froze. In a high, thin voice, she said, "Guys? What's that?"

CHAPTER 6

I followed her gaze. Past the dock, something dark was moving through the mist. It rose and fell with the waves.

"We should run," Jenn said quietly.

"What?" Clay said, his teetering voice betraying his bluster. "It's probably just a—"

A ship appeared out of the fog. Modest in size, the boat was covered in fading white paint. Rust lines trickled from the bow.

"See," Clay said confidently to his wife. "No need to worry."

She didn't look any less panicked.

The ship pulled up to the dock slowly. I noticed there were words written along its side: *Omnia Aeterno.*

I gasped, not believing what I saw seeing—I knew those words. Fingers freezing from the cold, I fought to unclasp the pocket watch from my medal. There, written along the bottom of the Dembroch brooch were the same words. Long ago, I had deciphered this Latin phrase, which meant *all timeless and eternal.*

Dembroch, I realized, my stomach doing a leap. This boat must go to Dembroch.

By the time I had explained this to my friends and they had all grumbled their misgivings, the ship docked and a man strode down the gangplank. The dock's boards creaked as he came to a stop before us. He was dressed in ornate clothing with filigreed designs sewn into the material. He smiled kindly, a flicker of green in his eyes.

"Seeking passage on the ferry?" asked the man, his voice thick with a Scottish accent. "Where to? Ireland? France? Further?"

None of us said anything.

The man scanned over us. When he looked at me, he spotted the Dembroch medal in my hand and practically fell into a bow.

"My sirs and ladies," he said, his Scottish accent suddenly replaced with a twangier one like Page Hybore's. "Forgive me! I am Sir Liliford, the ferryman of Dembroch." He glanced over us. "Page Hybore?"

"He passed while delivering my summons," I explained.

"I thought he might," Sir Liliford said, knocking his chest. "I shall deliver you to Dembroch in his stead. Before we embark, do you have any belongings you wish me to store onboard?"

There was a beat of silence. I hadn't even thought about packing a change of clothes or toiletries.

"W–we don't," I finally stammered.

Sir Liliford raised an eyebrow.

"I must be mistaken," he said, his voice straining as he regained his composure. "The seer anticipated you would be bringing plenty of...what was the word...ah, yes, baggage. I am inclined to believe the belongings you carry are unseen and far more powerful. Dembroch's hope rests upon it. Now, please, allow me to give you a hand."

He helped us onto the dock and, before we boarded the ferry, asked to see our Dembroch sigils. I was pleasantly surprised to see that even Jenn and Clay still had their medals.

As I passed the ferryman, I noticed again that he had a flicker of emerald green in his eyes, just like Page Hybore. I wondered if it was a Dembroch thing.

"Settle in. The passage takes some time, but I promise a safe journey," Sir Liliford said, leaving us at the bow of the ship.

"Where are we going?" Meg demanded to know.

"Through the Norwegian Sea," the ferryman called back over his shoulder. "Past the Bolts of God to the harbor of Dembroch!"

Within minutes, the morning sun began to thin the mist, Sir Liliford pulled the boat away from the dock and set us out to sea. The green, mist-hewn slopes and cliffs of Scotland shrunk away. We approached and passed a set of tiny islands. Jenn let out the occasional sad sigh. Meg glared at her every time she did. Clay was all smiles and gusto.

"Fascinating," he kept saying. "Interesting. Wow, look, over there. What an adventure we're on, Jenn!"

Meg glanced at me and rolled her eyes.

CHAPTER 6

"Hold on," Jenn said tremulously some time later. "Shouldn't we be...avoiding that?"

Ahead of us, perhaps a quarter mile away, was a wall of clouds. I thought about calling out or warning Sir Liliford, but our ferryman was staring at it with a confident, green gleam in his eye.

We entered the veil of mist. It was thick. My friends disappeared from view. I heard Jenn clambering to find the railings. I stiffened too.

Suddenly, something tall, sharp, and dark passed by the starboard side of the boat. Hair stood up on the back of my neck. I spun, searching the fog.

Another one passed on the left. Jenn squeaked.

The cloudbank thinned enough to reveal spindly rock spires surrounding us. The spikes protruded from the grey ocean like broken, decaying teeth. Around some, I saw broken masts and ship ruins.

"Never you fear, my friends," Sir Liliford called from the steering wheel. "I've never led a traveler to danger. These are the Bolts of God! They guide us home."

We sailed on for what seemed like hours, weaving slowly but expertly through the rocky spires and storm. The roaring waves pushed the ferry like a toy boat, but Sir Liliford used this to his advantage, sweeping in pirouettes around the rocks that had claimed so many other vessels. Then, when it seemed we'd never arrive, Sir Liliford called to us again.

"My sirs and ladies," he said. "I ask you to direct your gaze to the bow!"

My heart skipped a beat. My skin flushed with goosebumps. At last, Dembroch!

We passed a thick cluster of rocky spires. The veil of clouds evaporated like magic.

And there, right in front of us, was an island. *The* island.

I couldn't help it. I gasped. But it wasn't out of amazement. It was shock.

Heavy, dark clouds blocked out the sun. Gloom reigned across the Norwegian Sea, making the waters a murky black, and over the island too.

Roughly elliptical in shape, the shadowy landmass loomed before us. Surf crashed into steep, craggy cliffs. Wind swept across blackened rolling hills and thick, dead forests. The land pitched and rolled like the most dramatic Scottish landscapes, rising to sharp bluffs in the west, sloping to inlets and narrow beaches in the southeast, but it all looked steep, harsh, and uninviting.

Far off, perhaps an island of its own beyond the one before us, was the clouded tip of a steep mountain. It was covered in snow and obscured by clouds of brewing blizzards.

I couldn't take it all in at once. There was so much to see, and a feeling of dread was creeping into me. But one thing caught my eye, one tiny, beautiful thing.

In the middle of the haunted-looking island, or perhaps just a bit off center, were the turrets of a castle. Sticking out of the dead trees, the fortress' towers looked like a crown upon the head of a giant human whose brow was just breaking the surface of the ocean. Golden flags flapped on spires, the one spot of color in the monochrome wasteland. This was surely the castle of Queen Coralee, the capital of Dembroch. But, even with the bright beacon of the castle, this place didn't seem like a timeless kingdom. If anything, it seemed like a desolate one.

My heart sank. I knew without a doubt: we were here. This was Dembroch, the place of my dreams that I had so avidly longed for in my youth. And it had already fallen.

CHAPTER 7

The Fallen Kingdom of Dembroch

The four of us sailed in silence. There were no sighs from Jenn, senseless chattering from Clay, or sarcastic grumbles from Meg. The sight of Dembroch, wasted away and barren, had arrested us and left us in shocked, horrified stillness.

I gaped at it. All these years, I'd imagined Dembroch as this beautiful island paradise of forests, waterfalls, and mythical creatures. After all, it had been called the Timeless Kingdom. But this was not a beautiful, enduring place of childhood fantasies. This desolate kingdom was a land of nightmares waiting to unfold. The forests and grassy meadows were withered and black. Riverbeds were gutted and dry. I half expected to see vultures over the trees or beady eyes peeking around trunks, but the creepy, dead island was empty, further perpetuating the eeriness. Not a soul, animal or human, walked its land.

I wondered if it had always looked this way. Surely the island had been beautiful once. Surely it's unappealing appearance was a byproduct of whatever famine had befallen it. Surely?

Beside me, Meg tapped her wristwatch. I glanced over. Curiously, the second hand would tick forward one second and then pause for several more seconds before moving just one second more.

"A gear probably slipped," I offered.

"Or it died," Jenn said morosely, looking over Meg's shoulder.

Meg groaned and pulled her sleeve over the malfunctioning watch.

Before long, we were a stone's throw away from the southwest edge of the island, approaching a wooden dock extending from a sandy beach. Buttressed between steep, eroding cliffs, the beach rose to a hill, at the top of which waited a horse-drawn carriage without any attendants.

In due time, we docked. Sir Liliford lowered the gangplank and ushered us off the ferry.

"Follow me, my friends," he called, walking down the dock and toward the shore. "Your queen awaits your arrival."

My friends shambled after, but I stood frozen for a moment. Everything I'd ever wanted was beyond this beach and slope, and the glimpse I'd gotten had already shaken my expectations. What would I find over the hill? Did I want to know?

Meg noticed I'd stopped and hollered for me to catch up, her tone clearly indicating that I had dragged her into this and if she had to follow the ferryman, so did I.

We crossed the sandy shore to the steep hill, tracing a trail through patches of dead, leafless shrubs until we stood at the top of the hill beside the horse-drawn carriage. The horses considered us with nervous trots of their hooves.

My eyes were drawn to the island beyond. It hadn't changed, but I still couldn't believe it. Dembroch stretched out before us in all its haunted forsakenness. There were no birds or rustle of life. Everything was still and quiet. Far to the east, white steam shrouded the land and rose to the sky. A path twisted to the north, following the natural curves of the land toward a gaping canyon and gnarled forest. Tiny, blue-tipped towers were just visible above the twisted limbs, at least two or three miles away.

"Is this...Dembroch?" Clay asked.

"The main island of the three," Sir Liliford said matter-of-factly.

"Three?" I repeated.

"Ah yes, a brief refresher on the lay of the land," our ferryman said. "The Timeless Kingdom is made of three islands: Dembroch, Ryderwyle, and Whittlesea. We stand upon the largest, called Dembroch after the realm's namesake. The two smaller isles, Ryderwyle and Whittlesea, are separated from our main island by a channel of the sea." He pointed to northwest. "You cannot see it from here, but beyond the trees and the waves is Whittlesea. It is home to our pages, philosophers, and high thinkers. The isle is only accessible during low tide across a sand bar." Then, he pointed at the snowy mountain to the northeast. "The mountain right there is Ryderwyle, perhaps the most dangerous area in our territory."

"Dangerous?" Jenn asked feebly.

"Notwithstanding its current weather conditions, it is home to the Horror Hollow," Sir Liliford said simply. "Many a beast lives—or lived—in the Hollow. As such, it is also where the kingdom's defenders train. Or did before the winter descended. And the skybridge was destroyed. And the monsters relocated here. And all the defenders died."

I tried not to let these last details perturb me but I felt fear creep through me like snow slipping down your collar and onto your back.

"Why is it snowing?" I asked, trying to distract myself.

Sir Liliford seemed surprised I did not know. "Have you not heard? An errant knight caused the winter storm to assault the isle. He has since perished and left us with yet another problem to solve." The ferryman shook his head. "Now, chop chop. It's off to see the queen."

My heart did a somersault of joy and shock. The queen? We were going to see her? Right *now*? I suddenly felt self-conscious how round my belly had grown and the stubbled cheeks I hadn't shaved in a few days. Would she remember my letters? Did we have to meet her right now?

Sir Liliford instructed us to board the carriage. It had room to seat eight and carry all their luggage, so we barely filled it. Sir Liliford took the reins and gave them a flick. The horses whinnied nervously and, with a tug, we were off.

CHAPTER 8

The Famine of Timelessness

We rode across the barren, rolling hills and meadows, crossing rocky ravines where rivers once ran and a wide field full of gnarled, brown vineyards. Not a single vine bore fruit.

"It has been a difficult time as of late," Sir Liliford said. "The season has been harsh."

"A famine?" I asked, remembering Page Hybore's words.

"Of sorts," the ferryman replied.

"Are the vineyards your main source of economy?" Clay asked.

"As well as fruits and fishing," he added. "The Civium cultivate the land and, from the surplus, have me sell the wine, fish, and fruits to the Scots as an independent farmer."

"What do you do with the money?" Meg said, her tone far from generally curiosity.

"The kingdom keeps a small fund for transactions with neighboring countries and our sister kingdoms, such as the purchase of meats and fabric. I broker most of these transactions."

"As an independent farmer?" I assumed. "Why?"

"Dembroch is one of the world's best kept secrets, of course! We pretend to be a small farming and fishing community in occasional need of protection from seafaring hostiles, but we are so much more."

I felt my brain cloud with confusion.

"Why?" I asked.

"Much of the work done on Dembroch is unprecedented," Sir Liliford replied, "and beyond the understanding of the outside world. If our true nature was known to the world at large, many a beggar, crook, and monger would be upon our dock, begging for our services, even demanding. We have dealt with this firsthand and, as a result, actively avoid revealing our true presence to the world."

My brain seemed to short circuit.

"What do you do exactly?" I asked, trying to get a straight answer.

Sir Liliford gave me that funny, green-eyed smile he had.

"Why, we aid those who need our help," he replied as though it were the most obvious answer in the world.

I stammered, trying to ask too many questions at once. Sir Liliford cut me off with a shake of his head.

"Perhaps you've never heard the full account of our origins," he offered. "Allow me to weave you the tale. Long ago, Christians fled Roman persecution and found the shores of Dembroch. The mage and his wife, the only residents at the time, welcomed the vagrants and provided them sanctuary. Those values were the founding tenants of the kingdom when King Peter formed the monarchy, and the same values we observe today."

"Which are...?" Meg grumbled.

"Shelter and healing," the ferryman replied, unphased by my sister's tone, "for the injured, afflicted, or cursed. They are called the Hospites: good-spirited, strong-hearted individuals from the world beyond who are incurably sick, unfairly afflicted, or untenably, tragically cursed. We permanent residents, the Civium, seek out these poor souls, the Hospites, and offer them a temporary home while we heal them. If they stay long enough in our kingdom, they live in the village of Amaranthine."

"Why is this place any better at healing than a hospital or surgeon?" Meg asked, crossing her arms.

"Come now, do not play the fool," Sir Liliford said. "You know of the magic."

"Right," Meg said with an arrogant chuckle. "Does your kingdom have trolls and fairies and elves too?"

Sir Liliford didn't even turn around.

"There is magic in this kingdom sure enough," he said, his tone still even and cool.

"No way," Clay said, laughing boisterously.

"It is all around us, accessible to you and me if we know how," Sir Liliford continued. "Some can bend and manipulate the magic to do their will, others bottle it for later uses. But the magic of Dembroch has one specific effect that is given to all, one that requires no manipulation to access. It's in the very air we breathe, coursing through the land."

He paused. We waited. I half expected him to start laughing at our gullibility.

Then, with all the seriousness of a doctor diagnosing an incurable disease, the ferryman said, "The magic of Dembroch suspends time."

There was silence for a moment as the words sunk in. Then, Meg laughed. Clay joined in, his chuckle boisterous and unbecoming. I shot them a look.

"What?" Meg replied. "You can't be taking this guy seriously."

"I would not lie to such stellar, formidable dignitaries," interjected Sir Liliford. "Do any of you possess a standard, analog watch? Look upon its face. You will see the suspension of which I speak."

I looked back at Meg, raising an eyebrow. She smirked back but didn't look at her wristwatch because she knew as well as I that her wristwatch was still ticking forward one second, then pausing—or suspending—for several more seconds. It was the only proof we had that we were truly in a timeless realm or that magic existed. Besides the chroniseal that had transported us to Scotland.

"But," Jenn, ever the logical one, finally said, "look. Up in the sky. The sun has been moving. The shadows are changing. Time is still moving."

"Nature of the world beyond continues on," Sir Liliford agreed. "The globe spins. The planets, stars, and moon continue their paths. But on this island, time stands still. We are locked in a beautiful summer day until the world itself stops. Nothing grows, nothing dies. Time is averse. Suspended. That is why Dembroch is called the *Timeless* Kingdom, and that is also why we offer shelter to Hospites. No matter the injury or malady they face, their fate is forestalled the moment they step on the shores of this kingdom. Their injuries stop progressing, their diseases stop spreading. We can heal them while their bodies have stopped aging."

"So then...*we've* stopped aging?" Clay asked incredulously, touching his chest.

Sir Liliford nodded.

"If this is true," Jenn mumbled, glancing at the scorched land around us, "does the kingdom always look like this? For all time?"

"No, no, my dear," Sir Liliford said with a chuckle. "Dembroch was once a lavish land full of people. But much has changed. The magic I spoke of has been dying. As a result, the vegetation has perished. The food supply has run short. Water is scarce. Time fights to reclaim the land."

I nodded, grasping this detail. That must have been why Meg's watch was moving. If this timeless magic had been at full strength, her watch would have been frozen.

"What about the Hospites?" Jenn asked, sounding surprisingly interested in something other than our imminent demise.

CHAPTER 8

"Gone," Sir Liliford said, his tone growing somber. "Many perished before we could save them. Others fled the kingdom in hopes of saving themselves before it was too late. Even many Civium have fled. Less than a dozen remain on the isles."

"Page Hybore's family?" I asked.

"Hidden, like most of the other Civium," Sir Liliford replied.

"Is there a way I can see them?"

"Perhaps. But first, the queen."

"What about the defenders?" Clay asked. "Did they run away too?"

I looked at him from the corner of my eye. Had he forgotten what the summons read?

Sir Liliford didn't mince the words.

"Most of the original order perished some twenty years ago in the Siege of the Shallows," Sir Liliford said. "One hundred strong became six. Shortly after, another one hundred Reserves were called to the isles...all of which have perished over time. The last of them were lost recently in the Clash at Cliffside Tower. You four are the last."

Jenn gave one of her trademark morose groans. Clay gulped. Meg just sat there with her arms crossed. I sat back in my seat, the terrible reality sinking in. We four had been called to Dembroch to save it...but it seemed to have already fallen beyond repair.

"Take heart, my sirs and ladies," Sir Liliford said, his tone unreasonably cheerful. "Our kingdom rests in your hands, and I have no doubt you will succeed. The seer has seen your actions and the queen has vouched for your formidable skill and strong hearts. If anyone can save the kingdom, it will be you four."

"Hold on," I said. "You said the magic is dying. As in not gone yet. Why?"

Yet again, Sir Liliford gave us all a look, as though we were pulling his leg and feigning ignorance. Nonetheless, he explained.

"A witch attacked our kingdom decades ago," the ferryman revealed. "Though she was imprisoned after the Siege of the Shallows, the damage was done. Her actions caused the kingdom's magic to fail and it has dwindled ever since."

I felt my eyebrows crease—I'd almost forgotten that Page Hybore had mentioned a witch. Was all of this because of her?

Meg chuffed arrogantly. I could tell she was waiting for the opportunity to make a joke about the magic and prove the ferryman a fool.

"What can we do to fix it?" I asked.

"The queen knows," Sir Liliford said. "And the magic isn't even half of it. There are a great many other terrors burdening Dembroch. You four have your work cut out for you, but the queen will set your right."

Sir Liliford gave the horses another flick with the reins and we hurried on. As we did, I mulled over what the ferryman had said, trying to understand. If he was to be believed, Dembroch was everything I'd wanted in my youth, but nothing I wanted in my adulthood. In fact, that very moment, the information wasn't sitting well in my mind. It all seemed impossible, like a beautiful lie meant to ensnare the weak-minded. Magic? Timelessness? A witch? I had believed in magic once, even hoped in my youth that Dembroch had it, but I had forgotten these fantastical beliefs long ago. I had grown up. The prospect of magic was now naïve, childish, and farfetched. But then, how else could I explain the watch transporting my friends and I to Scotland in the blink of an eye? What else could explain Meg's watch ticking forward a second, then pausing for several more?

Either way, I decided, the real problem wasn't the magic. It was this witch. Magic or no, she'd singlehandedly rid the realm of its prior defenders and sent the rest of the kingdom's citizens running. Only a few remained, and they'd needed ex-defenders to come help them.

It was then, as we trundled ever closer toward the castle and the queen and the imprisoned witch, that I fully realized that I, who had never thrown a punch to defend myself or fought to protect someone else or faced any type of violent threat, was extremely underqualified for the job I'd volunteered for so long ago and was about to undertake.

CHAPTER 9

The Castle

Our carriage crested the last hill and descended toward the edge of a steep inlet named Coral Canyon. Far below, Sir Liliford said, the Siege of the Shallows had taken place.

The canyon was truly awesome in scope. Spreading from its broad opening to the ocean in the west to the narrow end in the trees around the castle, it was hundreds of feet across at our crossing and just as deep. Chunks of its walls had been blown away in several places, perhaps by erosion or a great rock slide or a battle. A treacherous path was carved into the steep sides, leading all the way down to an inlet of pools aquamarine in color. Way down there, I thought I could see a black rock, incongruous with the limestone rock and colorful coral.

A drawbridge was lowered across the gaping canyon. Once we'd crossed, the horses stopped at a squat cabin. Other horses whinnied from nearby stables. A portly man who called himself the Bridgemaster—he too had green in his eyes—asked us to dismount the carriage and proceed by foot into Amaranthine, the capital city of Dembroch.

Before we left, the Bridgemaster fished into a barrel full of water and pulled out a baby turtle with big eyes and cute little flippers. At the sight of the cute animal, Jenn cooed like a baby.

The Bridgemaster handed the turtle to Sir Liliford.

"An offering for the queen," Sir Liliford explained when he saw my questioning glance. "She likes the little creatures."

He held the turtle gingerly and led us by foot back into the decayed forest. Behind us, the drawbridge retracted across the canyon with a mighty creek. The gnarled trunks swayed above us. I half-expected a werewolf or other bloodthirsty monster to jump out at us, but as before, there was nothing—no birds, deer, bugs, or people.

Homes began to appear out of the woods, little cottages fit for fairytale characters. Empty wells interrupted the cobblestones, buckets and rope laying unused.

Above, through gaps in the branches and the village's rooftops, I saw flashes of blue steeples and golden flags, cobble walls and windows. In a few moments, I knew, the castle would be wholly visible in all its glory.

And then, I saw her.

Glimpsed just for an instant through the trees, but seared into my mind's eye like a flash of light, I saw the castle's tallest tower. There was a balcony near the top and leaning over its edge was a woman with long, golden hair.

My heart skipped a beat and I nearly tripped. The next second, the canopy of dead branches became too thick and I lost sight of the tower, the balcony, and the woman.

The queen, I thought to myself. *It must have been the queen. And she was looking right at me.*

We rounded a final bend. Mighty stone walls stood before us, extending into the trees and out of sight. Directly ahead was a massive arch filled with gargantuan oak doors.

CHAPTER 9

Sir Liliford opened one of them and ushered us to enter. I expected a burst of cheers or a few people welcoming us, but beyond was an expansive, empty courtyard. Two massive water fountains sat in the center, dry.

My eyes were drawn skyward. Towering above us all was the castle.

It stood magnificently, an elegant mass of ornate columns and chiseled basalt-hued stones. Rounded windows overlooked the courtyard from every level. Flying buttresses and gargoyle sculptures punctuated the walls, awnings hung over various entrances. The main structure of the castle was directly opposite of us, stretching out around the courtyard like the open arms of a mother and forming the walls we'd entered through. The castle, I realized, was a giant, thick circle of stone.

High above, towers were topped with rounded spires of sapphire blue. Golden flags bearing Dembroch's sigil flapped to and fro. The tallest tower indeed had a wraparound balcony close to the top, but there was no woman up there anymore.

My eyes came to a rest at the foot of the fortress. Steps led into the castle's largest and surely main entrance, beyond which were a cluster of columns blocking my view of the interior. Sir Liliford led us across the courtyard, up those steps, through the columns, and into a very tall room. It was cylindrical in shape and stretched up at least ten stories. I automatically assumed it was the interior of the castle's tallest tower. Walls were adorned with tapestries, staircases, and thresholds to the inner reaches of the fortress. A staircase wrapped from the bottom floor where we stood to the very top where the ceiling glistened with intricate paintings. Midday sunlight shone through windows, illuminating the circular floor where we stood.

I spun around and around, marveling at the architectural wonder. At last, my eyes were drawn to the center of the floor. There, inlaid in a circular stone and about three feet in diameter, was the crest of Dembroch. It was made of beautiful, glistening gems.

Drawn to it, I reached out to touch one of the colored stones.

"Not yet, Sir Nicholas," Sir Liliford called to me.

I pulled my hand back as though scolded by a parent.

The ferryman gestured to the hall around us.

"This is the Rotunda," he said simply. "The crest at your feet is our Aerary. For now, we are headed to the throne room."

We followed him across the Rotunda to another hallway and into a maze of corridors. I quickly lost my sense of direction as we twisted and turned through torch-lit hallways and past elaborate rooms. There were many closed doors and nary a person in sight. I saw an extravagant ballroom with chandeliers and foreign musical instruments, then a large, vacant space that seemed to be a hospital of types with cots, fresh linens, containers, and bowls with crushed herbs.

At long last, we stopped. Before us was a large wooden door no different than any of the others we'd passed.

"If you will stay here," Sir Liliford requested, "I will prepare the queen for you."

He entered the room beyond, shutting the door quickly behind him.

My friends and I exchanged glances. We all looked nervous, but it seemed for entirely different reasons. Jenn seemed ready to faint, Clay was running his fingers through his hair, and Meg was whispering under her breath. I thought I heard her say, "Two rights, left, straight, straight..."

Before we could share our concerns or second-guess our meeting with the queen, Sir Liliford returned. The baby turtle he'd been holding was gone.

"My sirs and ladies," Sir Liliford said, holding open the door for us to enter, "the queen of Dembroch."

My friends and I entered a room long and rectangular in shape. Tables were pushed up against the walls. On the opposite side of the room was a throne, and sitting atop it was a woman with long, golden hair.

CHAPTER 9

I knew her instantly, even from across the room. It was the woman from the balcony, the maiden of my childhood daydreams. She was more beautiful than I'd ever imagined.

It was Queen Coralee.

CHAPTER 10

The Queen

Seeing the queen, my stomach dropped. In my mind appeared the countless letters I'd written to her. Suddenly, I wanted to turn around and go die of embarrassment alone in the hallway.

Behind us, the door shut. I glanced back—Sir Liliford hadn't entered with us. A second later, I heard the slide of a lock.

"Please," the queen called, her accented voice echoing around us. "Approach."

We walked to her awkwardly, footsteps loud on the stone walls. My cheeks seemed to burn hotter with every step. I noticed an empty turtle shell on the arm of the throne, but my eyes were drawn irresistibly back to the queen.

At last, we came to a stop before the throne. The queen stared at all of us, not smiling or frowning, just observing. But when she looked at me, her lips curled into a slight smile. My palms started to sweat.

CHAPTER 10

She was violently beautiful, in an overbearing, yet arresting kind of way. Oddly, though I'd always assumed she was much older, she appeared to be our age, perhaps her late twenties or early thirties, most likely thanks to the supposed timelessness of the island. She had thick locks of hair, a slim bodice gowned in green, and sharp features accentuated by the midday sun. There were white scars along one of her hands from a bad burn long ago. A sword hung from a belt slung low on her hips. From her poised posture to the filigree crown atop her brow, she breathed power and demanded respect. She was not the fair, mourning queen I'd imagined, but shrewd, calculating, and steely in the eyes.

"My knights and dames, you are the last defenders?" the queen finally said, her smile twisting into a strange smirk. She paused, almost smugly, before saying, "It is a pleasure to meet you all. Where are your sigils?"

"Here," I said, fishing the medal from my satchel. My friends did the same. The queen took each brooch and placed them on the throne's armrest, right beside the empty turtle shell.

She descended the steps leading up to her throne and began to circle around us, all the while still smirking. It seemed to me she was sizing us up.

"I will admit," she said, her voice echoing around the chamber, "you are not what I expected. You wrote to me with such conviction and heart. I had heard much tell of your skills and abilities. Yet, you four seem—"

"Hey!" Meg suddenly shouted.

The queen flinched, as though terrified we would suddenly lash out and become violent.

"You're the one who called us," Meg said, her voice loud and obstinate.

"Indeed I did," the queen replied, still circling us.

As she passed, I thought I saw an edge of paper sticking out of her neckline. It was old and wrinkled with the scrawl of a child's messy handwriting. I couldn't have been sure, but I thought I recognized it. Was that one of my letters? She had it? On her person? Why was I even looking that closely at her neckline?

"So let's get to it," Meg said. "What do you need us to do? Are you going to convince us there's magic that needs saving too?"

I couldn't believe my sister's nerve, nor could I fathom why the queen was treating us like street rats. Or why she had my letter held so close.

"Oh, fix the magic?" the queen said. "You're doing all you need to do right now. I called you and you came running."

The queen smiled, sinister now.

All thoughts of my letters and the queen's odd behavior fled my mind. I sensed danger.

The queen drew her hand back as though reaching for her sword.

"Watch out!" I shouted.

But the queen wasn't reaching for her sword, nor were my friends the quick-minded and swift-footed heroes we'd been in our youth. We stood there dumbly, me cringing, as the queen whispered words I didn't hear and racked a clawed hand through the air. Mirages of green light flew from her hand and blasted us off our feet. I was flying, twirling through the air, and then I slammed back onto the stone ground.

"Taking your titles didn't do the trick," the queen said. "But taking your life certainly should."

Suddenly, I was flying again. My friends and I were launched across the room. I slammed into the ground hard. My back lit on fire.

The queen marched toward us. Green light gathered around her hands. From the corner of my eye, I saw movement and suddenly Meg had me by the leg and was pulling me behind the throne. A blast like a grenade went off where my head had been. Chips of stone bit my scalp.

The next second, I was behind the throne with my friends. Blood ran from Jenn's hairline. Clay's jacket was torn on the shoulders. We were all shaking from head to foot.

CHAPTER 10

"Don't hide, my knights and dames," the queen sneered. "It's unflattering of your reputation."

Meg glanced over the edge of the chair and her eyes got wide. The queen was coming, I knew, and there was no way to stop it.

"I could have sent assassins to kill you in your sleep or poison your drinks," the queen called, her voice growing ever nearer. "But I heard of your strength and skill. I knew only *I* could rid the kingdom of you. I had to have you here before me, see the whites of your eyes, and then I could face you. But where is your strength? Where is your skill? You cower behind the throne like little children. You seem little more than amateurs pretending to be soldiers. Do not make me work too hard for the slaughter. If you are warriors, face me now, and give me a show, or suffer a thousand pains cowering for your lives."

The throne we hid behind suddenly lifted off the ground and exploded into a thousand pieces. Our Dembroch sigils and the empty turtle shell went flying. The queen glowered at us and then, her eyes rolled into the back of her head. Her fingers twitched like she was playing an invisible instrument. Green light danced around each digit.

"Bleed you dry of air so sweet," she said, "death will approach with swiftest of feet!"

As if bidden by the queen's words, the air left my lungs. My throat tightened. I clutched at my windpipe, but there was nothing there constricting my airway.

My friends collapsed too, raking at their throats. We gulped like fish, unable to inhale. Green light danced around their necks, untouchable yet compressing upon their flesh.

Suddenly, a loud voice roared through the room.

"Silence, witch!"

There was a distant clang and bang. The queen shrieked words my oxygen-deprived mind didn't understand. There were bursts of ivy green light. It looked so familiar, so bright and shining—and that's when it all clicked. The queen was wielding magic, real magic. It had physicality, an emerald green that sparkled in the light. It was the same color of green I'd seen in Page Hybore and Sir Liliford's eyes. Somehow, she'd been controlling them to lure us here, just as it was killing us now.

My eyesight got blurry. My limbs felt heavy. My heart beat painfully, obstinately.

This was the end, I knew. I had reunited my friends and brought them here just to die. I had finally made it to Dembroch, this awful, trick of a kingdom, just to suffocate to death.

All at once, there was a great quake. At first, I thought it came from me, some internal fracture of sanity or final tremor of death throes. But then I realized I could breathe again. Air, blessed air, was rushing back into my lungs. At the same time, my friends gasped, sucking in the air.

The world came back into focus. I realized the castle was shaking. Far off, a horn was sounding. Somewhere in the room, a deep, booming voice was crying out in agony. Then, as suddenly as it had started, it ended. The castle and air lay still.

"What have you done, witch?" shouted a new voice.

I sat up. What was going on?

Across the chamber I saw the queen, but she was facing off with five newcomers.

"Your defenders are dead," cried the queen at the five strangers, her voice a shrill cackle. "Your magic is gone!"

"You're going to have to try harder than that!" Meg exclaimed, her voice raspy.

The queen spun around, face contorted in confusion and loathing. Before our very eyes, her blonde hair was turning white and her fair face was wrinkling. She seemed to be aging on the spot.

"Curious," the queen mouthed. She wiggled her fingers. They moved like spiders, green light dancing around them.

"Don't you dare!" one of the newcomers, a humanoid creature covered in moss, croaked. "Civium, provide the defenders care."

The moss man lunged at the queen. She swatted him away with lances of green magic, but he kept pressing on.

Meanwhile, the other newcomers ran to my friends and I.

CHAPTER 10

"Off your arse," a mountain of a man with a thick beard and axe hollered at me.

I tried, but too slow apparently. The behemoth grabbed me and threw me over his shoulder.

Across the room, there were shouts and bangs. A flash of green light. A pained shriek. The moss man stumbled back, but he got back to his feet, eyes locked on the queen. His persistence knew no bounds.

"Come on, mage!" my rescuer cried.

We—whoever *we* were—made it to the door. My helper held it open, ushering everyone through. Hanging over his back, I had a good view into the throne room. It was a disaster, tables shattered to splinters, the walls impacted and torn apart. Quite a battle had been waged while I'd been incapacitated. In all the chaos, there was a yellowed, folded piece of paper laying on the ground.

The queen was still fighting the man of moss, but she didn't look the same. She wore the same green dress, but she was shorter and her face was completely different. It was a totally different person, except she wore the same garb.

I saw a flash of waxy, gaunt skin and sunken eyes, a hideous woman that should have only been in haunted houses or horror stories. My would-be murderer. Somehow, she'd become someone new.

"Mage!" my rescuer cried again.

The man of moss body-slammed the queen, green daggers cutting right through his chest. While the queen was down, he half-ran, half-limped over to us and ran through the door. He looked winded from the battle, though the holes in his chest did not bleed. My rescuer followed the moss man, slamming the door shut. He stepped over a fallen body—I recognized it as Sir Liliford, knocked out on the ground—and took off at a run after my friends and their saviors, followed by the fading shrieks of the defeated queen.

CHAPTER 11

Magic and Its Mage

The moss man, who was apparently a mage as his comrades kept calling him, let out a sharp gasp of pain and crashed to the ground. When he hit, it sounded like a rock slamming down and breaking, though he appeared to be made of nothing but moss.

"What's going on?" Meg shouted.

"Quiet," my rescuer replied, his voice a gruff whisper. "Mage, we must hurry."

But the mage wasn't getting up.

"Get off," my rescuer said to me, sliding me off his shoulder. He went to the mage's side, followed by our other rescuers.

There were four of them besides the man made of moss. The largest of the lot was my rescuer, a thick, broad, lumbering man with a face full of hair, an axe strapped to his back, and a belt of golden pocket watches. The other two men were smaller but nonetheless intimidating, the youngest wearing belts of swords around his scrawny hips, arms, and legs. The other was a roly-poly of a man in mustard yellow robes with scabbed knuckles and deep scars lacing his arms. The woman was a dainty thing wrapped in dirty folds of clothing. Her eyes were glassy, and her grey hair stuck out like she'd been struck by lightning.

"Mage," the mountain of a man whispered, turning the moss man onto his back. "We must continue on. The witch—"

The mage inhaled sharply, painfully.

"Decipher the gears," he murmured, his voice deep as the ocean but light as a butterfly's wings. "Power she has come to fear."

"Mage?" my rescuer said, cradling the mage's head. "Are you with me?"

"Cliffside's keep, Dreadnaught's reap," the mage replied nonsensically. "Heart's core. Hidden door."

"We're losing him," the woman said.

"We can't," the young, scrawny boy with belts of swords said, his sweat-soaked face turning white. "He's the only one—"

"He's known," the man in yellow said softly. "He left us everything we needed."

"The magic," the mage breathed, his voice growing creaky. "Gone. I too. Fallen echelon."

The young boy gaped.

"Did he say—did he mean?"

The woman nodded, depressed. "The magic is gone."

The boy pointed at us.

"But they're—"

"They're alive," my rescuer interrupted. "The mage is dying. Focus, page!"

"He can't die!"

"He will. He was born of the magic. He subsists off it. He dies with it." The mountain of a man patted the mage's back tenderly. "Rest easy, mage. We will see brighter days."

The mage suddenly sat up. His eyes found my friends and I. The moss around his eyes and mouth were turning black and drying out.

"Have heart, you four, for what's in store," the mage said, "or Dembroch will be lost forevermore. Ignite six sparks before it...all...goes...dark."

The mage's eyes lost their light and turned oily black. Each curl of moss withered and died. He slumped and lost form. A million bundles of moss collapsed on themselves, scattering across the hallway, covering the laps of his comrades.

We all stood there for a moment, shocked. I couldn't believe what I'd just seen. The mage had...died.

As one, without exchanging glances, our four rescuers beat their fists over their heart. Their fabric clothes clanged like armor.

"Come on," my rescuer grumbled a few minutes later, "he's gone. We need to keep moving."

He got to his feet, glancing over my friends and I with a sneer.

"Anyone want to explain what's happening here?" Meg said, her tone overly arrogant.

"You could do the same," he replied.

"Look, buddy," Clay interjected. "We just got here and—"

My rescuer spun on Clay. A gigantic hand slammed him into the wall.

"How is it you live?" he growled in Clay's face. "How? While the mage dies?"

"I don't know!" Clay replied.

"The queen—" I stammered. "She called us here—then she tried to kill us—"

"That wasn't the queen."

Clay and I stammered, not sure what to make of this or what it meant.

"Speak, boy!" the man shouted at Clay.

"Okay, okay," Jenn said. "Everyone calm down. We all need to communicate."

CHAPTER 11

The mountain of a man, once my rescuer, now Clay's attacker, grumbled under his breath. He loosened his grip on Clay, letting him slide back to the ground, and loomed over Jenn.

"That wasn't the queen who summoned you or tried to kill you," he explained. "It was a witch named Sorgana."

"What?" Meg spat.

"She's been imprisoned for years," explained the young, thin man with swords sheathed around his limbs, "but recently broke free and took the queen's place. She lured you here to—"

"Kill us," Meg interrupted. "Yeah, we got that."

"What do you mean *lured* us?" I asked.

"She summoned you all," he replied. "She bewitched Sir Liliford to deliver you and Page Hybore to collect you, God rest his soul."

Our rescuers hung their heads and pounded their chests as they had done for the fallen mage. The woman let out a muffled sob.

In the back of my mind, I felt the pieces fall together. I'd been right: Page Hybore and our ferryman had been controlled by the witch, the only clue being their green eyes. When Page Hybore had been revived, he'd been momentarily free of the bewitchment and tried to warn me of the witch and the dangers, but he hadn't had enough time before passing on.

"Why would she want us dead?" Jenn bemoaned.

"To kill the magic," replied the woman.

"Which she accomplished," the behemoth grunted.

I glanced at Meg's wristwatch. The light of a torch caught the brass of the clock's hands. The second hand was moving unhindered, ticking away second after second without pause. I gulped.

"She wanted to kill us to kill the magic?" Clay asked.

Our rescuers nodded.

"Why would killing us—" I began, but Meg cut me off.

"If that was the witch, where's the real queen?" she asked, crossing her arms.

"Locked away in the prisons, yes, yes," the man in yellow said.

"We're taking you there now," said the younger man.

"If you lot would keep quiet long enough to get there," the imposing man grumbled. "She'll have plenty of questions for you. I suppose I'll wait till then to hear a good explanation from you lot."

Our rescuers started to head out, but I called after them.

"Wait, what about the...the mage?"

The woman glanced back mournfully.

"There's nothing we can do now," she said dreamily. "We'll give him a proper sendoff when it is safe to do so."

She began to walk away again.

"Hey!" Meg called after them. "Who are you? How can we trust you?"

I shot her a look, but her demands got the job done. The four strangers returned.

"Page Trey," said the scrawny young man with all the weapons. He bowed. "I am one of the kingdom's combat instructors, apprentice to Master Malleator. He—"

"We don't have time for this," grumbled the largest man, and the grumpiest apparently.

"Sorry," Page Trey said, smiling sheepishly at Meg.

"I'm Sir Rignot, the librarian, yes, yes," said the squat, roly-poly of a man in yellow. He glanced over his shoulder warily, rubbing his scabbed and bruised knuckles.

"I am Lady Sinclair, the seer," said the woman with glassy eyes, "but you may call me the seer who does not see. Or, if it is simpler, just the seer. Yes, perhaps, just the seer. Pleased to meet you, Lady Jennifer."

Something about her rang a bell in my mind, a distant reminder of something that I just couldn't quite remember, but I didn't have time to figure out what it was. I realized the woman had been staring at Jenn the whole time, and in turn, Jenn was sliding behind her husband.

"Watchmaker," said the mountain of a man, running his finger along the chains of the dozen golden pocket watches hanging from his belt. "Now come on. We have places to get."

CHAPTER 11

The Watchmaker took off, followed by his three compatriots. My friends and I trailed them slowly, trying to wrap our heads around what had just happened.

"This is ridiculous," Meg said under her breath.

"I'm quite enjoying myself," Jenn said.

"Of course you are," Meg replied. "We were nearly killed, some walking piece of moss just died, and we're being hunted by a crazy lady. You must be right at home. You with your death, death, death."

"What do you mean hunted?" Clay repeated, chuckling nervously. "We're safe with all these people, right?"

I noticed the woman called the seer eyeing us—well, Jenn—with a raised eyebrow.

"It'll be okay," I said, more to get the seer to stop listening. "We'll be fine, Clay."

"For once, I agree with you, Nick," Meg said quietly. "We will be fine. Once we get off this island."

"What?" we whispered in unison, all of our voices scratchy from nearly suffocating to death.

"We're leaving, aren't we?" Meg asked. "First chance we get, we'll grab that ferry and get out of here."

"We can't just—" I began.

"Yes, we can," Meg said. "We're not knights and dames anymore, Nick. We're under no compulsion to help these people out. Best if we just get out of here while we still can."

"What about the magic?" I asked.

"What magic?" my stepsister chuffed.

"They said it was dead," Jenn said sullenly. "All the way now."

"And then they blamed us," Meg said. "I know one thing for sure. This isn't my rodeo. So I'm out. Who's with me?"

There was a brief pause, then Clay said, "Can I come with you?"

"Me too," Jenn echoed.

My head swiveled between the three of them.

"You all want to leave?" I said, aghast.

"You dragged us here," Meg said. "None of us wanted to come."

"We just wanted to say hi to some old friends at the diner," Clay said honestly.

"I just don't want to die," Jenn said.

"What is it with you and death?" Meg grumbled.

I gaped at them, completely shocked. For the first time since reuniting at Dave's Diner, I realized I was amongst strangers. Gone was Clay the brave, Jenn the carelessly happy, and Meg the staunch stepsister. Before me was a coward, a depressed pessimist, and an impatient, self-reliant soul. All they could think about was their recent scrape with death and how badly they wanted to avoid further confrontation.

"What happened to you all?" I suddenly spat.

Meg's lips grew thin.

"You may not remember this, Nick," she spat back, "but fifteen years ago, you chose Dembroch over me."

"Over all of us," Jenn added.

"Dembroch never wanted you," my sister said. "But I did. I still do. I may not particularly like you somedays, but I don't want you dead."

"Come on, Nick," Clay whispered. "Come with us."

"Let's make a run for it," Meg suggested.

"I'm no good at running," Jenn bemoaned.

"Whatever, Jenn."

They all stopped and pushed me back the way we'd come—only to screech to a stop.

The seer stood behind us. She stared at us with her glassy eyes.

"Do not go the way of Solomon," she whispered harshly.

She waved her hands. We all cringed, Jenn squawked, expecting to be flung across a room. But there was no green light or magic. The seer was just shooing us along. So I spun around and hurried after the Watchmaker, page, and librarian. My friends followed suit, Meg mumbling under her breath. The seer slunk behind us, watching us like an eagle-eyed teacher monitoring her preschool subjects.

CHAPTER 11

At long last, after passing through the Rotunda and twisting through more corridors, we found what must have been the castle's prison. On the far side of the chamber were four cells. Dying sunlight streamed through one window. Cobwebs hung from the corners. The putrid smell of spoiled food and bad plumbing oozed from the space.

While the seer and Page Trey kept watch down the corridor, the Watchmaker approached the leftmost cell.

"My queen," he said.

A bundle of cloth on the floor stirred. I thought I heard sniffling.

"Do not despair, my queen," the librarian said. "Your defenders are here, yes, yes."

There was a gasp, then the bundle of cloth was thrown aside. A woman stood and ran to the bars, clutching them.

Clay and I stutter-stepped backward. Jenn yelped.

The woman behind the bars was the same woman I'd seen a glimpse of in the throne room. She was wrinkled and furrowed, more bone than flesh, a skeleton wearing human skin. I could see every vein, knuckle, joint, and ligament.

"Do not be afraid," the woman said, her voice croaky and weak. "It is I, your queen. Please, come closer."

We didn't move a muscle.

"Sir Nicholas!" the woman cried, her weak voice full of desperation. "Sir Clayton. Ladies Jennifer and Meghan! Please, it is I, Queen Coralee."

We still didn't move, not willing to fall for another trick. This was surely the witch, pulling us in for another trap. We'd been fools to even trust our rescuers.

"It's the queen, you doles," the Watchmaker grunted. "The witch cast a spell to disguise the two of them. The witch looks like the queen, the queen looks like the witch."

"Yes," the woman begged. "As you are the last defenders, I am the true dowager of Dembroch. I am the rightful queen."

I didn't want to believe him, but I caught sight of the woman's eyes. They may have been sunken and glassy with considerable age, but they were pleading, kind, and brimming with tears. The witch's eyes, though disguised as the queen, had been overflowing with malice. Eyes were windows to the soul, after all. No disguise or magic could hide their true intentions.

"Queen Coralee?" I asked.

"Yes," she said, wiping the tears away.

I approached the cell. Clay warned me, but I knew now that the woman before us was our true ally.

The queen reached through the bars, holding out a hand. I took it and she squeezed it tightly.

At long last, despite all appearances, I'd met the queen of Dembroch.

CHAPTER 12

The True Dowager of Dembroch

"Bless you, Sir Nicholas," Queen Coralee said, holding my hand firmly. "I thought you had fallen at the whims of the witch."

"Almost," I acknowledged, forcing a laugh.

"How do you live while the magic has died?" the queen asked, looking over my friends and I.

It was the same question the Watchmaker had shouted at Clay, but none of us knew what they meant by it. I stammered.

"We must then celebrate these small, mysterious victories," the queen considered. "While you four still stand, the witch shall never succeed, nor shall Dembroch truly fall."

She glanced past us, surveying her four subjects.

"Where is the mage?" she said tremulously. When no one said anything, she cast her eyes to the ground. Slowly, deliberately, she knocked her fist against her heart and whispered quietly.

The Watchmaker cut in.

"Pardon me, my lady," he said, "but time is short and we have much to discuss. Has the witch been here yet?"

"Come and gone," the queen said. "She is hunting for you."

It was the librarian's turn to pipe up: "And the magic has truly died?"

The queen nodded sorrowfully, sharing a quick, dark glance with the Watchmaker. "The last flame has extinguished. The Gate Grounds are dark. Time has resumed."

Queen Coralee turned her attention back to my friends and I.

"My defenders, there is much to say, and little time to share it. First, let me apologize. I should have summoned you long ago rather than have you suffer through this storm. I shall make it up to you in due time. But we have more pressing matters. The witch wreaks havoc. Monsters roam our woods and the sea. Our Watchmaker's home has been devastated and his watches have been stolen. Our remaining Civium are under constant threat of attack. But the main root of the problem, what has caused much of this, is that the magic has been..." She took a breath and tried again: "Our magic is...dead. With it gone, time reigns over the kingdom once more. And its affects are swift and terrible. Our mage has already perished. Death looms over our precious isles and all who remain here. For Dembroch to survive, for us to defeat the witch...we must restore the magic."

No one laughed at the mention of magic this time. The queen's plea was as raw and honest as could be. Terrifying even. There was no denying her need or what she believed needed to be done.

"Restore it?" Clay asked. "How would that fix things?"

"The island's famine would end," the queen replied. "Our residents would once more be safe. But more than fixing our current problems, we must restore the magic to stop the witch. Whatever she intends for this kingdom, she can only accomplish it with the isles' magic extinguished. If it were restored, she would be powerless to accomplish her ends."

"Which are?" Meg goaded.

The queen shook her head to say she did not know, but the way she kneaded her hands, the way she seemed to draw into herself, the way she looked to the Watchmaker, I sensed the queen had a pretty good idea.

"The Watchmaker has been tasked with discovering her intentions, but the Dreadnaught has complicated that end goal," the queen said. "For the time being, our best hopes of saving the kingdom is to restore the magic."

Meg had finally had enough.

"Okay," she grumbled. "The gig's up. Where are the camcorders? Where's the audience? You got us! We almost fell for it! But this restoring the magic thing was a step too far."

The people of Dembroch, from the queen to the Watchmaker, stared at her.

"Lady Meghan," the queen implored, "it is the only way."

Meg chuffed.

"It may be difficult to accept," the queen offered, "especially for visitors from the world beyond, but let me assure you. There is—was—magic on Dembroch. And for the kingdom to see a future, we must reinstate it."

I knew the queen was telling the truth. In the last few hours, I had seen unequivocal evidence that magic was real. But Meg refused to believe it. She argued with the queen, demanding she drop the act.

"None of this is real!" Meg shouted. "It was a scam for kids. We paid you the money. Years ago. It's over!"

The Watchmaker shouted, his thunderous voice drowning Meg out.

"My queen," he said. "Did you not tell us that these four were the last of the original Reserves and, without question, the best of them?"

The queen locked eyes with the Watchmaker, her face hard as stone.

"Did you not beg us to save them should they need it, for they would be the only ones capable of saving our kingdom?"

I shifted uncomfortably, knowing where this was going.

"I saw it too," the seer said distantly.

"Who are these people the witch has brought to your island?" the Watchmaker shouted.

"Defenders," the queen said adamantly, but she was kneading her hands again.

"Defenders?" the Watchmaker echoed. "Perhaps once, but now?" He looked over Clay. "Tell me, boy, are you as good at fighting as you are at working up your hair? And you, girl. Do you shrivel at the sight of a witch, or every time a bird swoops by overhead?"

"Calm yourself, Watchmaker," the queen requested. "I intended to intimidate our enemy by making claims of our last defenders' skills and abilities. While they were exaggerations, they are no less true, nor do they undermine the people who stand beside you. These four came to Dembroch after all. They intend to help."

My friends and I exchanged nervous glances.

"You see!" the Watchmaker exclaimed. "They quibble and quiver like little children. Their chins are soft and guts are round. They have no better chance of saving Dembroch than an iceberg surviving summer."

"Mind your tongue," the queen said, never once raising her voice. "I have every confidence in our four last defenders. I ask you to trust them as I have."

The Watchmaker grumbled and backed up to stand guard at the end of the corridor. Queen Coralee returned her glassy eyes to us.

"Now, please," she said to us, begging Meg to accept the truth. "You must understand. The isles have always held magic within them, but they became concentrated into flames. There were six throughout the kingdom. But, as each of the flames died, so did the magic. To stop Sorgana, as the mage predicted, we must reignite these flames, thereby restoring the magic. And the way to do it is in the book I sent you four long ago."

CHAPTER 12

For the first time since arriving on Dembroch, I realized I had a way to help. The book, *The Knights and Dames of Dembroch,* was in my satchel.

I reached into it to pull out the book.

"Not here," the queen implored, pushing my hand back into my bag. "It holds secrets the witch should never know. I sent it to you for that reason. Therefore, you must find a quiet place, read of the origin of the isles' magic, and act on it. Only with the knowledge within this book and the mercy of time can you follow the mage's musings and save the kingdom."

"Can't you just tell us?" Meg asked, sounding irritated.

"There is much to know, and it is quite complicated," the queen said. "It will take some time."

"I have such a place to offer, yes, yes," the librarian offered.

"Excellent," the queen said. She reached out again and took our hands. "Now, my knights and dames. I must ask you... Will you save Dembroch?" She blushed. "I know you are no longer defenders in name and your titles were renounced. I was forced by the witch to do such a heinous thing in her first attempts to end the magic. Because of that, you have no responsibility to aid this kingdom. But my faith in you has never wavered. You have kept the book safe all this time, even after you lost your titles. And you continued to write letters."

Meg shot me a look, mouthing the word, "Letters?"

The queen continued: "Those writings and those of your youth attested to your pure hearts, aspiring ambition, and strong spirits. From those letters, I came to know the bold women and men who would someday stand before me, and I knew in my heart that you would never abandon your responsibilities. But this is no ordinary request. It is rife with more danger and burden than ever before. You are the last of your disbanded order. The challenges ahead are grim. To aid Dembroch may be to forfeit your life. Therefore, I must ask you. Will you reclaim your old duties? Will you save the Timeless Kingdom of Dembroch?"

"Yes!" is what we should have said. It's what I wanted to say. But none of us spoke. Something the queen had said had caught my attention and sent my head spinning.

Our hesitation was brief but telling.

"I see," the queen said, releasing our hands and taking a step back. "Watchmaker?"

The mountain of a man lumbered back into the room. There was a devilish smile on his face.

"Tell me, my last knights and dames," the queen said, "where is your childlike faith? What time do your watches read? Surely not midnight. Your conviction is surely not gone. You will not abandon your kingdom in its most desperate time of need."

She looked to each of us, searching for an answer, silently pleading for help, appealing to the humanity within us that she thought was still there. The Watchmaker loomed over us.

"I can't," Jenn finally said.

"Lady Jennifer, you must!" the queen implored.

"Why can't any of you do it?" Jenn asked, looking to our rescuers.

"We are trying," Page Trey said, looking younger and more scared by the minute. "But we four can only do so much."

"My aides have already been tasked with objectives to help save Dembroch as elucidated by the mage," the queen agreed, "but the magic is a matter of its own. You four—" she pointed to my friends and I "—are inextricably tied to the magic, and only you four can restore it. Now please, look within yourselves. Will you not help this kingdom?"

"I would if I could," Clay said, his voice full of bluster, his tone cavalier. "But...this is a lot for a few ex-knights and dames to handle. We're only four people. We have no experience with this stuff."

The queen's wrinkled brow furrowing with confusion. Then, terribly, she looked to me.

"And you, Sir Nicholas?"

I should have agreed to help, should have been the first one, but red flags were popping up into my head. The queen made it sound like the witch had taken control of the realm, then the queen had sent the book...but we'd received the book long ago, right before the order had been dissolved. Sorgana had just broken out a week ago or so. Maybe the mail system was to blame, or the kingdom's time magic, but I sensed the queen wasn't telling the full truth.

And then there was the matter of my letters. I'd seen one of my letters on the witch's person and, after the battle, lying on the floor of the throne room. And the queen had just mentioned the same letters. She'd received them and, worse, read them. And she'd never responded to us. Not once.

My blood boiled. How could the queen ask us to help her when she had denied us these twenty years? I couldn't even begin to put my thoughts into words.

"What's in it for us?" Meg interjected when I didn't say anything.

The Watchmaker shot Meg a look. Page Trey raised an eyebrow. The librarian clucked his tongue.

"Lady Meghan," the queen said, scowling at her. "I am surprised at you. What of the people? The kingdom? Your duty?"

Meg crossed her arms.

"I have no duty to help you," she said. "You took my titles, whether that witch forced you or not. I don't *have* to do anything. But if we're talking a reward..."

I ogled at my sister. Where did she get the nerve?

"I see," the queen mused. She paced her cell, rubbing her hands again. "My sirs and ladies, do you know the rich history of Dembroch's defenders? While protecting this kingdom, they have also served the world beyond for millennia. From the Knights Templar to the Ghost Army, the Principality of Sealand to the unified safeguard of the Arx, from the Monuments Men to the Order of Holy Sepulcher. Our history is steeped in a rich beauty and a steadfast devotion to good. But one comes to mind at this moment: the Hibernians. Protestors sought to burn down churches in early New York City. Our order of defenders came to their aid and kept the church safe for decades. At last, when the protestors had given up and the Hibernians had succeeded, we left the church's safety to the parishioners. And do you know what happened? A few nights later, a clumsy Hibernian priest knocked over a candle and burnt the whole place down."

She glared at us, her face pressed against the bars and temper growing.

"Do you see the irony?" she asked, her tongue sharp. "Like the old church of your world beyond, Dembroch has stood the test of time and refused to yield to any aggressors. But what has broken our kingdom? What has ended our magic? Not the witch, nor any antagonizers seeking our shores for ill will. Rather, we have fallen from within." The queen frowned deeply. "My knights and dames, you disappoint me. You are no better than the Hibernians. You have gone the way of Solomon before you even stepped foot on our shores."

There it was again, that name that the seer had mentioned. I didn't know what it meant, but it clearly wasn't a compliment.

The queen wasn't finished. "It is no wonder the magic has died," she said, not meanly, but matter-of-factly. "You four are no more than dead men walking. The death of the mage is on your hands, as are any further catastrophes that should burden this withering kingdom built on the backs of such foolish men and women."

"I guess there's no obligation to help you then," Meg spat, turning to walk away.

The Watchmaker was still right behind us, blocking Meg's way.

"Consider your life to be your obligation," he growled. "If you fail, you die. We all will."

A thick hand fell on my shoulder. The Watchmaker grabbed onto Meg too and pushed us toward the other prison cells. We ran into Jenn and Clay, and though we were four fully grown adults, we started skidding forward.

"The choice is yours," the Watchmaker told us. "Help your queen and kingdom or spend the last of your days in these cells. And believe me, if you do not help us, your stay here will be painfully, unmercifully short."

Jenn and Clay started stammering.

"You can't—" Meg argued.

"He can," the librarian said. "The Watchmaker and all Civium act under the queen's authority. If you refuse to accept your old responsibilities, you are trespassing visitors to our kingdom. And we dictate the comings and goings of such aliens. The choice is yours. You shall either aid us or die with us."

The Watchmaker pushed again, stronger. I dug my feet into the ground. The queen was biting her lip but doing nothing to stop this.

"Okay!" I shouted finally. "I'll help!"

Jenn and Clay echoed my agreement with quiet, desperate voices. It was not a hard choice, but it was not exactly one made from the bottom of my heart.

"Fine," Meg said.

The Watchmaker grunted in acceptance. He released my shoulder. I felt uneasy, yet again realizing that my childhood fantasies of Dembroch had been tragically naïve. Sure, the witch had deceived us and tried to kill us, but the queen and her aides, the ones who I assumed would be friendly and helpful and welcoming, had just pressganged us into service.

The queen gave a curt nod, her wrinkled face tightened and stern. "It is settled then. You will save this kingdom, and should you survive, you shall be sent home happy and healthy, never to return. Farewell, my last defenders. God speed."

Everyone else seemed to breathe a sigh of relief—the tenseness was over, as was our meeting with the queen. But not me. I alone stood frozen, struck by what the queen had just said. Had anyone else heard it? She'd exiled us. If we just so happened to save the kingdom and not die in the process, we would be banished from Dembroch and never be allowed to return. This was my first and last trip to the kingdom.

No one seemed to notice or care. Queen Coralee nodded to her Civium and they guided us away. The meaning was clear: we had our orders and it was time to go. But I wanted to stay. There were so many questions I still had, so many things I needed to say, whether it was a conversation or an argument.

I glanced back as I was dragged along. The queen was lost in her own thoughts, but as I watched, she nodded curtly to herself, looked up, and locked eyes with me. Deep within the wrinkled visage of the witch, the queen's eyes flashed with a strange expression of hope and apology. She was hoping for the best and, despite blackmailing us and feeling bad about it, was sticking to her guns. In that moment, I realized I had to do the same. I'd made my choice, no matter how coerced, and I had to commit if I were to survive.

At the very least, I figured, out of the available options—imprisonment, death, or exile—my friends and I had chosen the one that offered a slim chance of life after Dembroch.

CHAPTER 13

The Birth of the Isles' Magic

"Sir Nicholas," Sir Rignot said. "Your book, please."

The Watchmaker and Page Trey were no longer with us. They had left to complete their own errands—Page Trey had even asked Meg to accompany him to the Gate Grounds, which she'd ever so impolitely declined—despite the librarian and seer begging them to stay. Now, my friends and I stood with the seer and librarian in the library fit for the thirstiest bookworms. Books and scrolls filled the room from floor to ceiling, wall to wall. The rich smell of vanilla and old pages wafted through the air.

Sir Rignot held out a hand for my book. In the other, he held a vial of gold liquid.

"What's that?" Jenn asked.

"Magic," the librarian replied simply.

Meg raised an eyebrow.

"I thought the magic was gone," I said.

"True, true," the librarian said. "The magic of the island is gone. Only stored and preexisting magic remains now."

"Preexisting?" Jenn echoed.

"Curses and promises linger no matter where you go," Sir Rignot explained, "prized possessions are conduits and harbor power over an owner's life such as prolonging life, altering your appearance, and healing wounds, and stored magic always keeps. This right here—" he shook the vial "—is bottled magic. Extracted from the flames' sparks, then modified for a specific use. In this case, to bring written word to life. Now, Sir Nicholas, if you please, yes, yes, we need to see that book."

I pulled it from my satchel. The edges were foxed and worn, the pages yellowed. Within were countless tales about Dembroch's past defenders, though the only story I remembered with any clarity was about the late King Arthur's fruitless search to break a curse. All of the stories had been written in Latin, but I'd translated all of them over the years and written the English in the margins.

Sir Rignot placed the book on a nearby table and flipped it open to a story near the beginning—*The Birth of the Isle's Magic*. Then, he uncorked the vial of golden liquid and poured a few drops on the page. Smoke furled from where it landed, growing and expanding above us. Lightning flickered on its edges.

"Watch and listen, watch and listen," the librarian said. "The written word can be deceiving, but, yes, yes, together we can *see* history unfold before our very eyes."

The cloud began to descend on us. Jenn let out a whimper. Clay stiffened, prepared for the worst. I saw Meg smirk at us all and then my vision was lost in white.

Right when I was about to ask Sir Rignot what was going on, the white smoke gained color and substance, painting a scene around me. The next instant, I was outdoors. Sun beat down on my face, though I couldn't feel the heat. Grassy meadows stretched as far as the eye could see, rolling into hills. There wasn't a single building, forest, river, or vineyard in sight. Miniscule, golden sparks floated through the air like pollen. It gave the air an ethereal, almost alien yellow haze. Distantly, I heard the crash of waves.

Though it looked different, I recognized the general shape of the land: it was Dembroch. We stood on the northwest headland before the castle had been built or the land had become desolate and dark.

I looked around, searching for the ocean, and yelped—I was standing over it. The ocean crashed on cliffs miles below. I scampered like a cartoon character, trying to push myself through the air to safety. Impossibly, my feet touched ground though I hovered in open space. I raced forward, reaching the grassy ground, and—"Careful, Sir Nicholas," the seer called after me—ran right into something invisible and very solid. I fell onto it, groaning in pain. I had a strong suspicion I'd run into a table stacked high with books.

"Calm down, calm down," called the librarian, standing a few feet away with my friends and the seer. "You're still in the library, Sir Nicholas. Only your mind has travelled somewhere new. Now, now, pay attention, everyone, yes, yes. We must watch and listen, but the magic must be guided. Sir Nicholas?"

"Uh...," I murmured as I walked slowly back to my friends, careful to avoid any invisible tables or bookstacks.

"Do you remember the tale?" he asked.

It had been years since I'd read it. I would have needed the book, but I could no longer see it.

"Fair enough, fair enough," the librarian said. "Allow me, allow me." He cleared his throat and, in a voice becoming a narrator, said, "The isles of Dembroch, first of the Arx, have always been magical. For many millennia, it was home of the mages—"

"Whoa, whoa, whoa, what's happening?" Meg interrupted, her voice straining. "What is this?"

Two figures had materialized right in front of us. I recognized their unique appearances instantly: they were mages, human in form, but composed completely of moss. There was a male and a female. The two danced around one another, plucking golden sparks from the air and collecting them in baskets.

At the sight of the male mage, the seer knocked against her heart and bowed her head. This must have been her fallen comrade.

"Be calm, be calm," Sir Rignot told Meg. "They will not harm you. You have not left the library. You are simply witnessing history. The magic allows us to *see* what has been written. You must only watch and listen. Now, now, if I may continue, yes, yes, these two mages, husband and wife, mage and his magesty, lived alone on Dembroch for millennia until, one day, vagabond Christians found the island."

Bidden by the librarian's account, the air became less dense with sparks. The once green island yellowed. The mage and his magesty stood stock-still, watching the southern end of the island suspiciously.

Humans, olive skinned and wary, approached the mages cautiously. The two mages held their arms open in welcome.

The librarian continued: "Mage and human lived in harmony for several years. The families grew in safety and numbers. But the island began to fall into famine due to the dwindling magic and excess of citizens."

All around us, the isles changed with the librarian's words. A small gathering of cottages was built near the eastern end of Coral Canyon. But even as this grew, the face of the island darkened. The grasses became dust. The hazy golden atmosphere lightened to the point of nonexistence.

"And then," Sir Rignot continued, "one day, several generations later but still long before our time, when it seemed this would be the final generation to live on the island, two citizens shared a kiss on the cliffs."

A dashing boy and button-nosed girl popped into existence, chasing one another toward the cliffs. They wrapped one another in a strong embrace and kissed. It was long and passionate. Sparks flew off them—and not just figuratively. Literally. Golden embers exploded out of that kiss, filling the air like a million tiny fireflies.

CHAPTER 13

"At their feet," the librarian continued, "grew a plinth."

So it did: a rock tore through the grass. It was made of black stone like the castle's walls, about the size of a man's chest cavity, and tapered up to a flat top the width and length of a human palm.

"And from the sparks of their kiss...," Sir Rignot said.

The sparks around the couple amassed on the plinth's top and blossomed into red and orange flames. Golden-red sparks sputtered in every direction and the flames' tongues danced wildly.

"...was born the first magical flame of Dembroch," the librarian concluded. He took a deep breath—the kissing couple froze in their liplock of the century and the waves below stopped crashing—and said ponderously, "From this moment, the magic of the land was not just in the ground and the air and the water, but concentrated in the flames. Because of this, though they wouldn't discover it until much later, the magic was accessible and tangible for humans to use."

"And the flames were started by them?" I assumed.

Sir Rignot nodded.

"How?" Clay asked.

"They are SparkSources," the librarian said contritely, "so named because they were the *source* of the *spark* that started the flame and concentrated the magic."

The word SparkSource sounded familiar to me. I knew I'd heard it or read it in my youth, perhaps elsewhere in my book, but I couldn't remember its importance.

"Let us move on with the story," the librarian said, "to when the magic was officially discovered."

Beckoned once more by Sir Rignot's narration, the scene around us changed fast and frequently. The sun and moon rose and fell in quick succession. Rain and wind assaulted the flame, but it continued to burn. At the same time, the couple kept returning to the cliffside, sharing meals or talking or kissing. Ever so slowly, they grew older.

Then, all at once, the tide of time stopped. With the sun at the height of the sky, the couple returned once more to the plinth, but this time, they had several people in tow, including the mages and an elderly, regally dressed man. The mages and elder inspected the flame. Sir Rignot bowed at the sight of this older gentleman, hand thudding against his chest.

"King Peter, our first ruler," he whispered. "The late father of our late King Richard."

My friends and I bowed disjointedly at the man though he couldn't see us.

The librarian continued his narration: "Over the course of several years, the couple aged less rapidly than their friends and family. The leader of the land, soon to be King Peter, deduced with the island's mages that the flame exuded a magic of timelessness. Anyone within arm's reach of the plinths stopped aging. To preserve the peculiar, unexpected magic, fearing it could be put out by a storm or wind, King Peter ordered a shelter to be built around it."

Quick as a flash, a tower was built before us. It was cylindrical and at least fifty feet tall. The flame was visible through the bottom window.

"Cliffside Tower," the librarian proclaimed. "Impressive, yes, yes? Once a shining beacon of our humble beginnings. Now sunken, sullied, and the site of our defenders' defeat."

I approached the tower's window and looked in on the plinth. The flame seemed ordinary, but on the black stone, I noticed indentations. It took me a second, but I realized they were words.

"Ca...ri...tas?" I sounded out.

It took a moment, but I placed the word. *Caritas.* It was Latin for a love deeper and truer than any simple friendly, brotherly, or familial bond. It was the type of love that could change the world. And if that word was on the plinth of the flame started by a couple kissing... The gears in my head turned, putting two and two together.

"Some time later," the librarian continued, "as humans began to understand the magic of the first flame and began using it to accomplish other means, five more flames came into existence with the aid of other SparkSources."

CHAPTER 13

Suddenly, we were deep in the Coral Canyon. A woman floated in one of the shallow pools.

Sir Rignot explained what we were seeing: "A woman, shunned by even her family for her opinions and open-mindedness, found peace with herself, a greater peace than any on Dembroch had known."

The woman smiled serenely. A spark of light flew from her, as though it had been within her. Just as had happened before at the cliffs, a black plinth rose from among the shallow pools. The sparks amassed on its flat surface and burst into flames. The golden tongues of fire danced, spitting out sparks.

I squinted. There were words on this plinth too. Was it *pax*?

I didn't have much time to look closer, because the second the flame lit, we were taken somewhere new. Coral Canyon became a barren, white wasteland of hot springs and geysers. Before us, a man held out a hand to another.

"Come with me," he said. "Trust me."

Sir Rignot filled us in: "Two friends discovered gates to distant lands and trusted one another enough to discover the unknown together."

One friend took the other's hand, and together, they leapt forward toward a hot spring. Before they landed in the torrid water, they disappeared from view. The only thing left in their absence was a sparking flame upon a plinth. This one had the word *fides* carved into the black stone.

We were off again, flying to the northern reaches of Dembroch. We saw a woman deep in the woods, a man upon the sandy shores of Whittlesea, and a lone figure atop Ryderwyle's mountain. All the while, the librarian narrated, and we saw what he said: "A generous woman took the first steps into Dembroch's newly grown woods and tended to a hideous monster none dared to heal. An embittered man who lost his wife during childbirth found joy in the new life he was to care for. A man, the last of his line, lost everyone he loved, but with much effort, saw the goodness in the world still."

We saw each of these—the hideous mushroom-colored monster licking the woman's face in thanks, the man holding his newborn with tears of joy and sorrow in his eyes as the sun rose over a sandy shore, and a man overlooking Dembroch from a towering mountain as he cast his burdens from himself—and in each of these places, sparks gave birth to flames on plinths. On each, I saw carved words, but they were long and difficult to remember.

"Each of the flames exuded the same small aura of timelessness, though each had been started by different means," the librarian said. "The power of the flames spread across the isles, and many sought it as their own. Fighting ensued."

All at once, we were back at Cliffside Tower. Hordes of people came running at us, pushing and fighting for entrance into the tower. Those who got inside fought for space around the plinth. One woman cleared enough room to hold a wooden torch in the fire. The torch did not light. Then, someone pushed her and she fell onto the plinth, her hands landing in the fire. She cried out, pulling back burnt hands. The torch clattered on the ground, flameless and unburnt.

"Yes, yes, notice," the librarian observed. "Anyone near the flame is free to bask in the magic, but most anyone who tried to touch the flame was burnt and no one could light a torch from the flame. Well, none of these people."

"Could someone else?" I asked.

"Indeed, indeed," Sir Rignot said. "As the book's account states... To quell the fighting of his people, King Peter and the mages devised a plan to spread the magic throughout the island and make the blessings of timelessness available for all. King Peter organized the isles into a kingdom and, on a beautiful summer's day, sent out the new monarchy's defenders to collect the flames."

Above the shouts of the mob, I heard the whinny of a horse, then its approaching gait. From the corner of my eye, I saw that the Dembroch castle had been half-built near the center of the island.

CHAPTER 13

Over the hill came two horses, and upon them was a knight and a dame. They wore heavy armor and the knight bore a hefty metal torch.

The mob parted in the presence of the two defenders. Together, the knight and dame entered the tower and, each holding the torch, lowered its brackets into the flame.

They waited a moment. The crowds hushed.

When the knight and dame lifted the torch, it was alight with golden flame and spewing sparks. Fire still burnt on the plinth too.

The knight and dame exited the tower, holding the burning torch high for all to see. The people clapped and shouted.

I marveled at the two. They looked impressive with their armor, weapons, and—

"Hold on!" I shouted.

The scene froze. The crowds and the knight and dame stopped moving. I approached the couple, careful to not run into anything else in the library, and peered through their visors. Within was the dashing boy and the button-nosed woman, the ones who had first started the flame by the cliffs.

"Hey," I exclaimed, pointing at the knight and dame. "They're the first SparkSources."

"Indeed, indeed," the librarian said. "After much trial and error, the eight SparkSources were the only ones who could spread the flames. As such, the eight became the founding knights and dames of the defenders. Each went to the flames they'd originally started and spread them back to the castle."

The knight and dame mounted their horses. Bearing the torch and leading the masses of people, they took off for the half-built castle in the distance. As they went, hundreds of sparks filled the air and hung there. Soon, the entire island was shining with billions of orange embers like a million suspended stars.

We arrived in the bowels of the castle, standing upon an oval, metal platform that hung from a stone ceiling. Railings circled the edge. Below was oily blackness and the eerie silence of a great, open expanse.

Eight knights and dames stood around the balcony, holding up six torches of flames. At their feet, arranged in a tight circle were six rocks, the same size and shape of the black plinths we'd seen rise throughout the kingdom.

"This is the castle's Aerary," the librarian explained. "Accessible only through the kingdom crest in the Rotunda."

I recalled passing the crest when we had first entered the castle and admiring it before Sir Liliford had hurried us along.

"In the Aerary, the defenders spread the kingdom's flames, and by extension, the magic, throughout the realm. From that moment forevermore, the Timeless Kingdom of Dembroch was suspended in a summer's day."

Beckoned by the librarian's words, the knights and dames lowered their torches toward the plinths on the balcony. There was a burst of light. The Aerary was filled with the orange glow and a million tiny sparks. The flames grew into full force, each burning so bright that they met one another and formed a circle.

At the same time, the room below us had become lit. It was a massive cavern. There were trees growing from the ground, their leaves glowing lightly. Wine barrels and stores of food were stacked in piles far below.

"Omnia Aeterno," the defenders chanted.

"It means—" the librarian began.

"All things eternal," I interjected.

He nodded. "Sadly, sadly, all is not truly eternal on Dembroch. The space below is no longer a wine cellar. It has been converted to catacombs. Many now lie beneath the castle."

My heart fell. All this beauty and splendor, I'd almost forgotten that it had all come crashing down.

The librarian cleared his throat and, forcing a tone of cheeriness, announced: "The knights and dames, having successfully spread the magic throughout the kingdom, were tasked with tending and safeguarding the flames. Wielders and philosophers alike began to use the magic to benefit the kingdom."

CHAPTER 13

Suddenly we were outside, hovering high above Dembroch. Before us, the island became bountiful. Vegetation grew from the ground, producing food. Rivers and springs carved into the land. The golden haze fell upon the whole island once more. Six flames flickered around the whole kingdom.

I couldn't believe my eyes. This place…it was stunning and far different from the desolate isles we had discovered.

My heart fell. What had happened? How had it fallen so far? Could it be this paradise once again?

"It was quite the wondrous feat," Sir Rignot continued, "but one that did not go without notice. The appearance of such powerful, timeless magic and the development of the kingdom attracted the attentions of darker forces in the world beyond. Many a dark soul sought Dembroch's shores to corrupt it or use its magic for their whims."

We were swamped in darkness. I sensed something watching us, something immense and bloodthirsty. And then, there were eyes in the darkness. Many of them. Some were human, others reptilian, others clustered like a million spider eyes, others alien and foreign to me. Each and every one stared at us with the wide, thirsting, longing of a predator seeking its prey.

Jenn let out a squeak. The seer shuddered. Sir Rignot went on, his voice shaky with fear.

"The order of defenders called for assistance from throughout the world to defend the kingdom. For each one who offered, they were trained rigorously by Master Malleator and, when ready, to prove themselves worthy of the flames."

The scene around us remained dark, but the eyes were replaced by dozens of new recruits running past, diving, jumping, swinging, and running their way through obstacles and trainings, right back into the Aerary. The dozen gathered around the ring of flames. Overseeing the ceremony were the mage, the magesty, and a stately man and woman, their expressions observant.

"Our queen and her late King Richard," the librarian said, kneeling. The seer knelt too, knocking on her chest in reverence. Jenn and Clay copied them, but I only had eyes for the woman beside the king.

It was Queen Coralee. She looked the same as she had in the throne room—or as the witch had—young, elegant, and shrewd. Her eyes, though, were full of kindness. This was the true queen of Dembroch, both in mind and body.

"What happened to King Peter?" Jenn asked.

Sir Rignot was quick to explain: "After spreading the flames and creating the kingdom, King Peter did not feel it was his right to lead such a nation. He gave the kingdom to his son, King Richard, who was born with a lion's heart and deep love for goodness. Afterward, King Peter left the isles and lived out the remainder of his days in the world beyond, aiding those in need and pointing the persecuted to the haven of Dembroch. In standard time, this was millennia ago."

I nodded in understanding, eyes passing over the king. He looked impressive dressed in deep purple. Upon his brow was a thin, black-and-gold flecked crown. He looked strong, confident, bold, and breathed fairness and justice. It was no wonder the queen had loved him. Maybe she still did.

Before us, the king gestured at the ring of fire. The dozen recruits reached out their hands and placed them directly into the flames closest to them. A few leapt back, shouting in pain, while the rest did not scream, nor did the flame burn their hands. These lucky, unburnt dozen began to circle the plinths, continuing to hold their hands in the flames. Many shouted at one point or another, but four of them made a full circuit without being burnt.

"Those select few who were worthy of the flames were invited to join the ranks of the defenders and share in their responsibilities," the librarian said.

From their scalps, the four remaining recruits pulled tufts of hair. They held the hairs over the plinths and dropped them in the flames. The follicles disappeared in bursts of sparks. The recruits' eyes glowed the color of the fire for a moment. Queen Coralee presented the four with a Dembroch medal—just like the one we'd had.

As I watched this, I remembered that my friends and I had sent our hair to Dembroch. Our hair must have been cast into the flames. Had this created some type of magical bond? Had my eyes glowed at some point in my youth?

"The defenders grew one hundred strong," Sir Rignot said, "each dedicated to preserving Dembroch's magic. And so long as the defenders stand, the magic of the isles would continue forevermore, bound in the age of knights and dames."

Something about this last statement struck me, as though it meant more than what was stated or immediately understood, with Sir Rignot's final word, the Aerary, its flames, and the defenders of old faded from view. Bright white smoke surrounded us again. I squinted, and then, with a blink of an eye, the story ended, the smoke disappeared, and we had returned to the library.

CHAPTER 14

The Age of Knights and Dames

"Do you understand, yes, yes?" Sir Rignot asked us, closing the book and handing it back to me. "Do you see now what the witch must never know?"

He watched us expectantly, as did the seer. My head was spinning with flames and Latin and SparkSources, the answer eluding my grasp like words to a song you can't quite remember.

I glanced at my friends. To my surprise, they didn't look scared or bored. Clay and Jenn seemed awed. Meg's face was strangely vacant. Something within them had stirred, even if they, like me, didn't have an answer for the librarian.

Sir Rignot cleared his throat. "Allow me to nudge you ever closer. Do you recall the final line from the tale? 'The kingdom's magic persisted forevermore, bound in the age of knights and dames.' The Latin for this final phrase is *milites flammis animam*, or the flame protector's age. But it is not age in the meaning you may first assume. *Animam*—age—has several meanings. It can be translated to mean a time period, a person's years of life, a person's youthfulness, and even parts of the body: mind, heart, soul, life. It could mean any of those...or—" he looked pointedly at us "—all of them."

Jenn caught on first.

"So 'the age of knights and dames' could be translated to the youth and heart of the defenders? As in us? *Our* youth?"

Sir Rignot nodded. "Even when your titles were stripped, you were still tied to the flames, acting as a fuel source with your youth."

"Well, no wonder the magic died," Meg interjected. "We're humans. We grow older. We die."

"But we're not dead," Clay said.

"Not yet," Jenn said, rubbing hand sanitizer generously over her hands.

"Uh, guys, I said. "I don't think it's just our *physical* age. I think it's our..."

I didn't know the word for it.

"*Metaphysical* age," the seer offered.

Meg rolled her eyes. "What a crock of—"

"Do not underestimate the invisible," the seer said sternly. "Just because you can't touch it or see it doesn't mean it's not there. In fact, the unseen often has more influence on us because we ignore it, and, consequently, is often more powerful than we give them credit. They are—"

Meg chuffed. "Invisible? Like what? Name one thing."

"Love," the seer replied simply. "Caring. Trust. Empathy. Apathy. Bonds between friends or family. Curses. Promises. All unseen. All the more potent for it."

"So our *youth*—" Meg made air quotes around the word as she said it with disdain "—acts as fuel for flames? That's not even scientifically accurate. Flames can't be fueled by *youth*. Even if it could, we're not on fire. We're not close to the flames. It's not possible."

The librarian and seer both screwed up their faces, words sharp on their tongue. They had a lot to say on this matter, but I cut them all off. My brain had been spinning for the last few minutes and I'd just realized what Sir Rignot was trying to say.

With everyone's attention on me, I flipped open my book until I found the story I needed. It was the musings of an old Dembroch knight and his dissertation on the truest traits of a defender.

"Guys, listen to this," I said. " 'Only through these truest traits—faithfulness, love, peace and patience, gentle generosity, joy, and goodness—may a SparkSource and defender truly be worth his flame,' " I read. I pointed at the Latin translation for the traits. "*Fides, caritas, pax, modestia, guadium, bonitas.* Those were the words written on the sides of the plinths when the flames started. Because those were the traits exemplified by the SparkSource to start the flame, *and* the same traits you had to have to become a knight and dame. Just as they start and fuel these magic flames, these truest traits are the substance of our youth. To have these within us keeps us young."

Jenn and Clay looked confused. Sir Rignot nodded eagerly. Meg was eerily silent. I had a feeling she knew where this was heading.

"I don't get it," Clay said.

"Let me back up," I said. "Remember the two who kissed on the cliff? They started a flame of *caritas.* That's real, true, deep love. Their kiss was the perfect example of it, and so their *love* created a spark, which became a magical flame. It's the same with all the others. All the SparkSources acted in a way that fully embodied a venerable trait and, as a result, flames were born. But the SparkSources didn't just start the flames, they fueled them. It was a permanent, unseen bond. As they continued harboring those traits, the fires continued to burn. So when the SparkSources became knights and dames, anyone who joined their ranks and put their hair in the fire had to exhibit those traits too. If it was within them, the flame wouldn't burn them. And then, once part of the order of defenders, they joined in the responsibility of fueling them."

CHAPTER 14

"So the fuel for the flame is our youth," Jenn said slowly, thoughtfully, "which is composed of these truest traits?"

I nodded, dreading the gravity of this truth.

"That's it, yes, yes?" the librarian interjected. "The flames are not tied to your years of age, but to the age of your soul. If you hold the six truest traits within you and embody them fully, you will be forever young."

"This doesn't make any sense," Clay said. "I have love within me. And happiness. All those things Nick read. I'm still young."

Sir Rignot pushed on, hell-bent on making us understand. I already knew what he was saying and knew it would hurt to hear. Meg was biting her lip, the first sign of tepidness I'd seen from her.

"A person must grow old physically," Sir Rignot said, "but they need not grow *up*! Even when an elder has brittle bones and failing organs, they may choose to smile, share kindness, and seek out the silver linings. That is their soul choosing to stay youthful. A soul's age—yours, mine, anyone's—is dependent upon the presence and constant training of the truest traits. The more love and goodness in your life, the younger your soul. But each of you?" He pointed at us all. "I saw it while you were talking to the queen. She saw it. The Watchmaker saw it. You are dead men walking. Dead women. Your souls are dead as brittle leaves, faded and extinguished as the fires it once fed. Your youth, that invisible quality you dismiss so easily, is gone."

"Well, forgive us for our glaring flaws," Clay chuffed. "We're only human."

"Flaws you choose to embrace," Sir Rignot retorted. "You choose sloth over initiative, cruelty over gentleness, pessimism over hope, tepidness when asked for dedication. Don't you see? You four were the last ones bonded to the flames and as your youth died, so did the magic. The witch didn't have to kill you. You killed your spirit and ended the magic for her."

The weight of this hung heavily on my conscience. I'd known it for a few minutes now, but to hear it out loud was like a hammer hitting your finger: you see it coming and it hurts even worse. And this truth, this revelation, cut me to my core.

After all my longing and searching, the kingdom I'd loved so much in my youth had been in danger because of...me. Not Sorgana the witch, not because we weren't knights and dames anymore, but because my friends and I had lost our way in life. In the past decades, we had all grown old before our time, skeptical, easy to anger, cowardly, and pessimistic. As our spirits had died, so too had the flames. Once fueled by the truest traits of love and faith and patience, the fires had died as our hearts were filled with anger, boredom, and hopelessness.

I remembered when the witch had tried to kill us. Leeched of air, suffocating to death, I'd intentionally dismissed Dembroch and its promises, abandoning my hope to be part of it and save it. At the same time, I'd felt an internal tremor. I'd thought it was external, but perhaps it had been my soul letting out its dying gasp. That, I realized, was the moment that the last flame had extinguished. That was the moment the last of my youth had died, and as a result, Dembroch's magic had died too.

I had ended the magic, I realized. My friends had contributed, but I had put the final nail in the coffin.

Terribly, in my mind's eye, I saw Page Hybore lying before me, eyes pleading, voice whispering, every ounce of his being begging me to save his home. Though he'd been bewitched to retrieve me, he'd given his life to get me here in hopes I'd succeed. The mage, too, had died trying to tell us what to do, to impart some knowledge as to how the magic had died and what we could do to fix it.

These people, I realized, knew no limits to their sacrifices. To them, this land and what it represented was worth dying for. It was time I gave it the same weight. I *had* to save this place. Not because I was being forced or coerced, but because I genuinely wanted to. Because I chose to. I, who had avoided commitment and mending mistakes my whole life, had to fix what I'd destroyed and restore this kingdom to its former glory.

CHAPTER 14

"Yes, you see it now," Sir Rignot said. "Look at your pocket watches."

We pulled out our pocket watches. When I clicked it open, I saw that the minute, second, and hour hand were no longer at 11:00—where it had been stuck since Page Hybore gave it to me—but now pointed at the numeral twelve. As before, the gears in the back were still moving. A quick glance at my friends' watches proved that theirs read the same: midnight. I wasn't sure how, but it seemed obvious. These watches didn't tell the time of day. They were tied to our souls somehow. And though we were still alive and the gears were still turning, our souls had struck midnight. We, like the magic, were dead inside.

"You see," said the librarian. "That is why the magic died. The witch got exactly what she wanted without hardly lifting a finger."

I couldn't have felt any lower. By the looks of it, my friends felt the same way. Clay hung his head. Jenn was crying and rubbing hand sanitizer over her palms. Meg was biting her lip and blinking hard.

"Sir Rignot," Jenn said, breaking the quiet. "You and the queen said the witch can't know any of this. But the magic is dead, so what does it matter?"

"True enough, true enough," the librarian said. "But what the witch does not know and you now do is *how* the flames were started. If she were to know this, she could have severed your bond to the magic quicker. She could have created her own magic. There is no telling what she could have done. But she does not know and never shall. Only you know. And with this knowledge, you can start new flames."

"Bring the magic back?" Clay asked.

The librarian nodded.

"And bring the Hospites back?" Jenn asked.

Again, the librarian nodded.

I felt my heart leap. There was a glimmer in the darkness we'd created.

"Great!" Clay said, his bravado returning. "So how do we do it?"

"Like the SparkSources," Sir Rignot said simply. "Each of you must exemplify the truest traits and bear a spark. And the mage knew exactly how it needed to be done."

He began rummaging through maps and books covering the nearby table.

"Some time ago," he said as he searched, "when the witch first arrived and was imprisoned, the queen consulted the seer and the mage."

"I wish she never had," the seer said with a heavy note of melancholy.

"The mage," the librarian continued, "ascertained four threats to Dembroch that must be eliminated, four tasks that must be resolved. In so doing, the kingdom would be saved and the magic would be reignited."

"The mage can see the future?"

Sir Rignot chuckled. "No, no, my good sir. In this kingdom, only the seer sees the future." The seer hung her head. "The mage is gifted with wisdom beyond years given his substantial age and can see evident truths where we see murky waters. While the seer predicted doom, the mage foresaw a way to save the kingdom. And that task falls to you four."

"Can't it be someone else?" Jenn asked.

"There is hardly anyone left on the island, and of the few left, most are attempting to complete what the mage commanded," the librarian replied. At last, he found what he was looking for and pulled a roll of paper from under a stack of books. He held it close as he faced us, speaking with dire intensity, "Truly, as you will hear and if the mage is to be believed, which he should be, you four must take up these tasks and aid us in our struggles. And if you four cannot help us, then the kingdom is truly lost."

Hand heavy with the weight of the words on the paper, the librarian handed it to us. There on its surface were five groups of verses, presumably spoken by the mage and recorded quickly by a listener.

I took it and, taking a deep breath, read aloud as my friends looked over my shoulder.

"The last day begins when the magic is gone and I too shall join the fallen echelon. Have heart, last defenders, for what's in store. You have until noon next day before Dembroch is lost forevermore. Start six flames, ignite six sparks, return them to the Aerary before the sun is highest in the dark."

I paused. These were similar to the words the mage had spoken before he'd died, but there was a new piece of information: a deadline. According to this, from the moment the magic died, the kingdom had until tomorrow to be saved...or it would be gone for good.

The only way to prevent that, I knew, was to do what was written below. Hands shaking, I read on.

"Hopeful defender of her choosing, aid the seer, return to her the power she has come to fear. In the imposter's grave within hallowed halls confined, discover sight to aid the blind. In your hand will be the power to see what can be done to save Dembroch in its final hour."

"Lady Jennifer," the seer said airily. "Of the four, you shall be my dame."

Jenn let out a sad whine.

"One down," I murmured, and kept reading: "Another, whose bravery runneth over, must claim the treasure from the cliffside's keep. Recover the Watchmaker's most prized possession, cull the Dreadnaught's reap. Decipher the gears of the broken clock, face the fate of two roads you dare to walk. Should you persist past a promise's cruelest tricks, you alone can complete the six."

Clay, Meg, and I exchanged glances.

"The Watchmaker doesn't like us," Meg said. "You're up, Clay."

"I c–can't...I...," he murmured, looking ready to soil himself.

"What else, Nick?" Meg asked.

I shrugged apologetically to Clay and read on: "To another most patient, you are tasked to find the hidden door. Aid the man abandoned, master and apprentice, restore. Only together can you overcome their trial. Reunite master and apprentice, liberate Ryderwyle."

Meg groaned. I winked at her.

"That one has your name all over it," I said, remembering Page Trey asking for her help with this very task before we'd come to the library.

Terribly, lastly, I read the final verse, which I knew would be my task: "Most faithful defender, discover the broken heart and mend it to its core. Break the curse, free the sister, the safest shores restore."

It was as if the mage had whispered the words into my ears. These commands may have befuddled other defenders, but I knew immediately what I was called to do and what should be done.

So that was that, I realized. My friends and I, the last defenders of Dembroch, now knew our responsibilities and what must be done to rectify what we'd destroyed. Before us lay four quests that must be completed by noon the next day.

Meg glanced at the verses.

"There are only four quests," she noted. "I thought we had to light six flames."

"Right, right," the librarian said. "I observed the same conundrum, to which the mage promised that these four would yield the six. It can only be assumed that the more trying tasks will produce more than one magical flame."

I wasn't quite ready to wrap my head around this, and nor was Clay.

"N–Nick," Clay said, his voice tenuous. "I'm not sure about this. Starting a flame is one thing. But the Dreadnaught?"

Jenn stepped away from the seer too, looking wary.

"You don't have a choice," Sir Rignot said.

I held up my hand, quieting the librarian. Forcing my friends headlong into this wouldn't be right. But I knew I could show them the way.

"I know this is scary, guys," I said. "I know this seems daunting. But all of this mess is because of what we've done. Somewhere along the way, we all lost ourselves. I know I did. And for anyone else, it would just be the end of chivalry. An unhappy, miserable life. But for us, there's more to it. This whole kingdom depended on us to be...better. And we let it down. Right here, right now, we have a choice. We can leave and never look back, or we can stay and fight. And we're the only four who stand a chance."

"Nick," Jenn said slowly. "I don't want to die."

I looked her square in the eyes.

"I'd rather die here, fighting for something, than go back to Midvale, where I was already dead to the world, living that way I was." I looked to my friends and stepsister. "I know you feel the same way. Isn't there something here worth saving?"

They cast their eyes around. I tried to think of what else to say to convince them, but I knew they had to make up their own minds now. I'd dragged them this far. The queen had forced us along too. Now, it had to be their choice.

A moment later, Clay looked back to me. Miraculously, or perhaps it was the torchlight from the library's walls, I saw a spark in Clay's eyes. Then, Jenn gave us a ghost of a smile.

"These people," Jenn murmured. "The people who had to flee. They need Dembroch. And Dembroch needs us."

She stepped closer to the seer, taking her hand.

"And we need them," Clay said. "Maybe helping them...will help us." His voice had changed. It wasn't in his confident, boasting way, but rather a determined, quiet voice I'd known in my youth.

I couldn't help but smile. There was a glimmer in their eyes, some personal epiphany that had finally convinced them to stay.

We looked to my sister. She was biting her lip still.

"Come on," I pleaded with Meg, desperate to have everyone on board. I knew that, without her, we couldn't possibly complete the mage's quests.

Meg frowned at the ground, her gaze lost in the middle distance. I could practically hear the gears turning in her head.

Finally, she looked at me. In the faintest voice, she said, "Yes."

I gave her a nod. If I still knew my sister, I knew she couldn't stand being blamed for something, particularly something she knew she'd been responsible for. Without a doubt, she was staying to set the record straight and wash her hands of it.

We looked back to the librarian, once four individuals, now unified as one.

Sir Rignot didn't smile or applaud. He gave us a curt nod and, from his desk of books, produced a map, which he unfurled for us. A hundred notations were scribbled across it, identifying beaches, villages, and homes.

The librarian pointed at a tower on the northeast headland of the main island.

"Cliffside Tower," Sir Rignot told Clay. "You will find the Watchmaker there."

The seer pointed to a cottage in the northeastern forest.

"My home," she said to Jenn.

"Page Trey will be here," the librarian said to Meg, tapping the southeast area. "The Gate Grounds. Tread carefully." He looked to me. "Sir Nicholas? Where are you headed?"

"I know where I need to go," I said.

Sir Rignot gave me a nod, rolled up the map, and handed it to Clay. Then, he handed me the vial of golden liquid.

"There may yet be more secrets within your book," he said. "This magic, perhaps the last in the kingdom, may be what you need to find the answers you seek."

I obliged, storing the vial and book back in my satchel.

"Come, Lady Jennifer," the seer said.

She gave each of us a strained, nervous look.

"I love you," Clay said to her.

"Be safe," I said.

With a final wave, Jenn and the seer walked off into the aisles of the library.

CHAPTER 14

Clearly seeing we were at an end to our discussion, Sir Rignot bowed to each of us.

"You have learned much, sirs and ladies," he said. "Now, for the sake of an old man's head and for our kingdom, please, be on your way. Save our kingdom before it is truly too late. And beware the Dreadnaught. It roams the woods. Take heed to not cross its path. It is indestructible."

With that, the roly-poly librarian bowed and disappeared into the aisles of bookcases. Clay, Meg, and I gave each other knowing looks and went on our way. It was time to save the kingdom we'd doomed.

A few bookstacks away, when sure everyone was gone, the seer tugged on Jenn.

"What are we doing?" Jenn asked.

"Escaping," the seer replied.

"What—no!" Jenn said. "I have to help you—"

"That's what the mage wants," the seer replied. She guided Jenn toward a door, one that presumably let out of the library. "But I know what you will help me with. Leaving Dembroch!"

Clay, Meg, and I stopped just beyond the exit of the library.

"Are we all on the same page?" I asked.

"One more time," Clay said. "Slower. In English."

I tried one more time. If anything, it helped my brain sort it out too.

"Six flames were started on Dembroch by eight people who exhibited the truest traits of peace, love, joy, gentleness, goodness, and faithfulness," I said. "The flames were tied to their creators, the SparkSources, who became the kingdom's knights and dames. Anyone who joined their ranks shared in the bond of fueling the fires. We were part of those ranks. But...because we all gave up on our youth—the truest traits—the flames went out. Now, the only way to stop the witch, whatever she's planning, is to go start new fires. We do these things—stop the Dreadnaught, free Ryderwyle, help the seer, mend the broken heart—and we exemplify the truest traits, and the flames get relit. We bring them back here to that Aerary thing and the kingdom is saved."

Clay sighed deeply, nervously. Meg bit her lip.

"Alright, let's do this," I said.

I took a step, prepared for the quest ahead, but there was one little thing we had forgotten: the witch.

And she was standing at the end of the hall.

CHAPTER 15

Light in the Library

Sorgana the witch glowered at us. She looked like the queen again, but you could see her true self in her eyes. It was not royalty who stood before us. It was chaos personified, a woman who knew only suffering and the need to cause more. And her sights were set on us, the three would-be defenders trapped at the end of the hallway.

"You have been immensely helpful," the witch said, her voice harsh and unbecoming of her alluring form. "You ended the magic for me and now, so helpfully reveal its true nature. Six flames tied to defenders. But not their lives, rather their age..."

She slunk closer, slow and confident. Clay drew behind me. Meg breathed hard. I prayed she didn't do anything stupid. At any minute, I expected the witch to fling us through the air or choke us to death with the flick of a finger.

"Love," the witch spat. "Patience. Joy. These are the virtues of children, of weak minds and bent spines, those who kneel and bow to higher powers while refusing to claim it as their own. It is no wonder this pitiful kingdom fell if its magic was built on such weak foundations."

She sneered at us.

"Rest easy, destroyers of Dembroch," the witch said. "The kingdom will have magic once more. *I* will do it. And I will rebuild upon firmer foundations. Your skeletons."

This was the moment, I knew it. She was about to attack. Unless we attacked first.

I did the only thing I could think of. I pulled my book out of my satchel, threw it open on the ground, and, quick with the vial, spilled several drops of golden magic onto its pages.

The effect was instantaneous. Smoke exploded out of the book. I was bathed in white light.

Not waiting to see what happened next, I turned and ran through the door into the library. My friends followed, as did the smoke. It filled the library in an instant, blocking our view.

Suddenly, the scene materialized—sun beat down on us, crusty white earth spread as far as the eye could see. There was a black castle set far away in ivory cliffs. It was the setting of the one story from the book I still remembered well.

I glanced back. Meg and Clay were right behind me, but Sorgana was there too. And she could see us.

She glowered at us, easily overcoming the sudden change in scenery. If we were to live, I had to distract her.

"Once," I shouted, "King Arthur fought his greatest foe, Morgan Le Fay!"

Two beings—a knight in shining armor and a witch in swirling rags—materialized out of thin air, appearing between us and the witch. The two fought viciously across the salt flat.

CHAPTER 15

Sorgana gave the two figures a strange look, almost one of recognition, then she returned her focus to us. She made to walk through the duelers after us, but she bounced off an unseen wall. I nearly laughed—she was still in the hallway outside the library.

"Come on," I said to my friends.

We ran the opposite direction, holding out our hands to feel any obstacles that would get in our way. The witch went the easier route. There was a flash of emerald green and the entrance to the library blew apart.

"Any last words?" King Arthur asked from behind us.

"I curse you," Morgan Le Fay replied, her aggressive voice carrying all the way to my ears, "and I curse your lineage."

There was a burst of green over my head. I spun around to see the witch—she was much closer, in the library now, and charging right for us.

"Shoot," I said under my breath. We had to get better concealment than this salt flat. In a commanding voice, I said: "Burdened with the curse and his spoils of war, King Arthur...uh..."

I couldn't remember what came next, but it didn't matter. The salt flats disappeared, and King Arthur was walking into a dark, stone room. There were loud cries of a child or infant...or worse. My friends and I were concealed in darkness.

Huh, that isn't how the story goes, I thought, but that didn't matter. The witch did.

"You can't hide forever," the witch crooned, her voice echoing off the walls around us.

"This way," I whispered to my friends, feeling an opening between two aisles of bookcases.

We crept along. It was so dark, we could hardly see anything. The only light was from the room King Arthur had entered. A second later, King Arthur walked out of it, clutching something to his chest. Shocked by his sudden appearance, Clay hit a stack of books. They tumbled to the ground.

The witch jumped out of the darkness, appearing right in front of us. Clay yelled, I cringed. Sorgana muttered an incantation and sent green daggers right at us—

They exploded before they hit us, colliding with a bookcase in between the witch and us.

"Go!" I cried.

We were off running, carelessly this time. I bounced off bookcases and tables. The witch was right behind us, muttering enchantments that couldn't find their mark.

"Bleed you dry of air so sweet," I heard her say.

"Oh, no you don't!" Meg cried.

She wrapped her hands around a book, invisible to our eyes, and heaved it at the witch. There was no obstacle in the way this time. It smacked her face, silencing her incantation. We ran off, finding another aisle, and running further into the darkness. Behind us, the witch shrieked. Flashes of green flew all around us. Unseen bookstacks exploded, peppering us with splinters.

Suddenly, I slammed into something hard and solid. Part of it gave. I saw a brief rip in the scene, a hallway lit by torchlight. We'd found a door out of the library!

Meg and Clay saw it too. They pushed through it, I followed. We emerged into a hallway of the Dembroch castle and slammed the door shut. The sounds of breaking bookcases and shredding books were muffled behind the door.

We raced down the hallway. At an intersection, I looked back. The witch hadn't made it out yet.

Down one of the other hallways, I saw a wall of white clouds. My book must have been down there.

Fighting the impulse to run, ignoring the pleadings of Clay and Meg, I ran down the hallway. At the bank of clouds, I stooped to the ground and reached around for my book. I found it and snapped it shut. The second I did it, I knew it was a mistake. The cloud of white disappeared with it, revealing the hallway and the broken door leading into the library. Within, the crashes of the witch's rage ceased.

"Nick! Run!" Clay shouted at me.

I turned and booked it, fast as my unexercised body could carry me. Clay and Meg ran too, leading me into the labyrinth of castle halls. We didn't stop, even when we ran into Sir Liliford. We all screamed. Meg wound up to force the ferryman out of the way.

"Wait!" I shouted.

There was no green in the ferryman's eyes anymore. He was free of the witch's enchantment, though ashen and disoriented.

"She's coming!" I shouted at Sir Liliford. "Run!"

This he understood. He turned tail and ran, leading us on. We chased after him, our sides aching.

Sorgana the witch fumed, barely containing her rage. She paced the destroyed library.

The defenders had escaped her for the second time. Despite their overall lack of composure and fighting prowess, they were resourceful and fortunate. They would pay for that. If her Dreadnaught did not devour them, she would personally see to their demise.

But to do so, she knew, would be costly. Her internal magic was intrinsically tied to her stamina and lifeforce. The more she used, the weaker she became, particularly when she used it upon a living being—because murder and harm were the hardest acts to produce and inflict. She did not need to kill the defenders anymore. She only wanted to kill them out of coldblooded wanton and revenge, but to do so would have been wasteful. There were greater things to be accomplished—and now, thanks to the defenders, she knew the final puzzle piece that even her informant hadn't known: the kingdom's flames had been started by the truest traits. And with this knowledge, she now knew how to complete her spell. She would have to work quickly if she were to beat the defenders.

There was a sharp gasp across the library. The witch froze.

"Help," a weak voice said. "Help me."

The witch spotted the source: the librarian lay under a pile of splintered bookcases and torn pages. He was bleeding from his nose. She could drown him in it if she wanted. But to do so would be wasteful of her energy.

She stepped back into the shadows of the last standing bookcases. Someone would return for the librarian and when they did, her own quests would begin.

At long last, we burst back into the Rotunda. Dying sunlight cascaded down from the upper windows. The inlaid kingdom sigil flashed by as we ran—the Aerary was down there, I knew now.

Sir Liliford ran through the columns and off into the coming night. Meg and Clay noticed I'd stopped. They turned, demanding I come with them.

"My quest is here," I explained. "Go. Watch your backs."

"Same," Meg said.

They disappeared into the cluster of columns that led to the courtyard. I ran off in search of the prison where I knew a certain broken-hearted woman lay wait.

It may have taken a deadline to doomsday and a few blows to our egos to rekindle our friendships, but at long last, the quests of the last defenders of Dembroch had begun.

PART 2

The Quests of the Last Knights and Dames of Dembroch

CHAPTER 16

The Seer Who Would Not See

"We can't just leave," Jenn said.

"We most certainly can," the seer replied, tugging Jenn through the castle.

"The mage told us—"

"Yes, yes, I know what he wants."

"So we should stay—"

"We should *leave*. The Civium left in droves years ago, taking all the Hospites with them to safety. A few loyal remained, but they left a week ago, after the witch escaped. So many chances, but I knew I had to wait for you. You alone, Lady Jennifer, can escort us to safety."

Jenn wasn't sure what to make of this.

"Don't be so surprised," the seer said. "I saw it long ago."

Seeing Jenn's confused expression, the seer stopped tugging and dug into her shawl, pulling out papers. She unfolded each of them and, after looking closely at them, cast them to the ground one-by-one. Jenn saw hand drawn sketches of the Dembroch insignia, sparking flames of red and others of black, knights and dames fighting a giant worm and dragons and walking skeletons. There were so many, she lost track.

"Ah-ha!" the seer cried.

She unfolded a paper and showed it to Jenn. It was a scenic picture of Dembroch's main island from a southern viewpoint. The castle stood above a fallen forest. Dark figures lingered on the tallest tower's balcony. But in the forefront of it all was a stunning portrait of Jenn herself. Her face was wrinkled, and her golden hair was the same as it was now, but her eyes were unusually youthful and exuberant. It seemed the artist, presumably the seer, had taken Jenn's younger face and drawn it onto her thirty-two-year-old body.

"See? See?!" the seer pleaded. "This is the moment. You take me to the docks. To the ferry. We flee."

"You *saw* this?" Jenn asked, reading between the lines. "Is that the power you have come to fear?"

The seer's face fell. She folded up the paper and hid it within her shawl again.

"I won't," she said darkly. "I can't. I mustn't." She grabbed her hair exasperatedly. "It was a burden, Lady Jennifer, that none should bear. I rid myself of it and shall never seek it again."

"Again?" Jenn goaded.

The seer hesitated for a moment as though scared to explain herself, but finally spoke.

"When I was a young, foolish girl, I sought out the Sight," the seer said, still playing with her hair. "The last seer passed them on to me. Two mirrored talismans. Every time I held them in my hand...I could See."

"What could you See?" Jenn asked, sensing that this type of sight was far different from standard twenty-twenty vision.

"The invisible," the seer explained, her face becoming stony. "Recent pasts. Potential, immediate futures. In the present, I could see emotions. Strong thoughts. Things that wished to remain hidden. It was a more densely populated world around us than you realize. And with the Sight, I could see all of it."

The seer closed her eyes and grimaced.

"But it was a terrible gift," she continued. "I saw beautiful things...and terrible things. My mind became so crowded, I tried to draw much of what I saw. And then...all futures turned dark. I saw what it was all leading to. I began to fear looking. I began to leave my Sight unattended."

The seer let out a sob and sank to the stone floor. Jenn sat with her.

"I'm here to listen," she said, "if you want to talk about it."

The seer didn't need much more prompting.

"Some twenty years ago," the seer said through her tears, "I had left the Sight unattended. The queen arrived and requested I look to the future for a way to safeguard the kingdom. I had already seen much more than I wished, but I obliged. But my sight had been taken by another. My little Emily found them. What she saw..." The seer shuddered. "I found her screaming and tried to pull the Sight from her. But in so doing, I saw everything she was seeing. Pain. Failure. Untold sadness. Death. The sky turns red and the tallest tower falls. The isles crumble into the sea and sink into the earth. The queen, the defenders, the Civium...no one can stop it. There is death, doom unstoppable, a curse no one can break. Dembroch falls. The queen falls. The defenders fall. My husband..."

Jenn swallowed hard. It was as Sir Rignot had mentioned: the seer had seen a glimpse of the future—of Dembroch's end, of her lover—and the terror of it had turned her into a shut-in. The same thing had happened to Jenn, but with less magic and more nightly news.

"It has all come to pass," the seer muttered. "There has been little I've seen that I could prevent. To recover the Sight...it would do more harm than good."

"I'm so sorry," Jenn said.

CHAPTER 16

They sat in silence for several minutes. The seer rubbed her thumbs in the palms of her hands. When she spoke, her voice was dry.

"I couldn't bear it.... So I decided no more Sight. I rid myself of it."

"You destroyed it?" Jenn assumed.

The seer's face crumpled.

"Would that I could," she said. "The Sight cannot be destroyed. Only lost or hidden."

Jenn's shoulders slumped. This quest was over before it had begun.

"What would you have me do?" she asked.

"Take us far from this place," the seer pleaded. "As I was shown with the Sight. Guide us to safer shores."

"And the kingdom?" Jenn inquired, thinking of the beautiful isles of the past that she had glimpsed in the library. "The queen? The other Civium?"

The seer's face fell.

"I can't abandon them," she said, then sighed heavily. "But how would the Sight save any of them?"

Jenn grasped at straws: "Seeing the invisible and immediate futures could be a powerful tool to prevent a misstep or know the right course of action."

"Only if you can interpret what you See with enough time to act in a way that circumnavigates what you have seen," the seer chided.

Jenn paused, letting this statement sink in. A second later, the seer frowned, knowing the trap she'd just fallen into.

"A devilish trick," she spat. "Insidious. Cruel." She sighed again. "Yes, I alone could decipher what the Sight showed. But I do not wish to See again. I cannot."

"We must," Jenn implored. "I...I used to sit at home every night. Watching the world burn. Getting lost in the misery of it all. This is the first night in a lot of years I'm doing something different. And if I can get off that couch, if I can face the future, so can you." She took a deep breath, measuring her words. "If I find your Sight, if I recover the talismans, would you be brave enough to look one last time? To See what can be done? And then...no more."

The seer's glassy eyes teared up again.

"Only once more?" she asked.

"Once," Jenn agreed. "Where are they?"

"Under the castle," the seer confessed after a moment of silence. "In the catacombs. I hid them in the open, unmarked grave of Solomon."

Of course, Jenn thought. Because the seer couldn't leave the Sight somewhere warm, pleasant, clean...

"Hold on," Jenn said. "Who is Solomon? Earlier, in the castle, you said—"

"Don't go the way of Solomon," the seer repeated. "Yes, Lady Jennifer. Do not go his way. You will see when you visit his grave. His way is to suffer greatly."

"But who is he?"

The seer frowned deeply. "The Poison Priest of Pavidus. Then a Hospite. Then a defender. Then an exile. But truly, he was but a damned knight, one of the worst. He used his authority to wreak havoc, and as a result was ultimately stripped of his titles and exiled from the kingdom."

That sounds familiar, Jenn thought bitterly.

"It didn't stop him," the seer continued. "He went on, lost in his ways, after glory or power. No one really knew. But he was fast and effective. He gained supporters, toppled cities and kingdoms, decimated our sister islands, his home of Pavidus, even a military of a thousand. He was feared by many. Except by Dembroch. We knew him in his beginning, who he still was deep down. So, King Richard set out to put a stop to Solomon's acts and returned home with his body...or the remains of it. They rest in infamy below, a reminder to defenders and all Civium of the poisonous perils of power."

"And that's where I'll find the Sight?"

"The last place anyone in this kingdom would want to look," the seer said.

"How do I get there?"

"Any descending staircase will lead you there eventually. The cleanest entrance is through the library."

"Will you come with me?"

The seer shuddered. "I cannot. I mustn't. The catacombs are no place for the living."

"*I'm* living," Jenn said.

"But you are a dame," she replied. "You have prepared your whole life for a moment like this. I am only the seer and I must attend to my daughter."

Jenn wanted nothing more than to run, but knew she must stay. She wanted Dembroch to live on. Its purpose was good, a bright ray of light in the world that Jenn only wished she could be. No matter the danger, no matter the terror ahead, she had to do this. Even if she had to do it alone.

She helped the seer to her feet.

"I'll meet you at your home," she promised. "Look once more for me and I will take you and your daughter to safety."

The seer beamed from ear to ear.

"You were always my favorite, Lady Jennifer."

Jenn found her way back to the library. Inside, she found stacks overturned, wooden cases blown to splinters, pages torn and strewn, books rent into hundreds of pieces. Only a few bookcases remained standing.

"Some temper tantrum," Jenn mumbled, making a personal note to never cross the librarian.

She circled the library, looking through doors until she found one with a descending staircase. A cold draft blew out of it.

Jenn felt her bravery ebbing away. Why was she pretending? She wasn't brave or good or hopeful. Why would she voluntarily go into the catacombs, where there would be corpses and death and disgust? She should just—

"Help me," a voice called.

Jenn nearly jumped out of her skin. She spun around to find Sir Rignot pinned under a heap of splintered wood. He had a fresh bump on his head and blood running from his nose.

"What happened?!" she cried as she worked to free him.

"The witch," he replied. "She attacked shortly after you and your friends left. She seeks you vigilantly. I fear she lingers close. And you?"

"The seer," Jenn explained. "She left her Sight in the catacombs."

The librarian frowned. "Of course she did."

Jenn pushed away the last, largest piece of broken bookcase and helped the librarian up. He weaved on his feet for a moment.

"I'm afraid I'm not much use here," he said, looking around his destroyed library. "May I accompany you, Lady Jennifer?"

She was all too eager to accept the offer. They pulled two torches from the wall and Sir Rignot unlocked the door. Together, they descended into the catacombs.

Perhaps, Jenn decided, she could face the darkness. With a little bit of help.

CHAPTER 17

Rescuing Royalty

I slunk through the castle, jumping at the sound of every creak and crack.

At last, I found my way back to the prison. In the last cell was the queen, looking like the old, frail, ugly witch, but worse than when I'd last seen her. Blood tricked from her mouth. She had a black eye and long scrapes in her arms. The witch had obviously been by and vented some of her frustrations.

"Sir Nicholas," the queen rasped when she saw me. "You should not be here—"

"We already have our quests," I explained. "You are mine."

For a moment, I thought I saw the queen blush, but it was hard to tell on such a ghastly appearance.

"If the witch returns, she will show no mercy," the queen whispered.

"I'd better get you out then," I replied.

“Careful,” the queen said. “The witch cast a spell on the door of my cell. Should anyone open it, she will surely be alerted.”

I pursed my lips, thinking hard.

“She may have done that to your cell,” I thought aloud, “but I doubt she did it to these ones.”

I opened the door to the cell beside the queen’s slowly. Nothing happened, so I entered it and inspected the makeshift wall of bars separating the queen’s cell from the one I stood in. Four rusted bolts secured the bars to the stone wall.

“I have an idea,” I said.

From further down the hallway, I retrieved an iron torch. I snuffed out the flame and took it back to the prison cells. There, I wedged the pointed end of the torch between the bolts and the stone wall. I began pulling and twisting. Slowly but surely, the bars began to bow and tremble. It would take a while, but it would work.

As I worked, the queen paced her cell.

“Given your presence and insistence to aid me,” the queen said, “I assume you intend to heal what cannot be mended?”

“Well–uh,” I stammered, not sure what to say about this.

“I have given it much thought,” the queen said when I didn’t speak. “If the mage’s musings mean me, and my broken heart must be mended, we must go to the source. My heart was first broken by the loss of my king. Perhaps the only way to mend it is to avenge his death.”

“The witch?” I assumed.

The queen nodded. “I do not take the task lightly. But the king cannot die in vain. The witch shall pay penance for her transgressions.”

There was a fine line hidden in her words. I didn’t sense she wanted to harm or execute the witch, only to make the witch own up to her crimes.

“Tell me about the witch,” I said as I popped one bolt and began to work on another. “The magic of Dembroch is gone, but she’s still throwing magic around. And she keeps aging.”

CHAPTER 17

"She is a mystery unto herself," the queen replied, kneading her hands. "Prior to arriving on Dembroch, she managed to internalize her magic, a task not easily accomplished or lightly taken. It causes great strain on your heart and mind. But she has accomplished this feat nonetheless. As a result, she is her own source of magic. So long as she can speak an incantation, her will can be done."

"And the aging thing? Back in the throne room, she went from thirty to ninety in a few seconds."

"As you may have seen, the use of her magic puts a strain on her body and ages her terribly," responded the queen. "Like many witches and warlocks before her, she consumes the flesh of the incorruptibles to stay young."

"Incorruptibles?"

"Innocent, long-living creatures. Whales, turtles, elephants, the like. By eating their flesh, Sorgana consumes their lifeforce and uses it for her own."

I remembered the turtle Sir Liliford had retrieved for her from the Bridgemaster's home. I gulped. The witch had eaten the poor creature.

"Does that mean...humans?" I gulped.

The queen shook her head. "Unlikely. Humans are much more complex creatures. She wouldn't be able to simply—"

"Eat us?" I interrupted. My skin crawled and I decided to change the subject. "How did she get here?"

"My husband," Queen Coralee replied. "She arrived on Dembroch covered in his blood, possessing his chroniseal."

"The witch killed him?"

"We can only assume, though she has never claimed responsibility. I also believe she tortured him for information. The witch knows Dembroch intricately—the geography, the castle, the magic—though she has never been here. I believe she learned these secrets by way of force."

I winced, my imagination running wild to picture King Richard, the once proud monarch, strapped to a chair in the freezer of a butcher's shop, the witch using her magic to torture him until he spilled every secret she wanted to know.

"So why is she here?" I asked. "What is she trying to accomplish?"

The queen kneaded her hand like she was trying to polish off her fingertips. I sensed she was choosing her words carefully.

"She has yet to say," the queen answered. "Whatever she intends, it required ending our kingdom's magic and its safeguards."

"The timelessness?" I assumed.

The queen bit her lip and nodded. I sensed she knew something more that she was not sharing, perhaps because it was only a puzzle piece that did not complete the full picture or some personal matter that put her in a bad light.

"Whatever she does next," Queen Coralee continued, "I believe it to be a matter of reprisal."

"Revenge?" I echoed. "For what?"

The queen paused. "Sorgana...claims to know me."

"Do you know her?" I asked.

The queen shook her head earnestly.

"If I ever knew her, I cannot recall. Whatever slight she believes I paid her, or however Dembroch has failed her, I cannot possibly know. It must have been long ago."

"Long ago?" I said. "As in before... Before you got here?"

She nodded. "I was not born on Dembroch. Like many others, I was brought here. Long ago."

I couldn't help asking. "How long *have* you been alive?"

Queen Coralee smirked at me.

"It is impolite to ask a queen her age," she said with a wry smile. "I stopped aging right before my thirtieth birthday. But, I can say with reasonable assurance that I have been on Dembroch for at least two thousand years."

My jaw dropped. I was speechless. Sure, I'd figured the queen was older than she looked, maybe a hundred years, but two thousand? I couldn't even fathom this. That meant when she'd been born, the

Roman Empire had been falling, King Arthur had been seeking the Holy Grail, and chess had been invented.

I returned my attention to the bolts, which I had been neglecting the last few minutes, my mind spinning. Given I'd messed up my life in a matter of twenty years, I couldn't begin to imagine the things Queen Coralee had seen in her thousands or what small crimes she or her kingdom may have committed to warrant the witch's assault.

CHAPTER 18

The Dreadnaught

Deep in the woods to the north, Clay jumped behind a tree. His pulse raced. He clutched a broken tree limb, unsure what to do with it. If Jenn could seem him now...

The sound of a million ticking clocks was all around him. It was so dark and the canopy of gnarled, dead trees was so thick, he could hardly see a thing. A hundred paces away was a clearing, bright with the setting sun, but he didn't dare go for it. Whatever was moving through the trees, it was headed right for Clay. The ticking was growing louder.

Then he heard it. The scuttle of legs. Many of them, light as a whisper of wind. They grew closer. He held his breath.

There was a gust of air behind Clay. It wrapped around the tree, tossing his hair and tie. The breath was rancid and acidic, like a vat of overactive stomach acid turned loose in a belch.

CHAPTER 18

The ticking was overbearing now. Clay couldn't even hear the creature's movements. He squeezed his eyes shut. There was nothing to be afraid of. It was probably a friendly beast, surely not the Dreadnaught.

But when he opened his eyes, prepared to make a run for the clearing, his blood ran cold. Hovering in the darkness in front of him, blocking his view of the clearing, was a set of eyes the size of cars. They were pumpkin orange and staring right at him.

The creature roared at Clay. He was bathed in a ghastly acidic stench of mold and decay and undigested food. A billion ticks were drowned out in a horrendous, screeching roar.

The eyes lunged at Clay. He was done for, he knew it—

Something big and fast slammed into Clay. Suddenly, he was moving, held not by teeth, but by an arm. The monster roared and chased after them. Trees fell as the massive, shadowed body smashed through them.

Branches slapped Clay's face and tore at his clothes as his rescuer raced out of the woods and into the clearing. His rescuer dropped Clay and belly-flopped onto the ground.

"Don't move," the Watchmaker whispered gruffly.

Clay breathed a sigh of relief, sure that if anyone could protect him, it would be this burly, axe-wielding, giant of a man. But the Watchmaker wasn't ready for a fight. He lay flat, weapons holstered, looking out of the corners of his eyes.

The pursuing monster charged into the clearing only to scamper to a halt. It roared angrily, rearing its head skyward. Clay gasped. The monster—it was surely the Dreadnaught.

It was repulsive, like a slimy insect you'd find under a rock. Wormlike in shape with centipede legs, the Dreadnaught was at least fifty feet long and as many feet around. It must have had muscles in its back, because its top half was rearing up like a cobra ready to strike. Its skin was gelatinous, slimy, and ghost white. The gigantic orange eyes were two of hundreds, though the others were black and beady like a spider's. Pincers and jaws gesticulated hungrily. The tick of a million clocks emanated from its body.

Shaking with fear, Clay felt the ground around him and grabbed a rock.

"Drop it," the Watchmaker whispered. "You'll just get its attention. Lay still."

Against his better judgement, Clay lay prone in the dead grass.

The Dreadnaught, pasty white and bug-eyed, scanned the clearing. Its nose slits opened wide. A thousand fangs clicked together, a many-forked tongue flicked out. The pupils of its eyes dilated and expanded sporadically in the dying light. A tense second later, the Dreadnaught roared and lumbered off, nearly stepping on Clay as it went.

Once the monster had disappeared into the shadows of the forest, the Watchmaker pulled Clay to his feet.

"How did it not see us?" Clay gasped.

"Bad eyesight," replied the Watchmaker. "Can't see well in the light. Makes up for it with impenetrable skin."

"Well, sheesh, thanks," Clay breathed. "I owe you, big guy."

"Don't forget it," the Watchmaker said gruffly. "You get eaten by that thing, you get digested over a couple seasons. Slowly. Painfully. So, best be more observant of your surroundings."

The Watchmaker pulled his gigantic axe from his back and walked off.

"Wait!" Clay shouted.

The Watchmaker didn't even stop, letting out a chuckle as he went. Clay ran after him.

"I'm here to help," he said. "I'm supposed to come with you."

"Supposed to?" the Watchmaker echoed. "Big man you are, then?"

"I *want* to come with you," Clay insisted. "Together, we can—"

"I'm not a fool, boy. You no more want to be here than the last poor sap who was told to come help me," the Watchmaker said. "And the last. And the last."

The Watchmaker saw Clay's whitening face.

CHAPTER 18

"That's right, boy," the Watchmaker growled. "I'm as good as cursed. At least a dozen of your fellow defenders fell on my watch. I won't drag you along to die, too."

Clay felt his hands begin to shake again. Cold sweat formed on his brow. But he couldn't shrink away out of fear. He had a reputation to uphold.

"They may have failed you," Clay said, forcing himself to sound bold, "but I won't."

The Watchmaker bellowed with laughter.

"I don't need a knight. I need a thinker. A shrewd eye. A fierce mind."

Clay stammered, now in quite the conundrum. Here he was, pretending to be a fighter to win the Watchmaker's favor, but the Watchmaker needed exactly what Clay was: a thinker and analyzer.

"Be on your way," the Watchmaker said. "Bother someone else for their troubles."

Clay didn't move.

"I am here to help you," Clay insisted. "You want to kill the Dreadnaught, but you need something from the cliffside keep."

The Watchmaker gave Clay a look.

"You heard the mage's musings. So have a hundred other defenders. How do you think they died?"

Clay shuddered, but kept walking with the Watchmaker. After a few strides, the mountain of a man grumbled.

"Alright, shorty. Here's the rough of it. The Dreadnaught needs to die. It's killed plenty, destroyed more, and took something of mine. But I can't just cut its head off. No manmade weapon can pierce its skin. However, there is a sword, a fortissium blade, that was crafted long ago that can cut through any material, wood or metal, flesh or stone. It resided in the Horror Hollow on Ryderwyle for centuries and was nigh impossible to retrieve. The metal gives off this scent that lures in monsters. I made a few attempts, but the little beasties guarding it weren't too keen on letting it go. A few defenders tried to help me, but...well, they're in the catacombs now. Then, a few days ago, that fool of a knight, Sir Kenneth, finally did something right. He got the sword. Whole lot of good it did though. It caused the winter wonderland on Ryderwyle and all the little beasties pursued it to the mainland. The sword didn't work for Sir Kenneth, so now it's somewhere in Cliffside Tower, guarded again by the monsters of Horror Hollow. I tried to retrieve it a few days ago, but the queen ordered us remaining Civium to stick together. Probably because we're all part of the mage's quests. But enough of that nonsense. I have a task, and I'll be cursed twice if Sir Kenneth could get the blade from Horror Hollow and I can't get it from the Cliffside Tower."

So that was it, Clay realized with another shudder. The Dreadnaught was to die, and the only way to do it was a sword in Cliffside Tower after failing its previous owner. Didn't seem too bad...except for the monsters. The Dreadnaught was one thing, but the "little beasties" of Horror Hollow now gathered in Cliffside Tower, intoxicated on the smell of the sword, willing to fiercely protect their prize... That was enough to shake the bravest man's soul.

"Let's do this, then," Clay said, forcing the bravado in his voice.

The Watchmaker gave him a raised eyebrow.

"You'll die for it," the Watchmaker replied.

Clay puffed up his chest.

"Then I'll die for Dembroch," he said, his voice straining.

The Watchmaker let out a bark of a laugh. "I misjudged you, boy. You're brave *and* stupid. Come along then. If you must follow through with this task and die like the others, who am I to stop you?"

And so they walked into the woods. Clay's heart thundered with fear, but also the prospect of adventure. Dare he say it, or even think it, he felt young again.

CHAPTER 19

The Gate Grounds

Wind blasted Meg in the face. She hunkered down and pressed on, the light of the sunset lighting her way.

The southeast lands of Dembroch were alien and strange compared to the rest of the mainland. Limbless, burnt trees stood among plates of sandstone. Wind raced across the flat expanse, creating winding trails of sand and salt. Dark waves splashed chaotically on the sandstone cliffs and inlets.

The otherwise uninteresting landscape was punctuated by pools of boiling water and glistening cones of mineral build-up. The scent of sulfur hung in the air. At varying times, the pools boiled over and colorful steam of various colors poured from the surface. The air was filled with faint greens, blues, yellows, and reds. It was enough to give anyone pause, but Meg was in no mood to gawk. There was less than twenty-four hours to save this kingdom, and she would save it if it was the last thing she did.

As she had expected, Page Trey stood in a ring of hot springs some hundred feet ahead. His eyes were closed and he was murmuring under his breath. The wind tossed his golden hair and mustard yellow robes. A couple walking sticks lay at his feet. The swords gleamed in the sunset.

When she was next to him, Meg cleared her throat.

Page Trey's eyes snapped open. He frowned heavily, quite the contrast to the jovial, youthful expression he'd demonstrated earlier.

"Try not to move, Lady Meghan," he said, some of his words getting lost in the wind. "We wouldn't want you to fall into the wrong door."

"What?" Meg shouted, her patience growing thin.

Abruptly, all the geysers fell still. Burning hot water splashed back to the ground and only white steam emitted from the pools.

The page exhaled sharply.

"What can I do for you, Lady Meghan?" he asked, frustration oozing from him.

"I'm here to help you," Meg replied. "With whatever it is you're doing."

Page Trey stuck his nose in the air.

"Thank you," he said. "I am honored. However, you may carry on with your tasks. I am in no need of assistance, I assure you."

"That's not what you said back in the castle," Meg reminded him.

"And you *politely* declined my request," Page Trey replied.

Meg grumbled under her breath. She knew what the page was doing.

"I'm sorry," she said, rolling her eyes. "Please let me help you?"

"No need," he scoffed. "I can do this on my own."

I've heard that before, Meg thought angrily, having said the same thing several times a day to her incapable employees.

Meg forcibly removed her ego and politely said, "I'm sorry for offending you earlier. May I help you now?"

"You have had a change of heart?" he asked. "You believe in saving my master?"

"Yes," Meg said solemnly.

"You'll have to change more if you hope to stir the Gate Grounds."

"Try me."

Page Trey considered her for a moment.

"You will help me find the gate?"

"Whatever that means, yes."

"You will come with me to Ryderwyle?" he asked.

Meg bit her lip.

"If I have to," she said.

Page Trey sighed heavily.

"Fine," he said. "But only because you insist." A smirk tugged at the edges of his lips. "Now, to business. I am here to seek my master, a magician in his own right and the combat trainer of the kingdom's defenders. He was trapped on Ryderwyle after that idiot knight took the fortissium blade—a sword—from Horror Hollow. Then the Dreadnaught destroyed the skybridge."

"What? Speak English, please?"

Page Trey scowled.

"On Ryderwyle, there is a hollow which holds a storm stone. When the fortissium blade was taken, the stone was disturbed, thus the winter storm sieging the island. The knight who did this escaped before the surrounding ocean froze over. My master has been trapped ever since."

"For how long?"

"In standard time," the page mused, "perhaps a week."

"And he's still alive?"

"You doubt my master?" the page asked. "He is quite accomplished with survival techniques and can bend the kingdom's magic to his every whim. I have no doubt he survived this last week. But since the magic has fully died, I fear he is in danger. I need to find him before he freezes to death...if he has not already."

"Don't you need to find the sword first?" Meg asked, thinking this seemed obvious. "Get the sword back to the Hollow thing and the storm goes away?"

"Saving my master is my priority," Page Trey said. "Fixing the weather can come later."

"So just row over to the island—"

"You would freeze before you reached the one accessible shore on the northern edge. The rest of the island is steep cliffs."

"Okay, then," she said, trying to hide her arrogance. "Why are we standing here then? How does this get us to Ryderwyle?"

Page Trey motioned to the land around them.

"We stand in the Gate Grounds. There are dozens—nay, hundreds—of gates that lead to elsewhere in the kingdom and the world beyond."

Confused, Meg glanced around. She saw ocean and rocks, dead trees and hot springs, steam and far-off castle turrets, but no gates.

Before she could say anything, Page Trey added, "They're invisible."

Meg nearly laughed, but bit her tongue hard.

"You're trying to find an invisible gate?" Meg asked. "As in a doorway?"

"Not just any," Page Trey said. "The one to Ryderwyle."

Meg began to roam around the circle of hot springs, looking for any sign of a doorway or gateway.

"Careful, my lady," Page Trey said. "Just because you cannot see them doesn't mean you can't walk through. Some are stationary, others orbit the grounds. It's a miracle you made it to my side without stumbling through one. I myself use the staves to prevent falling into a gate." He motioned to the walking sticks at his feet. "Once through, there is no return trip. I ended up in Scotland not long ago."

Impatience ground away within her. This all seemed so ludicrous, so outrageous, so impossible... But in the last few hours, she'd seen too much she couldn't explain. And if those were real, these invisible doors must have been too.

"Okay, okay," she said, standing still. "So how do you find a doorway you can't see?"

CHAPTER 19

"The geysers," Page Trey explained. "There is a chemical in the eruption vapor that illuminates the doors. Once they're visible, we can see which to walk through and which to avoid. But the trick is getting the geysers to explode at the same time. Only then is there enough colored steam to illuminate all the doors. At least...that's how it worked when the magic was thriving."

"You're just standing here, waiting for geysers to explode simultaneously?" Meg asked.

Page Trey nodded. "And stay that way. The longer the geysers gush, the longer I can see the doors."

"That seems like a waste of time. And if it doesn't work anymore because your magic is gone..."

"Nothing is a waste of time," Page Trey implored. "There is merely the march of time and how we decide to use it. As for myself, with the kingdom on the verge of collapse, I know I must reach my master. It is time-consuming, yes, but I cannot just hope to stumble around the Gate Grounds and miraculously fall through the right gate."

"Seems faster—" Meg began, circling the geysers again, reaching out to see if she would feel an invisible door or if her hand would miraculously disappear.

"Lady Meghan! Wait!" Page Trey suddenly shouted.

Meg felt a lurch in her stomach. It was like an invisible blanket wrapped around her arm and pulled. The world around her became alarmingly blue. The next instant, she landed with a splash in a shallow pond.

She shook her head, confused. She was no longer on the white flats of the Gate Grounds, but instead at the bottom of a deep, steep canyon, waist deep in a shallow pool of water. Dozens of other pools surrounded her, baby turtles and crawfish wandering lazily from one to the next. The setting sun was shining bright in her face now, reflecting off the sea. High above, past the canyon walls and gnarled trees, she could the tips of castle turrets.

She knew instantly what had happened: she had found a door, an invisible one, and fallen right through it into the shallows of Coral Canyon.

Meg waded out of the pool and began searching for the invisible door. She swept the shallows for it, looking absurd with her outstretched arms. A few minutes later, she remembered what Page Trey had said: the doors were one-way trips. Once you walked through them, you couldn't get back.

"Dammit," Meg grumbled, and she began her long walk out of the Coral Canyon and back to Page Trey and the Gate Grounds.

It took her the better part of a half hour to get back, only because she borrowed a horse from the Bridgemaster's stables. Her thighs were chaffed, she had a blister, it was dark, and she was in a foul mood.

At the edge of the Gate Grounds, Meg dismounted the steed and began walking in. Page Trey was a quarter of a mile away, still in the center of the springs, arms stretched to the sky. The entire ring of geysers spat up colorful columns of water and steam. And there, scattered around the pools of water, Meg saw doors. Seven feet tall and four feet wide, she saw at least twenty rectangular doors, some standing still, others moving slowly in orbits, all illuminated green and blue and brown by the colorful geyser mist.

"Wait!" she shouted at Page Trey. "I'm coming!"

"Patience!" Page Trey called to her, motioning for her to stop walking.

But patience had never been Meg's strong suit. Time and efficiency was her master, and she was its slave.

She felt it too late, the tug and pull. The next instant, she was pulled through another door. The Gate Grounds disappeared, and she was in darkness, laying at an incline on cold wood. Her impatience got the best of her and she let out an infuriated shriek.

CHAPTER 20

The Catacombs

Jenn and Sir Rignot's footsteps echoed off the stone walls as they descended the stairs to the catacombs. The further they went, the colder and danker it became. Chiseled black stones became stained with moss and dew.

The librarian was surprisingly silent. Jenn sensed he was more scared than her.

At last, they reached the foot of the stairs. It was freezing cold. The librarian's hands shook as he fit the key into the metal door and opened it. Beyond was a hallway of oily blackness. There was a dim light at the far end.

Jenn motioned for the librarian to lead her, but he insisted she lead the way. Any other day, she would have turned and run but she had to complete her task. She had to save Dembroch and all the good it stood for. Maybe, just maybe, she could be part of it and help people in a way she had always wanted. But not without finding the seer's Sight.

Despite her fear and panic, she gulped and, holding her torch ahead of her, led the way.

Through the hallway, they emerged into an immense cavern. High above, Jenn saw the glistening edges of stalactites, tiny rectangular windows dim with sunset, and the foundations of the castle. There were glimmers of light up there too, in the middle of the ceiling, perhaps lightning bugs or stars or reflective surfaces.

On the cavern floor were aisles of coffins, all hand carved out of dark wood and stacked three high and two wide. Sprouting amongst the aisles were immense trees with black bark and luminescent leaves that dimly lit the cavernous catacombs.

"Do you know where she hid the Sight?" the librarian asked.

"In an unmarked grave—"

Sir Rignot hissed his obvious disapproval. "Such a gift placed in a dwelling of inequity?"

"She said it was Solomon's grave," Jenn said.

The librarian grumbled under his breath.

"Lead on," he said. "We'll find the wretch somewhere down here. I might break one of his bones while we're at it."

They began to roam the aisles in search of Solomon's open, unmarked casket. It was a simple, if not time-consuming, task. Most of the coffins were sealed. In the few that had missing lids, Jenn saw skeletons of pure white and corpses of inhuman colors, but also small nameplates scored with the name of the dead defender lying within.

Jenn and Sir Rignot reached the opposite side of the cavern where there was another door of wrought iron bars, presumably another exit, and a giant statue of King Richard atop a crypt.

The two turned back and wandered new aisles. They were halfway through when Jenn came upon an atrocious mess. A stack of coffins had collapsed atop each other. Goo leaked from the middle one, saturating the ground with a dark, sticky mass. The topmost coffin had lost its lid, and within, Jenn saw a horrific corpse. Half-eaten and half-disintegrated, the corpse was dressed in the chainmail of a knight. The half-decayed face still captured an expression of absolute agony.

Jenn turned away, gagging. Maybe this task wasn't for her. Maybe she could wait at the exit while the librarian did the searching for her.

No, she told herself. She couldn't rely on her husband or the librarian or others to do her work for her. She had to do this on her own.

Suddenly, there was a thump. Jenn and Sir Rignot spun to its source. One row of coffins away was the stone wall of the chamber. Caskets had been propped upon the wall.

There was another thud. This time Jenn saw the coffin tremble. The body inside was trying to escape.

Her imagination was on fire, already predicting what would happen next. The dead would arise. The many knights and dames would seek out Jenn, bringing another into the fold and deep into the grave.

That's when, as if beckoned by Jenn's fears, the trembling coffin let out a bone-chilling scream.

Jenn screamed, too. She tried to run, but tripped on Sir Rignot. They scrambled to her feet just as the coffin broke open. A skeleton flew out at Jenn. She swung with her torch and the skeleton exploded into pieces.

Jenn shuddered, breathing hard. Movement caught her eye.

Another being emerged from the coffin. But it was a human, not a skeleton.

Jenn gaped.

"Meg?" she shouted.

Meg stumbled into the catacombs, eyes burning with rage.

"Jenn," she grumbled. "Where are we?"

"Catacombs," Jenn said. "How did you get here?"

Meg furrowed her brow. "Invisible door. Page Trey is trying to find the one to Ryderwyle to save his master. He's stuck there in the snow since someone stole the fortissium fork or something or other."

"Sir Kenneth," the librarian said. "Unburied. His body is still in the Dreadnaught's stomachs."

Jenn cringed in disgust.

Meg sighed irritably. "What are you doing down here?"

"The seer sent me," Jenn explained. "I have to find her Sight that she hid down here."

"Gross," Meg said. "Any idea where it is?"

Jenn glanced at the librarian, who shrugged his shoulders, and then she gasped. Just behind Sir Rignot was the row she'd been wandering before Meg arrived. And in that row was the grotesque corpse in an open grave. She realized now that there had been no nameplate on the coffin. It was surely Solomon's tomb. Jenn could grab the Sight and get out of here with Meg and the librarian.

But the witch had other plans.

Hiding in the shadow of the entrance to the catacombs, watching Meg, Jenn, and the librarian, the witch placed a hand on the ground.

"Long dead bones, awaken from slumber," she whispered. "Take up your weapons, add to your number."

CHAPTER 21

The Queen's Protection

Metal and stone screeched against one another as I popped another bolt from the inner wall of Queen Coralee's prison cell. Halfway done. Only two more to go.

"With everything going on, the witch and the Dreadnaught and the defenders and...you know, all of it," I said, broaching a topic I'd been scared to mention, "why didn't you call us sooner? Get all the defenders on the island, all of the Reserves, and put a stop to her."

"I called a majority of the Reserves," the queen said. "But even a force of a hundred could not stop the witch and her Dreadnaught."

"But you didn't call us," I said, trying to hide my apprehension.

Queen Coralee inclined her head with a tight smile. She started kneading her hands again. I popped off the third bolt and began prying the final one.

"It was most admirable for you to volunteer as children," she said. "Of all the Reserve, you and your friends were the most passionate and adamant in hopes to help. But I could not possibly call you then. It would have been most inconsiderate and unconscionable of me, a queen, to call upon the youngest and most vulnerable knights and dames first. A sound mind should never call children into battle."

"What about when we were older?" I asked. "Wasn't the witch locked up until just a few days ago?"

We locked eyes for a moment, at a stalemate. After a moment, Queen Coralee reached for my hand through the prison cell.

"Sir Nicholas," she said, her voice pleading. "From your first letter—" my heart skipped a beat at the mention of those old childhood letters, but I didn't have the guts to say anything "—I knew you yearned to protect the kingdom. I knew your heart, though I had never truly met you. Because of that, no matter your age, I knew that you must never face the witch. I entrusted you with the book, but did not dare call upon you. To put you in such danger..."

I gaped at her, suddenly realizing something.

"The witch didn't force you to take our titles," I realized. "You did it." I was flabbergasted and angry. "Why?!"

"To protect you!" the queen cried.

"From what?" I shouted back.

The queen bit her lip.

A thousand thoughts ran through my head. Perhaps fearful of being accused of favoritism of her defenders over her kingdom, the queen had secreted the book away that could inform the witch of the kingdom's secrets and disbanded the order herself. The witch hadn't forced her hand. But why? Was it truly to protect us? Favoritism? Compassion? Something else? All in all, it was a dangerous move on the queen's part. Stripping my friends and I of our titles could have backfired and killed the magic sooner. But had the queen really done it to protect us poor, little children? Or was there something more to this story?

CHAPTER 21

I was trying to figure out what to say next, when suddenly, with a pop, the queen transformed before my very eyes. One second, she was the hideous witch, the next, she was the queen. The true queen. Long locks fell over fair features. She was beautiful in a tender yet authoritative way. Her eyes, I realized, were a captivating brown, full of kindness and knowledge. She had scars of a burn on one of her hands.

"What just happened?" I asked.

"The witch," the queen gasped. Her voice was different too, a light, lilting voice with the accent of her kingdom. "She must have parted with my most prized possession. It was the key to her disguise. Without the letter, we are ourselves once more."

At first, I wasn't sure what the queen was talking about, but then I remembered the fold of paper I'd seen sticking out the witch's neckline. It was a letter, surely one I'd written to the queen in my youth. Had that been the source of magic that made the queen and witch switch physical appearances? Was one of my letters the queen's most prized possession?

At this prospect, I should have felt giddiness, maybe pride. But instead, anger bubbled inside of me. How could she have received our letters, read them, cherished them, and abandoned us? Just to protect us? That wasn't good enough. There had to be another reason, a deeper one, and I swore to myself I would find it out.

Through all this, I had still been working on the last bolt holding the inner wall of the queen's prison cell to the stone wall of the castle. As I was thinking, the last bolt popped off. The wall sprung open. A split second later, a shrill alarm sounded. I clutched my ears, but it did no good. The siren was loud enough to alert the whole island.

After three blares, the alarm fell silent. The queen and I exchanged glances.

"That's not good," I said. "We gotta move. The witch will come looking for you."

But the queen stayed in her cell. She kneaded her hands and now, I realized she was rubbing the burn along her fingertips.

"I have deceived you," she confessed. "I truly apologize, Sir Nicholas. I only acted in your best interests at the risk of losing my own titles. Is there any way you can forgive me?"

I couldn't begin to answer that honestly. There was layers and layers of secrets on Dembroch and plenty around the queen. I had a hunch I'd only seen the surface.

"I have a lot of questions," I said honestly. "But for now, we need to save the kingdom. And my job is to save you."

"Where will we go? What will we do?"

"Find the witch," I said. "Stop her. Avenge your king."

This gave the queen pause, but not for long. She pushed the cell door open and joined me. Her presence, so close and uninhibited by prison bars, made my insides do flips.

"There's the knight I knew," Queen Coralee said. "Lead on, Sir Nicholas."

CHAPTER 22

Dead Men, Dead Men, Come Alive

Deep in the catacombs, dry bones popped into place, the clicks and snaps echoing off the walls. The lids of the coffins pushed open. Bodies rose. Jenn, Meg, and Sir Rignot gathered close together.

"What, what?" the librarian stammered.

"Jenn, we gotta—" Meg began.

A coffin next to them broke open. From it, a moldering corpse, forgotten by life and romanced by death's decay, came forth. It shambled, learning how to walk again, then lunged. A dozen other skeletons rolled out of their caskets too, charging at the women and librarian. They didn't stand a chance and were pinned to the wall, overcome by the sheer number of attackers. Jenn's torch was torn from her hands and cast out of sight. A few seconds later, a hundred other corpses garnered in swords and decaying armor gathered around them, their frosty eyes staring right at Jenn, Meg, and the librarian.

A cackle rose through the cavern. The witch—disguised as the queen—strutted into view, a pernicious smile on her face. She crossed the catacombs toward her prey with the slimy smoothness of a snake.

"Girls, girls, girls," the witch crooned. "All this unrest has upset the dead."

She surveyed them with a sneer.

"Not having much luck with your magical flames?" she asked.

The librarian yelped in surprise.

Jenn shot Meg a look. "She knows?"

"She kind of heard everything," Meg rasped against her captors' bony holds. "Not really important right now."

"Precisely," the witch agreed. "More pressing is how best to kill the both of you. Shall I leave you here to rot or hoist your bodies for all to see and make trophies of your spines. Or perhaps..."

She glanced back at the coffins, a sinister cackle coming from her belly. But it was cut short.

Meg had managed to break free of her captors and socked the witch right in the face. The corpses and skeletons clicked and clanked as they pulled Meg back, slamming her into the wall again.

Sorgana hit the ground hard. A small, folded letter fell from her bosom—at the same instant, the witch transformed into her true, hideous form of deep wrinkles, sinewy skin, and thin, white hair.

The witch sprang back to her feet, eyes wide with anger, the fallen letter unseen, her transformation unnoticed. She raked her hand through the air, tips sharp and spiky with broken nails. They sliced into Meg's chest, drawing blood. Meg squealed in pain. The witch dug into her flesh, relishing in the cries.

"Most believe that deep wounds, lethal wounds, hurt the worst," Sorgana seethed as blood dribbled down Meg's front. "But they're wrong. Flesh wounds nick the nerves, leave them raw. They burn long after. And this—" she ran her broken nails over Meg's fresh wound, extracting a scream "—will never leave you. Not until you die. It's what you get for crossing a witch."

CHAPTER 22

The witch's eyes snapped to the librarian.

"Speaking of," she spat. "You meddlesome little fool. Bussing a book of secrets away from the kingdom so I would never see it. As if I would trouble myself searching old texts in that pigsty of a library for the answers to my needs."

She grabbed Sir Rignot's throat, squeezing. The librarian began to choke. Jenn cried for her to stop.

"It matters not," the witch spat, aging on the spot as she strangled the librarian. "I know the secret of the flames. Your efforts were for naught."

The librarian garbled a retort.

"Oh, but I will succeed," the witch wretched. "I'll let you in on my secret. What I plan to do to your little kingdom."

She whispered in the librarian's ear. All color left his face. A tear formed in his eye.

"You'll—you—never—" he rasped.

"I will," the witch seethed. "And do you know why? Because Dembroch is doomed. Cursed. It always has been."

The witch was wrinkled and grey now, having aged decades as she strangled Sir Rignot.

"Don't you see, now?" she asked, wiping a tear from his cheek. "The futility of it all? You did all of this for your queen...for nothing... Your kingdom will fall for nothing. Your defenders will die alone down here while your body rots. At least you shall be spared the kingdom's final desolation."

The librarian fought against her, dangerously close to running out of air.

"Take them!" the witch cried.

The skeletons and corpses pulled Jenn and Meg from the walls and dragged them to the open coffins. The women screamed and bucked their bodies.

Sorgana focused only on the librarian.

"You die for nothing," she spat in Sir Rignot's face. "What futility. What misery. What...woe."

Meg and Jenn were thrown into the open caskets. Lids were slammed onto the top. Jenn pounded on the wood for all it was worth, screamed at the top of her lungs, but she was trapped.

There was a sick crack followed by a wet thump, then the witch crowed with laughter. Jenn started banging on the casket again, but it held tight. The dead defenders must have been holding it closed or have secured it somehow.

Suddenly, the air was rent with the shrieking blare of a siren. It rang three times, drilling into Jenn's ears and then it was dead quiet. She lay silently, listening, but all she could hear was her own heartbeat.

What had happened? Had the witch killed the librarian? What was that alarm? What was—?

Jenn wound up to start banging on the coffin again, but her arm touched something cold. She felt around, wrapping her hands around the tip of a broken sword. She wielded it uncertainly in the darkness of her coffin and wedged it between the lid and the casket. She pulled and pushed, prying the top off. Its sharp edge drew blood from her fingers, but she refused to lay here until she suffocated or died of starvation.

The lid popped open just enough. She pushed hard and it flew off.

She came out fighting. There were two skeletons standing watch and she bowled them over. Their bodies shattered into a couple hundred pieces each.

Breathing hard, holding the broken sword tip like a machete, she spun around, quickly taking in her surroundings.

The witch was nowhere to be seen. There were about two hundred dead defenders circling around Jenn. Meg was still trapped in her coffin, the lid shuddering with each hit from within.

Jenn glanced behind her and squinted, not sure she understood what she was seeing.

CHAPTER 22

Hovering in the air between her and the wall was a sphere of black specks. The iotas swirled around one another like a million little bugs. She didn't know what it was, but it couldn't have been good.

On the ground, she spotted the letter that had fallen from the witch's dress. She stooped quickly, unfolding it. She recognized it instantly and stuffed it into her pants pocket.

The dead defenders were creeping closer, none quite ready to attack her. She pointed the sword tip at them, keeping the skeletons and corpses at bay. She glanced again at the wall, looking for the librarian. At last, she found him and her heart seemed to break.

Sir Rignot was standing, his back to her, but he wasn't alive. His head was backward on his body, the eyes bloodshot from burst vessels, his face vacant. He stumbled toward her, walking backwards, body slave to the witch's magic like the dead defenders.

"No," Jenn moaned. "No."

The librarian, tears of the living still fresh on his face, broken neck bruising, came at her. The knights and dames of old pressed in from the other side, drawing their swords, black pits locked on their prey.

Much as she wanted to curl up and die in that moment, Jenn could not go to the grave again. The librarian could not have died for nothing.

Jenn turned her back on the librarian, unwilling to hurt him, and charged the dead defenders. With the broken sword tip, she fought for all it was worth. Corpses fell around her, their atrophied muscles unable to compete with her quick, if inexperienced, jabs and slices.

She made it to Meg's coffin and pried it open. Meg came out swinging and knocked the sword tip from Jenn's bloody hand.

"Calm down," Jenn said, pulling Meg from the coffin.

"Where is she?" Meg shouted, scanning the masses of dead men and women pressing in around them.

"I don't know," Jenn replied. "She left after she killed the librarian."

"Didn't even have the dignity to wait for us to die," Meg grumbled. "Have you gotten that Sight thing?"

Jenn groaned a no.

"We can't leave without it," Meg said. "Can't let this all be for nothing. Where is it?"

Jenn swung her head in the direction. "That collapsed one over there."

"I'll have your back," Meg said. "But we need weapons."

A skeleton lunged at them. Meg sidestepped it and punched, knocking the skeleton into pieces. She grabbed the skeleton's sword, pulling its arm from the hilt and offering it to Jenn.

"Thanks," Jenn grumbled, taking the severed skeleton arm feebly.

"Okay," Meg said doubtfully. "On three."

They didn't have the time to count to three. The zombified knights and dames charged.

Moving with the bravery of an armored soldier, Meg lunged at the attackers. She cleared a swath. Jenn fell in after her, halfheartedly swinging at attackers with the skeleton arm. A few terrifying moments later, they were by the open, unmarked coffin of Solomon. The half-melted corpse still lay within.

"Don't go the way of Solomon," Jenn reminded herself with a shudder. He was the only dead defender who had not been resurrected, and perhaps for the best.

With Meg standing guard, Jenn grabbed Solomon's upper body—his burnt skin crumbled like ash under her fingers—and pushed the cadaver aside. Underneath him was bare wood. There were no talismans or mirrored eyeballs.

"No," Jenn gasped. Where was the Sight?

Then she saw it. There was a hole in bottom of the coffin, a large one. And below it was another lidless casket.

It's down there, Jenn sensed. *They rolled down into the next casket.*

With a heave, she pushed aside Solomon's top casket, revealing the coffin below. She nearly retched. Inside was a pile of red and brown gelatin. It stunk like rotten eggs. But suspended in the goop, just below the surface, were two spherical, mirrored rocks.

That was it, she knew. The seer's Sight.

CHAPTER 22

Jenn considered what must be done. She didn't want to. She hated goo. Mud. Germs. But particularly goo.

But she loved Dembroch more.

She dug her hands deep into the slop. It was warm and thick, congealing around her fingers. She squealed, but pushed deeper, reaching for the eyes.

The dry cries of the undead knights and dames filled the air. Jenn looked up just in time to see attackers getting past Meg. They ran at Jenn, mouths gaping, swords held high, bony hands reaching to strike.

Something shiny caught Jenn's attention. Buried in the coffin, presumably with the knight or dame before they had been turned to Jell-O, was a sword.

Without a second thought or hesitation, she dove deeper into the goo and pulled the sword free with a wet plop. She swung at the nearest incoming knight, cleaving his head from its shoulders, and kept swinging, determined to survive for Clay and for Dembroch. With each strike, bits of goo flew off the sword and her hands. In seconds, her clothes and face were spattered with it. She could have cried—this was going to take a lot of hand sanitizer to clean.

The librarian was the last attacker to make it past Meg. Jenn hesitated for a moment, not wanting to hurt Sir Rignot. But, she realized, this was no longer the sweet, knowledgeable librarian. His soul was long gone, and he would not have wanted his body to be used against Dembroch and one of its last dames.

She struck fast and true, freeing the librarian's corpse from the witch's magic.

Free again of imminent attackers, Jenn plunged her hand elbow-deep into the goo and, with another sick plopping sound, pulled the Sight talismans free.

"Got them!" Jenn shouted—right as an errant piece of flying goo landed on her lips. She doubled over, gagging and spitting.

It took her a while, but Jenn finally regained her composure. She joined Meg, slicing and dicing their way through defenders. At last, they cleared a path to the catacombs exit. They slammed the door behind them, wedging their swords into the bars to keep the undead defenders locked up for a few extra minutes. Together, they raced up the stairs and through the library. The witch was nowhere to be seen, so they kept running, through the castle and to the Rotunda, out into the courtyard, and past the castle gates. Once through, they paused. Jenn was headed northbound toward the seer's cottage; Meg was headed east toward the Gate Grounds.

"I've got to—" Meg breathed, pointing over her shoulder.

"I know," Jenn gasped back. "I've got to—"

"I know," Meg called back.

"Thank you," Jenn managed to say.

"Don't mention it," Meg said, her ego surprisingly mellow.

"Wait," Jenn said. She pulled the letter from her pocket and handed it to Meg. "You should have this. It's Nick's."

Meg took it with a raised eyebrow, opened it, and read. She smirked. "He'll need to see this," she scoffed. "Be safe out there."

"You too," Jenn replied.

With a nod, the two ran their separate ways.

Back in the catacombs, the undead knights and dames—still at least one hundred strong—broke through the door. They surged out of the catacombs like rats out of a flooded sewer. A few moments later, the catacombs were empty, leaving only the corpse of Solomon that had never awoken and the hovering flurry of black specks. The mass sank to the ground and burrowed into the soil where it burst into a small tongue of black flame.

CHAPTER 23

Escape the Castle

"She's coming," I whispered to Queen Coralee.

A second later, Sorgana burst around the corner. She had regained her natural appearance of ghastly pallor, but she looked significantly older than usual. Her eyes were bloodshot and frosted over. Her hands tremored. Her hair was grey. She hadn't had any turtles lately.

"My *queen*," the witch simpered, her tone so thick that the distaste practically jumped off her tongue. "And Sir Nicholas. Of all the knights and dames, you were the last, best protector. When you fell, you took Dembroch's magic with you."

She charged. The queen and I tensed. We'd have to fight. We were trapped in the open prison cell.

Magic flew from the witch's hands, right at us. The green daggers cut right into us—and shattered the mirror.

Hiding in the corner, I ran the distance to the cell and slammed it shut. The walls jangled more than usual thanks to my work getting the queen out earlier.

Sorgana turned, glaring at us.

"Clever, clever," she growled.

She approached the bars, green light forming around her hand. The bars glowed in reply.

"It is still sealed against magical interference," the queen said, joining my side.

"Time is running out for you, my *queen*," the witch whispered. "You can't keep me in here until the end. And your little knight is running out of time to finish his quest...if you let him."

"You know nothing about my kingdom or my heart, Sorgana," the queen spat back at the witch.

"Oh, but I do," the witch replied. "I know you weep for your king. I know you pine for your knight. I know you would give anything to save this wretched little kingdom that took you in out of pity."

I traded looks from queen to witch.

"Answer me, witch," the queen said. "Who are you? How do you know me?"

The witch drew close to the bars, and though she whispered, I heard every word.

"You didn't recognize me the day you locked me up," the witch seethed. "You didn't recognize me when I took your throne from you. And you don't recognize me now. No surprise. I don't recognize myself most days. But I hoped your heart would tell you. You see, blood is thicker than water. It stands the test of time. Even still, you don't know me. Did you try to forget? Did you try to bury me in the sea of time while you sat on the throne of opulence?"

"I don't know who you are!" the queen implored.

"Did you ever try to find me?" Sorgana inquired, her voice growing in volume. "Did you ever search for me? Did you ever seek me out? No.

I know the truth. You forgot about me. You left me behind and washed me from your memory. You abandoned me—your own sister!"

It was a second that lasted a lifetime. My jaw dropped. Queen Coralee's knees went weak.

"Edith?" she gasped.

I looked between queen and witch, sister and sister, hearing but not comprehending the information.

The witch took advantage of our surprise. She summoned up a blast of magic—her wrinkles furrowed deeper. Green light flashed and when it cleared, the prison cells had disintegrated to ash. Sorgana lunged at us, swatting me aside and taking the queen by the throat. She circled around Queen Coralee, holding her in a headlock.

"You forget," the witch seethed. "You enchanted the prisons against *ordinary* magic. Not mine."

I got to my feet but didn't act. The witch could kill the queen in an instant. I had to reason with her.

The witch turned her murderous eyes back on me.

"Don't you see, Sir Nicholas?" she crooned. "This is not a kingdom worth saving, not a queen worth loving. She has lied to you from the moment she asked for volunteers to defend her. The truth you cannot see is that her mere presence has cursed the kingdom and doomed its people. That's why they have all fled. They know it. Do you? To save this land is to preserve a petty little girl who will cast you to the winds when it best suits her."

My heart ached, I felt dizzy. Horribly, terribly, the witch was making sense.

"Walk away, Sir Nicholas," the witch demanded. "I can see it in your eyes—you don't want to be a part of this. Do what you do best. Run. Get off this island and save yourself from helping this treacherous queen."

It was as though the witch had been the dark voice in my head all these years, insisting that I forget it and walk away from anything too troublesome. I'd done it all these years, why break the habit? This situation was getting more complicated by the second. Why not just run away?

I locked eyes with the queen. She looked so small in the witch's hold.

"I looked for you," I choked out. "I spent two years searching for you. And I wrote to you every day, asking to be part of your world. I thought you didn't get them. That you were ignoring them. That you had better things to do. But you had them? All of them?"

The queen deflated right before me. It was as if I was striking her on the cheek with each word.

"Was I like Sorgana?" I asked. "A drowning victim waving their hands while you looked away? You knew I wanted to be here all this time, but you only call me when you need saving? When it best suits you?"

Actual tears were streaming down my face. The queen was crying quietly, and the witch had unwittingly loosened her grip on the queen. Best of all, neither had realized how close I stood to them.

I acted quickly. I swung a fist, punching the witch where there was already a bruise. She stumbled back as I pulled the queen from her grasp.

"Come on!" I shouted.

I pulled the queen after me, disappearing down the hallway. The witch roared behind us.

We ran for all it was worth, emerging into the Rotunda several stories above the Aerary. I led the queen upward.

"No, Sir Nicholas," she breathed. "We will be trapped."

"And if we go down, she'll catch us," I replied.

We staggered up the stairs. Right as the witch burst into the Rotunda, we shimmied through the upper trapdoor. I slammed it shut and ran to the balcony's edge. Though there wasn't time to look around, it was a stunning place to be. The whole kingdom isles lay beneath us, separated from us only by a balcony railing. The tip of the tower was above us, held up by a dozen columns.

"Sir Nicholas," the queen said, following me as I circled the balcony. "I am sorry—"

CHAPTER 23

"I didn't mean it," I said quickly, wiping the tears off my cheek. "I had to fool the witch somehow."

"But—" the queen began, unconvinced.

I spotted what I was looking for. There were a couple turrets below us, protruding from the exterior of the Rotunda. One of them was only a dozen feet below the balcony we stood on.

"Follow me!" I cried.

I climbed over the edge. A bolt of vertigo hit me, but I lowered myself down. When I was positioned over the turret, I let go of the railing. For a heart-stopping second, I was freefalling, then I hit the shingled tower. I scrambled quick, grabbing onto the edge and stopping the fall. After I'd steadied myself, the queen followed suit. Right as she dropped onto the lower turret, the witch emerged from the trapdoor.

"Come back here, you fools!" she cried. "I won't kill you...yet!"

"The walls," the queen breathed at me.

I realized what she meant: there were nooks and crannies between the large stone blocks of the castle's outer walls. They were just big enough to fit our hands and feet into.

We started our descent, hugging the wall and climbing down the Rotunda's exterior. My arms ached more with each second.

"Suffer the consequences, Sir Nicholas!" the witch cried after us.

She mumbled an incantation, but nothing happened. The witch shrieked in rage and began to climb after us. Queen Coralee and I descended faster, skipping stones in the rush to escape.

Another three stories below us was the catwalk of the castle walls. The queen and I inched toward it as the witch called after us.

"Don't slip, sister!" she crooned. "Or perhaps you'll use your knight as a pillow. Go on, flatten him like you have every other citizen of this kingdom! Use him until he gives his life for you!"

"Ignore her!" I insisted. "We can beat her."

And we did. Though the witch was strong of tongue and magic, she was slower and less sure of her movements. We beat her to the catwalk with time to spare.

I raced for the door back into the castle, but it burst open. A mob of skeletons and bloody corpses charged out at us.

Queen Coralee and I turned and ran, now pursued by the undead defenders of Dembroch *and* the witch. But there was nowhere to go. The catwalk circled around the courtyard, terminating at the wall of a tower over the entrance. I couldn't see a door or window. We were running straight for a dead-end.

I glanced over the edge.

"Queen Coralee," I yelled over the shouting mob. "Do you trust me!"

"If you trust me!" was her breathless response.

"Jump!" I shouted.

I grabbed her hand and pulled her hard. We both leapt over the edge into the courtyard. In midair, I slung out my satchel. The strap caught around a protruding gargoyle's head. I held tight to the satchel and the queen—

There was a sickening pop. The queen's weight pulled hard on my arms, and my shoulder popped out of place. I screamed in agony. My whole body seemed to wrench with pain. My heart pulsed sharply.

The satchel strap tore. We plummeted to the ground, now only a few feet away. We landed hard, rolling with the impact.

For a moment that seemed several minutes, we lay on the cobblestones. My shoulder screamed in agony, but deep inside, my heart hurt. Each beat seemed painful and fast, but thankfully, mercifully, it began to fade.

The queen got to her feet first and extended her hand to me. I sat up and we locked eyes.

It was a split-second decision full of meaning. If I took her hand, I showed my agreement to follow her and help her, to overlook previous accusations, and believe in the best of her. It was not a choice I took lightly. There were so many questions that I needed answered, so much anger and resentment burning inside, and so much fear about the path ahead and how complicated it could all become, but even with all these reasons to not follow the queen, I felt compelled to trust her. She was extending her hand to me in this moment to show once and for all, despite her past choices, she needed help. That she wanted to tell the truth, even if it scared her. That she needed...me.

I took her hand with my good arm. She pulled me up.

At the same moment, there was an eruption of sparks. The golden-red embers shot out from our hands. Beside us, a pyramid-shaped rock grew out of the courtyard cobblestones. The sparks gathered at its tip and a fire burst into being.

The queen and I exchanged a quick glance. I scanned the courtyard for some type of torch—there were frayed banners and empty torches—but I couldn't get to any of them fast enough. Dozens of skeletal defenders emerged from the castle's Rotunda and charged at us.

"Later," the queen insisted.

"Later," I agreed.

Abandoning the freshly made magical flame, the queen and I ran. My chest ached dully with each footfall. The mob of skeletons were hot on our heels, but slow and rickety. We quickly outpaced them, passing the courtyard's barren fountains.

A terrible shriek echoed down to us. I glanced back to see the witch hanging from the tallest tower. She raked her hands at us as though to pull us down, but her magic was drained. There was no green light; nothing happened.

The queen and I raced out of the courtyard, the witch's screeches following us deep into the forest, the king's death unavenged, the queen's home abandoned to the witch.

CHAPTER 24

Cliffside Tower

Clay and the Watchmaker emerged from the dead forest into bright moonlight. Yellow grass meadows stretched out to steep bluffs. Waves crashed far below.

Cliffside Tower stood over them, stunted and twisted. The grounds around it were saturated with moisture and the tower had sunken into it, blocking most of the entrance. Its outer walls were coated in dried blood. Several cobblestones were missing, there were deep claw marks on the walls inside, and the top of the tower seemed to howl slightly in the wind.

"This is where it gets hairy," the Watchmaker said. "It's tight quarters in there. No telling how many beasties are hiding. Keep with me, stay safe, and be brave."

Clay chittered nervously.

"You mock me?" the Watchmaker grunted.

CHAPTER 24

"No," Clay blurted out. "Not at all. Just trying to find where I left my courage."

"You're scared?"

"Of course not," Clay boasted, avoiding eye contact with the mountainous man.

"You're a fool if you aren't," the Watchmaker said. "The bravest men and women fight their deepest fears. There are no acts of courage without horror. Just need the right tools to take it on."

He pulled the axe from his back and flipped it expertly in his hands.

"An axe is all it takes?" Clay asked.

The Watchmaker shrugged. "That's the trick, isn't it? Get the right tools, nothing is too scary. My weapon is an axe, my reasons are my own. But truly, to fight the good fight, you need something in here."

He thumped his chest.

"If a good man or woman of Dembroch passes," he mused, his tone no longer grumbling, but deep and pondering, getting dangerously close to sentimental, "we knock our hearts and whisper our kingdom's motto, *Omnia Aeterno.* Means 'all things under God, forever'. It doesn't mean we expect everything to last forever. We hope, certainly, but don't expect it. Everything goes in the end. Truly, when we pound our hearts and speak those words, it's a promise and a prayer that we carry the fallen in our hearts forever. Their lessons, their love, within us keeps us going. Keeps us fighting, keeps your heart beating. And maybe it's not just loved ones we carry in our hearts. For some, it may be aspirations and ambition. Others, it may be treasure or prized possessions. Whatever it is that matters most to you, keep it close, hold it deep within. You'd best have your own for what lies ahead."

Clay didn't know what tools he relied on, but knew he must follow the Watchmaker. He nodded nervously.

"Right, then," the Watchmaker said. "Stay close."

They entered the tower, shimmying through the narrow, rounded entrance. It was strangely warm inside; the ceiling hung low. The flame and plinth of the past were nowhere to be seen, likely buried under the moist ground.

On the far side was an ascending stairway, which they crawled toward. The ground was spongy. Clay's hands and clothes became damp and maroon. He tried not to think about its source.

At the stairs, Clay heard whispers of snarls. He got to his feet shakily.

Come on, he told himself. *Get it together.*

"Age before beauty," the Watchmaker said, pushing Clay forward.

"I don't have anything to fight the...the monster things," Clay said tremulously. "Can I have—"

The Watchmaker chuckled. "This is *my* axe, boy. You should have brought your own weapon. Now, hurry on. We have places to get."

Weaponless and defenseless, Clay ascended slowly. With every step, terror filled him more. He felt like a child—one he had never been—quaking in fear, terrified of what was to come. He could practically feel the monsters lunging, biting, drawing blood...

When he entered the upper room, relief flooded him. There wasn't a single monster, large or tiny, bug-eyed or sharp-toothed. It was an empty, circular room. Small, narrow windows were spaced evenly on the walls, the moonlight barely illuminating the area. On the opposite side was another ascending staircase leading to the topmost room. Louder growls and snarls came from those stairs, and, as if in reply, Clay's fear returned tenfold.

Where had his bravery gone? he wondered. Where had he misplaced it? Was it lying beside his youth, abandoned years ago and forgotten in the monotony of adulthood?

Grumbling about the dimness, the Watchmaker tore a thick root from the wall, scraped a flint on his axe, and lit the root. The fire flared brightly, illuminating the room fully. Which was the last thing Clay needed.

The room was not empty. Not really. Spattered across the ceiling, walls, and floor were layers upon layers of gore, the larger piles still wet.

CHAPTER 24

Splintered bone chips hid in blood-drenched clumps of clothing. Broken swords glimmered in the torchlight.

"How does this happen in a place like Dembroch?" Clay stammered.

"Monsters exist all over the world," the Watchmaker said. "Dembroch is no different. For every flower, there is a poison. For every well-meaning person, there is a witch. For every deer or horse—"

"I understand," Clay stammered, trying and failing to inject gusto into his words.

"Aye. Now hurry on. It is best not to linger in such a place."

And so, quaking in his boots, urged on by the Watchmaker, Clay tiptoed to the next staircase. He ascended painstakingly slow, nerves jangling.

The steps were dark and sticky with blood. He entered the final room slowly. At the last second, he saw something long, dark, and wet reaching to touch his extended arm. He nearly screamed, but the Watchmaker clapped a hand over his mouth.

"It's moss," he whispered harshly.

Clay slowed his breathing and, heart beating a mile a minute, took in his surroundings.

More so than any place Clay had visited, the topmost room of Cliffside Tower was a disgusting place. It smelled of rot and death. Mounds of skulls and skeletons were lumped into huts and nests. Moss hung from the pointed ceiling in wreaths of varying length. Hidden in them were the forms of dark creatures. The Watchmaker's torchlight caught glances of their form—slimy skin, black talons, rippling muscles. And then there were the eyes. They were crimson, as red as the blood they had spread through the tower.

"They don't know what to make of us," the Watchmaker whispered, then pointed. "Look, there."

Clay followed his finger. On the far side of the room, sticking out of a decomposing corpse, was the glinting blade of a sword. Its metal gleamed a shiny black, its hilt covered by the burnt husk of a hand.

"That's it," the Watchmaker said. "Go."

"What?" Clay whispered.

"Go, run, grab the sword, run back, I swing at any of the beasties who come after."

"N–n–no," Clay stammered. "I...I can't."

The Watchmaker sighed.

"Fine, then," he said. He thrust the axe into Clay's hand. "You get the hard job."

Clay spluttered in disagreement, but it was too late. The Watchmaker walked into the room as though on a casual stroll. The crimson eyes shifted to him. Angry growls echoed around them.

The Watchmaker wandered disinterestedly, kicking at bones and dismembered limbs. When he was next to the sword, he kicked at the hilt. The burnt hand fell away but the sword clanged loudly, not budging. The Watchmaker doubled over, cursing under his breath, but kept walking.

"The blasted thing is stuck," the Watchmaker whispered as he strolled by.

He kept going, circling the room again. The growls and grumbles grew louder. Crunches of stone echoed through the tower as the monsters shifted.

The Watchmaker didn't try to take the blade this time. Instead, as he passed by it, he looked it over, taking in every detail. When he returned to the stairs, he settled next to Clay.

"There were words on it," the Watchmaker said. " 'Pure of heart, pull me forth; my loyalties are yours henceforth.' What the devil does that mean?"

Clay shook his head uncertainly. He was too distracted by the crimson eyes. He gripped the axe tight enough to form the leather.

"Lot of help you are," the Watchmaker grunted. "One of us must be pure of heart. Let's give it a go."

CHAPTER 24

The Watchmaker grabbed Clay by the scruff of the neck and pushed him into the room. Clay wheezed in protest, grinding his feet into the sticky ground. The monsters growled ever louder, but none approached.

"By God, you'll be brave, boy, even if I have to make you," the Watchmaker said.

A second later, Clay and the Watchmaker were next to the sword. Up close, Clay could see the inscription carved into the hilt amongst a dozen glittering jewels. It indeed called for a wielder of pure heart.

"Better you than me," the Watchmaker said.

Wanting to get out of this place sooner rather than later, Clay set aside the axe and wrapped his hands around the hilt. It was stuck firm as though it was pinned by a boulder instead of a corpse.

Clay tightened his grip and pulled—and an electric shock shot through his hand. He jumped back, biting back a yell.

"Not quite the knight you thought you were?" the Watchmaker said with the hint of a laugh.

Just then, there was a soft thud right behind them. Clay spun around. Sitting on the ground was a small, hand-sized lizard. Its maroon eyes stared at them. It had unnaturally long and rounded dorsal spines that resembled porcupine quills and there were bumps between its front and hind legs, like masses of folded skin.

"Ah, look at him," the Watchmaker said, his voice coddling and sweet. "A little baby dragon."

Clay's jaw dropped. A dragon? What was it doing in here with the monsters?

While the little dragon stared at them, the Watchmaker placed his axe on his back and reached for the fortissium blade. He pulled and leapt back with a shout.

At the same time, the dragon shrieked at Clay and charged. As it did, the folds on its back puffed up and expanded. Wings swung out wide. It flew right at Clay.

"Watch it!" the Watchmaker shouted.

Clay dove to the side, narrowly avoiding the dragon.

"The baby ones are deadlier!" the Watchmaker continued. "More venom, smaller body."

The dragon flew around the mass of hanging moss and torpedoed right at Clay again. He yelped and dodged. Quick in the air, the dragon turned and followed him. It opened its mouth wide and a jet of a fire shot out. By luck or misfortune, Clay tripped on a skeleton—the fire missed him and hit a tangle of moss. He fell hard. The baby dragon tried to avoid him, but it was flying too fast. It collided with him right before he hit the ground and squealed as Clay landed on it. He shimmied away, fearing a venomous bite, but the baby dragon skittered off into the shadows, whimpering.

A monstrous bellow echoed through the tower. Then another. The whole tower shook with roars.

"Oh, no," the Watchmaker murmured.

Clay gaped up at all the crimson eyes. They were drawing closer and closer, their bodies fully illuminated by the burning moss.

"Dragons," Clay breathed. "The monsters of Horror Hollow are dragons."

There were hundreds of them, each black as night, fire growing in the back of their throats, snake tongues flicking the air.

"Watchmaker?" Clay said nervously.

"You'd best have something worth fighting for, boy," the Watchmaker said, his voice still audible over the growing roars.

A mama dragon, twice the size of the baby one, shrieked at Clay and launched itself at him. Clay screamed bloody murder and ran. A dozen dragons took to the air, zooming around the moss to breathe fire at Clay.

"Get the sword!" Clay shouted.

The Watchmaker tried again, pulling hard as he could, his arms, big as tree trunks, bulging with the effort, but the sword would not free itself.

Meanwhile, Clay ran erratically, dodging and ducking and weaving, never daring to strike one of the dragons. Fire and snapping teeth barely missed him. He was sure he was using up any and all luck his life would have.

Slowly but surely, the other hanging tangles of moss caught fire. The whole place was becoming an inferno.

Clay grabbed one of the hanging moss strands. He swung on it, evading the closest dragons. They spun after him. Fire singed the greying hairs on his head.

"Watchmaker!" he cried.

The Watchmaker screamed in the effort. He freed a hand and felt along his belt, grasping an empty space where two chains hung free of pocket watches.

Suddenly, impossibly, miraculously, the sword pulled free. And not a moment too soon.

An errant dragon smacked into Clay. He fell to the ground hard. The dragons screeched in glee and descended upon him.

The Watchmaker made it to Clay first. He brandished the fortissium blade, a jet-black, bejeweled sword, the knife-edge gleaming with golden filigree. The sword sliced clean through the dragons like a knife through butter. Blood gushed out, raining down on Clay and the Watchmaker.

"Up you get," the Watchmaker called. "Fight with me."

From his back, he grabbed the axe and threw it to Clay. He dropped the massive weapon and fumbled to pick it back up. All the while, the dragons attacked in droves, falling by the dozens to the unstoppable fortissium blade.

A wingless dragon caught Clay off-guard and tackled him to the ground. Its sharp claws squeezed into his flesh, drawing blood. It snarled, opening its mouth wide. Golden fire appeared in the back of its throat. Clay tried to lift the axe, but it was heavy and he was pinned.

"No, you don't," the Watchmaker growled.

He smacked the dragon off Clay with a sweep of the fortissium blade. Not missing a beat, the Watchmaker grabbed Clay's shirt, and dragged him across the room, striking down the dragons as they went.

With the fortissium blade, the job was effortless. The Watchmaker made it to the stairs in no time and pulled Clay after him.

Two terrifying minutes later, they were crawling out of the tower. The Watchmaker filled the exit with mounds of bloody dirt, trapping the dragons inside.

Clay backed away, breathing hard, the axe shaking in his hands. The tower shuddered before him as the dragons shrieked in rage. They would be coming for them, once they got back into the topmost room and through the broken ceiling.

"Thanks for the help, boy," the Watchmaker growled. "We'd best get moving...and keep moving."

He marched off into the forest. Clay followed, pride sinking lower than the Cliffside Tower. He was a coward. A terrified, disappointing coward. He hadn't even been able to wield the fortissium blade, let alone defend himself against dragons. Those had been his favorite once upon a time. If ever there was a place to start a magical fire of his youth, it should have been here.

How he longed to be the old Clay, brave and honest and true to himself. But he'd forgotten what it was to be brave and Dembroch would be the one to pay for it.

CHAPTER 25

Doors to Distant Shores

"It's a witch's mark," Page Trey said.

He was with Meg in the inner ring of the Gate Grounds' hot springs, examining the cuts running over Meg's collar bone. They were oozing puss and dribbling blood as though she had just been cut.

"Means you're marked for death," said the page.

"Figured I already was, being as she's been trying to kill us all this time," Meg considered.

"Yes, but now more so. The cuts will never heal, nor will they ever go away. They act as a beacon for the witch. She will be able to track and pursue you no matter where you go or what you do. And if she does not end your life, another will."

"Like the Grim Reaper?"

"A reaper, surely, but of unknown identity," the page explained. "The witch has doomed you to death, whether by her hands or another.

There are plenty of historical accounts demonstrating both outcomes. Mark my words, Lady Meghan. Every person in history who has been marked by a witch has perished."

"Doesn't everyone die eventually?"

"Indeed, but not typically in such horrific ways."

"Wonderful," Meg mumbled. She pulled her shirt back up to cover the nasty, oozing cuts. "All the more reason to stop the witch. I'll meet my maker another day."

"Right, right," Page Trey said. "Let's begin. As I was saying, the geysers of the Gate Grounds react to high quantities of melatonin, a chemical produced by humans when they are relaxed. Let us put our minds at ease and call for the gates."

Page Trey shut his eyes and stood in resolute silence. Meg waited and watched. The moon was rising high above them. Midnight was approaching according to Meg's watch. The hot springs frothed and foamed. Sulphur burnt Meg's nose. The cuts on her chest stung. White steam rose in puffs. No doors were illuminated, no destinations were revealed. The seconds ticked by so achingly slow, Meg wondered if the kingdom's timelessness had returned, but it couldn't have. Because Meg hadn't started a flame. Because she hadn't found the right gate. Because these geysers weren't erupting!

Anxiousness boiled in Meg's gut more fervently than the hot pools around her. After what felt like an hour, though it was only a few minutes, she sighed heavily. When Page Trey did not react, she sighed again.

"My lady," the page finally said, his voice grating with irritation, "prayer and meditation are often done in *silence*."

Meg stamped the ground. "This is pointless!"

"I had no problem stirring the geysers earlier this morning or this afternoon or earlier this week," Page Trey admitted. "Tell me, Lady Meghan, have you ever tried to calm your mind? Have you ever exercised your patience? Have you ever found inner peace?"

Meg bit her tongue. Of course she had, but not in recent memory.

CHAPTER 25

"Peace and patience are siblings," the page said. "They go hand and hand. To have one is to have both. And to possess it within you, peace and patience, is a tranquility of the soul, an assurance of self. It is contentedness with the present and a just yearning for future prosperity, no matter the longanimity required." He searched her eyes. "If this is foreign to you, I implore you to look within. Think on an internal conflict in your mind or heart, one that does not have an immediately obvious solution. Dwell on it. Focus on it. You may not find an answer, but you will discover that, with peace and patience, all things can be riddled out. It just takes time. And, with peace and patience in your heart, nothing is truly a waste of time."

His wise words stirred Meg from her skepticism. As Page Trey once more bowed his head and closed his eyes, she felt compelled to do the same. She lost herself in the darkness and tried to quiet her mind.

But it was for naught. She tried, she honestly did, but her brain was hardly a silent place. A thousand thoughts swirled around: her quest to help Page Trey, the witch's death-bringing mark, how frustrated Meg was to have not yet succeeded in making her flame yet, how badly she wanted to mend her mistakes and wash her hands of the stains she had put there. It all spun round and round and—

Why was it so difficult to calm her mind? she demanded of herself. Would couldn't she just have some peace of mind for once?

Because she didn't have peace. Page Trey had told her as much. And, according to him, if she didn't have peace, she didn't have patience either.

She chuffed to herself. She was patient. She had peace.

Didn't she?

Just the fact she was considering it seemed to prove the point.

But, she considered, if she wasn't patient and peaceful now, when had she been?

Like the first rays of sunrise warming your face, a memory graced the fringes of Meg's mind. She was young again, deep in the woods of

Midvale, playing pretend with Clay and Jenn and her brother. She was Meghan and she was happy.

Those days, she knew, had been the best days of her life. She'd thought of her friends before her own needs and been a walking vision of persistence and amity. Nothing could rattle her.

But that had been before the divorce. Before her brother had chosen Dembroch over her. Before moving to Seattle. Before her mother had kicked her out of the apartment without a dollar to her name. Before she'd been forced to survive on her own, to stop thinking of others and patiently wait for the tides to turn. She'd had to forge ahead and, as a result, she'd shed the past and become Meg, queen of impatience and impoliteness, slave to the march of time, and forgetful of her old self's yearnings, ambitions, and hopes.

How miserable she'd been all these years as Meg, she realized. How chaotically and desperately she'd scrambled to survive, to succeed, to overcome, and all at the expense of her family, friends, and happiness.

Meg heard a loud belch and bubble of water. She squinted, seeing deep blue steam venting from a frothing pool nearby. Had she done that? Was the spring responding to her? She closed her eyes again and dove back into the muck of her mind.

She was not at peace, she fully realized. She hadn't been since she'd been a child. And, worst of all, she didn't know how to fix it.

It hurt to admit. The yearning and determination to fix things was practically engrained in her DNA. She saw problems and fixed them. She thrived off it. And to know that she could not fix that which she should have known most intimately cut deeper than any witch's mark.

I have to fix it, Meg thought dreadfully. *There must be a way.*

If there was, it was not immediately evident, and this scared her more than anything. It was an unknown, shrouded path of change that seemed more daunting than witches, invisible doors, and wrapping her head around magic. Could she really find her way back to her youthful self? Could she reconcile the Meg she had become to the Meghan she had been?

CHAPTER 25

I can't do it alone, she realized with a skip of her heart. As Dembroch needed defenders and Jenn had needed Meg in the catacombs and Page Trey had needed Meg to find Ryderwyle, Meg needed Jenn and Clay and Page Trey and her stepbrother to help her. Friends had been the source of her contentedness in her youth. They could help her find it again.

Somehow, deep down, though she knew this was the first step in a long walk fraught with obstacles and personal peril, she was at peace with it. With her friends and with Dembroch, she would one day feel peace and patience again.

There was a loud blast of gurgling water and steam. Meg's nose was assaulted by a fresh wave of sulphur.

Her eyes snapped open. She was bathed in color. All around her, the hot springs were spraying steam into the air. Invisible doors became visible. But, as Page Trey had suspected, the destinations beyond were hazy and unclear. Without the kingdom's magic, the geysers weren't illuminating the gates' terminuses, only their presence.

Meg marveled at the many doors. They were everywhere, numbering at least a couple hundred—and that was just the immediate area around her. No two were alike. Some were tall, others short and squat. Some remained still, others moved lazily in grand, circular orbits around the area, disappearing from view once beyond the colored geyser mist.

But the gates weren't the only thing to gawk at. She saw a flicker of orange. Page Trey let out a shout.

Protruding from the sandstone a few feet in front of Meg was a black, pyramidal rock. A flame sputtered on the top. Sparks shot out and then hung in the air, some disappearing into gates. Carved into the foot of the plinth was a single word: *pax*.

"Peace," Page Trey translated, squeezing her shoulder. "You have returned magic to the Gate Grounds."

Meg gawked at it, not believing her eyes.

"But," she stammered. "I'm not at peace. I just decided that."

"Exactly," Page Trey said with a wink. "By admitting such a bold confession to yourself, you are at peace with such a conclusion. And there is no greater piece of peace than a mind and heart knowing its current place and where is must go in due time."

Meg squinted, absorbing the page's words.

She gestured at the flame.

"Now what?"

Page Trey held out one of his walking sticks to Meg. She took it and dipped its tip into the flame. It flared, instantly lighting the torch. When she held it up, the tongues of flame burnt wildly around the walking stick's tip, not truly burning the wood, but dancing around it. Sparks spat out of it like the tail of a firework.

Enthralled, Meg swung the torch through the air. The flame weaved, but did not waver. It burnt strong, even when she plunged it into the hot spring. The fire, it seemed, was magical in every way, and could not be extinguished by natural means.

She approached one of the illuminated doors, holding the torch near it. The world beyond became startlingly clear, though tinged in a rainbow of colors. She saw a canyon filled with shallow pools—it was the gate to Coral Canyon.

Meg beamed. She'd never felt so giddy in her life, or at least not since she'd been Meghan. She had started a flame and now, with the geysers and springs erupting and a magic-spewing torch in her hand, she could help Page Trey find the door to Ryderwyle.

"What does Ryderwyle look like?" Meg asked.

"Steep cliffs," Page Trey replied. "Frozen waterfalls. Tall, thin trees covered in snow. Anything that looks like a blizzard."

Holding the torch before her, giving the gates plenty of berth, Meg led their search. When gates neared the aura of Meg's magical flame, they peered through to dozens of destinations. Meg saw thick woods, sandy shores of Whittlesea, deep blue ocean, a sprawling hillside leading to Cliffside Tower. For a second, in this last gate, Meg thought she saw

Clay and the Watchmaker admiring a sword, but she hurried on. She had to find Ryderwyle.

They kept looking. The steam became lighter as the geysers and springs began to dwindle in strength. Meg pressed on, desperate to find the door before it was too late.

Not desperate, she reminded herself. *Peaceful. Patient. We'll find it.*

And just then, she saw it. She pointed. Page Trey let out a shout of joy.

Spinning in a lazy loop around the Gate Grounds was the door to Ryderwyle. It slid past the plinth where the flame burnt strong. So close to the magic, the door was illuminated—there was a steep cliffside covered in snow, a frozen waterfall, a tangle of thin, snow-wreathed trees.

"That's it!" Page Trey shouted.

The two raced toward the gate to Ryderwyle. The door swung in a wide arc, headed toward a large hot spring.

"They're fading!" the page declared.

He was right. The geysers were settling. The colored vapor was becoming white and dwindling. Doors were disappearing. Meg's torch illuminated doors a few feet away. The path ahead became infinitely more treacherous. Meg tried to memorize the layout, picturing where the various doors were, but the moving ones were hard to track. All she knew was the gate to Ryderwyle was sliding right over the hot spring and would disappear in a few seconds.

They made it to the edge of the hot spring. Meg and Page Trey leapt—

It happened in an instant.

Meg's torch illuminated another moving door, this one moving fast, sliding diagonally at them. Page Trey was tugged into the door to Ryderwyle, but Meg was pulled hard and fast toward the new door. Their hands were torn apart. The act jarred Meg. She dropped her torch and it clattered to the ground. A second later, Meg and Page Trey flew through separate doors to their own destinations.

Back on the Gate Grounds, the walking stick torch clattered to the sandstone. The geysers and hot springs fell still. The invisible doors roamed silently. In the middle of it all, the new magical flame of peace flickered.

CHAPTER 26

Wandering the Woods

Across the island, Jenn was lost. She'd been shuffling around the woods for hours on end, trying to find her way to the seer's cottage. Like her husband, directions were not her strong suit.

In her hand, she held the seer's Sight. The two mirrored talismans were comparable to steel marbles. Shallow grooves were carved intricately into the reflective surfaces, all encircling an iris and pupil. The more Jenn looked at these stones, the more she felt the engraved pupils were looking right back at her.

Just get to the seer's cottage, Jenn kept telling herself.

But such an easy task that would have only taken an hour or two in the daylight was taking Jenn all night. She was lost in an unfamiliar, dark forest. The thick canopy of dead tree limbs made for difficult navigating. There was no telling what other terrors lay ahead or if she was even headed in the right direction.

She pressed on. Eventually, she figured, she would stumble upon a shore or landmark to indicate which way she should go. Nonetheless, she had to have hope. It was something she'd long forgotten and only recently rediscovered, but she held onto it like a toddler fighting for a blanket by holding onto the tattered strings on the end.

Suddenly, there was a snap of twigs, then the sound of something large moving toward her. Too late, she heard the ticks of hundreds of clocks. She saw eyes, giant orange orbs with black slits for pupils.

Before Jenn could scream or fight, the Dreadnaught's jaws were around her, digging into the earth. They snapped shut. A crooked tooth sliced through her calf, drawing a river of blood. Up she went, dead grass and dry soil smothering her, teeth crunching, cutting into her skin, then a thick, slimy tongue pushed her into its throat. Her scream was cut out as the hideous beast swallowed her whole and scuttled off into the woods.

CHAPTER 27

Crossed and Cursed Paths

"What was that?" I said.

Queen Coralee and I scanned the surrounding forest, but all was calm and unmoving. The scream had come from far away.

"It would be best to keep moving until we find shelter," Queen Coralee offered.

We continued on, walking blindly through the dark. I held my dislocated arm, the joint burning with every step.

"So," I said, trying to distract myself from the pain, "your sister seems...nice."

Queen Coralee chuffed. "All this time Sorgana...Edith...has been in my kingdom, taunting me that she knows me, and I never once realized it was her. My own sister..."

"She looks like she's aged quite a bit," I offered.

"Which is impossible," the queen said. "It has been thousands of years since we parted ways. Any person would have passed millennia ago. I never thought she could be alive, let alone be *here*. Or be so..."

"Mean?"

"Different," the queen corrected. "That was *not* the sister I knew."

"She wasn't always bent on killing you and your kingdom?"

The queen shook her head.

"We were sisters," she revealed. "The best of friends. Until..."

"Until you left her?" I assumed.

"I didn't *leave* her," the queen said, eyes fiery. "I was taken." She hung her head. "And lo and behold, she has found her way here to wreak havoc."

"We'll stop her," I insisted.

"I fear this curse is too strong."

"Your curse?" I asked, not sure what that meant.

The queen's lips went thin.

"What do she mean 'Dembroch is cursed because you are'?" I pressed.

After a long pause, the queen said, "There is much to explain, Sir Nicholas. Let us find shelter from the night and I shall tell you all you wish to hear."

I wasn't altogether satisfied with this answer, but figured it was good enough for now.

We pressed on through the darkness, coming to a patch of brambles. I pushed them aside and screeched to a halt. The black tip of a sword pointed right at my nose.

I held up my good arm to show surrender. My voice caught in my throat. How had the skeletons caught us?

Queen Coralee appeared beside me and froze too.

"My queen?" a voice called.

"Nick?" another said.

CHAPTER 27

Past the point of the sword and across a narrow, dry creek bed was Clay and the Watchmaker, my friend bearing a broad axe, the latter holding the sword pointed at my nose.

The queen rushed to the Watchmaker with a shout of relief. I met Clay in the middle of the river, wincing when he gave me a hug.

"Nice axe," I commented.

He shrugged, straining to lift it.

"What have you been doing?" I asked, looking over Clay. He had remnants of blood and slime on his clothes. His tie had been burnt to a stub.

Clay explained his harrowing journey into the Cliffside Tower, leaving out the bits where he had run in circles of terror and had been unable to lift the fortissium blade or defend himself. When he asked me about my day and my limp arm, I explained my misadventure in the castle with the queen, witch, and skeletons.

"No flames yet?" he asked.

"Only one," I explained. "I have to go back for it. But my quest isn't done yet. I think I have to light another one. You?"

Clay hung his head.

"It's okay," I insisted. "We still have till noon tomorrow?"

"About twelve hours then?" Clay said dejectedly.

"What do you have left to do?"

"The Dreadnaught," Clay murmured.

"Perfect," I said, remembering that Clay loved chasing down imaginary monsters in his youth.

But the Clay before me didn't look too excited to face any beasts. His false bravado had melted away, exposing a raw nerve of fear.

"You can do this, Clay," I promised him. "If I can jump off a castle wall for a queen, you can fight the Dreadnaught. It can't be that horrible."

Clay looked off into the distance. He murmured something about bravery amongst horror, then gave me a hug. I yelped in pain as he patted my dislocated shoulder.

"Hey," he whispered in my ear, "what's going on over there?"

I followed his gaze.

Queen Coralee and the Watchmaker stood close together, whispering conspiratorially. The Watchmaker handed her a pocket watch from his belt. When the queen opened it, she looked dismayed. After handing it back to him, she started kneading her hands again, rubbing the burn on her fingertips.

"What was that about?" I wondered, but we didn't get the opportunity to theorize. The queen and Watchmaker joined us.

"The Watchmaker told me of your bravery, Sir Clayton," the queen said. "I commend you. It seems you have truly taken my words to heart and are striving to better yourself as you save our kingdom. For that, I am eternally grateful. You now have the means and the heart to slay the Dreadnaught."

As if in reply, there was a far-off shriek. It was otherworldly, guttural and powerful. For a second, I wondered if it was the Dreadnaught, but Clay answered my question.

"The dragons," he whispered, eyes wide and scared.

"Oh, you're favorite!" I shouted without thinking.

Clay shook his head slightly.

"You mustn't stay with us, my queen," the Watchmaker said. "The fortissium blade is the prize of the Horror Hollow. The dragons seek it for their own and will chase us through the night."

"I will stay by your side," the queen promised.

The Watchmaker shook his head, refusing.

"You have dangers and problems of your own to sort out, my queen," he said, casting a wary eye at me. "Rest assured, we will find the Dreadnaught and recover the witch's watch soon. But for now, for your safety, we must part."

Though the queen argued, the Watchmaker remained adamant. In time, he and Clay bid us farewell. I wished Clay luck, and the two disappeared into the woods, leaving the queen and I to find our own shelter and answers.

CHAPTER 28

Quite a Gruesome Spectacle

Horses whinnied nervously from the stables as Sorgana limped to the Bridgemaster's home. She was a sight for sore eyes, bedraggled and weak, old and frail, a walking corpse.

She stopped at the water barrel and, stooping, plucked a baby turtle from within. Hardly relishing the taste, she bit the turtle's head off and swallowed it whole. She toyed with the shell until she had all the meat. With each slurp, she grew younger. Her energy renewed.

Before long, she emptied the barrel, crushing the shells after she'd drained them. But now she was in a feeding frenzy. There wasn't enough food—enough youth—to slake her appetite.

By the trees, the horses neighed nervously. Sorgana swept to their stables, ravenous. She struck one down, feeding on it, then another, and another. Their braes were the thing of nightmares.

When she'd eaten the last morsel of meat from the horses and absorbed the last bit of lifeforce available to her, the witch, plump and young and invigorated once more, ascended the porch steps of the Bridgemaster's home. She flung the door open dramatically.

The Bridgemaster and Sir Liliford the ferryman were inside, armed with butcher knives. Both were free of the witch's enchantments, their eyes restored to their natural colors once more.

"Stowing away for the night?" she simpered at the men. "Nursing your wounds until daybreak?"

The men exchanged glances that confirmed the witch's suspicions.

"You would lower the bridge?" she glowered. "Flee to the ferry? Leave your kingdom and your queen? Such betrayal!"

"We'd never abandon our queen or our land," the Bridgemaster declared boldly. "We'd only ever leave to call for reinforcements against the likes of you!"

Sir Liliford cast his eyes to the ground.

"Ah, that's more like it," the witch said. "Betrayal is too cowardly for you, Bridgemaster. And truly...neither of you shall leave this kingdom or see the light of day again."

She attacked like a snake, quick and cruel. Furniture was torn to pieces. Shattered turtle shells flew into the house and rained down like razor blades. The men were knocked over and savagely beaten. Sir Liliford managed to get to his feet and made to pull the Bridgemaster out of danger, but the latter was too heavy.

"Take him back against walls of black," the witch intoned.

The Bridgemaster lifted off the ground and smacked into the wall. He hung there, struggling against forces he could not fight.

Sir Liliford held up a kitchen knife at the witch.

"No need to fool me," the witch said to the ferryman with a wicked smile. "I know you want to run. To flee. To never return. If you go fast enough, you might be able to get ahead of me."

The ferryman trembled on the spot, eyes darting between the witch and his friend, then the door.

"No, no, no," Sorgana sang. "You're not leaving the island. Not now. But you still have a chance to run and hide. Think of it as a game. If you get far enough away or bury yourself deep enough, you may make good sport and I'll kill you quickly."

Sir Liliford shook on the spot.

"Don't just stand there, run!" Sorgana cried.

He remained frozen in fear.

She lunged, striking the knife from his hand. Her broken nails cut into his wrist, marking him.

"Run!" the witch shrieked.

He finally did, sprinting off into the depths of the home. Intriguing choice, the witch noted. She wondered if he was truly running or seeking protection. Perhaps there was a secret exit within the house.

"Abandoned and alone," the witch sneered, turning her attention back to the Bridgemaster pinned to the wall. "Left to suffer at the hands of your master these past days. You did me well, retrieving my food and allowing the defenders to pass, keeping the bridge guarded against any fools trying to flee. And how can I repay such loyalty?"

The Bridgemaster rasped weakly, begging for mercy. He was helpless, defenseless. Innocent of his crimes, yet due to be punished all the same. It was cruelty of the highest degree.

The witch rose her hand. Green light emanated around her. Butchers knives and turtle shell fragments raised, points directed at the Bridgemaster.

"Your recompense will not be quick or painless," the witch sighed. "It shall be long, agonizing, and, in every sense of the word, cruel. Suffer well in your reward, my slave."

Several hours later, the Bridgemaster gave up the ghost and succumbed to his injuries. Covered in his blood, Sorgana went in search of Sir Liliford. In the basement, she found a hidden doorway leading into an underground cave system. This was the way the ferryman had run. She could smell it.

She pursued her prey, eager for more blood, tracking him by the stench of his fear and the mark she'd given him on his wrist.

Many twists and turns later, she emerged from the caves on the northern shores of the island. Her quarry, Sir Liliford, was far to the west, headed for the sand bar leading to the sandy island of Whittlesea. The witch pursued him, a reaper he could not outrun.

A flicker in the water around Whittlesea caught the witch's eye. She recalled overhearing Civium speak of a famished sea monster, the Gangrene, that lived in the small island's lagoon. It would aid her well.

Just as the ferryman slogged out of the surf and onto the sands of Whittlesea, the witch came down upon him. She was brutal and exact, assaulting him viciously as he screamed for mercy. When he couldn't even find his voice to plead, she ceased. With a snap of her fingers and muttering of an incantation, the witch caused a wooden cross to grow from the sand. She strung the ferryman to it like a scarecrow. He hung limply, jaw broken, sole good eye glaring at her as blood ran from his lips.

"Be honest, ferryman. Am I not wicked?" she cooed, wiping his bloody bangs from his eyes. "Yes. But the trick of wickedness is a heavy sense of irony. You must offer the expected solution, but the means must cause countless more...bloodshed." She cackled. "I shall give you what you want. Rest. Peace. No more ferrying. No more running. No more starving of hope and food and justice. I believe you know of...the Gangrene?"

Sir Liliford's swelling eyes got big. He looked past her.

The surface of the lagoon broke. Thick, sinuous tentacles crept toward Sir Liliford. Inside the green-tinged suckers were tiny, gnashing teeth and gaping mouths.

The ferryman screamed as the Gangrene's black and green tentacles wrapped around him. Blood spurted from between the appendages. He writhed in agony, his garbled words cursing the witch and her wickedness.

CHAPTER 28

And just then, as the ferryman thrashed helplessly, Sorgana got what she wanted.

As had occurred in the castle catacombs after killing the librarian, as had happened while she mutilated the Bridgemaster in his own home, a black speck was born. It burst from her, hovering in the air. Before Sorgana's eyes, the spark multiplied, becoming a hovering, quavering sphere of black specks.

She looked upon the millions of swirling specks with pride. What it was, what it meant for Dembroch—

"Quite a gruesome spectacle it would be to power this spell," her mentor had told her decades ago when they'd first devised this plan. "A root of sin to devour Dembroch."

She couldn't have put it better.

Sorgana walked into the lagoon. The waves washed the blood of the ferryman, the Bridgemaster, and the horses from her. She pet the Gangrene as it fed. All the while, she watched the ball of black sparks. It would be a while before it was ready, but she had time to wait. And she was enjoying Sir Liliford's helpless squeals that faded of life with each passing scream.

CHAPTER 29

The Watchmaker's Watches

Clay and the Watchmaker trudged through the night, dragon shrieks trailing them in the distance. If it hadn't been for the island native, Clay would have been lost hours ago, or stumbled into the Dreadnaught again.

"The Dreadnaught haunts the northwestern woods most frequently," the Watchmaker had explained. "We'll stay clear. Find suitable shelter near there, rest up, and prepare for the fight in the morning."

As they walked on, the Watchmaker offered Clay the fortissium blade. Despite his fears, the sword did not shock Clay when he took it. He examined the sword and took a swing—but it did not cut into anything. The blade clanged loudly as it bounced off trees, stones, and dirt. It couldn't even cut a withered flower from its stem. But when the

Watchmaker held it, just a jab would slice through a boulder and send a pine tumbling to the earth.

"Perhaps it only yields its power to the current user," the Watchmaker mused.

Clay shook his head. "It's the inscription. If you're pure of heart, you can use it. I'm not. Just like the knight who stole it."

The Watchmaker's eyebrows furrowed.

"You think so little of yourself," he observed.

Clay hung his head.

"I lost it once, too," the Watchmaker said. "The will. The bravery. Once upon a time, I had the opportunity to fight, like you did in the tower, but I fell. Life knocked me down and I didn't want to get back up. And, in the end, I lost it. But, you know what I did?" The Watchmaker watched him, expecting an answer. "I got back up. I decided to fight for what I lost. You're lucky. You fell down and had someone to help you get back up. You haven't lost yet. You still have a chance to make it right, to learn. But I lost my chance."

"And what did you lose?" Clay scoffed.

"More than you can bear, boy," the Watchmaker replied.

Clay's jaw dropped. Was the Watchmaker grieving?

"The Dreadnaught took something from you," he realized. "Not just the witch's watch. Something personal of yours."

The Watchmaker grumbled. It seemed Clay had hit a nerve.

"Is it another watch?" he asked.

"It carries *all* the watches," the Watchmaker grunted. "I've made watches my whole life, real ones that told time in increments of twelve hours over a twenty-four-hour day. Then, time stopped. Magic was spread across the kingdom. It seemed I was out of a job, but people still wanted to track time. Humans are funny that way, slave to their own constructs. So I met their demands. With the help of some magic, I created these watches that, instead of telling the time of the day, tell the time of your life over a twelve-hour period. It accounts for your body and soul. In a perfect world, every ten minutes on the clock would signify a year in a life. A whole hour could suggest five to ten years. The closer to midnight, the closer to death—most often of the person, but sometimes death of just the soul. Each watch is different and specific to the person.

"As you can imagine, King Richard found the watches invaluable. He asked me to make one for every soul in the world, and with it, Dembroch's purpose was forever changed. Using the watches, we were able to find the Hospites in the world beyond."

"How did that work?" Clay asked.

"Back in the glory days," the Watchmaker explained, "when King Richard was still with us, a waning soul's pocket watch would chime when the subject was close to passing. I would find the ringing watch, read it, and, with the king and queen, select who should be brought to Dembroch to be healed."

"You don't bring every person to Dembroch?" Clay asked.

The Watchmaker shook his head. "When we first started using the watches to find people in need of healing, the kingdom was a lot more accepting of guests. We took anyone in need and got a hold of some ungodly folk. Witches, wraiths, Fomorians, Solomon... It started small enough, but they took advantage of Dembroch's magic, went mad with the power. We had to get rid of them, one by one. Solomon was the breaking point. After him, we made a new rule: only good men and women on Dembroch. None should step foot on shore who are not allowed. So we're more careful with who we invite to save. It can be tricky, particularly when royalty is involved."

Clay sensed there was more to be told, but the Watchmaker was moving on.

"Anyhow, from the chiming watches, royalty would select those who should be brought to Dembroch. The Praesidio, a traveling sect of the defenders, would then seek out the poor souls in need and bring them here, by which point the healers and I had read the gears and determined what to do to heal them."

"What do you mean 'read the gears'?" Clay asked, confused.

CHAPTER 29

The Watchmaker unclipped one of the watches from his belt and flipped it over. Like Clay's personal watch, the back of this pocket watch was exposed, showing spinning gears.

"The gears tell you about the person of the watch. Who they are, where they're from, what made them..."

Clay felt his eyebrows knit together.

"See the tiny gear in the back?" the Watchmaker said, his voice strangely light. "That's always the first gear I make, the foundation of the person, their purpose." He slapped Clay's chest. "It's what we have in here, what we fight for. Now, see, this watch is mine, so it'll be easy to understand. You can see from the gear that I was a young boy, the apple of my mother's eye. She was a watchmaker, and I followed in her footsteps. Then the girl showed up. That's the gear beside it. The two glided so perfectly together. My wife, my mother, me...we were happy as we could be."

He pointed to a larger gear.

"My wife's love gave me purpose, as well as love from and for my mother," the Watchmaker continued. "But then, time stopped on Dembroch. That's the odd-shaped gear there with missing teeth. My mother thought the magic unnatural and sought to leave Dembroch. My wife wanted to stay. I was torn between the two women I loved most. And in the end, I chose my wife. When my mother left, I lost a piece of myself. That's why the upper gears don't grind quite right."

Clay watched the Watchmaker closely, sensing a layered sadness within him, as if he wished he could go back to that day and leave with his mother, perhaps take his wife, too.

"Time went on," continued the Watchmaker, "though there was no time on the island. I began designing timepieces for my fellow Civium and that of every soul on the planet. When I created my mother's, I saw that she had perished in the world beyond. I was heartbroken—that rusty gear there. My wife tried to console me, but I was never the same. I fell down and didn't want to get back up. And then, the worst of it."

Lastly, he pointed at the top two gears, both grinding hard against one another, skipping now and again.

"The witch arrived on the island," he explained. "She sent the Dreadnaught to my cottage. She knew, you see. She knew we made watches, and she knew we'd be looking for hers eventually. So she sent her monster after us."

The Watchmaker's gruff face fell. His eyes became red.

"My wife and I were in the time hall in our cottage. The Dreadnaught struck. It gobbled up every watch I'd ever made and...it took her."

He looked off into the distance, breathing deep.

"I saw it in her watch, knew one day she would pass, but I didn't know it would be like that." He cleared his throat. "Then, right after, the monster tried to take a chomp out of me too."

He ran his fingers along his belt of watches, pausing in the middle where two chains hung without timepieces.

"Took the watches of my mother and my wife and ran off into the night, leaving me for dead."

There was a moment of silence. The Watchmaker looked off into the woods, eyes reflecting the stars. He pounded his chest hard.

"But that was twenty-some years ago," he grunted, clearing his throat. "Old news. And that last gear—" he pointed at it, a crimson gear that seemed to be the shape of a human heart with a metal rod connecting it to the tiny, innermost gear "—it's how it all ends. Without the love of the two women I love most, without the last link to their lives, I'm lost. It's connected to the bottommost gear because it's what I'm seeking. The queen wants me to recover the witch's watch and reveal the secret of its gears, but first, I'll filet that monster and pull the watches of my mother and wife from its gut."

"I'm so sorry," Clay said.

"It was long ago," the Watchmaker grumbled. "And I shall have my revenge by next day or fall with my kingdom."

CHAPTER 29

Through all of this, Clay could see each of these gears, predict how they moved and worked with one another, but he could not see any indication of a boy, a man, his mother, his lover, or anything the Watchmaker had explained.

But, as fascinating and perplexing as it was, he had discovered the Watchmaker's true quest. His most prized possession, the Dreadnaught's reap, were the watches of every soul on the planet, including every Hospite in need, the witch's, and ultimately, the watches of the two women the Watchmaker had loved most and lost.

"Hold on," Clay said. "If it was twenty years ago, wouldn't the watches be digested?"

The Watchmaker shook his head. "The beast has four stomachs and a painfully slow digestive system. Any living souls will have perished, but the watches will still be in there."

The Watchmaker strode off, wiping his face. Clay hurried after, the axe heavy in his grip, a newfound admiration growing for the island native. Not the muscles or the beard or the axe or the sword, but the Watchmaker's courage in the face of his worst nightmare. He was the man Clay could have been and wished he was.

And then, more than ever, Clay wished he was with Jenn. He had so much to say to her that he'd neglected to mention. He wondered where she was, how she was faring on her quest, and if she was thinking of him. He wondered if she was being brave in the face of her fears.

Perhaps, he decided, it was time to stop pretending to be brave and to *be* brave. Like he used to be. To have something worth fighting for in his heart.

CHAPTER 30

Off the Reservation

Elsewhere, Meg landed hard on a steep hill of wet grass. She tumbled and twirled, vines and creepers wrapping around her, finally rolling to a stop at the bottom of the hill.

Grumbling under her breath, Meg got to her feet. High above was a canvas of black sky and twinkling stars she didn't recognize.

She climbed to the crest of the hill she'd just rolled down. From the peak, she took in her new surroundings. One thing was for sure—she wasn't on Dembroch anymore. But she recognized where she was.

Before her were steadily declining slopes that led to a pebbly beach. Small and hidden in the dark was a squat hut with a dock.

She glanced behind her. Far off, a dozen miles away, shrouded in the nighttime mist, were the lights of a tiny city.

She was back in northern Scotland, she realized, where she'd been when she'd first begun this adventure. A quarter mile to the north would take her to boats and back to Dembroch, and a dozen miles behind her was a city that would provide the means to go home.

Meg hesitated on the top of the hill, unsure what to do. She had succeeded in her task on Dembroch—her flame was lit, though it lay unattended in the Gate Grounds, not yet spread to the castle, and it was only one of six. All the same, her task was complete. She could go home now, like she'd wanted to in the beginning, and her conscience would be clean.

And if this had been twenty-four hours previous, Meg would have done just that in a split second. But she had lived a lifetime since she'd first arrived in Scotland. She'd seen too much to go back now. There was too much worth fighting for. And she only just begun her path. She needed her friends...and they needed her.

She balled her fists and ran toward the shack. Toward the rowboats. Toward Dembroch.

CHAPTER 31

Midnight Mystery

Clay and the Watchmaker emerged from the woods on the western end of the island near Coral Canyon and the Bridgemaster's home. The windows were dark. The horse stables were ominously quiet.

"Isn't the Bridgemaster under the witch's spell?" Clay asked.

"He won't be for long," the Watchmaker replied, wielding the fortissium blade.

They approached the cottage. Clay's legs ached. He wanted nothing more than to barricade himself inside and lay down.

At the door, the Watchmaker hesitated.

"Someone's been here," he whispered. "They entered with force."

Clay would have preferred to sneak into the cottage, but the Watchmaker kicked the door aside and charged in with the sword. Reminding himself to be brave, Clay ran after him, tensing his arms to wield the heavy axe.

But there was no need for bravery, only a strong stomach.

CHAPTER 31

The room was in shambles and reeked of death. Furniture had been splintered. Fragments of gutted turtle shells were crushed into pieces. Gobs of blood and flesh were splattered across the walls. The Bridgemaster, body maimed and cruelly tortured, was pinned to the wall.

The Watchmaker swore softly and knocked his chest.

"Who did this?" Clay gasped.

"Who else?" the Watchmaker countered.

A flicker of movement caught Clay's eye. He spun, tensing.

Across the room, Clay saw a dancing black flame. Dark sparks hung around it like a million baby spiders free from their eggs.

"What—" Clay stammered.

From outside, a dragon let out a cry. The flapping of many wings grew louder.

"Hurry, boy," the Watchmaker grunted, leading him through the carnage, deeper into the cottage.

"What about the Bridgemaster? Clay shouted.

"Leave him," replied the Watchmaker. "He's gone. The dragons will go for him first while we hide."

Sickened by the thought, Clay followed the Watchmaker. They charged through the house and past the black fire while, behind them, dragons burst into the cottage. They heard snarls and crunches as the beasts fought over their food.

At the back of the house, the Watchmaker threw open a trapdoor that led into a basement. They ran the length of the room and, in the corner near overturned barrels, found a tunnel burrowing deep into the ground.

"Caverns run the whole length of the island," the Watchmaker explained. "The beasties will have a hard time finding us down here. The smell of the blade will fill all the tunnels."

Into the caverns they went. It was hot and stuffy, like the belly of a volcano. Clay lost his sense of direction as they passed through grottos and passageways.

"We'll rest here for the night," the Watchmaker finally declared.

"You're sure?" Clay asked.

"You want to go further, be my guest. We'll be safe here until morning."

The Watchmaker settled into a small alcove, telling Clay to keep watch if he was worried. A few minutes later, the mountain man was sawing logs more efficiently than the fortissium blade.

Exhausted but unable to sleep with all that was on his mind, Clay set aside the Watchmaker's axe and pulled out his pocket watch. As before, the time read midnight.

He sighed in disappointment. How he had wished that his clock would move backward, that his soul would reignite with bravery, that he could fight the Dreadnaught and the witch and the dragons. But if anything, the fight at Cliffside Tower and his shock in the Bridgemaster's home had proven how far removed he was from his courage. Starting a magic flame for Dembroch seemed impossible.

Clay turned the watch over and examined the gears. He tried to relate the whirring circles and clicking teeth to his past, but nothing spoke to him. It was as perplexing as ever.

Sighing in discouragement, Clay stowed away his pocket watch. He glanced over at the Watchmaker and caught sight of the belt. A half dozen pocket watches hung there, letting out soft ticks.

Clay's eyes fell on the leftmost watch. That was the one the queen had looked at earlier. She had looked so graven, as though the ill fate found within were unstoppable.

Curiosity getting the better of him, Clay slunk to the Watchmaker's side. He unclasped the watch from the belt and examined it. Gears whirred within. Clay tried to read into the gears, to see what the Watchmaker could see, but nothing spoke to him and no secrets were revealed.

He unclasped the front. It sprung open, revealing the clock face. He blinked, not understanding.

The queen's watch read a minute to midnight.

Beside him, the Watchmaker grumbled in his sleep. Clay returned the watch to the belt and hurried back to the other side of the cavern, his brain spinning.

His own watch was at midnight due to the lack of childhood spirit within. His innocence was gone, as was his bravery. It was no surprise his watch said he was dead of heart. It was how he felt.

But the queen? She was full of vim and vigor, courtesy and spirit. Which meant, if her childlike spirit was well and alive, the watch revealed something else.

Was it the imminent end of Dembroch? Was everyone's pocket watch a minute from midnight?

No, Clay remembered. The Watchmaker's was at nine-o'clock. Dembroch's impending disaster was still twelve hours away. Whatever was affecting the queen was personal. But what?

For reasons Clay did not know and could only begin to guess, the queen was dying. And, based on the pocket watch, she had very little time left.

CHAPTER 32

Honest Hours

"This is going to hurt," Queen Coralee warned

"Just do it," I insisted.

I was laying on the cold, hard ground. A fire—not a magical one, just a normal sticks and sparks one—burnt close by.

We were at the mouth of the mage's caverns on the northern shores of Dembroch. The sand bar of Whittlesea with its far-off beach hut village and strange, dismembered scarecrow on its southern tip glowed under the moon. Ryderwyle seemed to howl at us with its swirling winter storm. Waves crashed onto the rock shore. I tried focusing on it to distract myself from the impending pain.

"Ready?" she asked.

I nodded, bracing myself. My poor little heart beat fast, but it ached a little with each beat, which was worrisome too.

The queen began to lift my dislocated arm, angling it to be perpendicular with my body. I bit my tongue; every inch sent spikes of agony down my body. My heart pumped painfully.

CHAPTER 32

"So you're cursed, huh?" I grunted. "From birth?"

The queen stopped.

"Must we talk about this now, Sir Nicholas?" she asked.

"I...well, no, I was...just trying to distract myself," I said through gritted teeth.

"Let us distract each other with a different topic," she requested. "May I ask about what you said while we were in the castle, when the witch held me captive?"

My stomach dropped. All the physical pain seemed to melt away for a moment, replaced by fear and guilt.

"Did you mean it?" the queen asked.

Her tone was far too innocent for what she was asking, and she was too smart to know it wasn't just a simple, distracting question.

"Can we just—just do it," I said.

The queen did as I asked, pulling on my arm hard. Pain shot through me and my shoulder let out a sick *thunk*. My arm popped back into its joint, bone grating against bone. I screamed in agony, a million daggers stabbing through my chest and down my arm. My heart thudded away, pounding harder than it should have.

"I told you it would hurt," the queen said.

As I fought off the pain, the queen tore fabric from her dress. She tied it around my neck and arm, forming a sling.

We moved to the fire and sat on opposite ends for a while, awkwardly avoiding eye contact, neither of us wanting to start the hard conversations.

There was so much swirling around in my brain. Sorgana the witch was the queen's sister. The queen had stripped my friends and I of our titles to protect us. And in seemingly unrelated news, there was a curse.

After what seemed like hours, Queen Coralee looked me in the eye. There was a pause between us, like the moment before you jump over the edge of a waterfall. It seemed the moment was finally upon us.

"I will be honest with you," the queen said, her hushed words full of honesty. "But only if *you*, in kind, will be honest with me."

I stammered a few words, trying to find fault with this, for a way out, but silenced myself. I had proven I was faithful to the queen and she was showing her willingness to trust me in return.

I nodded.

"It is settled," the queen said. "Owing to the fact that I was the first to hide any truth, I shall be the first. It is difficult to explain, so I must begin with the start. Dembroch is cursed, but only because *I* am cursed."

"But—" I began.

"Everything that has happened these last twenty years," the queen said slowly, not looking me in the eye, "has unfolded because of me. The death of the king, the flight of our Civium and Hospites, the end of the kingdom's magic... All of this is my doing. And what a shame it is. What a mark on my soul. The kingdom took me in and trusted me to guide them to prosperity with my king, none knowing I needed the isles' magic as much as any Hospite. But none of them knew what I brought with me to the kingdom. None of them knew the curse that would one day lay waste to their land. That I would lead it all to ruin."

My jaw was hanging. The queen was a Hospite? She had been welcomed to the kingdom to save her from a curse?

"What is it?" I asked tenderly. "The curse?"

The queen shifted uncomfortably.

"It is quite byzantine," she said.

I waited patiently. I wouldn't force her if she didn't want to say it, but she knew as well as I that an explanation would help shed light on...well, pretty much everything.

"If you insist," she said. She took a deep breath and began: "My father was cursed by a witch. Not Sorgana. Another witch of old. And the curse? It was a dreadful one that burdened my father and any children he should have. Therefore, it rests on my shoulders as it crushed his."

I felt a stirring in my memory. This story seemed familiar.

"He searched the world for a way to break the curse," the queen continued, "but he died in the process. Before the curse affected me—"

CHAPTER 32

"Wait," I interrupted, suddenly realizing. "Was your father...King Arthur?"

The queen looked impressed.

"Well, yes," she said.

I gaped at her. "You're the daughter of...of King Arthur. Wow. Just...wow. But...hey, wait. I thought King Arthur couldn't have children."

I was pretty sure I remembered my history correctly. In all the history books, King Arthur had only one child: Mordred, an illegitimate child from dalliances he'd had in his young adult years. Several years later, he had married Queen Guinevere and never been able to father another child. Their lack of children had been one of the reasons Queen Guinevere had found solace in the arms of Sir Lancelot, one of the Knights of Round Table.

"There is much more to the story than history cares to tell," Queen Coralee revealed. "And far more than I can remember. I only know what was told to me millennia ago."

"I may have a way for us to see it," I said.

From my satchel, I pulled out the vial of golden magic that the librarian had given to me and the history book the queen had sent long ago.

I showed the book to Queen Coralee.

"May I?" I asked, shaking the vial slightly.

The queen nodded contemplatively. For the first time, I wondered if, perhaps, the queen had sent the book to us not only to hide the secrets of the kingdom's magic from the witch, but to hide the secret of her curse, too.

"Ready?" I asked.

When she nodded, I laid the book open to the tale of King Arthur. I uncorked the vial of storytelling magic and poured it onto the page.

CHAPTER 33

The Curse of the King

White smoke blossomed from the book and covered the queen and I. Our surroundings became an expansive salt flat. Heat mirages danced across the expanse. Far away, set in a mountainside, was a castle of dark stone and sharp turrets.

"Once upon a time," I said, prompting the magical storytelling to begin, "King Arthur bested his most terrible foe, Morgan Le Fay."

Two figures appeared before us on the salt flats. Dressed in chainmail and bearing a sword, King Arthur fought against Morgan Le Fay, a sinewy woman with regal robes of green. They battled fiercely.

"My father," the queen breathed, looking at King Arthur with admiration and wonder.

Before our very eyes, Morgan Le Fay sent out a blast of green fire at the king. The effort appeared taxing. Her skin rippled and cracked. It reminded me of Sorgana and the physical toll when she used her magic.

CHAPTER 33

Weakened by her own spell, Morgan Le Fay let up just for a moment. King Arthur took advantage of it and knocked the sorceress to her knees. He held his sword an inch from her neck.

"Yield," he said.

The witch knelt, anger burning in her eyes.

"Morgan Le Fay," King Arthur said boldly, "you have been sentenced to death for your crimes against the kingdom. Before you pass through the gates of hell, do you have any final words?"

The witch clasped her hands, twisting her fingers together.

"You may have bested me on this day, king, but I shall raze the very legacy you have built," Morgan Le Fay spat. "I curse you and your lineage. Child shall be separated from parent. Grief shall break your hearts."

"Silence, witch," King Arthur demanded.

But the curse had already begun. Ivy green mirages of magic flew from Morgan Le Fay's hands into King Arthur's body.

"And when each of your descendants reach the age of thirty years," the witch continued, "they shall be stripped of their lands, people, royalty, and title, and spend the rest of their days knowing what they have lost."

King Arthur exclaimed in protest and swung his sword. With a sick thud, Morgan Le Fay's body hit the ground, free of life.

"The curse," I breathed, fully realizing the ramifications of what had just occurred. "It wasn't just on King Arthur. It passed to his descendants." I looked to the queen. "To you."

The queen nodded, her eyes still locked on her father. King Arthur stood over the witch's body, despair wrinkling his face.

We watched for a while before I remembered I had to prompt the storytelling.

"Burdened with the curse and his spoils of war, King Arthur..."

I couldn't remember what happened next, but the story was already moving forward.

King Arthur turned his gaze to the castle in the mountainside. A soft wailing came from within. The next second, the scene darkened to near black. When my eyes adjusted, I realized we were in the castle, watching King Arthur walk through its halls.

This was a deviation from the written story, I remembered, having first seen it while fleeing the witch in the library. It seemed it was time to find out the story between the lines.

King Arthur entered a large room with a balcony overlooking the salt flats. In the corner of the room was a bed of black satin and, right next to it, a cradle.

We followed King Arthur to the crib. Inside was a tiny, blue-eyed baby girl. The baby cooed and reached out for the king. He took her in his arms and held her close.

"Is that you?" I whispered to the queen.

"I don't think so," she murmured, enraptured with the unfolding scene.

"Child of a sorceress," King Arthur mused to himself as he regarded the baby. "What horrors you would have lived. What evil your mother would have pressed upon you."

The king walked to the balcony, overlooking the salt flats, and drew the baby close, embracing her as a father would a newborn.

"I christen you Edith of Camelot and take you as my own," the king said to the baby.

Beside me, Queen Coralee gasped. I was shocked too. The baby in King Arthur's arms would one day be Sorgana the witch. She was the "spoils of war" that the book spoke of.

"Did you know?" I whispered.

The queen shook her head. "I knew she was my stepsister, but not her true parentage."

King Arthur continued speaking to his new stepdaughter: "You are free from the tyranny of your mother's will, just as I shall never sire a child to be afflicted by my curse. Rather, my wife and I shall take you as our own. You shall live free of any curse or witchcraft, so long as I live."

CHAPTER 33

I couldn't help but be impressed by the king. His resolve to do good, to suffer so others could prosper, was admirable. The king was willing to raise someone else's child and never have his own to end the curse, spare his own future children, and save the offspring of an evil witch. It seemed a high bar that Queen Coralee was desperately reaching to emulate.

After a moment, I realized the scene had frozen again.

"You may continue," Queen Coralee said softly.

"Okay. So, uh...burdened with the curse and his spoils of war, King Arthur returned to Camelot," I said.

The scene transformed before our very eyes. King Arthur mounted his horse. Holding tight to Morgan Le Fay's daughter, the stepdaughter who would one day be Sorgana, King Arthur urged his horse into a trot and rode off into the sunset. We followed him across the sand flats, through mountains and woods, until he arrived at the foot of a castle. I knew at once that this place, with its thick brambles, the sweeping British hills, and the marked beauty, was Camelot.

King Arthur took his adopted daughter to the throne room. His wife, Guinevere, waited there for him. He knelt beside her and kissed her hand.

"My queen," the king said. "Our greatest foe has been vanquished."

Queen Guinevere's attention was on the baby in King Arthur's arms, now a few months older.

"The witch bore a daughter," the king revealed. "Left alone in the castle. The babe would have died. And you and I...we can raise this child as our own."

"You're a fool, my king," Queen Guinevere said, a wry look in her eye.

She stood—and that's when I saw it. King Arthur did too.

Queen Guinevere was pregnant.

I looked to Queen Coralee. She nodded.

The baby inside Queen Guinevere was the queen standing beside me now.

"Shortly after you left," Queen Guinevere said to her husband, "the Lord blessed us."

King Arthur's smile soon faded.

"What is it, my king?" Queen Guinevere asked.

He told her about the curse of Morgan Le Fay now upon him and his lineage. Never once did he shout or lose his temper. I envied his even temperament. He had the solidarity of a leader.

"Our child," King Arthur said, placing a hand on his wife's abdomen, "will be subject to the curse as well. By their thirtieth year, they will suffer greatly."

"What can we do?" asked the queen.

King Arthur's jaw flexed and his eyes grew steely.

"The Lord has blessed us with a child when doctors told us we could not. This child is a blessing. And, by my last breath, I shall ensure that this child lives a full life. They will not suffer this curse. I so swear it, my queen."

I looked upon the family—the gallant King Arthur and his promise, the steadfast Queen Guinevere bearing the miracle child that was already doomed, and the stepdaughter Edith, adopted with good intention but surely to be cast aside. It appeared to be the beautiful calm before the storm.

"After this," I said, trying to narrate again, "I think King Arthur went looking for the Holy Grail."

Prompted by my words, the scene before us changed, showing much more than I had stated. We saw Queen Guinevere giving birth, a wizened old man speaking to King Arthur, the king riding off with twelve knights while the queen watched him go, a cup hovering just out of reach of the knights, then two young girls playing together... I began to lose track of what was happening, but Queen Coralee took the reins.

"My mother, Queen Guinevere, gave birth to me," said the queen. "In hopes to avoid reprisal from Morgan Le Fay's sympathizers, Queen Guinevere and King Arthur struck my name from the lineage records. My father consulted his mentor and confidante, Merlin, and, spreading rumors he was hunting Sir Lancelot for his crimes against the kingdom and the queen, went off in search of a remedy to break or delay the looming curse. His focuses ultimately turned to the Holy Grail, a relic he had pursued for much of his life that allegedly could forestall aging and cure any illness. Meanwhile, back in Camelot, I grew older with my stepsister, Edith, though neither was ever told of Edith's true parentage. Only my mother let on. Her heart only had room for King Arthur and her rightful daughter, and she shunned Edith whenever the moment presented itself."

I could stand it no longer; I had to say something.

"Your father...he was afflicted by the curse as well. Yet he spent all that time searching for a cure...for you?"

The queen nodded.

"I never knew my father in person, but I knew his heart," the queen replied. "You remind me of him, Sir Nicholas. A good man with a bigger heart. Now, let us continue."

Racking my brains for the story details, I said, "The curse tolled terribly on King Arthur and, though he had discovered the secret..."

I hesitated as the scenes resumed, praying it would reveal something.

The dark world around us lightened. We found King Arthur hunched over a table in a dark room. The only light was a candle, which he used while pouring over a book. He gave a shout. A tear came to his eye.

Queen Coralee and I leaned over King Arthur to see what he had found. The text of the book was blurred apart from one sentence. I read it aloud, right as King Arthur did.

"Upon the kingdom isles where time is averse, the fairest magic can break the darkest curse."

My heart dropped. I had been hoping for an illuminating command, a magic spell, or helpful potion. This was more like a fortune cookie.

But King Arthur seemed to know what this meant. He slammed the book shut and hurried to a door. The next moment, we were outside a half-buried library, running to the king's knights. Before he could share his findings, one of the knights came running to him.

"My king," the knight said, kneeling quickly. "Your son, Mordred. He has taken Camelot. He has imprisoned your queen and intends the most savage harm to her. We must make haste."

King Arthur's face went stony. I could see the gears working in his mind, realizing that the curse was coming to bear upon him, working through his illegitimate son of yesteryear.

He held out the piece of paper on which he'd written the verse.

"Take this," he instructed the knight. "Safeguard it. Should I perish during battle, deliver it to Queen Guinevere. No matter what, save my daughter."

The knight took the parchment. Together, King Arthur and his men rode off.

We flew across the world with them until we stood at the edge of Camelot. A great army stood between King Arthur and his castle. Mordred mocked him from the castle turrets.

"No," I gasped.

I knew this historical event. It was the Battle of Camlann, in which King Arthur breathed his last.

"This isn't something you should see," I told Queen Coralee, but she would not turn away.

King Arthur and his knights charged. Mordred's army roared in return. Swords leveled against swords, the air was filled with screams.

We didn't get the chance to see the battle. Instead, the scene faded away and we stood among many fallen soldiers. Queen Guinevere, free from her captors, knelt on the ground, holding her king. He was dead, as was his first son, Mordred. Queen Guinevere let out a terrible, heart-wrenching cry that held an eternity's worth of pain.

It all faded from view, turning dark. The next moment, we were back in the throne room of Camelot's castle. The lights were low. King Arthur lay on a table in the center of the room, wreathed in flowers. Hundreds sobbed as a priest gave blessings.

CHAPTER 33

In the corner, I spotted Princess Coralee and Edith. They were in their teenage years, both crying into one another's shoulders. Two knights watched over them while their mother wept from the throne. One of the knights, I recognized, was the one whom King Arthur had given the slip of paper with the means to break the curse.

Beside me, the adult Queen Coralee began to sob silently. My heart broke for her having to relive this terrible moment.

We'd seen all we needed to, I realized. I had to make this end.

"If only," I said hastily, "King Arthur had sought out the kingdom of Dembroch, so that he and his family would be spared."

Just like that, we were surrounded by white smoke. It lingered a moment and then, we were back in the cavern.

I wavered on my feet. The fire burnt near the entrance. I went to the queen's side. Tears ran hard down her face.

"I'm sorry," I said.

"Don't be," Queen Coralee replied. "I lost my family a very long time ago. Thank you for letting me see them again."

She wiped her eyes. She had a strange, wistful glow about her now.

"I suppose," she said, "you would like to know what happened next."

"You don't need to—" I began.

"Please," the queen said. "It is time someone else knew."

Begrudgingly, not wishing the queen to suffer through any more distressing memories, I agreed.

"Heartbroken by my father's passing," Queen Coralee continued, "my mother Queen Guinevere abandoned her kingdom and joined the nunnery, where she spent the last of her days mourning her fallen king. My sister, Edith, and I were left alone, orphans and heirs to Camelot. Guided by my father's discovery, his knights sought out Dembroch. They searched for many years without any luck, though I never knew of their search. In the meantime, my sister became my surrogate mother, tending and caring for me. It was unfair to her, to grow up all at once and become the guardian adult, but she never let on how difficult it was.

She loved me as much as I loved her. Nothing would separate us, or so we thought.

"A few days before my thirtieth birthday, one of my father's knights requested a private audience with me. Edith insisted on being present. It was then that I discovered the truth: Edith was not my sister, and I was cursed. But the knight had glad tidings to share. He had discovered the strange kingdom called Dembroch where magic flowed and time had stopped. Citizens did not age. And the king of this land—"

"King Richard," I assumed.

"Indeed," the queen replied. "He was willing to welcome me to the kingdom...if I would be his wife." She shook her head, scowling. "I refused, wishing to stay with my sister and live out my remaining days. My father's knights, however, gave me no choice. They had sworn an oath to my father and were bound by duty to keep it. And, truthfully, I think they feared what more damage could be done to their poor kingdom of Camelot should my curse come to bear, too. As such, they stripped me away from Edith, refusing to take her because she was neither cursed nor royalty. By nightfall, I was in a strange land with strange people."

"Your poor sister," I said, though I still didn't think that this revelation excused the witch's actions of late.

"I sought to bring her to the kingdom," the queen revealed, "only to discover that Dembroch had strict rules. It was—and is—a small kingdom with a set population to ensure the proper amounts of food, water, and resources. Any visitors were meant to be the cursed, afflicted, diseased, and helpless, but of chaste heart and decent merit, an old rule established long ago. And so, when I insisted on welcoming my sister and we found and read Edith's watch all those millennia ago, though it showed a future of ailing and suffering, she was deemed unfit to come to the kingdom, and I was forbidden from bringing her. I argued and fought and demanded to see my sister, but it did no good. The rules of Dembroch are fast, and royalty cannot exercise favoritism at the expense of the good of the kingdom."

CHAPTER 33

"You gave up on your sister?" I gaped. No wonder Sorgana was so salty.

The queen looked guilty as sin. Her eyes brimmed with tears again.

"It is a decision I regret every day," she revealed. "And no doubt why my sister despises me so. But I had no say in the matter. My king forbid me from finding her. Dembroch had—has—rules for its people, but also ones for its royalty, as ordained by the mage. No favoring your needs over the kingdom's, spoken decrees must be executed, no deliberate endangerment of the realm... To break any of them was to abolish my royalty, and that of my king's. It did not help that King Richard sought to hide my cursed state from the kingdom's Civium so they would not question his authority or accuse him of bias."

"So, no one knows?" I surmised. "About your curse? About your sister?"

"The Watchmaker knew, but was sworn to secrecy," the queen revealed. "I believe the seer worked it out, but she never said a word. And it lasted that way for millennia. But with the witch's arrival, she spread word through prison bars of a curse on the island. Panic ensued. Civium left in droves, those who knew of my ailment and others who believed me an unfit leader. Truly, though the magic still reigned and time was suspended, my curse was coming to fruition."

She hung her head.

"In that way, the witch...my sister... is right. She claims I use people to preserve myself. And, though I have never done this intentionally, I have indeed done it. My king has fallen, my Civium, my defenders... They have all fallen unknowingly to the curse that surrounds me. The Timeless Kingdom of Dembroch will end not because of the witch or hapless defenders or dead magic...but because of me."

"Tomorrow," I said grimly. "The mage said we had until noon tomorrow. And you were brought to Dembroch right before you turned thirty. After all this time, tomorrow is your birthday."

And this, I realized, must have been the truth of it. Through her father's cursed lineage, Queen Coralee had been doomed to lose her kingdom, people, and royalty by the time she was thirty. Though she had escaped the seemingly unbreakable curse by living in this kingdom of timelessness, the curse had arrived anyway and was unfolding at the hands of the witch, her sister. Within twelve hours, the witch's plot would surely come to fruition, as would the curse. Dembroch would fall and the curse of King Arthur would claim everything his daughter had cherished.

CHAPTER 34

A Curse Unbroken

"We have to end the curse," I said. "Plain and simple. That verse your father found... 'Upon the kingdom isles where time is averse, the fairest magic can break the darkest curse.' We have to find it." I raked my brains, trying to remember if I'd heard or read the phrase anywhere. "Dembroch's lightest magic..."

Queen Coralee shook her head unknowingly.

"Your quest, Sir Nicholas," she interrupted "is to save the kingdom, not me."

There was a moment of silence. I felt my cheeks turn red.

"Actually," I said.

The queen's cheeks reddened too. She had forgotten the specifics of my quest, but now fully remembered them. I was to heal the most broken heart in the kingdom.

"That will not remove the curse," the queen said pointedly.

"How do you know?" I dared. To me, it all felt interconnected. To save the kingdom was to save the queen and vice versa.

The queen's brow furrowed.

"Because," she finally said, her tone curt, "I have been in love before, and it did not break my curse. King Richard was still—" Queen Coralee choked on her words. She took several deep breaths before continuing. "I have lost much, Sir Nicholas. No one can possibly heal that many hurts that even love cannot heal."

"I can," I said before I knew what I was saying.

If possible, my cheeks burnt hotter. My heart started beating faster. We were headed into dangerous waters.

"You care for me?" the queen said, the statement so bold and straightforward I almost died of embarrassment.

"I—"

"Then why," the queen said, her voice once again calm, "did you say what you did in the castle?"

And we were back, full circle. I'd known it was coming, that I would have to explain what I had said. But I didn't want to go down this road. There was too much hurt there, too much bad blood.

"I was just trying to distract the witch," I said.

The queen didn't smile or even blink.

"Even the greatest lie has an ounce of truth in it," she said.

It was my turn to pause and collect my thoughts. Then, unbeckoned and unwanted, it all came spilling out.

"Twenty years," I said. "I wrote to you twenty years ago. Dozens of letters. And you read every single one of them."

"I did," the queen replied.

"And you never answered me," I said. "Instead, you took our titles. You abandoned my friends and I. You abandoned...me."

My heart beat faster—all the cards were on the table now. I might as well have fallen to my knees and held out my heart for her. But, now that I was going, I couldn't stop.

CHAPTER 34

"I loved you," I spat out, anger making the words sharp and dispassionate. "I loved you from the first moment I read your letter, and I didn't even know you."

"You were in love with the idea of me," the queen corrected.

"And you're even better than I ever imagined," I shot back, angry with myself for feeling this way. "You're kind, caring, smart. More than I ever dreamed. Only to find out you got all my letters, every single one. That you read them. And one of them may have been your most prized possession?"

The queen's cheeks flushed too. I'd been right, and it made me angrier, reckless, justified.

"So why?" I begged to know. "Why didn't you say something? Why didn't you respond?"

Queen Coralee stammered.

"Why didn't you call me here to help you!" I shouted. "Just tell me why!"

"From the moment you wrote me, I knew your heart, Sir Nicholas," the queen said, still even tempered. "I could hear the knight within the boy. But what monster would I be to call a young boy into a battle that would cost him his life?"

It was what she'd told me back in the prison, that she'd kept us away to protect us, but I knew there was more to it.

"Tell me the truth!" I pleaded. "Why did you ignore us? Why did you disband us from the defenders?"

"I...," the queen stammered.

"Come on," I begged.

And at last, my wish was granted.

"Because I cared for you, too!" the queen suddenly shouted.

There was a beat of silence. She looked shocked at herself. Her gaze fell to the floor. Then, quietly, timidly, she spoke.

"I loved you," Queen Coralee said, "and I couldn't let myself."

I tried to slow my breathing. My relocated shoulder ached.

"What do you mean?" I asked slowly.

The queen wrung her hands.

"Do you know the worst part of losing someone?" she asked. "Missing them. Every day, every night, you ache for them. To feel them beside you while you sleep. To see their smile or to feel their embrace. I still ache for my love, my king."

My heart sank. I should have known. The queen still loved her king. She was still grieving. Her heart was still broken. And there was no fault in that. Some loves, great loves, last a lifetime and can never be replaced or forgotten. The queen obviously felt this way about her King Richard.

"Love has not been easy for me," the queen admitted. "When I first arrived on Dembroch, I wanted nothing to do with King Richard. Our marriage was an arrangement so I would be spared my curse. Love was the last thing in my heart. I harbored regret and sorrow and anger, but no love for the king or this land. And that was a problem for the king."

The queen started kneading her hands again, rubbing the burn on her fingers.

"You recall that Dembroch's royalty must abide by certain rules? One such rule was a demand that any member of royalty was expected to prove their worth to the flames. Within days of our marriage, I had to touch each tongue. As you may expect, the flame of *caritas* burnt me. I felt no love for my family who had lied to me or my new king who had saved me just to have a queen. King Richard made me hide the burns and paraded me around as his great love. It was a long, difficult marriage at first.

"But, in time, I found it in my heart to love him. It took centuries. I discovered the good man I had married. Manipulative at times, crafty, but good and steadfast. At last, it seemed I had found love...only for him to be taken from me and killed. I became lost and angry. While the kingdom fell into my hands and I struggled to keep it together, I mourned. But then, when I called for Reserves from across the world, who should write to me...but you, Sir Nicholas.

"From your first letter," she continued, "I knew your heart and soul. In every word, I could hear your determination, valor, wisdom beyond your years, a childlike innocence...and how you truly felt. I knew you cared for me. I had them when I was younger, too. Flights of fancy. Fawnings. I believe the term today you use are 'celebrity crushes'. For your character, I allowed you to become a defender, but I did not write back so as not to encourage you. And yet, you kept writing. I witnessed your growing love for my kingdom and my safety. It was heartwarming, and I could see how you were growing. I began to look forward to your letters and, before I knew it, I realized my admiration and interest in you had bloomed into something more. You were no longer a boy, but a young man and your words spoke to my heart in a tender way I hadn't ever heard. Somehow, I had fallen in love with you. And I knew it was wrong. I couldn't love a defender while I still mourned my king, but what had taken centuries to manifest with King Richard had overcome my heart in your words alone. I was conflicted and I realized, deep down, that I could never let you set foot on this island. And so I took your titles. I received one last letter from you, only one, and I never heard from you again."

"It was all I ever wanted," I replied. "Dembroch. To be a knight. To be with you." I paused, trying to collect my thoughts. "Why? Why couldn't I be here? We don't have to...be together, but I could have been your knight."

"My feelings would have still been there," she replied frankly. "Regardless of my conflicted emotions, I am also cursed to lose anyone who serves me or whom I hold dear. By inviting you here, I brought you to a kingdom on the brink of disaster, where you would certainly meet your demise. And what of the curse? By loving you, I sentenced you to death. So I took your knightship. I cast you from the ranks of defenders and struck your name from the records. To protect you. To save you."

"But once we were here, you begged us to stay," I murmured. "Pleaded. Forced us even."

"I was trying to scare you away," she admitted. "When the kingdom's magic died, I thought you were dead as well. My heart broke beyond repair. The kind knight I'd never met but had loved so intimately had died. But then...you were there. Alive. Not well, but alive. I was confused. I knew I had to protect you again, but I couldn't beg you to leave. Not in front of the Civium. It would reveal how I felt. A bias I could not have as queen. So I tried to scare you. I told you of the terrors and monstrous obstacles. Yet, despite my best efforts, the Watchmaker put the fear of the Lord into you and you stayed. Now more than ever, you four, particularly you, are in danger. The curse—"

"You talk about the curse like it has feelings and intentions," I interjected.

The queen screwed up her face. "Yes...and no. It is sentient magic, a cloud hovering over me, manipulating events to complete its purpose. Never overtly or directly, but subtly. You will never see the curse manifested into a physical form, but it will influence events and the people around me. It aligns all to fit its needs. It has even influenced me. In the choices I make, the actions of others. I did my sister wrong and she sought revenge. She sowed fear in my people until the majority fled. I dismantled the defenders to protect you from the curse and protect the kingdom's magic from the witch, but in so doing, undid the magic and returned the flow of time. Don't you see? Dembroch's timelessness was meant to protect me, but my choices have undone it, and the curse approaches unhindered. By next day, the kingdom that has stood for millennia will fall, the island will crumble into the sea, and anyone who has not abandoned me will perish."

"I won't let that happen," I insisted.

"You can't stop it," the queen said miserably. "No one can. I see it more clearly than ever. Freewill is an illusion. The future is immutable. This curse is unstoppable. It has taken everything from me, everyone I love." She inhaled deeply, fighting off more tears. "My father. My mother. My sister. My king. My people. I can't bear to have it take you, too. I...I care for you too much."

At last, the truth. And it wasn't anything like I'd imagined. All these years, I had thought the queen was irritated by me or hated me. But in truth, she had loved me as I had loved her. Hundreds of thousands of miles apart and we'd wanted each other. So much so, that I'd dreamt of finding her every day while she had fought to keep me away so I would not become another victim of her curse. So that I would live.

"No one has ever loved me that much," I whispered.

The queen put a tender hand on my cheek.

"I loved you, Sir Nicholas," she said with all the honesty this world could possibly have. "We have known each other for only a day, but I have known your heart for years. And I cannot have you die for me. That is why I cannot love you now."

My heart swelled. My queen—she loved me, even if she wouldn't let herself. It was as though she were locked in a cage by her curse and did not dare try to escape.

Suddenly, I remembered the words of the mage: "...break the curse, free the sister."

Right there, right in front of me, was the queen, a sister of the witch, trapped by her curse. And that, truly, was my quest. I had to heal her heart and free her from the curse.

"I promise you," I said, my heart beating confidently, "I will break your curse. I will save your kingdom."

"Sir Nicholas, you will not have a choice. The curse cares not about your steadfastness. Even if you do not run and stand by me, you will have your life taken from you by forces you cannot control or stop—"

I looked her in the eye, meaning every word.

"My queen," I said. "I am your knight. Maybe not in title, but in conscience. It is my duty to aid you. It always has been. And it is not your job to protect me. It is mine to protect you. I will save your kingdom and I will not fail. I will not die. No curse will stand in my way. Because I will do it for duty and for honor. And, truly, because I will do it for you so that one day, you can love again without the fear of losing anyone else."

It was a bold promise, but I meant it wholeheartedly.

We were very close. I could see that, in the queen's eyes, she believed every word I said, and she loved me all the more for it. Her tensions and fears melted away. She trusted me. She believed.

Firelight danced off the walls. Beyond the cavern and the shore, the sky lightened as the morning sun neared the horizon. The new light glinted in our eyes, making the queen all the more beautiful. Everything felt like a dream. I wanted nothing more than to wrap her in my arms and kiss her. She wanted the same, I could see it. We burnt like a fever for one another. The sparks between us could have lit the world on fire.

And they weren't just the sparks of chemistry and romance. They were literal sparks coming from both of us. As the queen and I neared one another, ever closer to a kiss, the sparks floated out of the cavern to a stone plinth that had risen from the pebbled shore. On the top of the rock, the sparks ignited, becoming a crimson fire as strong and bright as true love.

The fourth flame of Dembroch's magic was lit. And what was written on the stone? *Caritas* of course. A love deeper than any familial bond or chaste compassion. A selfless, devoted, unending, true love that dared to stand against the coming storm.

CHAPTER 35

Dawn of Dembroch's Last Day

Dawn broke over the isles of Dembroch. It was the kingdom's last day and few were left to see it.

The seer knew this day was the last deep in her bones. She'd foreseen much of this day with her Sight and knew it well. The way the sun shone on the tumultuous waves. How the trees teetered and fell one by one. How the ground quaked more with each passing moment. How she must escape if she was to live. But there was no sign of Lady Jennifer, her escort and savior. Fearing the worst, the seer hastened back into her cottage. She did not want to go without Lady Jennifer, but if she had to...

Deep below the surface of the island, dragons sought their treasure, drawn by the fortissium blade's intoxicating scent. No longer able to smell it in the labyrinthine, interlocking underground caverns, they clawed for the surface and their prize.

Elsewhere, the Dreadnaught prowled the woods, hungry for another snack. It stumbled upon a mob of long dead defenders. They raised their broken swords threateningly, but the Dreadnaught had no interest in eating prey already tainted by decay. The monster belched and scuttled on, smelling a far-off, fresh piece of living meat.

The monster's master, Sorgana, prowled the woods as well. She walked with purpose, wary of coming across any of her foes. She hadn't seen the queen or the last living defenders all evening. With any luck, the defenders had fallen off a cliff or been skewered by her dead puppets. The queen, she knew, would be hers shortly. But what if the defenders were still alive? Well, it was no matter. Her tasks would be completed soon and, whether the defenders were living or dead, they would be unable to stop the witch.

Emily, daughter of the seer, was the youngest of any on the island. She sat on her bed, packed for the journey, awaiting word from her mother.

You didn't have to look too hard at Emily to know she was scared. Like her mother, she had seen glimpses of this day and knew the meaning of these tremors and the way the sun reflected into her room. If only her father had been there to console her. But she knew where he was.

A shadow passed Emily's window. She glanced over and shrieked. A revolting woman, young but of dark demeanor, was peering through her window, staring at her. As Emily watched, the woman melted through the wall and into her room.

"Such a sweet, sweet girl, filled with such dread," the witch simpered. "What terrifies you so? Tell me, my sweet. Or better yet...show me."

The witch dropped a blanket of green light over Emily. The little girl screamed as the dread in her heart, the nightmarish visions from the

Sight, leapt out of her. It was all around her, assaulting her over and over. Her father's death. The desolation of the kingdom. The suffering of the remaining people. Sorgana relished in it as Emily screamed. The room darkened. Blood ran like lightning strikes down the walls.

The door to Emily's room shook in its frame. The seer cried for her daughter, but she could not get in to protect her.

As Emily cried and her mother helplessly tried to reach her, a black spark flew from Sorgana. It hung in the air, circling lazily as it doubled and tripled, creating a ball of dark flurries.

Cackling in delight, the witch snapped her fingers and Emily disappeared. At the same instant, the door finally broke open.

"Where is my daughter?!" the seer cried in horror, her glassy eyes wide, her flyaway hair standing on end.

"She is mine," the witch replied. "An incentive for you to follow my commands."

"Do not—"

"I shan't," the witch promised. "Your daughter will be safe from harm so long as you do as I say."

The seer fell to her knees.

"What? What will you have me do?"

The witch knelt too, locking eyes with the seer.

"I know the fear in your heart," Sorgana crooned. "I have seen it grow each day for the past twenty years. You think to flee, but you hold out hope for a savior, for your dame to escort you. But none of this shall come to pass. Your Sight has shown you the truth. You flee from here on your own. You run."

"What will you have me do!" the seer cried.

"Run!" the witch screamed in reply. "Run without looking back. Run and never return. Abandon your kingdom. Betray your queen. Only when you have fled this land will your daughter be returned to you."

Sorgana took the seer's arm. Green light glowed from between her fingertips.

"You have my word," the witch promised. "When you have left the island, your daughter will appear by your side."

There was a flash of green, binding the words into a promise. At this, the seer burst into tears.

"You know the way," the witch sneered. "Run to the Bridgemaster's home. Lower the bridge across the canyon. The ferry waits at the docks. Go now, before I reconsider."

It was a stalemate, but the seer was mad with heartbreak and fear. She turned and fled. The witch chased her into the woods, shrieking in her ear. She didn't stop until a spark of darkness erupted into thin air. As the seer ran off, crying and begging for forgiveness for her betrayal, the witch watched the dark sparks multiply.

It was Dembroch's last day, she knew, and it was going to be a glorious one.

CHAPTER 36

A *Snuffed Flame*

Queen Coralee and I were a breath apart from each other. The freshly risen sun lit up little flecks of gold in her eyes.

The next instant, my ears picked up strange scrapping sounds, like metal on rock. Then, a gust of wind. Something flapping. Was that...growls?

"Sir Nicholas!" Queen Coralee shouted.

We separated, throwing ourselves against the cavern walls as a hundred dragons came swooping toward us. They shot out of the cavern and into the open air. Not one paid the queen or I any mind. They were after Clay, the Watchmaker, and the fortissium blade, I knew.

"Wish I woke up like that," I said. "Happy birthday, by the way."

The queen didn't reply. I turned to see what was wrong, fearing that not all the dragons had left, only to find her staring at the cavern's exit. I spun around and gasped.

A SNUFFEFD FLAME

Hundreds of golden sparks hung in the air. Their source was a flame between the cave and the waves.

The queen knelt at the black stone plinth and read aloud the inscription she found there.

"*Caritas*," she said, her voice distant. "Love."

We both understood what that meant. From our moment as the sun rose, as we'd dared to dream of a kiss, we'd produced a spark.

I nearly shouted for joy. With the queen's help, I had officially started two of the six flames. My quest must have been completed!

"That's perfect!" I exclaimed. "I just have to take it to—"

"No!" the queen shouted back.

Hand on a dead root hanging from the cavern wall, I paused.

"You cannot," the queen said. "This flame cannot be spread. It should not be. This flame's existence only further binds you to me, just as I feared. When the curse comes to claim you, the flame will surely die and the kingdom's magic will once more be in peril."

"None of that will happen!" I insisted. "The curse won't come to pass! Stay here with the flame. The area around it has timelessness. You won't age. I'll carry the torch to the castle and oust your sister. It will all be okay."

It seemed a pretty solid plan to me, but the queen would not have it. She was a woman of action, and she would not sit idly by while her curse ravaged her kingdom.

"I cannot, Sir Nicholas," she insisted. "I cannot let you risk your life. I shouldn't have let myself fall for your charms. I—I shouldn't love you!"

There was a sharp pop followed by a rancid smell. The flame of *caritas* went out, its plinth cracked clean in two.

"What happened?" the queen asked.

"The SparkSource ran out of fuel," I said begrudgingly.

The queen wrung her hands.

CHAPTER 36

"I'm sorry," she said. "Perhaps it is better this way. I swear to you—if we return the magic to this land, we will seek out the means to break the curse, and we shall see if we belong together. But until then..."

I believed her, I really did, but it hurt. She was doing what she thought was right, keeping me out of harm's way, but all I wanted was to stand by her no matter the danger.

"I can't stay," I said. "We can't restart Dembroch's magic without that flame. And if we can't make a flame of love last, who else could ignite it? Who else on the isles has a broken heart?" I chuffed. "Who else is even on this island?"

The queen listed everyone she knew: "The witch, the Watchmaker, the Bridgemaster, Sir Liliford, Sir Rignot, the four of you, Page Trey and his master, and the seer and her daughter."

I shot her a look.

"The seer has a daughter?"

"Emily," the queen revealed.

I smacked my head. How easily I had forgotten.

"And the seer's name?" I asked. "Is it Sinclair?"

The queen nodded.

"Page Hybore's family," I breathed. "He asked me to save them."

"Lady Jennifer has been aiding the seer in recovering her Sight. She will be safe with your friend."

"But the seer won't accept it," I realized. "The seer didn't want her gift back. I could see it in her eyes. But Page Hybore...he told me something that she needs to know. I need to find her."

"Her cottage is just east of here," the queen replied. "In the woods."

"Come with me," I said.

"I cannot," she replied. "I must go to the castle."

"That's suicide."

"I have run from my curse for far too long, Sir Nicholas. I will stand and face it by doing what I should have done long ago: make amends with my sister."

"You can't go alone," I replied.

We started to argue. My heart broke a little more inside. As badly as I wanted the queen, I could see the handwriting on the wall. We were from different worlds and there was too much in the way for us to truly come together.

Our shouting was loud enough, we didn't hear our intruders until it was too late. One second, we were arguing, and the next, skeletons and corpses were running into the cavern. They surrounded Queen Coralee, dragging her away.

"Run, Sir Nicholas!" she cried.

There was nowhere to go but deeper into the caves. I took off running, a few corpses hot on my tail.

CHAPTER 37

Dragons, Daring, and a Dreadnaught

The ground shook as the Dreadnaught charged toward Clay. In the growing daylight, it looked sickly pale and its orange eyes were narrowed, but it was nonetheless terrifying to behold. A billion watches ticked in its bulging gut.

"Be brave," Clay told himself, hands tightening around the axe. "Be brave."

The monster loomed toward him, slowing down, its tiny black eyes watching suspiciously. Clay stood his ground, though he wanted nothing more than to run. He had to wait just long enough for the—

The dragons of Horror Hollow came sweeping overhead, cawing like ravens in search of their treasure. The Dreadnaught reared, unwilling to surrender its prey to the beasts.

"Now!" Clay shouted, diving behind a tree and out of harm's way.

Beckoned by Clay, the Watchmaker fell from the trees, wielding the black and gold fortissium blade like a spear. The dragons, finally able to see their prize, shot right at him. Before the Dreadnaught knew what had happened, the Watchmaker landed on its ribbed, spiny back. He sunk the sword to the hilt into the monster's flesh, but too deep. He fumbled, unable to get a good enough grip on the handle to pull it out and stab the creature more.

The dragons landed too, biting and chewing and clawing at the Dreadnaught's impenetrable skin.

Shocked by sudden pain it had never known, the Dreadnaught roared. It was an alien howl made of the tick-tock of a billion watches, the guttural screech befitting such a horrid creature, and the shriek of the tiny woman—still very much alive—deep within its body.

Clay jumped out from behind the tree, his heart thudding in his chest.

That scream. It was Jenn's.

The Dreadnaught bellowed again and he heard the scream of Jenn once more. She was indeed deep within the belly of the beast.

As Clay watched, the monstrous slug fell onto its side and began to roll. The Watchmaker jumped aside just in time, but so did many dragons. They collided with one another and the Watchmaker slapped onto the ground. He lay there unmoving, blood running from his nose.

The Dreadnaught scuttled around, snapping at the circling dragons, searching for the Watchmaker.

Clay stood frozen, watching it all unfold. His wife had been eaten alive. The Watchmaker was seconds away from being smashed or eaten. And he was helpless to save either one.

What could he do? he thought in a panic. He wanted to be bold, but he could not possibly face the dragons and the Dreadnaught.

But, he realized with a start, if he would not be brave for his wife and his new friend, what would he be brave for? And what better motivation to hold in his heart to fight this fight?

Courage of old flooded Clay. He ditched the unwieldy axe, took a run, and leapt onto the Dreadnaught's spiked tail. Gripping the ridged white skin and spikes, he pulled himself up the monster's back.

Distracted by this new threat, the Dreadnaught reared its head, reaching to bite at Clay. All the while, the dragons circled the Dreadnaught, breathing fire on its back and digging for the fortissium blade.

Clay climbed until he made it to the sword. Only the green jewel of the hilt was visible, protruding an inch above the Dreadnaught's skin. Yellow, pungent blood seeped from the wound. Two large dragons scrapped at the gash, digging for their treasure. Clay gave the beasts a hearty, courageous kick, sending them scampering, and reached for the sword. He felt a jolt of electricity from the sword, but he held fast. In his mind, he summoned the thought of Jenn and how, in his youth, he had fought for her.

He pulled with all his might. The electric shock faded and suddenly, easy as slicing butter, the fortissium blade pulled free from the Dreadnaught's skin. Its black blade glinted in the rising sun.

Clay shouted in surprise. A surge of bravery rushed through him. He swung the sword around and sliced into the Dreadnaught's flesh. The monster screamed and thrashed but couldn't reach him.

Dragons swooped in now, breathing fire at Clay. He did not run, duck, or try to hide. He swung at them, slicing them from the sky. The dragons quickly realized this was a lost battle, and they took to the skies, fleeing to a safe distance.

Clay turned his attention back to the Dreadnaught and drove the sword right into its arched neck. He plunged deep. Yellow blood spurted out, drenching Clay. When he could sink the blade no deeper for fear of losing his hold on it, he shook it side to side.

The Dreadnaught's body suddenly tensed. It let out a sharp cry, then its body sagged. Clay pulled the blade free just as the monster began to fall. He turned and ran down the ridged back, jumping free as the Dreadnaught's body crashed to the ground. Clay spun around, white-knuckling the blade, but the monster remained where it had fallen.

Lights flashed in Clay's eyes. Joy rippled through his body. He felt truly young, having conquered the terrible beast. To his benefit, the creature hadn't fallen on the Watchmaker either. The dragons hovered by the trees, watching Clay with an air of fear and respect.

Clay's heart swelled. He had succeeded. And now, for the dame.

Dragons circling above, Clay ran to the Dreadnaught's underside and sliced deep with the sword. The moment he punctured the monster's stomach, it exploded. A flood of decomposing prey and bodies and watches burst from within, the latter flying at Clay like bullets. He was buried in hundreds and thousands and millions of them—and a whole lot of slime. A second later, Jenn came flying out. She crashed beside Clay. They fought through the watches, wrapping one another into a passionate, slime- and blood-covered kiss.

"Jenn," Clay breathed. "Jenn, I love you."

"I know," she gasped. "And I love you more. I..."

There was so much to say but no way to put it into words. Instead, they kissed again, long and hard and true.

"Oy, you two better not break any of my watches," called the Watchmaker.

Clay and Jenn parted. The Watchmaker stood over them, covered in bruises and his face looking squished. Cheeks red, Clay helped Jenn to her feet—she fell into him before catching her balance due to a deep gash in her leg—and introduced her to the Watchmaker.

"Ah, you're the lass worth starting a fire for," the Watchmaker appraised. "Pleasure meeting you. Let's get that leg cleaned."

Clay gave the Watchmaker a double-take.

"What did you say? A fire?" he murmured.

The Watchmaker pointed toward the Dreadnaught's tail. There, just beyond the creature's corpse and the pile of watches, Clay saw the impossible.

A stone plinth had punctured the ground. The word *gaudium* was carved just below a blazing, sparking fire.

Clay gaped at it. There was no doubt in his mind where the fire had come from, but he still couldn't believe it.

CHAPTER 37

"Joy of a pure and brave heart has returned to the kingdom," the Watchmaker said. "Go, light your torch."

As though in a dream, Clay glided to the plinth. He grabbed a broken Dreadnaught spine from the ground and lowered it to the fire. With a flash of sparks, the flame spread to the spine.

Clay turned back to the Watchmaker and Jenn, holding the spiny torch high. Delight beat strongly in Clay's heart, a feeling he had long forgotten, but one he would never lose again. He had faced his fears and bested them. He had rediscovered his passion and source of joy in the world.

Embracing the moment, he crossed the distance to Jenn and planted a kiss on her that made the Watchmaker groan. He was too busy to look at his pocket watch just then, but Clay would have guessed it ticked backward a full hour.

CHAPTER 38

A Rowboat Return

Meg paddled furiously through the burn in her shoulders and exhaustion of her mind. But she was almost there. She had almost made it back to Dembroch.

Without magic disguising it, the isles were completely visible. At first glance, they appeared as she'd left them. Ryderwyle was masked in a blizzard. Sir Liliford's ferry was still tied to the southern docks. But upon closer inspection, the kingdom was a lot worse for wear. The cliff shores were crumbling, and the waves crashed ferociously into its walls. Winds blazed across the ocean, kicking up dust devils across the island. Trees fell sporadically, thinning the forests. It seemed the land itself was under siege from the elements, deteriorating into the sea.

It's the last day, Meg realized. By noon, unless they succeeded, the island would fall. Literally.

She rowed faster.

"Hold on, Dembroch," she murmured. "I'm coming."

CHAPTER 38

Once through the Bolts of God, much more avoidable when visible, she paddled for the southeast cliffs. There was a narrow inlet between the cliffs and a steep grade by which she could access the Gate Grounds.

After rowing ashore, she climbed the steep path through the cliffs and returned once more to the Gate Grounds. Though its barren land was only punctuated by geothermal formations and dead trees, she knew there was plenty of danger ahead.

The castle drew her eye and brought a smile to her face. She never thought she'd be so glad to be back.

From a nearby fallen tree, she snapped off two dead branches. She held them out, balancing them in her hands so she would feel any movement or pull of an invisible door. Mind set, heart patient, she walked slowly into the Gate Grounds. At least a football field away, encircled by hot springs and a hundred invisible gates, was the magical flame she had started. At the foot of its plinth was her torch.

The prize was before her if she had the patience to get to it.

CHAPTER 39

Which Watch is the Witch's

After cleaning Jenn's wound—"That's a deep one, lass," commented the Watchmaker—and giving the axe back to the Watchmaker—"You're sure you like the sword more than the axe?" he asked Clay—the three of them started digging through the billions of pocket watches covering the ground. Dragons circled above overhead, cawing and shrieking but not attacking.

"You've impressed them, boy," the Watchmaker commented when he glanced up at the sky. "They want the sword, but it's too risky. I'd say they're yours to command now."

Clay chuckled softly. "I'll test that out later."

"Well, eyes down, then. The witch's watch is down here, not up there."

Clay and Jenn did their best to help, though neither really knew what they were looking for. The Watchmaker claimed that, if they had the gift to read a person's watch, they would spot the witch's watch the second they saw the gears.

As they searched, Clay told Jenn about his adventure at Cliffside Tower. He held up the fortissium blade for her to examine.

"What did you call it again?" she asked. When he told her its name, she screwed up her eyes. "That rings a bell."

Clay waited a moment, but Jenn shook her head.

"I lost it," she admitted. "What happened after you got the sword?"

"Fought some dragons. Killed a Dreadnaught. Saved you," Clay finished. "But, hey! Did you find the Sight?"

Jenn pulled two eyeballs from her pocket. Their mirrored surfaces reflected the world around them in millions of splintered views.

"It wasn't easy," she said. "The librarian..."

Clay met her eyes and he saw the truth.

"I'm sorry," he said solemnly.

"I am, too. But he's still in the catacombs. The witch brought all these dead knights and dames back to life. I got away, but then in the woods, the Dreadnaught found me. And ate me. I don't even know how I'm still alive."

"Four stomachs," Clay explained. "The Dreadnaught digests its food slowly. You weren't even close to being digested."

"Closer than you think."

Jenn showed Clay some of the raw spots on her arms and face.

"You should probably wash that off," Clay suggested. "Acid can still burn if you don't get it off your skin. Is your leg alright?"

Jenn nodded. Her pant leg was drenched in blood, but the cut was scabbed over.

"I'll help you find that watch, then I'll be on my way. Maybe find some water on the way to the seer's."

Suddenly, the Watchmaker let out a cry of joy. The airborne dragons shrieked in reply. Clay hurried to his side, anxious to see the witch's watch, but the Watchmaker had found his late wife's and mother's timepieces. Eyes welling with tears, the Watchmaker gripped the two tightly and walked off into the woods.

"He'll need a minute," Clay said.

He met his wife's eyes and, daring to be brave, told her everything he'd meant to say for the last decade or so.

"I've been lost," he admitted. "Ever since Seattle, I've been stuck at my parent's shop, and it's the last place I wanted to be. I couldn't see a way out. I got jaded. Stagnant. I tried to force it, put up a front, fake it until it came back. But it just got worse. I lost my joy for...everything. I loved you still, and I always will, but I just got..."

He didn't know the word, but she did: "Settled."

Clay nodded with a grimace.

"It's not just you," Jenn said. "I'm as much to blame. I get so wrapped up in what's wrong in the world, it's hard to see the good things. Like you. You're the one wonderful thing I have going right now. The seer helped me see that."

Clay understood this in a way he couldn't even explain. For the first time in nearly a decade of marriage, he felt like they were really connecting on a level beyond words.

He pulled her close again, wrapping his hand in hers.

"With all that I am," he said, "unless you want to be rid of me and our marriage to implode—" they chuckled together "—I will never again let you forget how much I love you, and I will never let you go again."

Jenn blushed. They locked lips. It was the first kiss in a long time, and, though slimy, it was full of passion long forgotten. They seemed locked together, two becoming one. Neither of them saw the torch on Clay's back flare brightly and one of its sparks enter their bodies.

A few seconds later—or what felt like a beautiful lifetime to the couple—they parted, but did not fully separate. Clay's hand kept hold of Jenn's tightly. He loosened his grip, but still, his hand stuck to hers.

"Jenn," he said.

"Let go," she replied.

CHAPTER 39

They started to tug, but their hands were impossibly stuck together like two magnets happily conjoined.

"What the heck?" Clay gasped.

He studied their hands. There was no visible adhesive, and he wasn't squeezing tightly. Somehow, someway, his hand was wrapped lightly but immovably around his wife's.

"Hold on," Jenn said. "What did you say before we kissed?"

Clay raked his brains. "Uh, that I'd never let you go?"

Jenn bit her lip. "Oh, no."

"What?"

"Remember what the librarian said?" she said. "'Curses and promises linger...'" She pointed to the flame on his back and the sparks gathering around it. "That's magic. It just sealed your words into a promise. A magic one. You probably won't be able to let go of my hand unless you intentionally break the promise you spoke. Go on, try it."

Clay wasn't so sure about breaking a promise sealed in magic, but he gave it a try. He pulled hard as he could, goading his hand to let go of hers. There was a slight give, and he sensed that if he willed it through every fiber of his being, he would be able to let go, but he knew he shouldn't.

"Well, I guess it's you and me," Clay said.

"Or else," Jenn joked gravely.

Hand in hand, they returned to searching for the witch's watch. At first, being attached to Jenn was a bit awkward to maneuver and sift through the timepieces, but Clay found he liked it. He hadn't felt this close to her since...well, since the day they'd been married.

They turned over hundreds of watches. Clay began to fear he wouldn't know the witch's watch if he came across it. Nevertheless, they searched on.

"Clay...," Jenn said a few minutes later. "This one is...different."

She handed him a watch. It looked like any other and was badly corroded by the monster's stomach acid, but the spinning gears in the back were badly constructed from the start. Teeth did not align. Deep within, a tiny golden gear did not move.

He opened it up. The face of the watch read midnight and the glass was shattered.

"I think this is it," Clay said. In a louder voice, he called, "Found it!"

A grunt issued from far away.

While the Watchmaker walked back, Clay analyzed the watch's gears, willing himself to see some hidden truth, some secret inscription, or a broken gear that resembled a shape.

Deep within was a golden gear that didn't spin and wasn't connected to any other sprocket. The way it shone, it reminded him of the burning, golden feeling of joy in his heart. Its stunning shine was contrasted by the rest of the gears, which had missing teeth and sharp edges.

That bottom gear, Clay remembered, was the one the Watchmaker said often represented initial wills and motivations.

Through some inexplicable, bizarre hunch, Clay thought he grasped what the gear stood for. The witch, he decided, had once had great joy, but something in her life—perhaps whatever the broken gear closest to it symbolized—had removed her from that bliss. The feelings of happiness and joy were now buried deep within, uncultured, untouched, and unfulfilled.

The Watchmaker returned. He had clipped his late wife's and mother's watches to his belt again, strung tighter and closer to him than even the queen's watch.

"Sharp eye, Sir Clayton," he said with a nod. Then, he groaned deeply. "It's been fouled by the belly of the beast. The acids have eaten away at the gears. See anything obvious?"

Feeling stupid, Clay described the small golden gear and what he thought it meant.

"If joy was her original driver, what motivates her now?" asked the Watchmaker, looking impressed.

CHAPTER 39

Clay's eyes were drawn to the topmost gear, a gnarled piece of metal. Though it was badly tarnished, it seemed to be a master gear, driving the gears that still wanted to move.

"This one," Clay said, pointing to the large upper gear.

"What does it look like?" the Watchmaker goaded on. "If that gear were an emotion, what would you call it?"

"Hatred," Clay said, the answer flying to his lips before he understood it. "Corrosive, vengeful hatred." He looked to the Watchmaker. "But why?"

"You've made it as far as I at first glance," the Watchmaker revealed. "To know more will take some time considering its wear."

He gave Clay and Jenn a once over.

"Are you two stuck at the hip for the rest of the journey?" he asked with a tone of annoyance.

"Uh...," Clay stammered. He held up their magically interlocked hands. "We're kinda stuck together."

Jenn explained Clay's verbal promise to love her and never let her go, and the resulting handhold.

"Hmm," the Watchmaker said. "Cursed is the price for a promise denied twice. Just a saying in Dembroch. So what promise did you make exactly?"

They strung together the exact words.

"You're stuck," the Watchmaker said simply. "Forever. You hold hands until you die. If either of you let go, your marriage is cursed."

Jenn groaned.

"It's okay," Clay said. "We just won't let go."

"Easier said than done," the Watchmaker said. "Now, come. Your dame must return the seer's Sight and, if we must be attached to her, we will accompany her while we decipher the gears of the witch's watch."

CHAPTER 40

Seeking the Seer

With dragons still circling above them, Jenn weaved through the trees toward the seer's cottage. She had a bit of a limp from the giant gash in her leg courtesy of the Dreadnaught, and it felt like the scabbed edges were tearing. Thin strands of warm blood trickled down her leg.

Clay lagged behind, hand clamped to hers, studying the witch's watch with the Watchmaker. She thought about asking for a break to fix her leg, or at least stop in a river to wash off the lingering acid all over her skin, but she pressed on. Dembroch was running out of time and she was going to save it. Even if she didn't look amazing in the process.

Apart from how disgusting she felt, and the fact she badly wanted a dab of hand sanitizer, Jenn was overcome with a happiness she had not felt in decades. For the first time in years, she knew she was smiling. Nothing, not the burning ache of her tired body, nor the prospect of the kingdom's imminent doom, could dispel her happy heart. From the battle in the catacombs to the long hours in the Dreadnaught's belly, she had grown and learned much.

She shivered to remember her time in the belly of the beast. She'd been bleeding profusely from the leg and burning all over, crushed by watches and skin and darkness as the Dreadnaught roamed the woods. At least she'd had the good sense to tear her sleeve off and bandage her leg. The bleeding had stopped soon after, though she felt light-headed. Shortly after, unable to find a way out of the monster's gut, she'd fallen into the doldrums of depression. There was no hope of escaping, she knew. She was as good as dead. She had failed.

But then, like a beacon in the darkness, a sword had cut through the Dreadnaught's back, puncturing its stomach. Jenn had shouted, cried, screamed.

How foolish she had been, she had realized. The future was not—had never been—bleak. The worst outcome was *not* the most likely result. The future, truly, was what you made of it. If you believed good could happen and acted as such, it would.

Now, despite all her doubts, she had recovered the seer's Sight, escaped the Dreadnaught, reunited with her husband, and lived to tell the tale. She would continue that way. No matter what happened in the next few hours, she would face it boldly and happily.

They came into a clearing. On the far side was a cottage that looked less like a home and more like an oversized beehive made of dried mud and twigs. There were a few windows and only one door. *Hybore* was carved above it.

They entered the cottage and came to a stop.

"Oh, no," Clay said. "Not again."

The seer's cottage was a disaster, though it looked like it always had been. There were stacks of newspapers from various countries, money from many more, mirrors, and thousands of handdrawn pictures covering whatever wall and floor space was left. But the stacks that were perhaps once organized had been strewn around. Papers and pictures had been shredded to pieces. Dried blood stained every hung drawing, tainting the sketches in unnatural colorings. The red flames of the

Dembroch sigil were now black. Portraits of past knights and dames were smeared red.

But in the middle of it all, crackling atop the strewn stacks of paper, spitting black sparks, was a fire dark as the stained blood on the walls.

Jenn stumbled toward it, not understanding.

"Jenn, this isn't a good idea," Clay warned. "This is what we found at the Bridgemaster's and—"

She ignored him, spotting a familiar-looking folded paper on the ground and retrieving it. When she unfolded it, she gasped.

It was the drawing the seer had shown Jenn earlier: a portrait of Jenn with the Dembroch castle behind her.

"The seer left without me," she breathed.

"Looks more like she was forced," the Watchmaker noted.

"She's headed for the docks," Jenn realized. She looked meaningfully to her husband. "I have to go."

"I'll come with you," he replied, squeezing their connected hands.

"Oy," the Watchmaker interjected, holding up the witch's watch.

"You can't," she said. "You have to read the watch."

"I won't let you go alone," Clay said. "If the witch made the seer run, she could be chasing her or hunting her. It doesn't matter we're stuck together, I wouldn't feel right—"

"Quiet!" the Watchmaker whispered suddenly.

He dragged the two of them into a corner by the door. They heard approaching footsteps, fast, running. The Watchmaker pulled his axe off his back. Clay brandished the fortissium blade.

Someone burst through the door. The Watchmaker swung—

I came sprinting into the cottage.

"Nick!" Jenn shouted.

She lunged just in time, dragging Clay with her, knocking me off my feet. The axe sliced the air where my head had been. I crashed to the ground, Clay and Jenn landing on top of me, all of us gasping for breath. My arm ached in its sling.

"What the devil, boy?" the Watchmaker howled.

CHAPTER 40

We all got to our feet.

"Good to see you again," I groused at the Watchmaker. I smiled at my friends. "Jenn, how're things?"

"A bit bad," Clay said.

"The seer is gone," Jenn explained.

I glanced around the room. The streaks of stained blood reminded me of a lightning storm. My eyes fell on the ball of black flame. It seemed unnatural, unnerving.

"Great," I murmured. "The witch."

"Why are you here?" the Watchmaker asked. "Where's the queen?"

"She was captured," I explained.

He spun his axe in his hand and puffed up his chest.

"She's alright, she's alright," I shouted, calming him. "We can't save her by storming the castle. There's a lot of...dead people walking around."

"Still?" Jenn mumbled.

"The best thing we can do right now is light our torches," I said. "Before it's too late." I glanced at Clay. "Nice job, by the way. Jenn?"

She pulled out two mirrored eyeballs.

"Almost there," she said. "I have to get these to the seer.'

"I have to find her, too," I explained. "She's Page Hybore's husband, the guy who summoned us. I have to talk to her. I think she has to stay for my flame to be lit."

"We'll go together," Jenn said, giving Clay a look.

"Anybody run into Meg?" I asked.

"She ended up in the catacombs with me," Jenn said. "She didn't have any flames, but she was headed back to the Gate Grounds. She needed—"

Jenn gasped suddenly. She pointed to the sword in Clay's hand.

"That sword," she said.

"The fortissium blade?" the Watchmaker asked.

Jenn nodded. "That's why the name rang a bell. Meg was looking for it. Or needed it for something."

"What? How?" Clay asked.

Jenn explained it as quick as she could: Ryderwyle, the storm, the sword.

"Horror Hollow," Clay interrupted. "That's where the fortissium blade was originally. If the sword is returned, maybe it can stop the blizzard."

The Watchmaker let out a sad, wounded sound. It seemed he'd grown fond of the fortissium blade.

"You have to go to Meg," Jenn told Clay. "Nick and I have to find the seer. We have to go our separate ways."

Clay looked pained. "Can't we—"

"There's no time," Jenn said. "Remember, a promise denied twice. When we meet again, we'll stay together. For good."

Clay bit his lip. He could feel the pull between their hands, strong as a magnet, not wanting to be separated. But they had to.

"Okay," he said.

Just like that, their hands tore apart. A bite of pain shot through their fingers. Clay nearly fell but caught himself.

Jenn massaged her hand. There was an angry red mark across her palm.

"Are you okay?" she asked.

Clay nodded, but could already feel a tingling in his hand, a pull toward Jenn.

"Go," he insisted, holding his hand away from her.

We exited the seer's cottage, hesitating before we went our separate ways. The dragons still circled above.

"Good luck," I said to Clay and the Watchmaker.

Careful to avoid touching his hand, Jenn gave her husband a kiss farewell. She smiled, the taste lingering on her lips.

"See you at the castle," she said, and took off running.

I gave my friend and the Watchmaker a sheepish grin and took off after Jenn, holding my aching arm. High above, beyond the dragons, the sun rose higher and higher.

CHAPTER 41

The Queen's Path

Surrounded by her corpse escorts, Queen Coralee arrived at the entrance to her castle. She'd only agreed to come when one of the dead defenders managed to speak, telling her that the witch had an innocent girl in the castle, one whom would be slain if the queen did not come home.

Seeing the fortress, her heart fell—the castle walls and its grand façade had cracks running throughout. Tongues of a black flame poked out of the low windows that ventilated the catacombs. Storm clouds amassed high above, blocking out the midday sun.

An army of cadavers lined the front steps of the castle. A hundred knights and dames from all walks of life—or death—watched her approach. They cleared a path for her to enter the castle.

Slowly, deliberately, she walked across the courtyard, heart heavy. Her kingdom was all but barren of citizens and life, the remaining surely condemned to suffer in the coming hours. The castle—her sanctuary, the stronghold, Dembroch's symbol—was breaking. And all of it, all of this devastation, was because of her. Because of her curse.

Queen Coralee cast her mind like a net into the sea, desperately trying to think of a way to put an end to the destruction, to forestall the doom of Dembroch, and to save those still left on the island.

She could run. Far. She could easily overpower and outrun these dead defenders. But where would she go? She'd never be able to outrun her shame.

She could fight. Storm her castle. Slay the witch. But then where would she be? She would have killed her sister, the last family she had. If she did this, the queen would truly become the monster that her sister had always thought she was. And the curse would still be there. Waiting.

Heart thumping hard in her chest, Queen Coralee thought of her parents. Oh, how she missed them. How she wished she could bend her father's ear for his wisdom. If only she could hug her mother, be filled with compassion and empathy, and go forward with love in her heart.

But her beloved mother and father were in the grave. In the end, her father had fallen to the curse and her mother, burdened with a broken heart, had abandoned her children.

The queen was filled with disappointment and sorrow. For the first time, she felt an inkling of the angst that her sister Edith must have felt. To be abandoned. To know her parents failed.

I must forge my own path, the queen decided. She would not run, she would not fight her way through. She would remedy this terrible situation in her own way and, even if it meant giving up her life, she would not let this curse hurt anyone else. Her kingdom would survive, even if the throne was empty.

CHAPTER 42

A Sharp Sword and Worn Watch

After hundreds of cautious steps and careful probing with the tree branches, Meg made it into the ring of hot springs at the center of the Gate Grounds. The fire of peace still burnt upon its plinth, the torch laying on the ground beside it.

With the torch in her hand once more, she glanced at the castle. All she had to do was deliver it to the Aerary. But her quest wasn't done yet. Not really.

She glanced at Ryderwyle. It was stormier than ever. The mountaintop glittered with ice before it was hidden in clouds again. Page Trey and his master were somewhere on the island. They must be freezing. Meg couldn't just abandon them…

"Meg!"

She spun around to see Clay and the Watchmaker running toward her, about to enter the Gate Grounds. Clay held a black sword above his head. A lit torch hung over his back. And right behind them, like a black cloud chasing them, were hundreds of dragons.

"Wait!" she shouted.

Her voice was so desperate, Clay and the Watchmaker came to a grinding halt. The cloud of dragons gathered above them, watching Clay's every move.

"There are invisible doors everywhere," Meg explained. "I'll come to you!"

Wielding her torch once more, Meg walked slowly through the Gate Grounds. She almost fell into a few moving gates again and even saw the one to Ryderwyle circle past her.

When Clay was beside Meg, he held the sword out to her.

"It's called the fortissium blade," he said. "Jenn told me you were looking for it."

Meg put two-and-two together. The sword before her was the stolen one from Ryderwyle that had set off the blizzard.

"Can you send it to Ryderwyle?" Clay asked.

"I'll hand deliver it," she said.

Clay was at a loss for words. She could see surprise on his face, and knew what he was thinking: she had changed. But she knew the truth. They both had. Clay looked young again. Brave again.

"May I?" she asked.

"Careful with it," the Watchmaker said.

She took the sword from Clay. A shock bit her fingers.

"What—?" she gasped, but her words were drowned out.

Overhead, the host of dragons shrieked in excitement and careened toward Meg.

"Go!" Clay shouted.

Gripping the fortissium blade, Meg turned and ran. She held the torch before her, dodging doors left and right. Dragons descended all around her, shooting fire from their mouths. Invisible doors swallowed fire and fiend alike.

Meg beelined for the Ryderwyle door. It was orbiting the geysers in a lazy loop.

CHAPTER 42

A dragon batted her on the head, its claws drawing blood from her scalp. She almost fell, but caught herself and swung at it with the sword. It clanged off the beast like she'd hit a gong with a hammer.

She kept running. The remaining dragons screamed in her ear, clawed at her clothes.

At the last second, her torch illuminated the door to Ryderwyle. It was headed over another hot spring. She leapt for it and felt the familiar tug of a gate. The next instant, she was gone.

A few minutes later, Clay and the Watchmaker sat in the woods—or what was left of them—at the edge of the Gate Grounds, studying the witch's watch free of distractions and dragons.

Clay still could not decipher the watch. There was too much damage. To his benefit, the Watchmaker had not cracked it either. The watch's gear set was dense and confusing to begin with, not to mention the damage from being inside the Dreadnaught for twenty-some years.

Maybe, Clay thought, he needed more practice. He fished out his own pocket watch and opened it up to see, much to his surprise, that the time read five minutes until midnight.

"Hey," Clay said, nudging the Watchmaker. "I thought lighting that flame made me younger at heart or something."

Intent on the witch's watch, the Watchmaker did not reply.

Maybe it's a combo, Clay considered. His watch wasn't midnight anymore because he *had* reinvigorated his soul and found his joy. But the kingdom was in dire straits and the deadline to save it was imminent. Everyone, even Clay, was in danger, or five minutes from midnight.

Clay turned his watch over, examining the gears. His watch had far less gears than the witch's, perhaps seven in all. The innermost gear was large and, though it made all the other, smaller gears glide rhythmically, it kept spinning out and catching itself.

It's spinning its wheels, Clay considered.

It made sense to him because he, too, had felt this way long ago. Bound by loyalty to his parents, he had abandoned his dream of engineering and worked at the family business. But all the while, he'd felt as though he were spinning his wheels. He'd been waiting for the right chance to leave, then the next, then the next—until he'd been there so long, he'd lost his drive and yearning to do more.

There was a gear just like it, a lumbering gear that could not be goaded to move faster by any of the others. But the remaining gears clicked along at a good pace, working perfectly together. One resembled a heart.

It all suddenly became plain to Clay: these gears represented the most important aspects of his life. They were his love for Jenn, his desire to have a job that he enjoyed. All of these gears ran smoothly because of the innermost, skipping gear, which represented his drive and motivation. It was his joy. It kept spinning out, begging to override his insecurities and doldrums. It yearned to help him love his life and wife more fully. Joy was what made Clay tick.

Clay gaped at his watch. One second, they were just gears. The next second, they were a story. He just knew.

Feeling slightly reckless, Clay turned his attention back to the witch's watch. And it looked completely different. The gears were all the same, but now, he could see what they were. What they meant. What the witch intended.

"Holy moley," Clay said, stirring the Watchmaker. "I think I know what this means."

"What?" the Watchmaker shouted.

Clay was already on his feet.

"Come on!" he shouted.

He took off, the Watchmaker lumbering after. Clay aimed for the castle, flaming torch bouncing on his back, the secrets of the witch on his tongue.

CHAPTER 43

Ryderwyle's Liberation

Several miles to the north and many degrees cooler, Meg weathered the storm. Winter winds and flurries of snow surrounded her like an icy blanket. Her exposed skin was already numb. The flame of her torch danced wildly but didn't extinguish.

A twinge of fear set into her. How was she going to find Page Trey and his master in this weather? Let alone the Horror Hollow.

You'll find them, she reminded herself. *Be patient.*

An idea struck her. She held a magic torch and the sword. Maybe she could make them work together.

She held the sword to the torch. Flames licked its metal. Sparks flew out of the fire, disappearing into the winter wind.

Meg searched her memory. What had the witch done to get her magic to work? Of course, she realized. She had to speak.

"Uh," she murmured, the wind stealing her words. "Stolen sword from Ryderwyle, show me your resting place on this isle."

It felt as though her own body was powering the spell. Her veins ached and her fingertips went numb. She suddenly felt weak. But it wasn't in vain.

At the same instant, her torch flared wildly. There was a burst of sparks, but this time, they didn't fly off with the wind. The glowing specks hovered for a moment and then pushed against the howling gales. They lined up one after another like breadcrumbs on a trail.

Meg didn't need telling twice. She trudged through the snow after the sparks, sure that they were leading her the right way.

Above the roar of the wind, she heard a high shriek. At the last second, she saw a dark shape drop out of the sky. She ducked, narrowly avoiding a burst of fire from a dragon. The beast disappeared into the storm, shrieking madly. A hundred others called back, unseen, but alarmingly loud and angry. Meg pushed on, but the snow was getting too deep. She couldn't run fast enough and she had no idea where she was going.

Suddenly, out of the blizzard, a massive tree appeared, its thick, tangled branches wreathed in snow. The trunk had gaping holes resembling eyes and a fang-toothed mouth. At the foot of the tree, where the roots should have met the snowy ground, was a huge hole. The sparks from Meg's torch disappeared into it.

The Horror Hollow, Meg realized with relief.

There was a swoop of wings behind her. She felt heat. The dragons were hot on her tail.

Meg ran. She crossed the distance to the tree and, as she sensed a dragon right behind her, she dove into the hole after the sparks. She was airborne for a second, then landed hard on stone. She rolled down, bouncing off icy steps, and finally skid to a stop.

Shaking the dizzies away, she took account of her surroundings. She was in a deep, cavernous hole under the tree, the bottom of which held a fifty-foot deep auditorium. Carved benches and steps circled the floor. At the very bottom, tunnels led off to dark nether regions and a car-sized boulder sat on a raised dais. Howling winds and ice chips came from the rock, rushing past Meg. Golden sparks from Meg's torch gathered around the boulder, fighting to stay against the gales.

Meg scrambled to her feet right as the hundreds of dragons shot into the Hollow after her. They circled the base of the tree, wings sweeping hard against the winter storm. One of them spotted Meg and the whole lot of the dragons nose-dived for her.

The race was on. Meg ducked and dived, racing down the icy stairs. The storm pushed against her. Ice chips cut her cheeks. Dragons landed on her, biting and clawing at her hand, tearing her flesh. Her suit jacket lit on fire. She dropped her torch and tore it off, batting the dragons away with the sword that wouldn't harm them.

At last, she reached the bottom, stumbling toward the boulder. Through the snow and ice, she saw a dislodged dial on the rock's face. It had foreign figures written around it and, in the middle, a slit where the sword must go.

Dragons crawling over her like bees on their keeper, Meg lifted the fortissium blade and forced it into the boulder. It sunk in, snug as if she had put it into a sheath. She twisted the sword's hilt, tightening the dial to the boulder and—

There was a blast of heat. It threw Meg off the dais. The dragons scattered from her. Meg skid along the icy ground, slamming into the first step. The heat wave flew past her, instantly thawing the snow and ice. Her numb fingers and toes were warmed instantly.

Overhead, the dragons beelined for the fortissium blade. They collected around the boulder and purred like gigantic, fanged cats, intoxicated by its scent.

Meg got to her feet, nursing her burns and cuts. Assuming her work was done, she collected her still-burning, spark-spewing torch from the ground, walked to the top of the auditorium, crawled out of the tree's roots, and was met by a glorious sight. What had once been a world of white was now turning into a colorful canopy of wildlife. Purple tulips unearthed themselves, pines shrugged off their snow. A towering mountain appeared out of the clouds. Far off in the distance she could see the main island of Dembroch.

Meg breathed a sigh of relief. Ryderwyle had been liberated. The storm was over.

With her exhalation, a single spark issued from her. It drifted away, gracing the top of a black plinth, and it burst into a flame.

Meg shook her head and gaped at it. Carved into the black stone was the word *modestia.* Sparks amassed around the flame, shining orange in the sun.

"What? How?" Meg said to herself.

Deep down, she knew the answer. For the first time since her youth, she'd done something kind and generous for someone other than herself.

About time, she thought to herself with a small burst of pride that, for once, felt well earned. She had to get this flame and her other to the castle, but not without finding Page Trey and his master. But where could they be?

She spun, taking in her new surroundings. The mountain of Ryderwyle soared high above her. The tree of Horror Hollow gaped in the sunlight, still haunting in its own right. To the east and down a steep slope, was a collection of wooden buildings on the shore. It must have been the Combat Encampment, Meg remembered, where the previous defenders had trained. If the combat master had survived the winter storm, he had probably holed up there.

After lighting her new flame with a tree branch, Meg hurried down the slope toward the buildings. She slipped and fell several times, smearing her pants with mud and tearing her shirt.

At last, she made it to the encampment. The buildings surrounded her, their wooden fronts sweating off the ice of a week's winter storm. She shouted for Page Trey. There was no reply. She began kicking down the doors, searching for some sign of life—and that's when she found them.

CHAPTER 43

In the building that seemed to be living quarters, she discovered Page Trey—white as a ghost, with frost in his eyebrows—shivering in the corner by a dying fire. Beside him wrapped in layers of clothes and fabric from cots, was an older, meatier man with several battle scars across his face. The older man, presumably his master, shivered badly.

"Y–y–you came for us," Page Trey said through his shudders.

"Told you your plan was a little shortsighted," Meg said, beaming at them. "Come on, let's warm you up."

Feeling confident, Meg held her torches close, grabbed Page Trey's hand, and thought up a stanza.

"Cold begone with the storm, let these two once more be warm."

The sparks from the torch flared as Meg's entire body was leeched of energy. She saw stars, but fought to hold on.

Some of the sparks disappeared into the bodies of the page and master. A second later, their skin and clothes began to steam. The frost melted from Page Trey's face.

"You have magic?" he gasped.

"Just the right words," Meg said, fighting to hide her sudden exhaustion, indicating the torch in her hands.

"You ought to have thought better," said the master. "You have begun a treacherous path that few can remain on."

"He wields magic himself," Page Trey said.

Meg bit her tongue from the comments coming to her mind and ushered the two men outside into the sun.

"How did you survive?" Meg asked when they were out.

"We train defenders," Page Trey replied, rubbing his arms. "We're stronger stock than most. This is Master Malleator, the combat instructor of the kingdom."

Meg extended a hand to the master, but he did not take it.

"And who are you, liberator of Ryderwyle and magic speaker?" the master asked, his tone harsh, eyeing her torches. "One of the last dames?"

"Excommunicated," Meg said jokingly.

The master did not seem to find this funny. He frowned deeply.

"I will have words with the queen," Master Malleator glowered. "Our order has stood for millennia, and at her hand, we filled our ranks with fools and charlatans. And who should she choose to save our kingdom? The defenders she never saw fit to summon?"

He spat on the ground.

"Master Malleator," Page Trey said, "please. Lady Meghan saved us. And, after she saves the kingdom, the queen intends to exile them."

Meg shot the page a look while the master glared at her.

"Good then," he said. "Until such a time as we prevail and you leave, I shall repay your kindness of saving our lives. How shall we repay you?"

From the corner of her eye, Meg saw rowboats rocking on a treacherous dock.

Master Malleator saw what she was looking at.

"To the queen?" he asked.

"For Dembroch," Meg corrected. "We don't have much time."

Master Malleator considered her for a moment, as though trying to decide what Meg knew, then nodded curtly.

"Then, to Dembroch, we shall escort you."

CHAPTER 44

The Terrible Gift of Sight

Jenn and I ran for all it was worth. The back of her leg started to bleed, but even after I warned her, she kept running. I hurried after, my potbelly jiggling, my sides aching, my slung arm throbbing with my jolting heartbeat.

We raced past falling trees and across trembling ground, across the bridge over Coral Canyon and down the path that cut through the meadows and shriveled vineyards. At long last, as the sun rose behind gathering clouds, we huffed and puffed to a stop on the crest of the hill overlooking the southern dock and ocean. Down below, the ferry tugged hard against its ties. The seer was a switchback down, face shining with tears.

"Lady Sinclair!" Jenn shouted. "Wait!"

We ran to her. The seer was distraught, covered in tears and stumbling along the path. We held her still. I gasped for breath, hoping the pain in my shoulder and chest would fade.

"Where is your daughter?" Jenn asked.

"Gone," she moaned. "Like her father."

Jenn shot me a horrified look.

"She isn't—"

"She's as good as," the seer cried in distress. "The witch took her. She promised to return her to my side if I left the island. I flee this land and its empty promises to save the last of my family." She grabbed onto Jenn. "And bless you, dear child. You have come as I Saw you would. You shall take me to safer shores. To reunite me with Emily."

"Please," Jenn breathed. "You can't go. Not yet." From her pocket, she pulled the mirrored Sight talismans. "I found them. We have to look. Just one more time. Like I promised. We'll find your daughter and save her. We will save your home."

The seer shook her head obstinately.

"There is no way to change what is coming," she bemoaned. "Dembroch is—"

Jenn refused to believe that anymore.

"I've been where you are," she interjected. "I know the pain you feel deep inside. The bleakness. The despair. The overwhelming knowledge that you and the world around you is doomed no matter what you do. But you can't listen to that. You can't let it stop you from striving to fix it. If you don't try, the war is already lost."

The seer stammered incoherently.

"The future is scary, we both know that," Jenn said. "But we can't let uncertainty and fear of the future dictate our actions of the present. What you saw about the castle falling, the sky going dark... It's terrifying. But we can't let that possibility influence how we act. We must press on. The only way to make a brighter tomorrow is to build a better foundation today. So I won't back down. I will save your daughter, even if the castle falls on me in the process. At least then she will be free. We all will be. If we die today, we'll die ourselves."

True realization, heartfelt understanding, crossed the seer's face. Jenn felt a swell of pride. In all her years of psychiatry, she had never seen her words have such an impact. And now, Jenn knew, to fully convince the seer, she had to talk to someone else.

Jenn looked to me, a fire in her eyes I hadn't seen in decades, and nodded. I realized it was my time.

"Your husband," I said. "Page Hybore. I was with him when he passed."

"I know," the seer said wretchedly.

"That wasn't the end for him," I said, sensing that she had seen the page's first death before I resuscitated him. "I brought him back, just for a moment. His last wish was for me to find you and your daughter and remind you both just how much he loved you. That he did it all for you." I tried to remember his exact words. "He wanted you to find the safest shores where..."

My voice drifted off. I couldn't remember what else he'd said, but it didn't matter. The seer knew. She had covered her mouth, choking on tears.

"He always said..." After a few sobs, she tried again. "He always said that the safest shores were—" She was raked with joyful tears. "Whether a summer's day or winter's night, he swore Dembroch was the best place to be. If the flames are burning, there is good in the kingdom." She hung her head. "When the fires were flickering, I looked to the future and saw despair, but my page...he kept his eyes on the light. As the realm slipped into chaos over the decades, he conferred with the mage and learned of the defenders who would have a chance to save us all. Though it was not his station, he discovered the identities of you four, stole your watches, and prepared to summon you. And he knew that in doing it, he would die. He wasn't well before time stopped, you see. But he was going anyway."

The seer touched her lips where surely she and her husband had parted a week ago.

"Right before he left," she said, "the witch captured him, bewitched him, and forced him to deliver you. How ironic it was, that he was forced to do the very thing he intended to do from the beginning."

"The witch never had a true hold on him," I said. "In the end, when he broke out of the enchantment, he was so strong, so determined. He knew what he was doing and he didn't regret it."

The seer wiped her tears away.

"He got what he wanted in the end," she said with a wistful smile. "He found the defenders that Dembroch needed." She looked between us with newfound admiration. "This is the moment I saw. The grasses, the wind, the island dying all around us. And you, Lady Jennifer and Sir Nicholas, standing here, helping me find safety. I thought you would be taking me away from Dembroch, but I can see it now...you are bringing me back. To the kingdom I love. To my daughter. To the safest shores."

The seer touched Jenn's cheek affectionately, surely seeing the face she had drawn in her sketch.

"You truly are a dame and a lady," the seer said. "And you, Sir Nicholas. You have a love for this land and its people and its queen that has healed your heart. I need no Sight to see that, within both of you, are the sparks of flames, the Fruits of the Spirit. As God gave these gifts to us, you have rekindled them within yourselves and brought them once more to our kingdom. Your hearts overflow with those powerful, invisible truest traits. Goodness, patience, peace, joy, generosity, faithfulness, and, the greatest of all, love." The seer beamed at us. "And rightly so. The safest shores are restored by the fairest magic this world will ever know."

I shook my head, not sure I'd heard correctly.

"What?"

"My faith is restored," the seer said courageously. "Dembroch may fall this day, but it will not be without a fight. Not before I hold my daughter in my arms one more time. Page Hybore will smile upon us, whether we reunite this day or another."

"No, before that," I said. "The safest shores..."

The seer gave me a coy smile. "It is what my dear page told you before he passed. He said it to me for years as I slipped into despair, but not until today do I see he was right. The safest shores, he said, were the ones upon which the fairest magic burns forevermore."

My words caught in my throat. It was too much to process.

"I... I need a minute," I stammered.

"Nick?" Jenn asked.

"Just give me a minute," I said, wandering away from them, my mind spinning.

As I walked off, Jenn turned back to the seer. She held out the eyeballs once more. The seer hesitated.

"The Sight is a terrible and wonderful gift," the seer said. "I cannot bear it alone. But if you will join me, Lady Jennifer, I shall See once more."

"As you wish," Jenn replied without batting an eye.

The seer took one of the mirrored spheres in her hand and held it in an open palm. Jenn did the same.

"We shall See, we shall See," the seer chanted, "what shall be, let it be."

The eyeballs sunk into their hands. There was a flash through Jenn's sight and she started to shake. She stumbled, dizzy, blinking hard. Her eyesight seemed to vibrate. In her palm, a mirrored eyeball swiveled to and fro. The one in the seer's hand did the same.

"Relax," the seer told her. "Breathe."

Jenn took deep breaths, trying to understand what she was seeing. The world shook around her, auras of color oozing from every blade of grass and mote of dirt. When she looked at the seer, the woman's body tripled, creating three seers—one moving backward, one standing still, and one moving back up the hill.

"Give me your hand," the seer said. "I will guide you."

They linked hands and, together, their vision cleared. Jenn blinked furiously, but it was much easier to see. The world around her still seemed to vibrate and bleed multiple colors, but it was subtler and more controlled, a faint image she could overlook if she focused.

"Look to the docks," the seer commanded.

When she did, Jenn saw the ferry tugging against its moorings. But now there were two other boats. One crashed into the dock, splintering the wood, rupturing the boat's hull, and it sunk out of sight. The other ghost of the ferry pulled free of its ties and, manned by an unseen captain, cruised out into open water.

"Do you see it?" the seer asked. "Their immediate past, present, and foreseeable future. The ferry left unattended will crash. Guided properly, it shall sail away from the dock. But it currently floats, waiting."

"I understand," Jenn breathed.

"You are strong, Lady Jennifer," the seer said admiringly. "Perhaps with you, I can look upon the castle once more and face the dark future ahead."

They turned to face the castle and, together, they saw the future that had so terrified the seer.

The castle of Dembroch stood in the middle of the island, solid and immovable, a crown upon the land, the immutable sigil of the kingdom. But as they watched, its future unfolded.

The sky above darkened. Red lightning spiderwebbed across the sky and began to strike the castle. Chunks of stone and rock were blasted from the fortress. A thousand more bolts hit it and then, suddenly, terribly, the tallest tower collapsed. At the same time, the isles of Dembroch seemed to sink in upon itself like a black hole had formed underneath it. The castle fell, Dembroch was devoured...

The vision ended, and Jenn could see no further. She looked again, willing the Sight to show her the future, but when the castle fell, the vision stopped.

"The future," the seer lamented. "It has not changed."

The images took Jenn's breath away, but she could not abandon her cause. Not now. Not after all she'd learned. She had to run toward it.

"We can change it," Jenn said.

"If anyone can, I believe it is you," said the seer.

"Come with me," Jenn said.

CHAPTER 44

The seer looked terrified of the idea.

"Together," Jenn said.

Impossibly, the seer nodded.

"Together," she said.

They set off for the castle, a veritable force to be reckoned with, and nearly fell over walking into a black plinth bearing a golden flame.

As Jenn had seen the irrefutable vision of the castle crumbling before her yet still decided to face it and, against all odds, change it, a magical spark had come from her. Her obstinance and determination in the face of fate was a hope, a goodness, that Dembroch had forgotten some twenty years ago.

The fire from the spark stood before her now, the tongues flickering wildly. In the stone, written plainly for Jenn to see, was the word *bonitas*. She knew without understanding that this flame was fueled by goodness. Not just the benevolence of men and women, but the belief that there was goodness in the world, if you were brave enough to hope for it and bold enough to get a little dirty and fight for it.

CHAPTER 45

The Final Flame

While Jenn peeked into the future and started her magical flame, I stumbled across the barren foothills of Dembroch. My brain exploded like fireworks from everything the seer had said.

"The fairest magic forevermore," I repeated to myself.

According to the seer and Page Hybore, the shores of Dembroch were safest because it had the fairest magic. And that magic? It was the truest traits of a defender, the very qualities my friends and I were exemplifying to spark six fires.

My mind reeled. The flames of our quests were the way to break the queen's curse.

"...restore the safest shores," the mage had instructed me. I'd had the answer all along. Page Hybore had whispered it in my ear—though I'd misheard him—the queen's story had pointed me in the right direction, and the seer had revealed it for me to see fully.

CHAPTER 45

Suddenly, the way forward was clear. I had to relight my second flame. Not just to save this island, but to save the queen and whatever future we may have together. All I had to do was finish my quest: to mend the most broken heart of the kingdom. And at last, I knew exactly who it was.

The mage was quite the trickster, I thought with a laugh. All this time, I'd been racing after the queen. But hers had never been the most broken heart of the kingdom, nor had it been the seer's. It had been mine. The last twenty years had extinguished any love in my heart. I'd grown immune to it, uninterested, jaded even. It had taken finding out the truth from the queen to stir it, as a poker stokes the embers, but the seer had reminded me what love—true love—looked like. She had reminded me what Page Hybore had done for my friends and I.

The page had changed my life, I realized. He'd meant to, even if the witch had bewitched him in the process. And even now, in his death, through his wife, he had changed my heart. He had shown me love for something greater, and I felt it within me now. My broken heart was healing with a deep love for the kingdom I served, the people here, and the queen I could save.

Thinking of her, that spark rekindled within me. It came shooting out of my chest, a tiny speck of golden light. At my feet, the dead grass and sands shifted. A black rock rose from the ground, pyramidal in shape. My spark landed on the flat top and burst into flames. The word *caritas* carved into the rock.

I whopped with excitement. The flame of love had been lit once more.

From the grass, I pulled a piece of wooden framing for the vineyards. I lit it from the flame. It sparked like a welding torch.

I turned back toward Jenn. She was several hills away, holding a torch as well.

I cried for joy. She called back.

"Look!" the seer exclaimed, pointing.

I turned. Over the fallen woods to the east, I could see a pinprick of flame headed toward the castle. And further north, Ryderwyle was free of its winter blizzard. Dual pinpricks of light were floating in the waters, approaching the main island of Dembroch.

Meg and Clay had succeeded. They had three flames. Jenn and I had two right now, and I had another that I'd started in the castle's courtyard. All six of the truest traits had returned to the kingdom of Dembroch.

Though we were miles apart from each other, our hearts beat as one. We who had first destroyed the magic and doomed the kingdom were spreading new magic across the land. All that was left was to take the flames to the castle's Aerary, then timelessness would return to the land, the witch would be powerless to achieve her vengeance, the kingdom would be saved, and the queen's curse would be broken—

My brain came to a screeching halt. Something seemed off.

Six magic flames of the fairest magic had burnt once before on Dembroch and within the castle. Queen Coralee's curse hadn't been broken then, so just transporting the six flames back to the castle wouldn't be enough. There must have been something else required, some different way of making the queen interact with the flames.

Whatever the solution may be, I decided, my friends and I would riddle it out when the time came. But time was of the essence and we'd never been closer to achieving our goal.

Holding my torch high, love in my heart, I began the journey back to the castle and my queen. Jenn and the seer followed. Meg and Clay traveled from the north and east.

I was struck with the odd notion that we were all converging for a birthday party for the queen. The thought would have made me laugh had the circumstances not been so dire. Because high above us all, the clouds were darkening to black. Flickers of red lightning flashed. It was almost noon and, indeed, nearly the hour of the queen's thirtieth birthday.

PART 3

The Queen's Birthday

CHAPTER 46

What the Witch Did

Dead defenders escorted Queen Coralee to the castle throne room. Emily, daughter of Page Hybore and Lady Sinclair, was huddled in the corner, trapped by a wall of swords. Upon the throne was the witch. She was absolutely glowing.

"Release her," the queen demanded upon seeing the girl. "Lady Emily has no part in this, Edith."

The witch cackled. It was a high, shrill laugh.

"Inducement to ensure your arrival and your seer's departure," the witch sneered. She flicked her wrist at the dead defenders. "Take her to the Aerary. When we've had our fun, we'll cast her to the catacombs and let her rot like her father."

Emily was dragged kicking and screaming from the hall. Queen Coralee glowered at the witch.

"You would doom an innocent child to death?" she spat.

CHAPTER 46

"Be lucky I did not eat her," the witch crooned. "Though it would be for sport, not for longevity. Absorbing youth from humans is not so easy. It has been quite painstaking to arrange all of this."

"Stop now," Queen Coralee begged. "Please, Edith."

The witch raised an eyebrow. With a snap of her fingers, the defenders released the queen. Unhindered, she approached the throne slowly, stopping at the foot of the steps.

"My sister," she said, pouring every ounce of honesty that she could into her words. "I am sorry. I searched for you, but could not bring you here. I spoke for you, but was deterred. I gave up and left you to face the cruel world by yourself. And for that, I am truly sorry. As I ask for your forgiveness, I hope you accept mine. I forgive you for the lives lost, the terror spread. For my husband's death. And as I have made you pay, I know I must. Though no penance shall ever absolve my sins, I willfully surrender to you. Take my throne. Take my life. The kingdom of Dembroch is yours, if you should have it. All that I ask is that you spare the people still on this island. They have suffered enough. Let them leave in peace. Let Dembroch live on."

Fast as a cobra striking its prey, the witch swept down the steps to the queen and slapped her to the floor. She laughed at her sister. A blast of rancid breath assaulted the queen's nose, her ears rang.

"You think I want your kingdom?" the witch crooned. "Your *throne*? You think I killed your king for it? Oh, little sister, you know nothing."

The witch took the queen's hands, squeezing unmercifully tight, and led her out of the throne room. Through the corridors they went, the dead knights and dames trailing, all the way to the upper balcony of the tallest tower. For a moment, the queen thought she would be thrown over, but the witch stopped right at the edge.

"This is where we stood just a week ago," the witch simpered. "Look how far your kingdom has fallen, my *queen*. How much it has suffered. Just as I did not kill your wretched husband, I have not killed your kingdom. Your defenders have done that. You have done that. Your *curse* has done that. But I have done something more. There is beauty amongst the chaos. Look closely. Do you see it?"

Queen Coralee had already spotted it. Scattered around the castle—bursting from the Bridgemaster's home, from the shores of Whittlesea, from the seer's cottage, licking the fallen timber in the middle of the forest, and peeking out of a lower castle windows from the catacombs—were five black flames. They burnt wildly, spitting black sparks thick as gnats.

"What have you done?" the queen breathed.

The witch cackled again.

"While your daft defenders were wandering about trying to restart the kingdom's magic with the dalliances of children and fools, I created some magic of my own." She pointed to the fire below them, its black tongues poking out of the catacombs. "That one was started by showing your librarian how futile his actions had been. What woe he felt before I snapped his neck. And I started another by butchering the Bridgemaster while he still breathed. What cruelty! And the flame on the far island? I stalked your ferryman across the land, strung him up, and left him for the Gangrene. How he cried for mercy, how he cursed my wickedness. And the flame in the seer's home? The other in the woods? I showed the girl her worst nightmares and filled her with dread, then I convinced her mother to leave Dembroch forever. Five flames of licentiousness, of the darkest traits. Of misery and cruelty and wickedness, dread and treachery. And, though I took some small part in their creation, they truly came to be thanks to the people of your kingdom and how far their hearts could fall."

"How dare you!" the queen cried.

"There's no use lamenting it now," the witch sneered. "Your Civium are dead or gone. They're actions have spurred on their kingdom's destruction. Look upon your kingdom with pride, my queen. It was so easily manipulated. All five of these flames are the antithesis of everything your realm stands for."

CHAPTER 46

"Why?" the queen screamed, at a complete loss. "Why do you work so ardently to destroy this kingdom and create such evil? Take the throne! Take it and harm us no more!"

"I don't want your kingdom, your isles, or your thrones," the witch spat. "I told you from the beginning. It's all for you."

The queen frowned.

"For abandoning you?" she asked. "For the cold ignorance you believed I held in my heart for you, my own sister?"

The witch laughed a cruel little giggle.

"Oh, my sweet, simple sister," Sorgana sighed. "Have you not figured it out? All of this, the roots of sin spreading through your kingdom, the fires no one can quench, the spilled blood. It is to take back what could never be replaced."

The queen didn't understand.

"I gave my life for you," the witch spat. "I gave up my youth to help you all those years after your parents died."

"They were your parents too," Queen Coralee argued.

"They were my kidnappers, and I their hostage," spat back the witch. "And I wasted away my life raising their daughter. And what did I get for my years of servitude? What thanks did I receive? You left me. You disappeared. And I, an adopted orphan, was removed from Camelot. Only then did I begin the hunt for my true parents and discover that I, the daughter of Morgan Le Fay, had no obligation to love my dead father King Arthur or miss my sister. All those years, I'd spent my time fawning for the family I didn't even belong to. The family that left me. But now, I know who I should have been. Who I will be. Here and now, I have the chance to reclaim my youth from its thief and, when young again, live the life I never led. To be the daughter I never knew I was. When the sun is highest in the sky, sister, and your curse unfolds, I shall take your youth as my own and walk this world as the rightful daughter of Morgan Le Fay—as I was always meant to."

The queen's heart fell. Her sister was truly beyond reason.

"Five flames have been lit," the witch mused. "Only one remains. A flame of utmost hatred. Of murderous intent. And what deeper hate, what more treacherous intent, is there than killing your own sister."

A single spark, dark and foreboding, flew from the witch. It hung in the air, multiplying.

Flickers of light caught the witch's eye. She glanced over the balcony.

"Oh, what a surprise," she simpered. "There they are."

Golden flames raced across the kingdom, beelining for the castle.

"Your defenders have lit their flames," the witch spat. "But it is for naught. There will be no Aerary for them to spread the magic to. No castle to protect. No queen to save. They will only find a fallen castle and your corpse. Sir Nicholas will see your body and his heart will break beyond repair...and he shall be mine forever."

"No!" Queen Coralee cried.

The witch began to speak an incantation, a terrible one about walls and fire, to keep out intruders while she fulfilled her heart's desire. In reply, dark flames rose around the castle. Red lightning crackled across the sky. Thunder boomed ominously.

"Happy thirtieth birthday, my sister," the witch said. "My gift to you is the end of your precious kingdom. The end of Dembroch."

CHAPTER 47

Flames and Friends

Right as Clay and the Watchmaker arrived at the entrance to the castle, black flames encircled the fortress. They scrambled back, the tongues hot in their face.

Jenn, the seer, and I came running to them from the west. We shouted in delight at seeing one another. Jenn and Clay reunited with a passionate kiss. I watched enviously, thinking of the queen.

But Jenn and Clay had forgotten something. Their hands started to slide toward each other and then, before they realized what was happening, their hands clasped firmly together.

"Shoot," Clay said.

He started to pull away, but Jenn stopped him. There was something different about their handhold now. They weren't forcefully stuck together as though by magnetic forces. Now they were only tenuously connected. It felt as though they were holding hands like any other couple. But this time, to simply let go would turn Clay's promise into a curse. Neither wanted to know what that would mean for their rekindled relationship.

"Don't let go," Jenn said.

They nodded to one another, a promise made in silence.

"What do we do about this?" I asked, gesturing at the wall of black flames.

"Can't walk through it, that's for sure," the Watchmaker grumbled, rubbing his singed beard.

"How will we get to my daughter?" the seer bemoaned.

"Your daughter is in there?" the Watchmaker shouted.

As the seer and I explained to Clay and the Watchmaker, Jenn dared to look at the flames and the castle beyond. As she did, she glimpsed the future once more—fracturing stone, the red lightning, the crumbling castle, the black flames growing stronger, the swaying tower. She willed the Sight to keep looking as she peered up at the tallest tower. A group of people appeared there, ghosts of the future. She recognized herself, Meg, the queen... For an instant, she thought she saw Clay, but the world around him fractured. Half of him disappeared as though he was both on the balcony and not.

A bolt of fear ran through Jenn. Whatever future they were headed to, it led to the upper balcony, and Clay might make it, and he might not.

"Let's give this a try," I said, breaking Jenn's thoughts.

I leveled my torch at the wall of flame and pressed forward. The orange and black spat at one another, neither snuffing out the other. My torch started to get hot, followed by my hands and face. Finally, I backed off. There would be no getting through this wall.

Just then, Meg arrived. She bore two torches and had two people with her: Page Trey and Master Malleator.

"Combat extraordinaire," she said as she introduced the master.

"Good to see you again," the Watchmaker said warmly, clapping Master Malleator hard on the back. "Thought you'd be a snowman next I saw you."

CHAPTER 47

Master Malleator glanced at the wall of flames.

"What has our queen wrought, Watchmaker?" he lamented. "Did I not warn you all of crowning a foreigner."

"That you did," the Watchmaker grumbled back. "And I ignored you then. Keep up that talk, and you'll wish we'd left you on Ryderwyle a while longer."

Meanwhile, Meg eyed my slung arm.

"You alright, Nick?" she asked. When I nodded, she gestured at the wall of flames. "Any way through this?"

"Just tried a torch," I explained. "No go."

"Should have held onto the fortissium blade a little longer," she mumbled. She glanced at the wall again, and a spark seemed to light in her eyes. A verse formed on her lips.

"Lady Meghan," Page Trey said warningly. "It wouldn't advise it."

Meg looked hurt.

"What?" she asked. "It's worth a shot."

"Magic is a strain even under perfect conditions. To try such complicated tasks right now...," Page Trey said. "We need you in the fight, Lady Meghan. Do not expend your talents on this wall. We must do as the mage mused and return all six flames to the castle through safer methods."

Put out, Meg backed away from the wall of fire and glanced over all of our flames.

"I only see five."

I motioned to the castle.

"I have another one inside. The queen is in there too."

"And a whole lot of zombies," Jenn said.

"And a witch," Clay added.

"Speaking of the witch," I said, "she's the queen's sister."

Only the seer and Watchmaker seemed unimpressed by this revelation as everyone else gasped. Master Malleator swore curses at his queen.

"She's here to bring about the queen's—" I began.

"Curse," Clay interjected.

"What?" I gawked. "How do you know that?"

He held up a pocket watch. Exposed gears ground noisily. The tick-tock wasn't quite right.

"I read the witch's watch," Clay explained.

"Wait, what curse are we talking about?" Meg interjected.

Clay and I quickly explained that the queen was cursed, and the whole kingdom was in danger as a result.

Only the Watchmaker and seer seemed to know what we were talking about. Master Malleator whispered harshly to Page Trey. He looked pretty angry that the queen had kept such a secret from him.

"You have something to share?" the Watchmaker asked the combat master.

The muscles in Master Malleator's jaw flexed. "Only that this kingdom has been led to ruin by the queen we elected to oversee us. This is why we have rules for royalty, Watchmaker. Rules that must be followed. For the good of Dembroch."

"Saving your queen will be for the good of Dembroch," the Watchmaker replied. "Her curse affects all of us and the island we stand on. We crowned her. She calls Dembroch home. The queen is the land, Master Malleator. You save her or you let Dembroch crumble into the sea."

"Perhaps it would be better to save our own skins," the master shot back. "Head for open water. Let the queen fend for herself. It is her own doing, after all."

The Watchmaker loomed over the combat master.

"Don't test me, Malleator," the Watchmaker said, his voice booming. "You swore a duty to this kingdom, and God as my witness, you'll fulfil it. Or we will make you."

At last, this seemed to kick some sense into Master Malleator. He nodded brusquely and asked Clay to continue.

"Like I said," Clay said, eyeing the master nervously, "the witch was left behind when Queen Coralee was brought here to Dembroch to forestall her curse. After that, Sorgana lost her place in the world. She questioned who she was and everything she had learned. A mentor took her under his wing and helped her find her true ancestry: that she was the rightful daughter of Morgan Le Fay, who had cursed King Arthur and all of his lineage. The witch embraced this, rejected her adoptive family, and taught herself magic in the first steps to be more like her birth mother. With the aid of her mentor, she dedicated herself to extending her life unnaturally and seeking Queen Coralee and Dembroch. Revenge wore heavy on her heart. Her mentor was also the one who told her all about the kingdom and how it worked. That's how she knew to have her Dreadnaught eat the watches, to focus on the flames, to kill the defenders..."

"Well done, boy," the Watchmaker acknowledged.

"Who's this mentor?" Meg asked with a frown.

"I can't tell," Clay said. "He's his own gear, different from the rest, but he didn't follow her to Dembroch and I don't know who he is."

"Doesn't matter right now," I said. "What is the witch planning to do to the queen?"

"To kill her," Clay said simply. "The witch believes that Queen Coralee stole her youth and her chances to be something greater. As she consumed the youth of innocent creatures to remain young all these centuries, the witch wants to absorb Queen Coralee's youth. Then she'll be young again and have a second life to be the daughter of a sorceress in word and deed."

"How?" Meg asked. "How can you steal someone's youth?"

Jenn gaped at us. "Is she going to...eat the queen?"

Clay shook his head. "No. It's more complicated than when she ate the turtles. It takes a spell. A complex one. Her mentor made it."

"What is it?" Meg asked.

Clay shrugged apologetically.

"The watch shows motives, not exact details," the Watchmaker said.

"I think I know," I offered. "Look at the wall of flames in front of us. They're black. And we can't touch it or get too close. And there was black flame just like it in the seer's home. It had black sparks shooting out. It was really similar to—"

"Our flames," Jenn said. Then she gasped. "The witch is making her own flames."

"But they're dark ones," I said.

"Made from the same traits?" Meg asked.

"Murkier," Jenn corrected. "Our actions wouldn't have made these black ones."

"Darker traits," I said, nodding in agreement. "From darker acts. We made ours from peace, joy, patience, and all of that. She spent the last day mentally terrorizing the people left in the kingdom, hurting them and torturing them. She kidnapped the seer's daughter and got the seer to run away."

"She killed the Bridgemaster," Clay interjected.

The seer let out a sad, empathetic groan.

"I think she started one in the catacombs," Jenn said. "After she killed the librarian."

"Exactly," I said. "She made all these flames with acts of hatred, anger, terror... You name it. Six flames of evil magic to corrupt the kingdom and power a spell to suck the youth from the queen."

"How did she make them so fast?" Meg wondered. "It took us every minute of these last two days, and she gets her flames in a few hours?"

"The path of righteousness is narrow and the gate is small," the seer said quietly. "The road to destruction is broad and free of obstacles."

My friends and I exchanged quick glances. Only Jenn seemed to see what the seer meant.

"We can stop it," I said adamantly. "If we can get our flames to the Aerary, it overpowers the witch. It restores the timelessness. It fixes everything. We just have to get there."

"But we can't get into the castle," Clay interjected.

"There has to be a way," Jenn said.

"And we have to do it fast," I added. "The queen's curse hits when she turns thirty."

CHAPTER 47

"She's thirty?" Meg shouted.

I nodded. "That'll happen, like the mage predicted, when the sun is highest in the sky."

"Highest in the dark," Page Trey corrected, casting an eye to the dark clouds. "I'd say we have half an hour at best."

Meg glanced at her wristwatch. "He's right. It's a few minutes past eleven-thirty."

"It's okay," I said, seeing everyone's concern at the tight timetable. "We just have to get inside the castle. Anyone know of a door or underground passage or secret way around the flames?"

Meg's eyes got big.

"I know," she said. "In the Gate Grounds, there are invisible gates. They lead everywhere, all over the island. One of them leads into the catacombs of the castle."

"How do we find it?" I asked.

At this, Meg's shoulders slumped.

"There's too many doors," she said. "A group this size, it'll take us forever to get through there, holding out the flames. Even if I used the magic and made a trail to the door, one of us will fall through the wrong one before we find it."

Page Trey grunted in agreement, thumbing his sword.

"Invisible, you said?" Jenn asked. "I know someone who can see the invisible."

Jenn explained the situation—she and the seer shared the Sight, which allowed them to see the invisible, among other things. When the seer seemed timid, Jenn offered a hand. The seer took it and, after a brief shiver, agreed to help. Clay stared at them for a moment as though expecting the power of the Sight to transfer into his eyes as well, but nothing happened to him.

"We'll find the door, get your daughter, and get you out of there," Jenn promised the seer.

"It won't be easy," Meg said. "There's at least a hundred dead guys left in there."

"I know someone who can help," Clay said, nudging the Watchmaker.

"I'm ready for a fight," the Watchmaker said enthusiastically, flipping his axe in his hand. "There's a knight or two who got on my nerves right before they died."

"You won't be alone in this fight," said Page Trey. "We may not be able to forge you into warriors in such a short time, but we can certainly fight for you."

He glanced at his master. After a pause, Master Malleator nodded.

"I may not agree with the queen or her choices, but I will not let my home and kingdom fall," he said.

From his belt, he pulled a long, sharp sword and held it out to me. Page Trey did the same, wielding daggers and swords for us to use.

I felt a surge of hope. We had weapons, smarts, and some supernatural powers. At the very least, we stood a chance.

CHAPTER 48

What We Signed Up For

Our motley crew, eight strong, headed east for the Gate Grounds, conversing with one another nervously. Page Trey, his master, and the Watchmaker admired each other's weapons.

Limping from the pain in her leg, feeling faint from all the blood loss, Jenn clung to Clay's hand while her other held the seer's. Together, she and the seer shared in the Sight.

Jenn had never seen such strange, wonderful things. All around her, she saw invisible spectrums of color. Her compatriots exuded lights that seemed tied to their emotions. The trees and ground let out quivers of visible energy. And when Jenn looked long enough at something—one of her friends, a tree, her own feet—her sight fractured so that she could see the object's immediate past and future. She saw a tree falling and then regenerating out of rot, Meg racing across the fallen forest with her torch and then barreling into an invisible door, the Watchmaker skewering dragons and then fighting skeletons, her own feet moving backward and then racing forward along the ground. It was maddening and yet beautiful all at once.

Until she looked at her husband.

She'd been avoiding looking at him, for fear that some immediate future would show why he was not atop the tallest tower when it fell, that he had met some gruesome death. But she had to look at him eventually, and there was no better time to face the future than the present.

In the span of a second, Jenn saw Clay's past and future. She saw dragons and the Dreadnaught and the black fortissium blade. She saw him lighting his flame triumphantly, a past so bright it was almost blinding. But then she saw the Aerary. Clay hanging over the edge. Black fire and green magic. Death looming over him, grim and sure. A fracture running through him like a break in a mirror, one half tearing apart and the other disappearing over the edge.

She blinked and it was gone. Her heart was gripped with fear.

"Now you see," the seer said. "The Sight is a gift...and a terrible burden."

Jenn's head spun. Was Clay headed for death? Was it possible to save him? Would the same path lead to victory? But what if the path to save Dembroch was what led to his death? Her heart sank. Was this her fate? To finally stand up to fear of the future only to have it strip away her husband?

Clay caught her looking at him. His face fell with concern.

"What's wrong?" he asked, his voice that same tone it had been for the past twenty years as he'd seen his wife fall beyond the veils of depression and misery while he struggled and failed to help her. She hesitated for a moment, unwilling to tell him, fearing that speaking it aloud would ensure his fate. But this mentality—going alone, bearing the burdens of woe—was what had gotten her into this mess in the first place.

"The Sight," she said. "You...I think you..."

"Get hurt?" Clay offered.

CHAPTER 48

Her silence gave him the answer. He clenched his jaw.

"There may be a way to...protect you," Jenn said, tears forming in her eyes.

Clay gave her a confident smile.

"We'll find a way," he said. He squeezed her hand warmly. "We've found our way back to one another. And if we can do that against all the odds, we can save Dembroch. This future you see. It won't stop us. No promise or curse or falling kingdom will keep us apart. So long as one of us is breathing, Dembroch won't fall. I promise."

The flames on their backs flickered. A spark flew into Clay. His eyes flashed for a moment.

Jenn's heart fell. Clay's words had locked another promise into place, and it seemed to seal his life both to the fate of Dembroch and their ability to maintain contact with one another. It was as the mage had predicted, Jenn realized: Clay walked two paths, two promises, and time would tell which would win out. But Jenn saw the look of resolve on her husband's face and it gave her hope.

However, what Jenn did not know was the resolve upon Clay's face was not obstinance in the face of his fate, but acceptance of it. Having been slave to fear and desolation before Dembroch, Clay understood the death sentence upon him and faced it boldly. If he must die so his wife would live, so that Dembroch would persist, he would lay his life down.

Jenn, Clay, and the seer walked on, their minds marveling over futures and fates, promises and curses, and the witch that could undermine it all.

At the front of the group, I caught up with my sister, Meg. She seemed like a totally different person. The vibe coming off her was relaxed and peaceful, yet determined and vigilant.

"You've changed," Meg said before I could make a comment.

I chuckled. "So have you. You're using magic now?"

She took a deep breath.

"Nick," she started. "I...I just wanted to tell you... I'm sorry. For a lot of stuff, really. I was terrible to you and Jenn and Clay. I just...I forgot myself, you know. A long time ago. It was the only way I could get through back then. I couldn't care, I couldn't depend on anyone. I couldn't be Meghan. I had to be Meg. And seeing you three back at the diner, being here...it was the last place I wanted to be. I just wanted to get away from this place, from these people, from...you."

"What?" I breathed. "But—"

Meg grit her jaw and blinked furiously. "Being your sister was the best days of my life," she said. "We had each other through everything. And we had Dembroch. Until...we didn't." She sighed. "I thought you didn't want me as a sister anymore, that no one wanted me. So I left it all behind and, even when I was with you again in the diner, I refused to let it back in. Then, being on Dembroch...it made me look in the mirror and I didn't like what I saw. What I'd become. I just wanted to run." She sighed heavily. "I don't even know what I was running back to. Work? Structure? The prison I'd built for myself?"

A chill ran down my back. I remembered the mage's quest for me: to free the sister. All this time, I'd been sure it was the queen. But had I been wrong? The most broken heart of the kingdom had been mine, so perhaps the sister I needed to free was...Meg.

"I'm sorry," I said, my voice cracking. "I shouldn't have let you leave like that all those years ago. I let my best friend walk away when you left. And just to wait around in Midvale for nothing. Really...I am sorry."

"It's okay," she replied. "I forgive you. When I was in the Gate Grounds, I realized I was wrong."

"So was I."

"Maybe we both were," she considered. "But I forgive you, Nick."

"And I forgive you," Meg," I replied.

She bumped me in the shoulder and gave a genuine smile.

"Call me Meghan," she said.

CHAPTER 48

I beamed at her. We shared the silence like kindred spirits, brother and sister once more. The prison of Meg seemed to fall away as my sister, Meghan, emerged.

"So this curse," Meghan said. "What is it exactly?"

"By the time she turns thirty-years-old, she's doomed to lose her land, royalty, people, all that. Anyone who aligns with her could die."

Meghan's hand flew to her collar bone, gasping.

"All of us could die? Just by siding with her? Just like that?"

"Yeah."

"The curse just snuffs us out?"

"Not directly," I said, trying to recall what the queen had said. "It comes for us indirectly, ensuring our fates by other means. If it can't get us to abandon her, the curse will have manipulated events to ensure our demise. Blood loss. Dismemberment. You know, the good ol' stuff."

Meghan played with the collar of her shirt, mind on the witch's mark carved into her skin. Her heart raced.

"What about you?" she asked.

"Yup," I said. "Definitely me."

"Because you love her?"

My cheeks burnt, which was answer enough for Meghan.

I gave her a look. "Some quest, huh?"

Meghan chuckled lightly. "Not quite what we signed up for back in Midvale."

I was taken back in a flash to the moment Clay had first shown us the call for defenders on Dembroch. It seemed a million years ago. I'd been so naïve back then. Was I a fool now to think we had a chance of saving the queen and stopping the witch?

Like an old movie reel flashing through my mind, I remembered when the witch had first attacked us, how vulnerable and defenseless we'd been in the face of her magic. Was I not doing the same thing now? Were we not headed toward certain death?

Bolts of fear began to run through me. My courage and commitment faltered, as did the torch on my back.

"Oh, I nearly forgot," Meghan said, interrupting my panic. "Jenn found this in the catacombs. Thought you'd like it."

From her pocket, she pulled out a folded sheet of paper. I recognized it immediately. It was one of the letters I'd written to the queen in my youth. Intuition told me it was the one the witch had used to disguise herself, the one that had been the queen's most prized possession.

I opened the letter and was shocked to see it was the first one I'd ever written to the queen.

Dear Queen Coralee,

Hello. My name is Nicholas Hutchison. I'm very sorry to hear about the death of your husband and king. I've heard time heals all, but loved ones are always in our heart. My friends and I will be thinking of you, and I hope it hurts a little less each day.

As for your kingdom, my friends and I are thankful to be part of the Reserves. It's an honor, and we look forward to serving you someday. Hope you call us soon. You won't regret it. I promise you that my friends and I will help you and make your kingdom safe again. Clay is brave, Jenn is smart, my sister Meghan is a warrior, and I love adventure. But we're so much more than those things. We're best friends and we keep our promises. Whether you need us now or down the road, I promise we'll be there and we'll save your kingdom.

I can't wait to meet you.

Sincerely,
Nick

I smiled, remembering the chaste, loyal feeling in my heart I'd had as I'd written that letter. That burning loyalty had first endeared my queen. It gave me resolve now.

Perhaps my friends and I were headed to death's open arms, I decided. Maybe we were marked to die in our own ways. And if this had been twenty-four hours ago, my friends would have gone running the complete opposite direction. But we were different now. Younger, more resilient. We carried sparks of hope and determination in our hearts and in the torches we carried. Death may have been waiting for us in the castle, but we were going to put up a heck of a fight first.

When we arrived at the Gate Grounds, Meghan described the gateway we were looking for. Hands clasped, Jenn and the seer searched the barren land, guiding us through the invisible doors.

The trek was unmercifully slow—each second seemed to be another minute gone off the clock—but no one fell through a gate and, at last, Jenn and the seer pointed.

"It's there," Jenn said, a note of terror in her voice. Little did we know, looking into this door, she could also see the immediate past and future, full of swords, skeletons, Clay in the Aerary a moment away from death, Meghan screaming helplessly, the queen collapsing, me on the ground dead or dying.

But none of us knew this. All we knew was that there, invisible to our eyes, was the door into the catacombs of the castle.

"We just have to walk right through," Meghan said.

"Okay, once we're in there, it won't take long for the witch to find out," I said. "Watch each other's backs. Get your flames to the Aerary as soon as you can. I'll get my flame from the courtyard and meet you in the Aerary."

"Are you ready?" Jenn asked the seer.

She nodded wistfully. "We'll see."

"Everybody else?" I asked.

"Ready," Clay said, gripping his sword.

"Born ready," Meghan said, swinging the dagger.

"Hurry it on up," the Watchmaker insisted.

"Our blades are sharp, our wits sharper," said Page Trey.

"We've got this, guys," Jenn said.

"For Dembroch," Master Malleator declared.

I nodded.

"For those who came before us and those who will come after us because of what we will do today," I said. "Omnia Aeterno."

"Omnia Aeterno!" they all cried.

Together, we stormed the gate.

CHAPTER 49

The Catacombs Again

We emerged in the enormous underground chamber of the catacombs. I saw a glimpse of broken, overturned coffins, glowing leaves of trees, and dozens of desecrated corpses, but it was all overshadowed by a roaring black flame. It rose high to the rocky ceiling, licking the upper windows. Dark sparks filled the air.

Faces growing hot, we sidled around the flame. We'd hardly made it past when there was a scream from above and a flash of light. Jenn pulled hard on Clay, yanking him back with their locked hands. A blast of green, hard as a boulder, smashed into the ground ahead of him. Coffins were blown to smithereens.

"Run!" a desperate voice cried from high above us.

I glanced up just in time to see another flash of green light. It briefly highlighted the Aerary, a metal platform hanging from the ceiling of the catacombs. And standing up there, flinging blasts of magic at us, was the witch.

"That way!" Meghan shouted, pointing toward the far wall of the catacombs.

We ran for it. I raced past a few coffins and then jumped to the side as the witch's magic disintegrated the ground I'd almost run over. My friends did the same, dodging and jiving around coffins. It was a strange kind of dance.

But before we could get too far, the witch screamed an incantation and the black flame tore through the catacombs, expanding quickly, blocking our way to the far wall and the door out. My friends and I dove for cover behind coffins. Blasts of magic exploded over our heads as the black flames crept closer.

"Whoa!" Meghan shouted.

She had skid in between two coffins, one full of putrid jelly, the other lying upon the half-burnt corpse of an old knight. Her eyes were locked on the corpse, expecting it to rise and attack.

"It's fine," Jenn breathed, hands still tight around the seer's and her husband's. "It's Solomon."

The Dembroch Civium all muttered under their breath, casting suspicious eyes over their shoulders.

"Shouldn't he be alive or something?" Meghan asked.

"He didn't come to life when the witch first cast the spell," Jenn said. "I think we're okay."

"Doesn't matter," the Watchmaker grumbled irritably, wiping sweat from his face. "We're about to be fried."

"My daughter," the seer cried. "She was up there with the witch."

"So was the queen," Page Trey said.

"How do we get there?" I shouted.

"The crest in the Rotunda," Page Trey said. "It's the only way into the Aerary."

"What about getting out of here?" Clay asked.

"That was the only way," Jenn gasped, waving at the wall of flames separating us from the staircase.

I looked up.

CHAPTER 49

"What about the trees?"

There were a half-dozen of them, their glowing leaves reaching high over the catacombs, the thick upper branches offering plenty of protection from the witch's magic. None of them were close to the Aerary, but several of them grew toward the upper windows. That would be our way out.

"We have to climb," I explained. "Through the window, into the courtyard."

"The branches won't hold our weight," the Watchmaker observed.

"We could climb them over the fire and drop down—" I began.

"Too far a drop," Page Trey said.

I exhaled in anger. We were running out of options.

"We have to get through the flame," Jenn said.

"It will burn us alive," Master Malleator said.

"Not if we're dead first," Meghan said.

With great effort, she kicked aside the coffin and tore the armor off Solomon's half-burnt corpse. She threw it over her best she could, creating piecemeal armor. It wasn't a foolproof idea, but it was the best we had. The rest of us dug into the nearby coffins, pulling out spare, leftover pieces of armor until we were all wrapped in chainmail, helmets, and breastplates.

The Watchmaker picked up a coffin and held it in front of him like a shield.

"We'll need a distraction," he said.

Meghan held up Solomon's corpse.

"Got you covered."

Solomon's desecrated corpse launched across the catacombs. The next instant, his body was gone in a shock of green.

I barely had time to watch. I was too busy racing the other way, chasing after my friends and the Watchmaker. We barreled like a freight-train at the expanding wall of black flame. Overhead, I heard the witch shriek after us. I braced myself for pain, prepared to be savaged by the witch's wrath, but at that instant, we ran headlong into the black flames.

Sweat popped onto my forehead. The heat of the flame bore down on me like a hot blanket. My injured shoulder felt it worst. The armor over my body seemed like it was about to melt. I pressed forward, following my friends and the Watchmaker, who bulldozed his way through dismembered bodies and coffins.

My sword, heavy and sharp, fell into the dirt. I tripped, trying to grab it, and lost sight of my companions. Unable to find my sword, I ran in the direction I thought we were headed and bounced off a thick tree trunk. I stumbled, disoriented by the heat and black blaze. My friends were nowhere to be seen. I had no idea which way they'd gone.

There was only one way out. I ran for the tree and scrambled up it. The tree's trunk was knotted and wide, making it easy to scale with one good hand. A few seconds later, I was above the black blaze. I took a deep breath of blessed, cool air. My body felt blistered, but all of my limbs were still attached. The armor over my arms was indeed soft to the touch.

I looked around, trying to figure out where I was. Black flame filled nearly all of the catacombs. Going back to the ground was no longer an option.

"Nick!" Meghan cried.

I spun around to where she'd been calling. The far wall we'd been trying to reach was quite close. A branch above me hung far over the flames and drooped down along the wall. My friends must have been there, wondering where I'd gone.

"I'm coming!" I cried.

Over the flicker of flames, I thought I heard a shout of joy from my friends.

CHAPTER 49

But my voice had also alerted the witch. Blasts of green light flew over my head, causing branches to explode. Glowing leaves fell like snow, losing their light as they tumbled.

I disappeared into the branches, clambering up fast as I could, heart pounding in my throat and my injured shoulder. The witch kept firing away at me, unable to see exactly where I was.

At last, I made it to the drooping branch that would offer me access to the exit of the catacombs, if not a long drop. I peeked out of the branches, looking up at the Aerary, hoping I was concealed. When there was no flash of green, I took off at a run—which was exactly what the witch was waiting for. A lance of green light sliced through the air. The branch was cleaved from the tree. Suddenly I was falling, the black flames reaching up for me. I reached out desperately—my satchel went flying—the tangles of armor on my arm caught a stray branch and snagged. Gravity tugged on me, causing my slung shoulder to scream in protest. I lifted myself back into the tree and, once again sweating, started to climb again. There was only one way out now.

"Go!" I shouted at my friends. "Don't wait for me!"

My friends gave muffled shouts in dissent, but I couldn't hear them. I climbed and climbed. The fire chased after. Green light flared around me. Leaves and branches fell. It was a miracle I wasn't hit. The witch was throwing everything she had at me. It wouldn't be long before she chopped the whole thing down, but all I had to do was reach the top.

I made it unharmed, my shoulder aching. I could see the courtyard through the window. I ran along the tallest branch that could carry me—

And with an arc of green light amongst the black flames, the tree began to fall. It fell toward the window, then steeply away. I leapt for all it was worth—and slammed into the rock wall just below the window. Through some Herculean effort, and surely quite a bit of luck, I managed to wedge myself into the craggy foot and handholds. But I wasn't out of it yet. The fire was rising higher still. It wouldn't be long before it burnt me alive or the witch located me.

I climbed, crying in pain as my shoulder ached, finally reaching the window. I tried to climb through, but my armor was too bulky.

"Foolish boy," I heard the witch croon. "Watch, my queen, as your would-be defender falls to his doom."

I tore armor off me, casting the hot metal to the fire below. With each piece, I became more exposed. I nearly flung my torch off me, but I managed to grab hold, my heart racing.

On the Aerary, the witch raveled her hands and muttered an incantation. The breath caught in my lungs.

But she was too late. I heaved myself once more toward the window and slid out of her sight to the safety of the courtyard.

CHAPTER 50

The Duels of Dembroch's Defenders

Clay led the charge into the library, only to find it empty. Still destroyed, but empty.

They had shed their melted armor in the stairwell. Meghan held a half-burnt satchel close to her. Page Trey was nursing bad burns on his leg that would have warranted a hospital visit.

"Onto the Aerary," Clay instructed. "When we get there, Meghan and Page Trey, you should go help Nick in the courtyard."

They crept through the castle like thieves in the night, but their way was unimpeded until they reached the Rotunda. It took everything Clay had to not gasp in surprise when he peeked around the corner.

Thick as hornets on a nest, hundreds of skeletons and corpses filled the Rotunda. It seemed that every knight and dame who had perished in the name of Dembroch now stood protecting the Aerary for the witch.

Clay motioned for the group to back away. They retreated a few hallways.

"Our flames will give us away if we wait too long," he whispered. "We need a plan."

He was right. The torches were spitting sparks everywhere they went and were gathering thickly around them in the hallway. It would not be long before the glowing sparks traveled into the Rotunda and the corpse knights and dames went in search of their source.

"We need a distraction," Clay said. "Something to take them all by surprise or get them out of there."

Meghan patted the burnt satchel.

"I've got just the thing."

Out in the courtyard, I rolled to my feet just in time to see I wasn't alone.

Necks cracked as heads turned. A couple dozen pairs of eyes locked onto me. Skeletons and corpses of late Dembroch defenders raised their weapons and charged.

I drew my torch—a feeble vineyard strut—with my good arm and knocked the closest assailants back. A skeleton jumped on my back. Its knobby, bony fingers tore at my throat. My shoulder screamed in pain. I dropped my torch, threw the attacking skeleton off, then scooped my torch up again to defend myself.

For a millisecond, I could see the magical flame I'd started the previous day. It was twenty feet away, across the courtyard. Its orange flames danced, obscured by a thick cloud of suspended sparks. The word *fides* flickered in the light of the fire.

I pushed through, fighting for the flame. Once I was near it, though, I realized there was no hope. The dead defenders kept getting back up and fighting. I was a one-armed combatant and I couldn't keep my attackers at bay long enough to find another torch.

CHAPTER 50

One of the grislier corpses caught me while I was distracted. I tripped and slammed into the ground. Swords raced at my face—

The dead knights and dames stood at attention in the Rotunda. Hands gripped their sword hilts, ready to draw and skewer.

There was a strange sliding sound. The dead shuffled around as a worn book, open to its middle, slid across the Rotunda floor and stopped near the middle of the room. A second later, they caught sight of something overhead. A vial full of golden liquid fell out of midair and smashed onto the book. Golden liquid soaked into the pages, waterlogging it.

For a moment, the dead defenders hesitated. This did not seem to be a threat...

There was a war cry from the alcoves around the Rotunda. Clay and Jenn charged out first, hands linked, their free arms hoisting swords.

The skeletons and corpses drew their weapons, surging toward the intruders—right as a wall of white smoke exploded out of the book. A moment later, the Rotunda was filled with the sight of a new location: the mountaintop of Ryderwyle. A tall, muscular dame stood at the center, raising her weapon toward a massive, many-toothed dragon. All around her, creatures of the deep and monsters of the night crawled up the cliffs.

The corpse knights and dames fell into absolute disarray. Their poor, rot-muddled brains couldn't determine true foe from illusion. As they scuttled around the Rotunda, bouncing off walls and columns, they attacked the illusory monsters and dragon, slicing through thin air and cutting one another down.

Attached at the hand, Clay and Jenn ducked and weaved through the skeletons, cutting them down one by one with little effort. Their swords sparked against their foes and cut clean through their rotting limbs. Clay truly had a skill for it, one Jenn suspected he had harbored since his childhood.

The Watchmaker and Master Malleator joined the fray. The combat master was a blur of speed and skill. Lethal as a scorpion, agile as a ninja, he mowed through the skeletons, leaving splintered bone behind. Beside him, the Watchmaker shouted with glee as he swung his axe through the attackers. Bodies and bones scattered like waves crashing over rocks.

The seer lingered in the shadows above it all, watching the chaos unfold. She'd had her part in the fight and dropped the magic. But she was no warrior. She watched the defenders of old and new clash. And all the while, her Sight glimpsed the future. Her daughter falling. The witch victorious. The castle deteriorating upon them all. She wanted to stop it, but didn't dare have the courage to fight.

In the courtyard, I grimaced in the face of a dozen swords screaming through the air at my head. And just then, who should come to my rescue, but Meghan and Page Trey. They intercepted the blows of the dead defenders and knocked my attackers back.

"Up you get!" Page Trey cried, helping me up and giving my hurt shoulder an overly enthusiastic slap. "We'll fend them off. Do your duty."

Propping my one lit torch in the armpit of my injured shoulder, I grabbed a stray skeleton arm off the ground, ran to the plinth, and lowered the limb's fingertips into the flame. With a burst of sparks, the bones lit. The sixth and final magical flame had been transferred.

"Got it!" I shouted.

A dame broke past Meghan and Page Trey. She snatched the freshly lit torch away from me and ran across the courtyard.

"No!" I shouted.

CHAPTER 50

Meghan, Page Trey, and I chased after her, circling the courtyard. We pushed through the attackers until it was just the three of us and the dame.

It began to feel like cat and mouse. The dame couldn't be cornered. I sensed that she was stalling, trying to prolong our efforts as long as possible.

"Hold on," Meghan said. "Let me try something."

I gave her a raised eyebrow, but she ignored me. She held one of her flames close to her mouth and spoke in a soft voice.

"Dead dame dancing, live no more," she said. "Return your bones to where you were before."

There was a burst of sparks from Meghan's torch, but nothing happened to the skeletal dame. Instead, Meghan shouted in pain, grasping at her chest, and stumbled to the ground.

"Meg!" I shouted.

Before I could help her, Meghan had pushed me aside and gotten back to her feet. She looked pale and visibly shaken from the failed effort.

"It is as I told you, Lady Meghan," Page Trey said. "Magic takes much practice and energy. Such an act is beyond most wielders' abilities, least of all a dame who has just begun."

"Right," she mumbled. "I can make a trail of sparks and warm people up. Very useful."

As we talked, the dead dame circled around us, trying to make a run toward the black flames. We shambled in between, blocking her way again.

Beyond, I saw the white smoke filling the castle Rotunda. Clangs of swords were still ringing.

"Take this," I said to Meghan, handing her my vineyard torch. "Get it to the Aerary."

"It's your flame," Meghan retorted. "I can't spread it."

"You can," I insisted, sure of it. "I may have started it, but I know what this flame stands for, and I know it's in your heart as well."

This was clearly beside the point for Meghan.

"I'm not leaving you with her," she said, waving her sword at the dead dame.

"We can get her together," Page Trey said.

There was a sharp cry from the Rotunda of deep pain. It was undoubtedly one of our people.

"Go," I insisted. "I can manage one dame. We have to clear the Rotunda."

They finally obliged, my sister taking my torch.

"Meg," I called after her. "No more magic. Not yet."

"No more dislocated shoulders," she said with a wink and disappeared into the white of the Rotunda.

I turned on the dead dame. My heart thudded painfully, alarmingly, in my chest.

"I'll make you a deal," I said to the corpse. "Hand over the torch and I'll let you live."

The dead dame faked a run to the Rotunda and then spun the other way. I stumbled as she ran into one of the castle's side entrances.

I made chase after her into the castle's maze of corridors. Without that flame, the queen was as good as dead.

Back in the Rotunda, there weren't many dead knights and dames left, but the remaining fighters were the best. Their bodies were the least corrupted and their swordsmanship skills were the most perfected. It didn't help that one of them had kicked the book, turning it several chapters ahead, and changing the surroundings in the Rotunda. The monster-ridden mountaintop of Ryderwyle had transformed into the salt flats of Morgan Le Fay and King Arthur's final battle, making Jenn, Clay, Master Malleator, and the Watchmaker easily visible to the dead defenders.

A group of dames swarmed Jenn. They attacked savagely, taking advantage of her occupied hand. Clay was pulling against her too, busy with his own attackers. Their joined hand tugged back and forth, but Jenn refused to let go. She would rather die than let go of Clay's hand, thereby cursing their marriage, and it looked like death rather fancied her for it.

Across the room, the Watchmaker howled in pain and toppled. A dozen dead defenders surged over him like ants, fingers tearing at his flesh, broken swords raising for killing strokes.

Master Malleator tried to get to him, but he was held off by a few stubborn knights. Clay and Jenn fought their best, but they couldn't bat away their opponents.

Meghan and Page Trey burst onto the scene, Meghan holding three torches and her sword. They saw the unfolding catastrophe and ran to the Watchmaker, but they knew they would not be fast enough.

A savage cry rang through the Rotunda. Everyone looked skyward as Sinclair the seer, pacifist at heart and timid as a mouse, fell from the upper stairs and swept over the Watchmaker's attackers. She was no warrior, but she knocked them all away, plucking eyes from one corpse and throwing them at another with enough force to knock it over. The Watchmaker got back to his feet, pulling the broken swords from his torso and swung them at the corpses.

Invigorated by the seer's action, Jenn managed to dismember and decapitate the dead dames fighting her. She swung around and took out Clay's attackers as well. She kept spinning and spinning and spinning—right into his arms, heart thudding fast, hand still clinging tightly to his.

"I love you," he said.

She couldn't even form the words, her head was spinning so fast. All she could do was smile dreamily and—though it surely wasn't the best time—pull him into a kiss. If possible, her world swung faster.

When they parted, the last dead defender had fallen. The deceased warriors all lay still once more.

"Where's Nick?" Clay asked.

"Trying to get his torch back," Meghan replied. "He'll be here."

"Let's clear his way," Jenn said determinably.

Clay stooped to pick up the book. The second he closed it, the salt flats disappeared. The book twitched in his hands, gold light shining between the pages as the oversaturation of magic fought to be released. He handed it to Meghan who stowed it in her bag. Her hand shook with the effort.

The Rotunda returned into view around them. In the center was a gaping black hole where the castle crest had once been.

"She's waiting for us," Jenn breathed, her eyes dancing with a future only she and the seer could see.

The Watchmaker surveyed the entrance to the Aerary. The wrought iron staircase was just visible, disappearing in the shadows.

"Apologies for the bluntness, my ladies," he grunted, "but my portly figure will not squeeze through such a tight space. I had best keep watch here."

"We shall as well," Master Malleator said. "It will be too tight of confines if we all get into a fight."

Page Trey looked helplessly at Meghan—he had to obey his master, though he wished to fight beside her.

"Ten minutes," he warned, tapping Meghan's watch. "Remember, no magic unless it's the last resort. One more could wipe you out."

Meghan nodded, biting her lip.

"I will join you," the seer whispered. "My daughter will not be alone."

The Watchmaker handed his gigantic axe to Clay.

"She'll hit you the second she sees you," the Watchmaker said. "This won't hold for long, but it'll protect you just long enough."

"You remember what I did with the last weapon you let me use?" Clay said, but the joke was lost in the seriousness of the moment.

"Save our queen," the Watchmaker said. "Save us all."

Clay thanked him again and, holding the axe as a shield, gripping Jenn's hand all the tighter, five torches blazing around him, led his friends into the Aerary.

CHAPTER 51

Firefight

I chased the dead dame into the Rotunda, several stories up. The Watchmaker, Master Malleator, and Page Trey lingered below, circling the gaping entrance of the Aerary.

The dead dame raced up the steps toward the balcony above. My heart pounded from the exertion and fear—what if the dame got to the top with enough time to throw the torch over the edge? Where would it go? Would I be able to retrieve it? What if it got beyond the wall of black flames or rolled into the catacombs? There would be no hope of retrieval then.

I raced after her, my heart thudding more and more painfully, brain spinning with a thousand terrible possibilities, wishing for perhaps the umpteenth time that I'd made better use of my gym membership.

Green energy blasted into the axe, flecking its edges. The weapon shook in Clay's hands as the forces of magic fought against it. Jenn, Meghan, and the seer pushed against him, holding the axe upright.

At last, the magic let up. The axe was rent from Clay's hands and spun wildly at his neck. The women pushed Clay down as the weapon twisted over their heads and disappeared into the darkness.

Breathing hard, they got back to their feet. They had reached the Aerary. It was a metal platform hanging from the ceiling of the catacombs, some twenty feet under the stone floor of the Rotunda. Far below, the catacombs were flickering with black fire. Its heat and sparks moved around them. Glimmers of torchlight danced in the corner of their eyes from twirling mirrors.

Immediately before them was a ring of six plinths. Five of them bore black flames. Sparks dark as coal exploded out in violent, discordant eruptions.

In the center of the circle was the witch, returned to her former glory. Her skin was smooth and supple. Her green gown sparkled. She had the air of a conqueror who knew the spoils of war were hers.

At her feet was the queen, bound and gagged to the point of immobility, and Emily, the seer's daughter, a tiny little thing with round cheeks, pig tails, and a blade against her throat. Her scared eyes pleaded for her mother.

"Release them," Clay commanded, passing between the plinths to stand in the inner circle.

The witch held the blade tighter to Emily's throat.

"Surrender," she replied.

"You can't want this," Jenn implored. "To harm an innocent child. To hurt your sister and your own blood—"

"She's not my blood!" the witch screeched. "She's—"

"Your stepsister," Clay interrupted. "You gave her everything and she left you."

"Telling secrets, sister?" the witch spat at the queen.

Clay held up the pocket watch.

"We know you, Edith," he said. "We may not understand it, but we know your suffering. Causing more won't make it stop."

The witch exhaled sharply at the sight of the watch. "You...killed...my pet?"

Clay stiffened. This wasn't going as he'd expected.

"You'll die for that," she growled.

"Not if you go first," Meghan replied, and she lunged.

The witch flicked her wrists and sent Meghan flying over the Aerary's railing. Her torches clattered to the ground.

Jenn shrieked in horror as Meghan flew out of sight, but Clay couldn't spare the chance to look. He dove at the witch, pulling Jenn with him. The fight was on.

The dead dame made it to the upper trapdoor. She took too long to get the door open, and I grabbed her ankles as she stepped through. Surprisingly strong, the dead dame kept moving, pulling me after her.

We emerged into the open-air balcony. The corpse dame stumbled toward the edge, raising the torch over her head. I'd been right—she was going to throw it.

"No, you don't," I gasped.

I wrapped my body around her feet and twisted, pulling her to the ground. The skeleton arm torch clattered to the stone, its burning fingers moving on their own accord.

The dead dame rolled onto me, her bony hands wrapping around my neck.

From the corner of my eye, I saw the skeleton arm crawling toward the edge of the balcony. There was enough of a gap in the ballasts that the arm could walk right through.

I bucked my body hard, throwing the dead dame's weight off of me. She flew and smacked into the balcony's railing, her body exploding apart as I scrambled across the ground. I reached for the torch—it crawled like a burning, bony spider toward the edge—and grabbed it just in time. Heart pounding, I held it tight, breathing a sigh of relief. The flame was mine. I just had to get to the Aerary before it was too late.

Body aching, heart pounding, I got to my feet and headed for the trapdoor back into the Rotunda. But there was something in my way.

Clay punched the witch square in the nose. Her dagger fell from her hand. Jenn, dragged along in the process, squirted the whole bottle of her hand sanitizer into the witch's face. They swung sword and torch, pushing her back, keeping her from speaking a spell that would unleash her magic. She didn't even seem tempted though. She fought like a caged animal, swinging viciously for their knees and throats, reserving her stamina.

Jenn dared to look forward, to see what was to come. She stiffened in fear.

"Clay!" she cried. "We need to—"

But her words were lost as the future she feared burst into the present.

While they fought, the seer tore at the ropes tying her daughter to the queen. Once she'd freed her daughter, they embraced.

"Help me now, Emily," she implored, starting to undo the ties on the queen.

The two of them freed the queen. As they pulled the gag from her mouth, the queen gasped in thanks.

"Lady Sinclair," she said. "You have returned."

"I should have never run," the seer replied.

"Right now, you must. Take your daughter. Run!"

Grabbing her daughter, the seer ran for the staircase. At the same exact moment, the witch let out a burst of magic at Clay and Jenn. They were flung through the air and hit the seer and her daughter. The four of them went sailing, flying over the plinths and smacking into the balcony's far railing.

Jenn, the seer, and Emily tumbled over in one big mash of limbs. Clay managed not to go over and squeezed his hand with all his might around Jenn's, fearing the worst. There was a great pull as the weight of the three women tugged on Clay. He felt his shoulder scream, but he managed to hold them. They dangled over the great expanse of the catacombs. Black flames reached for them. Clay grasped tighter, refusing to let Jenn slip away. His fingers bled, digging into the metal of Jenn's wedding ring.

The witch giggled manically at the sight. She wound up her hands—but the queen jumped in her way. The witch barely batted an eye. She smacked her sister away and kicked her hard. She advanced on Clay again, immobile from holding up Jenn, the seer, and Emily over the catacombs and roaring black flames. She raveled her hands together, willing to spare some extra magic to put an end to them—

Suddenly, the castle trembled. The Aerary shook. The mirrors swung like pendulums.

The witch beamed at Clay, stopping her advance.

"It's time," she said.

Her eyes rolled into her head and she began to chant.

I was trapped ten stories above on the balcony. My way down, the trapdoor, was blocked by a mass of black particles. I'd missed it during my skirmish with the dead dame.

As I watched, the hovering mass burrowed into the stone ground and trapdoor and, with an explosion of black sparks, burst into a dark flame. It roared into life, growing across the balcony.

I backed away, the heat of the flame singeing my eyebrows. My clothes grew warm and my skin felt tight. The castle trembled.

Knowing the flame had been lit, the witch chanted. Far below, under the black flames and charred coffins and trees of the catacombs, red lines began to glow. They spiraled wildly across the ground, forming an ornate design of a pentagram.

Meghan hung from the dangling mirrors a dozen feet from the Aerary balcony. Having been thrown off it earlier, she'd managed to catch a mirror and swing her way from one to the next. She was one more jump away from the balcony, but the pentagram below gave her pause. It was sinister. The blood-red lines beat like a heart. Could she stop it somehow? Could she use the magic of the torches, speak a verse, and undo what the witch had done? What would it cost her? She was already exhausted from her magical attempt in the courtyard. Would it knock her out? What if she was still needed? If she was going to risk using the magic of the torches, thereby depleting her own energy, she had to know her actions would matter. But first, she had to get back to the balcony.

At the same time, Jenn pleaded with Clay as he held her above the catacombs.

"Let go of me," she begged. "Please."

"No!" Clay cried.

"There's a beam under here," she cried. "I can swing to it. We'll be safe."

"No!"

The witch stopped chanting and advanced once more on Clay, giggling frenziedly.

From the corner of her eye, the witch spotted Meghan hanging from a nearby mirror. With a wave of her hand, a bolt of magic flew at Meghan—*crash!* The magic bolt crashed into the mirror, exploding the glass, but there was no Meghan.

The witch shouted in surprise and, with a screech of rage, let a wave of magic fly from her. It rose at Clay like a tidal wave, sure to crash upon him and obliterate his very being.

Jenn's hand started to slip.

CHAPTER 51

Husband and wife locked eyes. They knew what was at stake. Their hands had been magically bonded by Clay's promise to never let her go. If he broke that promise, their marriage would be cursed. But if he didn't let go...

"I've got you," he gasped. "I won't let you go. Never again."

With the seer holding Jenn, they shared the Sight. They could see the immediate future. This far and no further. Fractures ran across Clay's body, the divergences of the paths he could take. But Jenn knew which road he would choose. She could see it in his eyes.

This was the moment, Jenn realized. This was where Clay died.

CHAPTER 52

Over the Edge

The wave of toxic green magic flew at Clay, the instrument of his death, the annexation of the two paths he walked.

If he let go of Jenn's hand, he could save himself, but their love would be cursed for the rest of their lives—which might be pretty short, given Jenn wasn't exactly sure she could reach the beam under the balcony. But if he didn't let go, he would be killed, Jenn would still fall, their flames would die out, and Dembroch would surely follow them.

It came down to a very simple choice: their marriage or their lives. Clay chose one path, Jenn chose another.

"I'll always love you," Jenn said. "Even if we let go for just a minute."

She released his hand. He grasped tighter, pulling the wedding ring from her finger as she slipped away.

A sharp sting pulsed through them as they separated. Gravity pulled Jenn, the seer, and Emily down. She reached for the beam underneath the balcony and missed it completely. They fell—

CHAPTER 52

Clay cried out, flinging himself over the railing after her. The green magic flew over him, blistering his hand still holding the railing, but not killing him. He screamed for his wife as she disappeared into the black flames.

Overhead, the hanging mirrors were hit by the wave of magic and exploded. But Meghan wasn't in danger. She'd already landed on the Aerary and, as the witch turned around, decked her right in the face.

Meghan scooped up her torches and knew what she must do. She had to use magic one more time. But it had to matter.

"Falling cease, no friends' demise," she cried. "Lift them up, let them arise."

It seemed every fiber of her being fueled her spell. The sparks from her flames shone brilliantly. For a heart-stopping moment, nothing happened. Meghan stifled a cry.

The witch got back to her feet, wiping blood from her cheek, crooning at the failed spell.

But then, Clay let out a shout. Far below, out of the black flames, Jenn and the seer and Emily began to rise. They lifted higher and higher.

Meghan fell to her knees, more exhausted than she'd ever been in her life. The queen crawled to her.

Clay hoisted himself back up to the balcony and, as the women lifted to the height of the Aerary, he pulled them onto the balcony. Making contact with Jenn felt like unbridled electricity was flowing through him, but it didn't matter right now.

Back on the balcony, a bit burnt, Jenn blinked hard, the Sight fragmenting into a thousand different futures. The talisman spun in her hand, thirsty for these new visions. It didn't want to look at Clay—it hurt too much.

"You've saved yourself from a quicker death," the witch crooned from across the balcony. "Tell me, seer. Has the future changed?"

Clay looked to Jenn, who squinted. Whether the future had altered or not, it was too fragmented for her to make sense of it.

Meanwhile, Queen Coralee and Meghan helped one another to their feet.

"It's exhausting, isn't it?" the witch crooned. "Pity you won't feel the real power course through you. Death has a way of cutting things short." She surveyed them all. "Don't you see? It's all been for naught. All your quests, your struggles, your failures and successes...nothing has changed. I still get what I deserve."

The witch slammed her hands on the balcony floor.

"Rise to the final prize!" she cried.

The red lines below turned maroon and, with an almighty screech, began to rise. It picked up speed, racing up toward them.

"Brace yourselves!" Clay shouted, wrapping around Jenn.

The ground from far below slammed into the bottom of the balcony. With a jolt, they began to rise.

"Watch out!" Emily shouted.

The Aerary balcony crashed into the stone ceiling and broke through into the Rotunda. At the same instant, the seer cried out—she and her daughter fell over the side. Clay and Jenn shouted after them, but they were buried in rocks and couldn't get to her. Thankfully, the seer and Emily didn't have far to fall. They landed on rubble a couple feet below as the Aerary balcony continued to rise.

Clay pushed stone off himself and Jenn. Meghan was close by with the queen, both of whom seemed to be rattled but unhurt. He felt dizzy looking over the edge as they rose higher and higher. Far below, he saw Page Trey, his master, and the Watchmaker running to the seer's aide.

They rose ever higher. Black flames licked their feet. Clay considered jumping over, but it seemed like suicide now. They were too high and headed straight for the ceiling.

The witch was still in the center of the rock ring and black flames. A shield of green protected her from the oncoming impact.

"We have to stop her," Meghan said to the queen. "She'll destroy this castle. She'll kill you."

The queen pointed to the black flames.

CHAPTER 52

"Replace her flames with yours!"

Meghan did her best. She angled one of her torches at the black flame, but the two fought against one another, neither yielding.

"We have to extinguish them first!" Meghan cried.

"Light the empty one!" the queen said, pointing.

But Meghan didn't have time. The balcony slammed into the upper rooftop. They were knocked down again by heaps of rubble as they erupted onto the upper balcony.

I was still on that upper balcony, running around the railing, trying to figure out what to do. How was I going to climb down with a torch and a recently relocated shoulder? How would I do it without falling?

But just then, the stones beneath me trembled mightily. The clouds above came to life with a million red lightning bolts. Thunder boomed, making my ears ring. The next instant, the stone ground exploded all around me. I was thrown back over the railing. I flew through the air, not a clue where I was headed, where I would land, or how long I would have to scream.

The Aerary balcony came to a rest upon the tallest tower. The upper tower tip shuddered above them, several of its support columns obliterated. Cool wind rushed past. Maroon light shone brightly from the stone foundation. Black fire burnt out of it, its tongues flickering through the metal platform. Black and orange sparks danced around them from the torches and plinths.

Outside the ring of stones, Meghan, Clay, Jenn, and the queen got to their feet again. The island lay beneath them. Red lightning flashed all around, striking across the island, blowing chunks out of the castle walls.

"Do it now," the queen murmured to Meghan.

Meghan made a run for the unlit sixth plinth, but the witch was faster. She scooped up a chunk of stone from the destroyed upper balcony, one with a raging black flame, and threw it at the sixth, unlit plinth. It lit and all six flames roared into a ring of fire. The witch was encompassed in them. Meghan was knocked back with a blast of heat.

Beyond, the isles groaned. The land began to tear apart. Hot magma began to seep through the tears, creating angry orange veins across the island. Black fire consumed the forest, burning everything to a crisp. The waves turned away from the island. Shores crumbled into dust. The cliffs cracked and fell in chunks.

"What do we do?" Meghan cried.

"We must exting—" the queen began, but her words turned into a shriek. Her body lurched forward, flying into the ring of black flames.

"No!" Clay shouted. He ran after the queen, but the flames flared. Unbearable heat pushed him back. He stumbled, blisters forming on his face.

"How do we get through?" Jenn cried.

"Can't you see the future?" Meghan shouted. "What do we do?"

"We—!" Jenn began, but her eyes grew hazy. "It's too much! I can't see the right way! Where's Nick?"

"We have to get rid of these flames," Clay interjected. "But if they're like ours, only the witch can extinguish them. She started the black flames. She has to end them."

"So we have to kill her?" Meghan asked.

"We can't even get through to her," Clay said.

"We need Nick!" Jenn cried.

There was a clang of metal behind them. They jumped, lifting their swords and torches to fight.

"Nick!" Jenn shouted with relief.

I pulled myself onto the balcony, bloody and browbeaten. My sling hung from my neck, torn and burnt to shreds. I held the sixth and final torch burning with bright orange flame.

CHAPTER 52

"Where is she?" I demanded. "Where is the queen?"

Meghan pointed at the ring of black flames.

"The witch," she gasped.

Anger filled my veins. I made a run at the flames but backed away as quickly, gasping in pain. Even a foot away, my skin felt scalded. My heart ached in my chest.

"Nick, stop!" Meghan shouted. "The flames will burn you."

"I'd rather burn than let her die," I said, taking my second torch from her.

I charged forward, an unstoppable force. The black flames assaulted me with heat and blistered my skin, but I would not be denied. I kept running, right through the pain, the heat, the dark magic—right through the flames.

"Run, Lady Sinclair! Tell others of this day."

Chunks of stone rained from the sky in the Rotunda. Holding her daughter close, the seer ran over the rubble and disappeared through the columns to the courtyard. The Watchmaker was hot on her tail—

But as nimble as he may have been for a man his size, the Watchmaker was still a large target. Several stones hit him hard on the back. The Watchmaker was smacked to the ground. More stones fell, heaping upon him, crushing him, burying him.

A few seconds later, all was still. The Watchmaker lay crushed under mounds of rock, all of it pushing down on him. He felt lightheaded, and something warm was pooling on his back.

The Watchmaker pushed against the ground, straining to lift the rocks. A sharp, stabbing pain ripped through him. Blood pooled faster and spilled over his sides. He went cross-eyed from the dizziness.

And then he heard it. The sound he never wanted to hear.

A watch on his belt—his own—let out a soft chime. It was not a warning of impending death, still a week or a few days away, not even a pressing warning of death in a few hours. This one was soft and melancholy, a chime signifying that he, the Watchmaker, had mere minutes, perhaps seconds, to live.

A calm came over him. He knew there was no way he could save himself. Perhaps Page Trey and Master Malleator were out there, still able to help, but the chances were slim. If this was the way it must go, the Watchmaker decided, at least it would be peaceful. At least, when he closed his eyes one last time, he would see the two women he loved most once more. He only hoped he had done enough for Dembroch and his queen.

CHAPTER 53

Stealing Youth

I burst through the flames. My skin was flayed and burnt.

The witch stood in the center of the ring, hands tight on her sister, who knelt at the witch's feet. Under the harsh light of the maroon pentagram and the black fire, the witch was a terror to behold. Her eyes gleamed madly. All her age had melted away, revealing the true effects of time. Her skin was gnarled and dead, her cheeks sunken. There were only spikes of broken teeth left in her black gums. Her body was wasted away, nothing but stretched flesh over bone and shrunken organs. All of her magic, all of her power, was being channeled elsewhere.

"You stole my youth, sister," she rasped at Queen Coralee, not noticing my arrival into the nexus. "Now, I steal yours!" She closed her eyes and, in a throaty tone, said, "Betrayal, hatred, treachery divine—"

"Stop!" I cried.

The witch broke her incantation. Her cold eyes found mine.

"Stop now, or meet your end," I exclaimed.

Shouts echoed behind me. My friends emerged from the flames, black and red burns lacing their faces. Their clothes were on fire. Jenn was pale as a ghost and Meg shook from the effort to keep herself standing.

The witch began to whisper again, restarting her incantation. I shouted for her to stop, that I didn't want to hurt her, but the witch persisted.

"Betrayal, hatred, treachery divine," she moaned, "let my sister's youth be mine."

The pentagram shone bright, blinding my friends and I. The black flames roared. Sparks swirled around us.

Queen Coralee screamed, and my heart seemed to shriek in tandem. The queen's skin withered and cracked. Her limbs and torso thinned. She shrunk on the spot, her body aging hundreds of years with each passing second.

At the same time, the witch grew younger. The ailments of time reversed and healed over. Her teeth regrew, her eyes cleared, her skin became plump and rosy.

"Stop!" I begged, my heart thundering in my chest hard enough to tear itself apart. "Please! I don't want to hurt you!"

"I won't!" the witch seethed. "I can't!"

"You can! Just stop!"

There was nothing for it. I knew what I must do.

I leveled my torches at the witch and pushed the orange flames toward her side. She shrieked in pain, but I didn't back away.

"The queen hurt me once too," I said. "She abandoned me. But I found it in my heart to forgive and to love. That is your only option now, Sorgana. Forgive her or perish."

The witch, now a vision of beauty and youth, screamed for me to stop. She threatened to flay me, grind me to bits, make me her slave, torture me unendingly.

CHAPTER 53

I pushed another torch toward her cheek. The flames of love licked her flesh. She writhed and screamed but would still not break her hold on the queen.

"This flame will not hurt you if you have love in your heart," I shouted.

My friends circled around the witch now. They held out their torches, nearing them to her skin.

"I was like you," Meghan shouted at the witch. "I thought my sibling abandoned me too. I was hurt and lost and decided to go my own way. But fate brought us back together. You can have the life you wanted, you just need the patience to seek it."

"Your brother is the queen's mindless pawn," the witch spat back. "He will abandon you like he did all those years ago."

"Have faith in the world," Jenn interjected. "Believe that good will come, and it will! You can change your path for a brighter tomorrow."

"Look at what the world has made of me," the witch screeched. "It has taken everything from me. There is no other way."

"There is," Clay insisted. "Be brave. Face the future and whatever it brings."

"Together," I tried to say, but a shock of pain in my chest cut my voice short. My left arm tingled strangely.

"Together," Meghan said.

"With the sister you love," I insisted, regaining my voice. "Let her go. Free her."

Something clicked in my head, like a light bulb turning on in my brain.

"...free the sister," the mage had said. He hadn't meant the queen. Or my sister. He'd meant the witch. She was trapped and I knew her prison.

"Look at where you are, Edith!" I shouted. "Destroying a kingdom of peace. Killing your sister. And for what? A curse? For the wrong done to you? It was not just your sister. Not just your choices. It was your curse."

The witch paused. She turned her youthful face upon me. Her beauty was betrayed by the cruelty in her eyes. The queen hung limply from her hands, barely breathing, ancient and worn, but still alive. The spell seemed to have paused.

"What?" the witch spat, her beautiful cheek burnt and bloody. "What curse do you speak of?"

"The curse of your father," I said. "The curse he fell to. The curse that afflicts your sister. If is upon you, too."

"Lies! The curse was upon the Arthurian lineage."

"To which you belong! King Arthur may not have been your blood, but he took you in. He was your father. You were his daughter. And like him, you lost much. Your family. Your kingdom. But you haven't lost it all. Not yet."

The witch seemed to be considering this. My friends pulled back their torches.

"You're with your sister now," I said. "You haven't lost her yet. She has it in her heart to forgive you. All you have to do is break the curse."

"It can't be broken, only completed," the witch spat.

"Your father found the answer," I revealed. "And if his knights had known you were afflicted, they would have brought you here. But you're here *now*. The fairest magic can break the darkest curse. I have the fairest magic in my hand. But you have to accept it."

I'd figured it out, I knew I had. This was the way to break the queen's curse and the witch's.

Impossibly, the witch stalled. She wanted to know more. I was convincing her.

And I would have told her. But in that instant, as we begged the witch to stop, as the queen clung desperately to life, as the whole kingdom seemed to hang in the balance, as my worn heart pounded its last painful beats, the sky suddenly lit up with a flash of red. The castle shook mightily. There was a smattering of soft chimes from my pocket watch and my friends'.

CHAPTER 53

Far below us, the Watchmaker was roused as the leftmost watch on his belt chimed softly. Though he could not reach it, he knew what it meant. The queen's watch read a minute to midnight. The sun was highest in the dark. The queen had turned thirty. Her curse was here.

CHAPTER 54

The Queen's Curse

A cold draft swept over me, like Death itself passing by, and then, deep in my chest, my heart was struck with blinding agony. My left arm went totally numb, followed shortly by knives of pain stabbing through my whole body. My veins felt like they were on fire. I fell to the ground, flopping on the metal. My torch fell from my hand, rolling to a stop at the witch's feet.

My fellow defenders toppled, too. Jenn collapsed, head spinning, face sickly pale. The wound on her leg bled like a waterfall. Meghan doubled over in agony, clutching at the wound on her chest. Clay, whose clothes had been on fire, screamed as the black flames ate at his flesh. Their torches tumbled away, orange flames fading to whispers.

Though they were weak, the flames of our torches had just enough flicker. Gathered around the witch's feet, the tongues licked her heels. The witch's dress caught fire and, in an instant, she was covered in orange flames. She howled, but it wasn't full of rage. It was a scream of pain, guilt, and lament. Her skin boiled and burnt.

I couldn't help her. I writhed on the ground, unable to scream, unable to fight for my life any longer. I was having a heart attack, I knew, a bad one, a widowmaker, and it was as much my fault as it was the queen's curse. My body had grown weak over the years, and all this running around Dembroch had put plenty of strain on it. Now, the queen's curse was unfolding, and the easiest way to dispatch me was with my already weakened heart.

My foolish, weak heart, I realized. It had pined for the queen, hardened in my twenties with skepticism and disbelief of the magical, broken loose in my thirties and hammered away as I ran across the realm, and now tore itself apart to save its true love.

But I was too late. The curse was unfolding and within a few seconds, the kingdom and everyone left on it would be gone. This was the terrible future that the mage had predicted, the one the seer had feared and Jenn had glimpsed. And we hadn't been able to change it.

As the witch burnt and the queen clung to life and her defenders lay dying, the isles of Dembroch trembled and began to sink into the sea. Red lightning burst from the storm clouds and struck the castle's walls. Great chunks of stone were obliterated with pops and cracks. The tallest tower began to sway. Thunder boomed like drums of doom.

In the Rotunda, stones fell. Page Trey and Master Malleator were buried. The Watchmaker felt his consciousness ebb.

Outside the castle, the seer clutched her daughter close as she ran for the shore, for the ferry. She wouldn't make it. Dembroch was being devoured.

Before us, though none of us could see, the burning witch writhed. The flames burnt deep into her flesh, eating away at her very existence, but the truth cut deeper.

As much as she despised the last defenders, there was no denying what had been said: she was truly cursed. By the age of thirty, she'd lost her adoptive parents, her sister, and her home of Camelot. As promised by the curse, no authority or land had come back to her, nor had any man or woman followed her unless enchanted. She had found her mentor who had helped her on the path to darkness, but he had never truly sought to aid her. She was simply a means to an end to accomplish his goals. In short, she had lived these long years miserably, stripped of everything she loved by a curse she didn't know she bore, doomed to lament and seek to reclaim everything she had lost. It was the curse to the letter, and oh, how she had fallen for it and let it twist her into ugliness.

But there was a solution, she knew now. A way to free herself of the curse, of this sorrow that had filled her for eons and turned her insides to rot. If only she hadn't been so filled with vengeance and hatred that she'd destroyed the only kingdom with the means to save her. If only she hadn't been killing the only person left in the world who might love her.

Through the tongues of flame, she saw her sister, frail and weak, a breath away from death, her eyes full of understanding of what was happening around her, but too weak to do anything about it.

Guilt swept through Sorgana, cutting deeper than any knife or burning flame. She lamented her choices, so irreversible now. The curse was not fully to blame. She had done all these things. She was killing her sister. She was fulfilling all the curse intended.

If only, she thought, she could stop it. Break it. End the curse. Undo all she had done.

But she didn't know how. She hadn't heard how to break the curse. She didn't understand what the fairest magic was.

There was nothing for it, Sorgana realized. She would not be able to break the curse by happenstance. But Coralee, her sister, could be saved. Of everything the witch had done, all the death she had caused and destruction she had wrought, she could at least reverse what she had done to her sister. Coralee, at least, would live.

"Flames of virtue, hear my call," Sorgana said. "From my body to hers, may the youth withdraw."

The color bled from the pentagram until it was black. She felt her lifeforce ebb as freshly gained youth was sucked from her. The witch aged as Queen Coralee became young once more.

The queen's eyes fluttered open fully. She gasped, sucking in air.

She had been weak during all of this, but she had heard every word. She knew the curse was unfolding—she could see her defenders dying around her, the black flames roaring to stay alive, the orange flames dwindling, her sister burning, the islands caving in. But she had heard what I'd said to the witch: that the only way to break the curse was with the lightest magic of Dembroch, the orange flames crawling over the witch and spreading toward the queen.

In years past, Queen Coralee had been able to touch every orange flame except the final one. The one born of love. She knew now that, to break her curse and save the kingdom, she had to accept each flame, even the one she'd never been able to touch.

It would be her end, she figured. Calling the flames to her would burn her to death, just as it was killing her sister. But it was a sacrifice worth making.

The flames travelled down her torso, covering her completely, as though called by her thoughts. They burnt deep, searing her to the bone.

Love, she told herself. She must feel love to break this curse, to save her defenders and what was left of her kingdom.

Her thoughts turned to me. She thought of how I had trusted her and stuck with her when I had every reason to abandon her. It was a love she'd never known. In the same way, she felt her heart swell with the realization that she felt the same way about me—having cared for me from words alone, known my heart without meeting me, and wanted nothing more than to save me, even if it meant she herself would perish.

And what of her sister? This terrible woman who had feasted on the innocent to prolong her life, who had sought only revenge and torture? The queen loved her still. She wanted nothing more than to care for Edith as Edith had done so long ago for her. No matter her trespasses, she could be forgiven. They could be sisters again.

And with that thought, with that realization that she could dare to love even if it threatened her very life, the cursed queen finally allowed herself to love.

As though invited to descend upon her, the flames seemed to burrow into Queen Corlaee. She gasped in agony. It felt as though she had been stabbed. And then, as though the blade had been pulled out, the pain fled her body. So did the fire.

She had died. She knew it. When she opened her eyes, she would be in Avalon, doomed or blessed, free of her curse and her tribulations.

Queen Coralee dared to open her eyes and gasped. She was still on the Aerary balcony. Much had changed. The black flames, both on the balcony and across the island, had gone. The pentagram had flickered out.

Her sister Edith still stood before her. Flames no longer licked her skin. She was alive though badly burnt and terribly aged.

Our curse is broken, Queen Coralee realized. They were free.

"My sister," she said, rising.

Edith flinched, but Queen Coralee wrapped her into an embrace.

"You will have much to answer for," she whispered to her sister, "but not a hair on your head shall be harmed. We are free. All is well."

But all was not well. From the corner of her eyes, the queen saw Clay get to his feet. But Meghan, Jenn, and I didn't stir.

Clay ran to Jenn's side. When he drew his hands away from her, they were bloody.

Beyond, the island of Dembroch was still collapsing. The damage had been done and the sea was swallowing the island whole.

CHAPTER 54

"The torches," Queen Coralee gasped at Clay. "We must spread the flames to the plinths."

Clay knew without asking. He scooped up the torches and swept around the ring of rocks, lighting the plinths one by one. As he touched the torches to the top of the stone, the flat tops lit with an explosion of sparks.

There was only one left to light, but as he ran for it, the ground beneath him pitched wildly. He was airborne as the tallest tower fell.

They all screamed, helpless and panicked. It seemed the very soul of Dembroch cried out as the castle collapsed, following the isles into the void.

CHAPTER 55

Dembroch's Deliverance

And that would have been the end of it—Dembroch, the queen, the last of the defenders, the Civium, the reignited magic, all of it—had it not been for Clay.

As the mage had foreseen, Clay truly walked two paths. After slaying the Dreadnaught, he'd promised Jenn he'd never let go with the intent of dying before he let her go again. Figuratively, yes, but magic is a spoken art and often too literal.

While walking to the Gate Grounds, he had made another promise: that so long as he breathed, Dembroch would persist. The two promises made two different paths, both leading to the Aerary. There, Clay had held his wife above the abyss.

If he'd held on, he would have died and Dembroch would have fallen. But Jenn had chosen a different path. She had let go of Clay, at a terrible cost to their marriage, and in so doing, made it so that Clay was present in this final moment atop the tallest tower. And because of their sacrifice, because of the path they'd chosen, the future was in his hands.

As the tower fell and Clay plummeted after it, he grabbed the final torch. He flung it at the last, unlit plinth. The torch's end hit the plinth's flat top and, with an explosion of sparks, the fire spread. The sixth plinth burst into flame.

The next second, the six flames erupted into a ring of flames, the orange turning into a rainbow of colors. Magic and its timelessness returned in full to Dembroch.

Below, in the Rotunda, a hand broke out of the rubble.

"Tower of Dembroch, fall no more," Master Malleator declared, "rise again, your foundation restore!"

Golden light swarmed around the master's hands. All around them, the roar of the falling tower dwindled.

The seer's shouts of fear became cries of joy. Before her very eyes, the castle tower stopped falling. The crumbling of the isles stalled.

In her bones, she felt a strange spark of light. She wondered for a moment what it was before recognizing it like an old friend.

Magic had returned to the kingdom.

She snapped her fingers and gold sparks flew around her like fireflies. The seer shouted again, overjoyed.

She turned her gaze back to the tower and truly looked. Not with her human eyes but with her Sight.

And then she saw the truth. The Sight had fooled her. It had looked to the moment the tower fell and no further because that was when the magic had returned. That was when the kingdom had regained its timelessness. And the Sight, the devious power it was, had only shown her the collapse, not the aftermath where time was suspended and magic returned.

Now, though, she could see it. And the immediate future was beautiful.

She set her daughter down and, bending the magic she had not used in years, called for the kingdom to heal itself.

The rubble in the Rotunda began to lift. Page Trey was freed. Holding his bruised ribs, he got to his feet.

Master Malleator stood amongst the rising debris. The Aerary balcony hovered a few feet above him, held up by golden light. As he watched, the balcony began to rise. All around them, the castle reassembled.

A weak voice called. The page ran to the side of the Watchmaker. He was badly hurt. Lying belly-first on the ground, he was inscribed in a circle of blood.

The Watchmaker turned just enough to see the hovering tower and murmured: "Well done, boy. Well done, indeed."

In his hand, he held the queen's pocket watch. The hands were spinning backward.

The Aerary balcony rose to the top of the tallest tower and rested into place. The upper tower settled back onto its columns. A ring of multicolored flames burnt brightly on the plinths.

Above, the clouds dissipated. The midday sun started to shine upon the isles of Dembroch. Healed by the return of its magic and with help from the seer, the trio of islands rose once more from the sea. The forests regrew and blossomed into thick tuffets. The vineyards sprang back to life, rivers ran full. Cracks in the land filled and sprouted flowers, colorful blooms of reds, yellows, and oranges. A billion golden sparks of magic spread across the whole land.

Upon the Aerary balcony, now permanently affixed atop the tallest tower for all to see, Clay and the queen rushed to the fallen. Meghan was rousing, holding her chest and hyperventilating.

"Just breathe," the queen said.

Meghan sucked in air slower, blotting the puss from her wound.

"She's lost so much blood," Clay gasped, tending to Jenn. "What can we do?"

Queen Coralee looked to her sister.

"You are more learned in the art than I," she said.

Edith, frail and toothless, looked unsure.

"Please," Clay begged.

The witch approached slowly. She held her hands close to Jenn's face.

"Her ring," the witch said. "Do you have it?"

Bewildered, Clay pulled Jenn's diamond wedding ring from his pocket. He'd put it there after he'd pulled it free on the Aerary balcony.

"Place a hand on her wound and the ring on her heart," the witch told Clay.

He did as asked, but the second he touched her, an electric shock jolted through him. He pulled back, angry welts on his fingers.

"Hurry now," the witch said. "She is suffering."

Clay placed his hands upon his wife again. A shock ripped through him, but he fought against it, maintaining a hold on her.

"Prized possession close to thine," the witch said, her words hard to understand with her cracked lips and broken teeth. "Heal the wounds for all time."

Jenn's diamond ring shone bright white. In an instant, the blood soaked back into her. The wound on her leg healed. She let out a gasp as she awoke. Clay wrapped his arms around her, kissing her forehead. She gulped in pain at his touch. When he tried to put her wedding ring back on her finger, the metal burnt her skin as though it had been left in a kiln. Clay held onto the ring, the both of them exchanging nervous looks, too scared to try to hug or kiss or hold one another.

Meanwhile, Queen Coralee scooped me up into her arms. My body was heavy, the muscles all relaxed. I did not respond to the movement.

"Sir Nicholas!" she called.

I still did not move. The queen's heart dropped. Was she too late?

Edith approached timidly.

"May I?" she asked.

"Please," the queen replied.

The witch ran her hands from my head to my toes.

"He was a breath away from death before the curse was broken and the magic restored," she said. "His heart was badly torn. He will be in agony unless mended."

"Can you—?" asked the queen.

The witch shook her head. "I cannot mend his heart. But he will not perish while on Dembroch. He lives."

Trembling, still holding her chest, Meghan crawled over and felt for my pulse. Pushing through the pain, she smirked.

"He always was a deep sleeper," she said.

CHAPTER 56

The King's Killer

I jolted awake to the screaming of my name, my chest aching in protest. My friends stood around me, tears in their eyes, giant grins on their faces. Behind them was a beautiful blue sky. The dark clouds and red lightning were gone. The midday sun was shining down on us all.

My eyes were drawn to the six plinths where a ring of multicolored fire flickered. Sparks hung in the air like stars.

And then there was the queen. She held me in her arms. Her face was an open book of emotion.

I knew more from intuition than fact what had happened. The queen's curse had been broken. Dembroch was saved. We were all going to be okay.

I rolled onto my feet and swayed, lightheaded. My heart didn't feel quite right, my whole body hurt with each beat, but I was alive nonetheless.

Then I saw the witch. At first, I thought I was hallucinating, but she was there.

"Don't you—" I began, holding up a hand in defense.

"Be calm, Sir Nicholas," Queen Coralee said, moving between us. "Edith is our enemy no more. She has forsaken her actions and the evil in her heart. Her curse, like mine, is broken. She accepted the fairest magic in her soul. And here on Dembroch, we offer our guests forgiveness, hope, and healing."

"Prove it," I insisted.

The witch hobbled to the ring of multicolored flames spitting sparks. She held out her hand timidly, fearfully even. When she touched the flames, her skin did not burn and she did not cry out.

I hesitated another moment, unsure. But there was no denying the truth. If the witch was touching the flames, she had truly changed. As my friends and I had rekindled our youth, the witch had seen the error of her ways. And, if I was being honest, the unsightly woman before me was no longer dangerous. She cowered and cringed, a raw human with no power and many sins to atone for.

I extended a hand to her. She reached to accept it.

Our hands met. We shook—and the witch screamed.

I tensed, expecting an attack, but the witch fell to her knees, thrashing and shrieking.

"What–what's happening?!" I cried. I looked to my friends. They were as much at a loss as I was.

Queen Coralee fell to her sister's side, holding her.

"Is she—?" Jenn began.

"We have to help her!" Clay shouted.

As he said this, the witch fell still. For a moment, I feared the worst, but then she opened her eyes and forced a pained smile. Before our eyes, her veins turned black and her skin flaked away.

"I made a promise," the witch gasped to her sister. "One I could not break."

CHAPTER 56

"You are protected by the kingdom's timelessness and magic," the queen said. "No curse nor death can reach you anymore."

"It was a poisoned promise with your king's killer," the witch breathed, agony raking her words. "He got me here. I promised him to end the kingdom. To end you. And if I failed..." She shuddered harder, her skin flecked away to show red, atrophied muscle.

"We have to...," I murmured, desperate but unable to think of a solution. "Meghan?"

My sister dropped beside the witch and put her hands on her chest.

"Poisoned promise break your tie, let the woman before me cease to die."

Meghan's last word became a cry of pain. Golden sparks flared around us, but the witch continued to fade. She smiled once more at her sister and her eyes found the ocean. Its light shimmered on her face.

"I'm sorry," she murmured. "For everything. Forgive me."

Queen Coralee let out a sob. Edith slipped lower in the queen's arms and exhaled one last time and lay still.

I didn't know what to do. Had the witch died? It shouldn't have been possible. Could we have done more to help her?

We knelt by the queen. I put a hand on the queen's shoulder, guilt heavy on my heart. The witch had been cruel, but she had shown true repentance. She had not deserved this. And yet, she had known of the promise she'd made and the consequences of not keeping it. She had chosen to let her sister live, knowing she would perish.

"Rest in peace, sweet sister," Queen Coralee whispered.

A gust of wind picked up. Edith's body disintegrated into ashes and was borne away as Queen Coralee cried. We all joined her, mourning the girl named Edith who had shown her face one last time.

CHAPTER 57

Many Happy Returns

When we descended from the upper balcony some time later, we saw the Watchmaker face-first on the Rotunda's floor, surrounded by a lake of blood. There was a jagged puncture wound in his back. It pulsed with an irregular heartbeat. Clay pushed past us, shouting for his friend. I feared the worst for the Watchmaker. As we got closer, I thought I could see ribs. My own ragged heart ached at the sight and I had to grab onto the queen to maintain my balance the rest of the way down the stairs.

Master Malleator and Page Trey were at the Watchmaker's side, offering comforting words. Clay skid to a stop beside them, eyes wide and harried.

"Come on, Watchmaker," he pleaded. "You're alright. You've walked away from worse than this."

The Watchmaker moaned in unbearable agony. He didn't even seem to register that Clay was there.

CHAPTER 57

"You've got something worth fighting for," Clay implored. "Fight for it." He looked desperately to Page Trey and his master. "Can't you do something?"

Clay shouted at the page and his master, pleading for them to make it stop.

"This is beyond our abilities," Page Trey said.

"We haven't much training in bending magic to heal," Master Malleator said. "We could wait for healers, but he will be in a great deal of pain."

"Would it not be better to let him go?" Page Trey offered tenderly. "We will ride with him along the shore, past the Bolts and the magic's scope, and let him pass with peace."

"No!" Clay shouted.

"Clay, he shouldn't suffer," Jenn said, her voice quiet.

Master Malleator knelt beside Clay. "There's nothing to be done. The poor man's heart has been crushed. A man can't live without a heart."

I felt dizzy with all this talk of hearts. My own still felt funny beating weakly in my chest. Thank goodness the magic had returned, or else the I would have been dead too.

Suddenly, Clay let out a shout.

"It's the things we love most that keep us going," he said, his mind somewhere else. "It keeps your heart beating."

He was onto something, I knew it, but I had no idea what he was doing.

"The witch healed you by having me place my hands on you," Clay said, pointing at Jenn. "Your wedding ring glowed. It's your most prized possession. We just need what the Watchmaker loves most..."

Clay began to feel around the Watchmaker's belt. The queen shouted in protest, but from the belt, Clay held up two small, golden pocket watches. Their gears were still.

"This is the watch of his wife," Clay said. "And this is his mother's. The two are his most prized possessions. They're conduits for magic, right?"

Master Malleator's eyes lost focus. Page Trey raised his eyebrows.

"He said so," Clay insisted. "It can prolong life, heal wounds!"

Master Malleator looked back at Clay and nodded. He took the pocket watches and, holding them tightly together, squeezed them as though trying to break them.

"Where your treasured watches reside, may a heart beat with pride," he muttered.

Gold light shone through his fingers. The next instant, the watches had reformed into the rough shape of a human heart. The gears, intricately reorganized within the shape, shook in their spots as though ready to spin again.

"If you have a weak stomach, I suggest turning away," Master Malleator said.

None of us did. We owed it to the Watchmaker to bear witness. Master Malleator reached into the Watchmaker, pulling apart skin and bone, yanked out his crushed heart, and placed the new heart-clock in its place.

"Do you know the witch's incantation?" the master asked Clay.

He shook his head. He hadn't heard it.

"Let me try," Meghan said.

"Lady Meghan," Page Trey warned.

"I'll be okay," she insisted and placed a hand on Master Malleator's. "Prized possession and blood entwine, beat for your owner, magic and life, combine."

Meg panted as she fueled the magic spell. She wavered on the spot, but maintained consciousness.

Before us, the Watchmaker's back healed over and his body jolted. He gasped for breath. His eyes shot open. The tick tock of a two-clock heart filled the air.

CHAPTER 57

"What the devil?!" the Watchmaker shouted. He got up quickly, spinning around and reaching for his back.

"Be calm, Watchmaker," the queen insisted. "You are badly injured. You may have broken bones or bruised organs."

"I've walked away from worse," the Watchmaker grumbled. He found Clay. "What did you do to me, boy?"

No longer intimidated by the mountain of a man, Clay said, "We saved your life. You have a new ticker. Your wife and your mother will live on with you."

The Watchmaker puffed up his chest and looked ready to scold Clay, but a tear grew in his eyes. He deflated and put a hand over his new heart.

"I can feel her," he said quietly. "I can feel both of them." He looked to each of us. With heartfelt understanding in his eyes, he said, "Thank you."

He looked to the queen. Tears in his eyes, he bowed to her.

"*Omnia Aeterno*," he said. "May you reign forever, my queen."

"Omnia Aeterno," we all repeated, except for Master Malleator.

"I hope to," Queen Coralee replied. "The kingdom has been saved. The curse is broken. The witch has passed."

The Watchmaker let out a whoop so loud, so joyous, the Rotunda seemed to ring with delight. I tensed, sensing sadness from the queen, but she didn't let it show for anyone else.

We heard the pitter-patter of footsteps and weaved through the columns to see who was coming. Running toward us was the seer and her daughter, Emily. My heart burst with joy at the sight of Page Hybore's family.

"My queen," the seer said, kneeling. "Forgive me. I was a fool tricked by my Sight and the witch. I doubted the kingdom and its future. I abandoned you when you needed me most. Words are not enough, but I ask for your forgiveness and, within my mortal abilities, I will never leave you again."

Queen Coralee beamed. "Welcome home, Lady Sinclair. A kingdom will always need its seer."

The Watchmaker gave Master Malleator a stern look.

"I believe you have words to share with the queen?" he said to the combat master.

Master Malleator looked to his queen for the first time, and it indeed seemed he had a great deal on his mind. But then, the moment passed, and his scarred face softened.

"I seek your forgiveness, as well," he said to the queen. "In our darkest, final hour, my faith faltered. I may not have always agreed with your choices—"

"Never would have guessed that," Meghan mumbled under her breath.

"—but my loyalty to you should never err. To serve you is to serve Dembroch, and I do so with honor."

Queen Coralee nodded, taking the small offering of peace that the combat master was extending.

As they spoke, Little Emily thanked Clay and Jenn, giving both of them hugs. When she came to me, I knelt to her level. I grit my teeth, fighting to keep my composure while pain radiated through my body with every heartbeat.

"Sir Nicholas," she said, her brown eyes gleaming just like her father's.

"Emily," I replied, my voice weaker than I wanted it to be. "Your father loved you more than anything."

"Even though I'm unconscionable?" she asked.

"Incurable," her mother corrected.

"Even still," I replied. "Without him, my friends and I couldn't have been here. We couldn't have saved Dembroch."

"He knew you would," Emily said with a smile and she kissed me on the forehead.

Meanwhile, Jenn reunited with the seer. When they embraced, they could see the near future, one of joy, happiness, and prosperity. They burst into tears, a bond forming that could never be severed, a hope that could never be broken.

With a burst of speed unfit for a man who'd just been crushed and had open heart surgery, the Watchmaker grabbed Clay, hoisted him up, and squeezed, popping the vertebrae in Clay's back.

"That's for taking my sword *and* my axe!" the Watchmaker said. He set Clay down and gave him a sturdy, appreciative thump on the back. "And that's for being the knight I knew you could be."

Page Trey wandered over to Meghan. They traded laughs about the hardships of rowing boats around the islands, and Page Trey invited Meghan to join him in training recruits on Ryderwyle.

"You have substantial skill," Page Trey commended. "Both in fighting and a quick tongue. With magic, I mean."

Dare I say it, Meghan blushed.

Clay and Jenn ended up next to one another after some time. They reached to hold hands, but a shock of pain made them hesitate. Blushing at one another, Clay pulled her wedding ring from his pocket.

"All this time, your wedding ring was your most prized possession?" he asked.

"For what it represents," Jenn said. "Every time I look at it, I think of you. My knight in shining armor."

"You did always like shiny things," Clay joked.

He tried to slide the ring on her finger once more, but Jenn pulled away, cringing.

"It's part of the curse, I think," Jenn said. "It burns. Maybe...for now...you keep it." She tried to laugh it off. "I don't need a ring to know you're mine."

Clay put the ring back in his pocket, but he knew better. His wife had always loved shiny things and what they represented. He could see the sadness in her eyes that she could no longer wear her ring. But it was a cost they had to pay for saving the kingdom.

"You knew," Clay said. "Down in the Aerary."

"I saw it," Jenn said, showing the eyeball in her hand. "But I couldn't let it happen. You would have died. Dembroch would have fallen."

"Thank you," Clay said. "At least I—well, all of us—will live to see another day. Even if we're cursed."

"It doesn't matter," Jenn said, a newfound optimism making her cheeks rosy. "No curse can keep us apart."

Through the shock and the pain, they embraced, locking lips. Deep down, their hearts fell slightly. Marriage was tough enough without physical pain when embracing one another. Though they didn't say it aloud, for speaking such a bold promise had gotten them into this mess, they vowed to find a way to break their curse and be together once more.

While Meghan and the Watchmaker groaned at Jenn and Clay, I made my way to the queen. I bowed disjointedly to her. We looked at one another for a minute, plenty passing between us that we didn't know how to say.

"Thank you, Sir Nicholas," she finally said. "This kingdom owes you and your friends a great debt."

"It's been an honor," I replied, suddenly remembering the queen's decree: that if my friends and I managed to save Dembroch, we would be exiled for our initial petulant behavior. In my quest, I'd learned that the queen's words were law. She couldn't show favoritism. My friends and I would have to leave.

She seemed to know what I was thinking.

"I hope you will not leave yet," she said. "There is much work to be done and many hard days ahead. And there is the matter of your heart. We must make efforts to heal it so you will survive beyond the realm of Dembroch's magic."

I gave her a nod. "My life is in your hands, however long you intend to hold it."

And I meant it. Whether it was a short day or longer, no matter the pain of living with a ruptured heart, I was going to enjoy every minute of being with the queen and the kingdom that we'd saved.

CHAPTER 58

Still Much to Learn

The summons was sent out the next day, calling for Civium and Hospite to return to the saved kingdom. The queen feared none would return, but Jenn and the seer said otherwise.

While we waited, the small group of us got to work. We swept the castle for the moss remains of the mage and collected them in an urn. It was buried with honor in the catacombs with the bodies of the deceased, including the Bridgemaster, ferryman, and librarian. Corpses of the deceased defenders were replaced back in their coffins.

Hanging from a limb of the catacombs trees, I spotted my satchel. I retrieved it and stored it in my quarters, hoping to find new secrets within.

Across the island, we began to rebuild. The skybridge to Ryderwyle was painstakingly reconstructed. I kept recommending we use magic, but the manual labor, as Master Malleator said, made a man honest. The magic of Dembroch was reserved for more important matters, not simple tasks that could be accomplished by calloused hands and a strong back.

Plank by plank, wall by wall, we reconstructed the village of Verum and Amaranthine, villages for Hospites who may have needed to stay on the isles long-term. The Watchmaker's cottage was rebuilt and every pocket watch was repaired. As my friends and I helped, we learned more of Dembroch's lifestyle and grew to love it for all its uniqueness. It really was an eclectic, well-meaning kingdom, and I was proud to have helped save it. All the while, I knew that one day very soon, the Civium would return, I'd be given a relatively clean bill of health, and the queen would have to ask us to leave. I just hoped I'd have the chance to talk to her before we were kicked out.

One afternoon, during a break between rebuilding another Amaranthine home, I got my chance. The queen asked me to join her in a walk around the castle grounds. We walked in silence until we found the flowers along the southern wall.

"I've been thinking about your sister…" I said. "I'm sorry we hurt her."

It was the first time we'd mentioned Edith since her passing. The queen was not perturbed by this though. She nodded to me kindly.

"You didn't," the queen said. "Simply put, you forced her hand. You guided her to the light and, with the help of the flames, pushed her in. And, in the end, she chose love over hate. In the end, I had my sister once more. But in so doing, she ensured her demise."

"The king's killer," I mumbled darkly. "How could this guy do something to Edith out there—" I waved my hands at the world beyond that I had grown up in "—that affected her in here? What about Dembroch's magic?"

"I have considered this as well," the queen replied. "Do you recall what Edith said before she passed? A poisoned promise."

"Like Clay and Jenn's?"

"Worse," the queen said. "Whatever promise she made with the king's killer, it was more powerful than Dembroch's timelessness. It utterly destroyed her." Queen Coralee hung her head. "We can only hope she has passed beyond the grasp of her mentor and her lust for revenge. If her soul was just and prepared, she may yet have reached Avalon."

I absorbed this information in silence, wondering about souls and their ability to grow old and dark or become young again. My own had renewed these last few days. But if I had died, where would mine have gone?

"So this guy, this king's killer," I said, the words like venom on my tongue. "Who is he?"

Queen Coralee shook her head. "I know not. I have asked the Civium as well and no one knows. Everyone assumed Edith killed King Richard. Alas, whoever he is, the king's killer is a formidable enemy to be sure. He has attacked defenders and Hospites to the point we closed our borders and dismantled our Praesidio. He sent my sister to our shores with knowledge and his promise brought about her death despite the protective nature of our magic. It's all too clear to me that our enemy is cunning and dangerous, but he shall pay penance for his crimes. We shall learn his secrets and identity, and strike swiftly and justly."

"Sounds like you have practice with this sort of thing," I joked.

"There is no rest for the wicked, and as a result, for the virtuous. We must never tire to do good. There have been many assailants in my few millennia here. There shall be many more. The mage, his magesty before him, and our seer have all foreseen many threats beyond Edith's attempts. Truly, it is as my late King Richard said. The isles of Dembroch and its sister kingdoms will always have enemies seeking to penetrate its walls and take its treasures."

I froze in my tracks, abashed.

"Sister kingdoms?" I repeated.

"The Arx," the queen said matter-of-factly. "There were seven."

"Were?" I stammered. A second later, I read between the lines and made an assumption: "For their treasure?"

The queen nodded.

"Do *we* have treasure?"

"Ours reside in the Reliquary," replied the queen, "the tallest room atop the tallest tower's balcony."

I gaped at her. "But...what's in there? What treasure—?"

"Keep up, Sir Nicholas," the queen called back as she walked on. "There is still much for you to learn."

She promised to answer my questions in the coming days and insisted we enjoy the fruits of our labor in the present, so I bit my tongue and we walked for a while longer, following the flowers to the eastern walls, taking in the renewed beauty of the kingdom. There was a haze over it, like the olden days we'd seen in the library. Magic was all around us, in every breath. I beamed, knowing what my friends and I had accomplished, but my heart grew heavy thinking of all those we had barely known and lost too soon. If only the librarian and the mage could have seen it. If only Edith had lived long enough to enjoy it.

"We should have a service for your sister," I decided.

"You are too kind, Sir Nicholas," the queen said. "I fear that only you and I would be in attendance."

"Let's do it then," I said. "Right now."

I knelt in the flowers and plucked two bright orange tulips, offering one to the queen. She held it out as if to a ghost, tears forming in her eyes.

"My sister," the queen said. "May you find solace in the quiet. Forgive me my sins as I have forgiven yours. Rest well, my sweet sister, and be free of your curse."

The queen's flower blossomed before my eyes and, as though tugged from her fingers, the flower drifted away on the wind.

I held up my flower in the same fashion. Though I had only known the cruel witch, I spoke to the little girl I had seen from the history book, young and full of love for her family.

"May you be everything you hoped to be," I said. "Peace be with you."

My flower, too, bloomed and was tugged from my fingers. It danced off lazily, as though the ghost of a young girl held it, lost in its simple beauty.

As we watched them go, the queen slipped her hand into mine. I held it tenderly.

"You saved her," the queen said. "And you saved me."

I shook my head. "You saved yourselves. I just laid around, having a heart attack, while you did all the hard work."

Queen Coralee laughed. It was a sweet sound I wanted to hear plenty more of.

"You are more trouble than I could have ever imagined," she said.

"And you more cursed," I replied with a laugh.

We grew near to one another. I longed to kiss her.

"We must proceed with caution," the queen said. "We are of different stations. The Civium, particularly Master Malleator, will not approve of such mingling. And there is my decree to consider. A royal's word is law on Dembroch."

"Meghan told me Master Malleator knows about your decree when we first got here."

"He has already spoken to me. He expects me to keep my word."

"Stickler," I grumbled.

A smirk teased the edges of the queen's lips.

"When it's time," I finally said, "I'll go. Dembroch needs its queen more than it needs me."

There was a spark in the queen's eyes, a surprise, a gratitude. She squeezed my hand tighter and leaned in for a kiss. My ragged little heart beat faster. My body flared in pain, but I didn't care.

Suddenly, there was a shout from Amaranthine. Clay came into view, pointing to the south. We turned to see a ferry slowly approaching the isles.

"The Civium," the queen breathed in surprise. "They have returned."

She took off at a gleeful run. I chased after her, pushing through the pain of my heart, sensing that I was chasing the queen across the kingdom and through life. I knew there was a long road ahead of us, notwithstanding my impending exile, but for a pained heartbeat or two, I felt that the queen and I hoped for the same thing: that somehow, someway, we could be together and see where the future led. I wasn't sure how, given her decree and her royalty and my lack of titles, but I dared to dream I would catch her. After all, what's a chase without a bit of struggled and what's love without a bit of hope?

CHAPTER 59

One Last Promise

It had been nearly a month since we'd saved the kingdom. The castle was a bit fuller. There were plenty of new faces and names that I struggled to remember. I was starting to lose track of the days—timelessness does that—but a new fear had grown in my heart. With forty-some Civium returned, the kingdom was well-staffed and the queen was in little need of us anymore. It didn't help that all of us had been inspected by the healers and, despite Clay and Jenn's love curse and Meghan's still unhealed witch's mark, they had been given clean bills of health. I too had been healed. After much manipulation, the healers had placed a spark of magic into my heart, mending it fully so it would continue to beat strongly even beyond the scope of Dembroch's timelessness. Which meant I could leave. We all could.

I knew it was coming—so did my friends. Our time on Dembroch was running short and we rued the day that was surely coming soon that we would finally be dismissed.

I tried not to let it get me down too much. It was how every great story went, I lamented. The heroes saved the day, received much thanks, and were sent home with the promise of returning another day when the helpless were in need again. Even if I had to leave, I knew—well, hoped—that I would see Dembroch again someday.

One evening with my friends gathered together by a fire, I shared this fear.

"We'll have to leave soon," I surmised.

Clay hung his head. Meghan bit her lip.

"I figured," Jenn said.

"There was still so much I wanted to do," Clay said. "Help out the Watchmaker..."

"Learn some magic," Meghan added.

"Restart the Praesidio," Jenn said.

"Maybe catch the king's killer," Meghan said—she'd obsessed over this idea since I'd told her my conversation with the queen in the flower garden.

I couldn't bear to say what I still wanted to do on Dembroch, though my mind jumped to the queen and the kiss we had missed.

"Where will we go?" I asked. "What can we possibly do after...?"

My friends looked as unsure as I felt. None of us could return home to our day-to-day routine after everything we'd done and everything we'd seen. Our youth was alive within us, our thirst for adventure unquenchable. Maybe, I dared to wonder, there were other kingdoms out there, other hidden islands, with quests and monsters and exploits.

But none of them, I lamented, would compare to Dembroch. None of them would be tantamount to the queen.

There was a knock at the door. When I answered, there was no one there, but there was a scroll attached to the door handle.

I brought it to my friends and unfurled it. My healed heart thudded heavily. I felt like I could have cried though I was a full grown, thirty-two-year-old man.

CHAPTER 59

Scrawled in the queen's handwriting was a summons. She expected to see each of us next day in the throne room.

"This is it," I realized. "She's sending us home."

I didn't blame her, I realized. But I ached for the chance to stay. To keep chasing after her.

Meghan reached out and grabbed my hand. I grasped Clay's shoulder. Before long, we were holding one another in a circle of kinship. I looked to each of my friends and felt a surge of pride and love. We had been through quite a storm together. We'd saved a kingdom and had our fair share of scars and burdens to prove it. None of us were unscathed, but at the end of it all, our friendships had been restored. Once separate, we four friends were together again.

"Wherever we go," Meghan said, "it'll be together."

"Promise?" I asked.

"Promise," they all said.

And somehow, I knew, it was a promise everyone would keep.

CHAPTER 60

A Fond Farewell

We gathered at the door to the throne room the next day at noon. Exchanging glances and steeling ourselves for the worst, we knocked on the door.

The seer appeared from within. She glanced us over with a surprisingly focused, stern expression.

"Where are your garments?" she asked.

We were dressed in common white clothes of visitors.

"Your armored garb," she said. "Where are they?"

She hurried us back to our rooms where clothiers handed us dark blue tunics with golden filigree designs. The garments were heavy on my chest, like a bulletproof vest.

I felt awkward in the armor. It was the color of the kingdom's defenders, and we had been stripped of those titles long ago.

CHAPTER 60

When we had returned to the throne room's door, the seer paused and gave us an uncharacteristically warm smile.

"Are you ready?" she asked.

"No," Jenn said morosely. "Are we going to die?"

The seer threw open the door and ushered us in.

As I passed, she gave me a dry smile and said, "You will not go the way of Solomon."

Not letting the compliment soak in, she prodded me forward, her face becoming distant and dreamy once more. I stepped inside, thinking deep about failed knights and what my friends and I had accomplished, and—I gasped.

The throne room was packed with every Civium who had returned. A dozen trumpeters burst into an exultant melody. The masses erupted into shouts and cheers, parting to form an aisle to the front of the throne room. And there, standing over us all, was Queen Coralee.

The seer poked me in the back, prodding me forward. I led my friends to the front of the throne room. As we went, Civium gave us smiles and claps on the back. There was the Watchmaker, Page Trey and his master, and even the seer's daughter, Emily. She gave me a toothy grin, one just like her father's. I beamed with pride, but my heart sank with each step. I had not expected such fanfare and did not want to be sent home with every eye watching, most of all Page Hybore's family.

At last, we gathered in a line before Queen Coralee. She surveyed us as she had done when we'd first met in the prisons: shrewd eyes, looking slowly from one to the next, assessing our appearance and potential.

"It is a glorious day to celebrate," she announced, silencing the trumpets and buzzing crowd. "The darkest day of Dembroch has passed and it shall stand the test of time forevermore. *Omnia Aeterno*!"

"Omnia Aeterno!" all of the Civium cried, knocking their fists on their chests.

"But it is not without loses," the queen declared. "Many have fallen. Many fled and never returned."

There was mumbling of agreement through the crowd. Some cast dark, suspicious looks at the queen.

"It is high time that I am honest with each of you," the queen continued. "This disaster was because of me. I was brought to this kingdom as a Hospite. I was cursed."

A shock of whispers swept through the Civium.

"But you took me in as your own," she continued. "For that, I will be forever grateful. And, truly, it opened my eyes to the kindness and awesomeness of this kingdom. I vowed to raise up this land with all my power. Even when the day was darkest, I sought to help you before I helped myself."

A smattering of applause echoed through the throne room.

"The witch who attacked this kingdom was my sister," Queen Coralee revealed. "She sought to ruin Dembroch to bring about my curse. As a result, the kingdom suffered, and for that, I am eternally sorry. Many of you feared crowning me would lead to Dembroch's ruin, and your fears were not unfounded. But my loyalty to this land never wavered. I sought, in everything I did and everything I do, to maintain our kingdom. If you will have me, I wish to continue guiding you and this glorious kingdom into a new era of beauty and healing."

There was no delay, no pause. Everyone let out a cheer. Queen Coralee wiped a tear from her cheek.

"And if you wish to stand by me," she said, "I welcome each of you back and reinstate your titles. We shall rebuild together, seeking out Hospites and healing the afflicted. We shall be a light on the hill for the world once more. Will you stand with your queen?"

Another cheer, louder than before. The broken and bruised spirits seemed to be healing over. Only Master Malleator seemed to be uninspired, though, to his credit, he wasn't booing.

"We are one again," the queen observed. "But we would not have this future without the four before you: Ladies Meghan and Jennifer, Sirs Clayton and Nicholas. Civium, look upon your saviors and show them your appreciation."

CHAPTER 60

I felt like a deer caught in the headlights. The entire kingdom erupted into joyous celebration. Trumpets and bells rang. They cheered, clapped, shouted, cried. They seemed so thankful. It was awe-inspiring.

"Their time on Dembroch grows short," the queen continued. "We must celebrate them this last day and send them off with full bellies and happy hearts."

For the first time, the crowd seemed to grow quiet. There were murmurings and raised eyebrows.

Then, the Watchmaker stepped out of the masses.

"I object, my queen," he said. "Sir Clayton slayed the Dreadnaught with the fortissium blade and braved the weapon's beastly guardians. He saved my life and was instrumental in saving the kingdom at the brink of destruction. Such a joyous warrior and shrewd thinker should not be banished."

Clay's face was bright red.

But then, the seer stepped forward too.

"Lady Jennifer recovered my Sight, tamed its power as her own, and changed an immutable future," she declared to the queen. "She has earned title of defender. I object to her exile."

There was a great cheer from the Civium. My heart beat fast.

Page Trey pushed past Master Malleator and walked up the aisle. His voice quaked with nervousness as he spoke.

"Queen Coralee," he said. "I beg your forgiveness to object your decree. Lady Meghan navigated the Gate Grounds and freed Ryderwyle from a storm started by her predecessors. She saved my master and I. She is a strong fighter, peaceful, patient, and generous. We need her."

The room buzzed. Everyone seemed to be waiting for someone to step out and testify to my abilities, but I knew it wouldn't be the queen. She could not show favoritism to a visitor, particularly one she'd promised to banish.

Silence came over the crowd. My heart beat loud in my ears.

But then, I heard the tiniest pitter-patter of feet. I turned to see little Emily, daughter of the seer and Page Hybore. She walked up to me and took my hand. With big eyes, she looked square at the queen and spoke clearly.

"I object, Queen Coralee," she said. "My father gave his life to find Sir Nicholas and his friends. He knew that they alone could save the kingdom. And he was right. Sir Nicholas freed three sisters from dreadful fates and ended the curse that could have destroyed our home for all time. But the most important thing he ever did was accept the summons. Promises are difficult to make and even harder to keep. He could have ignored our call or dismissed my Papa, but he answered the call. He laid down his own life to save this kingdom. Sir Nicholas is a defender in his heart, no matter his title or station. He should stay."

The throne room erupted with noise. Some cheered, others shouted, "Here, here!" Many began to cry, "We object!"

The queen raised a hand, calling for silence. She gave me a wry smile, and it was then that I realized this had all been the queen's plan.

"I hear your calls," she said. "As queen of Dembroch, my word is law unless overturned by the people. Do each of you object to my ruling?"

There was a mighty cheer of defiance.

Queen Coralee beamed.

"Then, on behalf of the kingdom of Dembroch, in agreement by its royalty, aides, and Civium, I renounce my previous decree. As is within my authority, I extend the offer of your titles and citizenship for this kingdom. Should you wish it, you may call Dembroch home all the days of your life."

My friends and I exchanged glances. None of us had expected this. I gaped, my heart thundering in my chest.

A purple-gowned aide brought forth a small wooden box and opened it for the queen. Within were four gold-flecked, black medallions, a castle inscribed in a ring of flames.

The queen plucked one of the medallions from the box and held it before Clay.

"Sir Clayton," she said. "For joy in the face of despair and bravery amid absolute horror, I reinstate your knightship. Do you so swear loyalty to the kingdom of Dembroch and fealty to your queen?"

"I do, my queen," said Clay.

He knelt to one knee. The Watchmaker let out a whoop and holler. The queen knighted him, placing a sword on each of his shoulders. When he stood, she pinned the Dembroch sigil to his chest.

I gaped. Clay was a knight again. We would all be defenders again!

Next, the queen addressed Jenn.

"Lady Jennifer," she said. "Fear is a powerful enemy, yet you faced it and, more, conquered it. For optimism in the face of our darkest hour, I bequeath upon you dameship. Do you so swear loyalty to the kingdom of Dembroch and fealty to your queen?"

Jenn curtsied and, with a sword upon each shoulder, she reclaimed the title of dame. Her face glowed as she admired the medal pinned to her cloak.

"I saw this!" the seer shouted. "I knew this day would come."

"Lady Meghan," the queen said, holding a metal brooch before my sister. "You came to us hotheaded and impatient, yet, beneath it, you demonstrated cool logic and a sound mind. For patience and a generous heart, I restore your dameship."

The queen asked if Meghan swore loyalty, and Meghan did without hesitation. She was given the sigil of Dembroch and grinned like a child. She let out a breath in satisfaction and I knew, deep down, she knew this was exactly where she was meant to be.

Then, the queen was before me. She held up a medal.

"Sir Nicholas," said Queen Coralee, her eyes saying more than words could share. "This kingdom will always be in your debt. It is a long, treacherous walk on Dembroch, and you have the steadfastness to take each step. For your initiative, your loyalty, and your unerring love, I bestow you with the knightship I once took."

The "yes" was playing on my lips, but she wasn't finished.

"Be warned," she said, "it is a duty few comprehend and even fewer can fulfill. Do you so swear loyalty to the kingdom of Dembroch and fealty to your queen in all that the future may bring?"

She looked at me meaningfully, searching for proof that I understood what I was being offered. It was the offer made to me as a child, now fully understood as an adult with a youthful soul, to be a defender. But, there was more to it. I could see in her eyes that it was not simply an offer to become a defender of Dembroch once more, but to be a defender of the queen's heart.

I proudly knelt, promising myself to the queen and Dembroch. Everyone cheered and my heart burst once more with pride. The queen knighted me and pinned the medal to my chest. Its weight was familiar—I had missed it.

As one, my friends and I stood, once more the four defenders of Dembroch, its people, its land, and is magic.

The Civium let out a cheer. The trumpets sang sweet tunes of victory. The magic sparks in the air burned brighter.

Emily squeezed my hand. Her look said it all—Page Hybore would have been proud.

Queen Coralee and I caught each other's eyes. Her face lit with an infectious smile full of thankfulness, hope, and love.

My heart swelled. I was head-over-heels. I could have kissed her, but knew there would be plenty of time for that later.

In that moment, seeing that look on her face, I realized the truth.

There wasn't much I could have afforded to do back when I was young. The orange cream malts at Dave's Diner seemed to be pretty good. But that $125 to become a knight, and all those struggles and heartbreak I'd experienced since, were worth every penny just to see my queen smile. She would be my queen, and I would be her defender, forevermore.

EPILOGUE

The Hope Chest
In the Attic

The grandchildren slept sweetly by the fire. Grandpapa closed the black book and checked his pocket watch. Though it was long past midnight, his timepiece still read nine-o'clock. He snapped it shut and kissed the foreheads of Robbie and Lucy.

"I love you both," he whispered.

"Littles and littles?" they would have replied had they been awake.

"Lots and lots," he would have confirmed.

He looked wistfully upon his sweet grandchildren.

Someday, he promised himself, he would tell them. Someday they would know. But six and seven were much too young. There was too much they did not know. And if they begged to go, he would not be able to deny them, despite the treacherousness of such a request.

Belabored by the weight of these truths, Grandpapa wandered off to bed.

EPILOGUE

But little Lucy and dimple-cheeked Robbie were not asleep. The moment Grandpapa left the room, their eyelids popped open.

"Did you get it?" Robbie whispered.

Lucy held up a tiny golden key, the one that had been hanging from the other end of their grandfather's pocket watch chain.

Quiet as mice, they snuck through the house. From Grandpapa's room, they heard snores.

Under the attic, Lucy grabbed the hook and pulled down the trapdoor. It creaked open and stairs descended from the ceiling to the floor with a dry screech of springs.

"Come on," Lucy whispered.

"I'm scared," Robbie said.

"Me too," Lucy said. "But we have to know."

Brother followed sister into the musty, dimly-lit attic. Lucy found the flashlight they had left close to the entrance after their last visit and lit it. The yellow light revealed a hidden world of furniture draped in sheets, framed photos caked in dust, and bookshelves stocked full of mementos. Dust spun lazily through the air like the snow falling in the cold winter's night outside.

The grandchildren probed the darkness, finding their way back to what they were looking for. In the furthest corner, where the spiders crawled over dense cities of cobwebs, was a hope chest. It was a beautiful thing, made of mahogany, expertly carved, and bound in metal framing. Set into its front was a lock.

"Go on," Lucy told her younger brother, handing him the key from Grandpapa's pocket watch chain. "Be brave. Like Sir Clayton."

He took the key, fed it into the lock, and turned it. The lid popped open.

Barely breathing, Lucy pushed the lid open all the way. The flashlight illuminated the contents within. There were no jewels or mounds of coins inside, but the belongings of a younger man from a younger time. There were navy blue clothes soft as silk but heavy as armor, swords of all lengths and widths, and black-and-white photos of people the children didn't know and places they'd never visited.

"Look!" Robbie squeaked.

He dug into the blue clothing and withdrew a medal. It was the size and shape of a silver dollar, the silhouette of a splendid castle inscribed in an ornate, red-hued circle that looked like a ring of flames. Carved along the bottom of the ring were the words *Omnia Aeterno.*

Lucy and Robbie exchanged a glance. Their breath caught. It was the sigil of Dembroch. A real sigil.

They dug deeper into the hope chest, finding more and more treasures. There was a complex drawing that looked like a star chart, a map of Dembroch's three isles, a blank diary smeared with blood and oil, and sheets of paper covered in half-finished maps.

Under these, Lucy found an old, yellowed certificate bordered with filigree and wax seals, confirming *Sir Nicholas Hutchison* as a *Reserve Knight* on the 13th of November, 1989.

Robbie and Lucy exchanged a glance, one full of incredulity and awe. These items were from hundreds of years ago—it was the year 2353 after all—and the subject of the papers, Sir Nicholas, was their Grandpapa.

"Dembroch is real," Lucy breathed.

"And Grandpapa has been there," Robbie realized.

"The story he told was his."

Robbie pointed. "And there's more."

Nestled into the very bottom of the hope chest were several leather-bound books, each a different color and bearing the Dembroch sigil on their front. There was a small space on the far left where Grandpapa had pulled out the black book of his first adventure.

Lucy and Robbie shared a knowing smile.

"Let's do it," they agreed.

They shut the trunk, Robbie holding tight to the Dembroch medallion. Down from the attic, the two tiptoed to Grandpapa's room. He was still snoring, his eyes moving under their lids.

His pocket watch sat atop his bedside dresser. When Robbie wouldn't go, Lucy slunk into the room. Grandpapa gave a stir. Lucy froze. But the old knight didn't wake.

She grabbed the pocket watch and crept back to Robbie.

He held up the sigil. She held up the watch. They connected the two, forming the chroniseal.

"Together?" she asked. "Like the defenders?"

"Omnia Aeterno," Robbie agreed.

They clasped hands together and pressed the winding crown on the pocket watch. There was a shock of electricity. The world blurred around them. Colors blended. They started to spin. And the next moment, Robbie and Lucy were gone, leaving the cold winter's night for a summer's timeless kingdom.

ABOUT THE BOOK

Though writing a novel is solitary work, its development takes a village. In that way, I must thank my editors (Fran, Matt, Jon, Mom, and Charles) and my consultants (Dwight, Lisa, Sarah, and of course, Melissa). You truly made this tale into something magical and you all have a place in Dembroch.

Truly, the concept of this tale came from my wife, who heard a story at work about the world's smallest country: the Principality of Sealand off the coast of Norway in international waters. Built during World War II to defend the shores against potential German invasions, the small military platform was later claimed by a retired British major who used the space to broadcast his radio show (Radio Essex). The Major, Roy Bates, and his family declared the platform a country in 1967, claiming the No Man's Land as their own. Several years of litigation and attacks followed, and in an interesting twist in 2012, the country allowed the world's public to become knights and dames to defend the principality in times of need.

My wife, her brother, and I discussed this over family dinner with fascination. What if we became knights and dames? Could we put that on our business cards? But wait—if we had said title, what if we were called into action? Would we be able to?

And thus, the story of Dembroch was born: a small country much in need of knights and dames to defend its honor. Plus...some magic.

I hope you enjoyed reading this first tale with Clay, Jenn, Meg, and Nick. Don't lament the end of this book, though. There are more adventures to come for our defenders, their queen, and the Civium of Dembroch. After all, the king's killer is out there somewhere.

Until next time, Omnia Aeterno!

obligatory chest thump

Patrick Harris – a man of faith, family, company, and country, with a dash of the written word. He is the author of *The Waterman Chronicles* and *Silver Rain*, and is currently working on further tales of *The Defenders of Dembroch* and an adult thriller, *A Toast of Blood.* To find out more, visit his website at AuthorPatrickHarris.com or connect with him on social media: @AuthorPatrickHarris.

When not exploring the closest theme parks and mountains, Patrick makes his home in Reno, Nevada, with his wife, Melissa, and their two puppies, Dixie and Penny.

AND NOW,
AN EXCLUSIVE SNEAK PEEK
AT THE OPENING PAGES OF

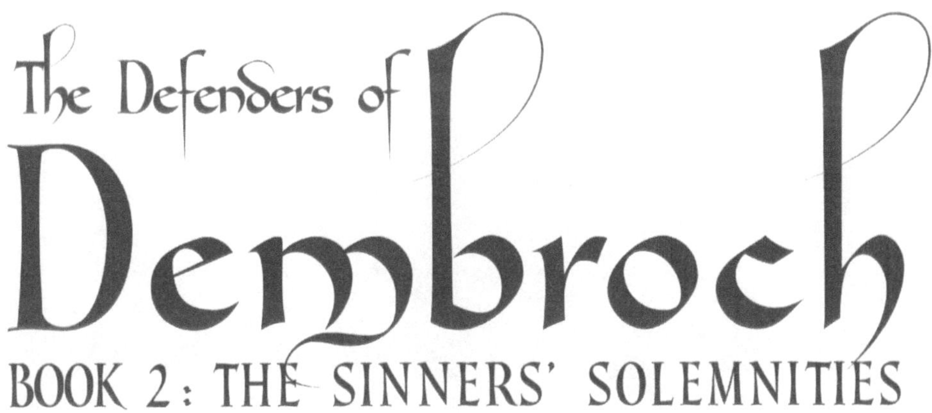

CHAPTER 1

The First Night

A gold-flecked pocket watch rang sharply, the desperate cry of a life cut short without warning or mercy. Clay ran to it, reading it quickly. The time was the death sentence of midnight and, as he flipped it over in his hands, the gears ground to a stop. He cursed under his breath. Dead before he even had a chance to find them. Suddenly. Violently.

He took a step back to see where he was amid the gigantic world map composed of pocket watches.

"Where is this?" he asked the Watchmaker.

"Paris," replied the giant of a man without even looking up.

His words were drowned out by another pocket watch ringing sharply. It came from the same spot. And a second later, another. Then another.

"What the devil are you doing?" the Watchmaker grumbled, finally giving the World of Watches his attention.

Clay stood on an elevated platform amidst billions of hanging pocket watches, one for every citizen on Earth. Each hung in the country of its owner and was bewitched to measure the length of a person's life. The closer to midnight, the nearer to death.

Amongst the millions of pocket watches representing Paris, France, a dozen timepieces rang for help. The Watchmaker reached into the mess and grabbed the closest. The hands were sliding toward twelve. The gears spun frenetically.

"It's an attack," Clay said. "They don't have much time."

"Most don't," said the Watchmaker. "You know the drill."

That he did. Long and lean, Clay took off for the castle. From his pocket he withdrew a tiny nautilus shell and yelled into its opening, calling for the queen and Council. The watch in his hand was one of a dozen nuns under siege in their convent. One of them, Sister Clarence, had been on Dembroch's list for years, a decent person in her bones and suffering a strange curse, one they had intended to help when the moment was right. And the moment was now.

The queen and Council gave their permission. Defenders of the Praesidio marched for the eastern walls of the castle. Clay skid into the room just as the defenders assembled in the central rings of the Navictorium. An elaborate, if impossible engineering feat, this machine called the Navictorium transported users to anywhere in the world. In this instance—Paris.

Clay helped program the coordinates into the Navictorium before running to the center ring. He joined his wife, Jenn, and his friends, Meghan and Page Trey. Queen Coralee and I entered the room just in time to bid them farewell and a safe journey, just as the Navictorium roared to life and the defenders disappeared in a swirl of light.

After decades of diligent study, prayer, and reflection, Sister Clarence knew this to be true: no matter the country or culture, the religion or riot, the king or the killer or the countryman, Death came for everyone. And when the final moment came, there were those who cowered and begged, and those who looked Death boldly in the face and dared to smirk.

Sister Clarence hadn't expected to be the latter, especially in this situation. After Fabinando, she'd led quite the sheltered life in the convent. Even still, in this terrifying, horrifying, nightmarish moment, her heart beat strong as when she'd been wild and in love in her twenties. Her sisters in God—those that annoyed her, those who irked her, but all those she loved—were dead. She was the only one left. And this man, the sinner who had pursued her so long ago, had come for her now.

The scarred man crept toward her, the fireplace poker scrapping along the floor. He watched her with a dark lust in his eyes. The blood of her sisters was speckled across his blistered, scarred skin.

A few feet from her, he lunged with the poker, stopping just short. The bloodied end pressed into Sister Clarence's neck.

"You chose the wrong haven," he said simply, his voice surprisingly human for how alien he seemed. "Now...beg."

Sister Clarence dared to smirk at the man, for she knew what lay ahead. Her chest was aching. If this horror of a man didn't kill her, her old heart finally would. She couldn't help but be happy—at last, the curse of the Costas would be ended. And she'd be with her sisters again. Not her sisters of blood, but the sisters of Sacré-Cœur de Montmartre. Perhaps she'd been one of them all along.

Sister Clarence closed her eyes and, in the face of Death, mocked it by turning to her faith.

"The Lord is with me, none shall stand against me," she said. "Blessed are the martyrs. Theirs is the kingdom of—"

She felt the poker pull back from her. The man was going to kill her now.

"Iugulo Innoxium!" the scarred man cried—and in reply, there was a bright flash of neon light, a rainbow of color.

Sister Clarence dared to open her eyes, just in time to see four newcomers appear in the hall. They were dressed in deep blue tunics, shining swords held tight in their hands. Light was fading from around them.

"Surrender yourself," said one of them, a woman with sharp cheekbones and hair pulled back tight.

"The words have been uttered," replied the scarred man. "The solemnities must be completed."

Before anyone could stop him, the scarred man thrust the poker at Sister Clarence. It sliced through her skin, crunching through her ribs, digging deep. The sister gasped. Shocks of pain ripped through her body.

There was a flash of movement, blurry in Sister Clarence's watering eyes. The newcomers swung their swords, knocking the poker from the scarred man's hand. Another scooped Sister Clarence into their arms.

"Go!" cried one of the women.

"Hold on," Sister Clarence's rescuer whispered. "I've got you."

Sister Clarence held tight as she could, knowing she was dying. There was a flash of color around her, bright and moving fast, and she smiled, welcoming whatever came next.

Page Trey disappeared with Sister Clarence, bound for Dembroch and the magic that would heal the sister's wounds. Meghan, Jenn, and Clay faced the Stricken Man, swords at his throat. The man heaved with every breath, spit running down his jaw.

"Ceremony's over," Clay said.

"One life," the Stricken Man sneered. "A drop in the bucket."

Clay pressed his sword into the man's neck, eager for a fight. "Would the King's Killer feel the same about you?"

Jenn waved Clay off.

"What do you mean 'the bucket'?" Jenn asked the Stricken Man.

"There's no point, Jenn," Clay said, knowing that this Stricken Man, like all the others, wouldn't reveal anything.

But, to Clay's surprise, the Stricken Man snickered darkly.

"The wait is over," he said, his eyes lighting with excitement. "It has been a long thirty years."

Meghan, Clay, and Jenn exchanged a quick glance.

"We'll play your game," Meghan said. "You give us answers, you get to keep speaking."

Surprisingly, the Stricken Man obliged.

"We sinners fast for such a festival," said the Stricken Man. "As tradition holds, on the last full moon before the new, I have spilled innocent blood and declared the words. The solemnities have begun and cannot be stopped."

"What are you planning?" Jenn asked. "What is the King's Killer planning?"

A dastardly smile curled across the Stricken Man's lip.

"Death," he promised. "Day by day, we will execute more. Innocents will gather in mounds. And on the night of the new moon, we will drench a nation in blood. So says the King's Killer. You remember him, don't you?"

"Which country?" Clay demanded to know.

The Stricken Man winked at him.

"Try as you might, you will not find us or stop us. The nation will fall, then the world. There will be no more lights on a hill. No more good men. No more czars or chiefs or Presidents, no more kings or queens. Watch and bleed. This will be a feast well remembered. But—"

The Stricken Man lunged suddenly. Meghan, Jenn, and Clay held firm. Their swords pierced his neck. Dark blood spurt from him, running down the metal of their blades.

"—the King's Killer will call off the ceremonies," the Stricken Man wheezed, air escaping from the gashes in his throat. "All of this can be stopped if you grant him one request..."

www.ingramcontent.com/pod-product-compliance
Lightning Source LLC
Chambersburg PA
CBHW020932310726
48980CB00007B/734/J

* 9 7 8 0 5 7 8 4 8 2 9 0 3 *